A PERSON OF INTEREST

ALSO BY SUSAN CHOI

American Woman

The Foreign Student

A PERSON OF INTEREST

A NOVEL

Susan Choi

VIKING

VIKING
Published by the Penguin Group
Penguin Group (USA) Inc., 375 Hudson Street, New York, New York 10014, U.S.A. ·
Penguin Group (Canada), 90 Eglinton Avenue East, Suite 700, Toronto, Ontario, Canada
M4P 2Y3 (a division of Pearson Penguin Canada Inc.) · Penguin Books Ltd, 80 Strand,
London WC2R 0RL, England · Penguin Ireland, 25 St. Stephen's Green, Dublin 2, Ireland
(a division of Penguin Books Ltd) · Penguin Books Australia Ltd, 250 Camberwell
Road, Camberwell, Victoria 3124, Australia (a division of Pearson Australia Group
Pty Ltd). · Penguin Books India Pvt Ltd, 11 Community Centre, Panchsheel Park, New
Delhi–110 017, India · Penguin Group (NZ), 67 Apollo Drive, Rosedale, North Shore 0632,
New Zealand (a division of Pearson New Zealand Ltd.) · Penguin Books (South Africa)
(Pty) Ltd, 24 Sturdee Avenue, Rosebank, Johannesburg 2196, South Africa

Penguin Books Ltd, Registered Offices:
80 Strand, London WC2R 0RL, England

First published in 2008 by Viking Penguin,
a member of Penguin Group (USA) Inc.

10 9 8 7 6 5 4 3 2 1

Copyright © Susan Choi, 2008
All rights reserved

LIBRARY OF CONGRESS CATALOGING IN PUBLICATION DATA
Choi, Susan, date.
    A person of interest : a novel / Susan Choi.
      p.   cm.
    ISBN 978–0–670–01846–8
    1. Korean Americans—Fiction. 2. College teachers—Crimes against—Fiction.
3. Bombers (Terrorists)—Fiction. 4. Serial murderers—Fiction. 5. Middle West—Fiction.
I. Title.
PS3553.H584P47 2008
813'.54—dc22   2007019873

Printed in the United States of America
Set in Celeste
Designed by Daniel Lagin

For Chang Choi and Vivian Choi

PART I

1.

IT WAS ONLY AFTER HENDLEY WAS BOMBED THAT LEE was forced to admit to himself just how much he'd disliked him: a raw, never-mined vein of thought in an instant laid bare by the force of explosion. Of course, it was typical in his profession for diminishing elders to harbor ill-will toward their junior colleagues. But Lee, who had been tenured in his department for more than twenty years, felt that he was exempt from the obsolescence that infected most other professors his age. He was still capable of the harsh princeliness he'd possessed in his youth, although now he was half through his sixties, and his hair was all white. That old aristocratic hauteur would return suddenly, and his loose, dowdy trousers, always belted too high, would seem to sit on a younger man's waist. The liver spots that had come to his face would be bleached by the glare pouring forth from his eyes. His wasn't the kind of temperament spouse or child or friend had ever wanted to cleave to, but for his students it had the power to impress; like most of their peers, they found the notion of mentorship fusty. Unlike Lee in his own student days, they shunned the emeritus aura. They mostly wanted teachers who acted like pals—this was why they'd loved Hendley—but they didn't scorn Lee quite as much, he felt sure, as they did the other professors his age, the old men with their elbow-patched tweeds, and their stay-at-home wives who made cookies and tea for the very few students who still bothered to seek professorial counsel.

Then again, there were times he was forced to believe the exact opposite: that his students had neither respect nor affection for him. He sat idle during his twice-weekly office hours, as did most of his aged colleagues, a crisp yellow legal pad squared before him on his clean desk, a Montblanc fountain pen with black ink in his hand— he'd always worked in black ink, an affectation he'd suffered since youth. A sign of arrogance, his first wife might have said; of humility, he might have parried. Ink kept one's errors on record. But whatever his Montblanc denoted, there were fewer and fewer to give their opinions. His office hours were an empty detention, unvisited and unproductive for him, no matter how he pretended. Each afternoon he would carefully stand the door open twelve inches, or the width someone needed to duck in casually and say hi; not wide open, as if in eager anticipation, and not merely slightly ajar, as if he begrudged this time for his students. He didn't; he sat poised on the brink of the legal pad, seemingly lost in his putative thoughts, the Montblanc in his fingers. Each set of footsteps he heard in the hallway launched him on a theatrical scratching of pen upon notepad; he would feel his face stiffen with self-consciousness and will his eyes not to dart toward the door. The footsteps were almost never for him. The rare occasions they were, he was always the same, as if reluctantly drawn from the pool of deep thought: "Ah," he would say, tempering his forbidding absorption with a lift of the eyebrows. But most often, as he twitched with unsure expectation, the footsteps passed his office—his door too little open for him to see who it was—and instead stopped at Hendley's, next door. There would already be lively murmur of whispers, students sprawled on the floor of the hall with their backpacks, awaiting their turns. And through the wall, the not-quite-comprehensible but very audible rumble of Hendley himself, holding forth, and a student's unself-conscious laughter, punctuated by the robotic bleeps and the primitive honks Hendley's two huge computers gave off.

His dislike of Hendley was all the more painful to him for his having until now been ignorant of it. Had he known, he might have forgiven himself his eager awkwardness in the face of Hendley's camaraderie, the oh-yeses he would hear himself helplessly blurting whenever Hendley found him at their faculty coffee events. As Lee carefully blew on his thin paper cup, Hendley would clap him on the shoulder so the hot coffee jumped, as if Lee were the person he'd most hoped to see. Hendley would launch into a long anecdote as if Lee were the person he'd most wanted to hear it, as if theirs were the sort of friendship that required no work, in which all was assumed. And in response Lee would hear himself saying "Oh, yes," would feel his head bobbing in dumb agreement, as if the past forty years hadn't happened and he was fresh off the boat with ten phrases of English etched painstakingly in his mind. His dislike of Hendley might have prepared him somewhat, if not for what happened, then at least for the dislike itself, the cold shock of his first, addled thought when he'd felt the vast fist of the detonation, like a bubble of force that had popped in his face. He'd felt his heart lurch, begin to flop in disorder and fear; he'd seen with his own eyes his wall of university-issue bookcases, the cheap metal kind with adjustable shelves, seem to ride the wall separating his office from Hendley's as if they were liquid, a wave. He had waited an endless instant, the eon between beats of his heart, for those bookcases so laden with waxy math texts to crash down in one motion and kill him, but they somehow had not. The explosion—he'd known right away it was a bomb; unlike almost all of his colleagues, he knew the feel of bombs intimately—had somehow not breached the thin wall through which, day after day, he'd heard Hendley's robust voice and his bleeping computer and the strange, gooselike yodel of Hendley's dial-up modem when it reached its objective. The explosion had not breached the wall, so that the work it had wrought on the far side was left for Lee to imagine, as he felt the force wash over him, felt his heart quail, and felt himself briefly thinking, *Oh, good.*

The bomb had arrived in a small, heavy cardboard box with the Sun Microsystems logo and address printed on it, but afterward it had been apparent to investigators, as it might have been to Hendley, had he examined the box with suspicion, that it had been reused—recycled, repurposed. A second layer of clear tape had been carefully laid on the first along the seam of the top set of flaps; the first length of tape had been slit neatly open by a previous, unharmed recipient. In the same way the mailing label addressed to Hendley had been the second, at least, for this box; but the previous label had been carefully peeled away, leaving only a soft fuzz of slightly abraded cardboard the second label had easily hidden. Hendley had ordered nothing from Sun Micro-systems at the time the box came to his office, but he was someone who easily might have, and who often enjoyed getting free innovative gizmos. He was a university professor at a midwestern state school only recently somewhat renowned, and only specifically for the com-puter-science branch of the math department, of which Hendley was chair. But he was also, to that part of the public that followed his work, an exemplar of a new breed of professor, worldly, engaged, more likely to publish in a magazine full of ads for a mysterious item called Play-Station than in a moribund university quarterly, read only by the frail, graying men (and rare woman) whose work was included that month. Lee knew that Hendley considered his appointment as chair of the computer-science division, for which he was paid far more than most other tenured professors, to be part charity, part evangelism; charity on the rare days when he grasped he was snubbed by the real mathe-maticians or held forth on his homesickness for the West Coast; evan-gelism, pure and exalting, on more typical days, when his work—not only "midwifing an unprecedented information-technology age that would transform the world as completely as had the industrial revolu-tion" but also "revitalizing the dying university"—made him feel like "the luckiest man in the world," even, these self-satisfied outbursts im-plied, mired at the featureless midpoint between the two coasts, on a faculty that was, other than him, laughable. Hendley was unique among his colleagues in gaily asserting what the rest of them sought to deny: that the rest of the school's departments were considered subpar by the rest of the schools in the country, an assessment that included the math department of which Lee was a member.

Hendley had been alone in his office when he opened the box; Lee had known that Hendley was alone, would later realize that he had al-ways been accurately and painfully aware of whether Hendley had stu-dent admirers in his office or not. At that hour Hendley had had his door closed to students, in part to devote himself to his mail. Lee, at his own desk, had had his own door open not the usual twelve inches—it had not been during office hours—but the inch and a half that allowed the pale light from his green-shaded lamp to sift slenderly into the hall and that would embolden anyone who sought him—office hours or not—to hazard a knock. Thus far on that day, no one had. The force of the explosion threw Lee from his chair, so that he found himself curled not quite under but against the cold metal flank of his desk. For all that he'd lived through a violent and crude civil war, he'd never been this close to the heart, the hot core, of a bomb. He'd been in the vicinity of far more powerful explosives, such as left steaming holes in the ground—and of course, if he'd been as close, barely ten feet away, to any one of those bombs as he'd been to Hendley's, he would not have lived to feel Hendley's at all. But he had never been so close to a detonation, to that swift bloom of force, regardless of size, in his life.

After the explosion Lee remained on the floor of his office, his body pressed to his desk, his eyes closed; they weren't screwed shut in terror, just closed, as if he were taking a nap. The building's automatic sprinkler system had been activated by the blast, and now regular, faintly chemical rain sifted down upon Lee with an unending hiss. Lee did not register the disorder of noise taking form in the hallway: the running feet, toward and away; the first shattering scream. The first person to get to Hendley was an undergraduate named Emma Stiles from Vinton, Iowa, who worked two days a week in the math department as an office assistant and who had been walking back from the women's bathroom when the bomb detonated. Emma Stiles was a known acolyte of Hendley's. If Lee had had the leisure to think as he lay on the tile, he might have thought that Emma had taken her job, which was dull as work-study jobs went, because it brought her into regular, casual, exclusive contact with Hendley. On her days in the department, Emma Stiles only worked from twelve-thirty to four-thirty, at which time the department officially closed, but she had won the privilege of using the student-assistant computer after hours to go on the Internet, a mysterious process the full-time secretaries did not understand but assumed was akin in some way to vocational training. Emma Stiles worked hard and so was very well liked, and she'd made a second home for herself in the math department, especially on the bright afternoons of April, when a four-thirty end to the workday felt like a vacation because there was still so much daylight, now that they'd finally come out of winter. On such afternoons Emma Stiles, walking down the deserted hallway amid great blocks of amber-hued light, betwixt spinning dust motes, past surviving ficuses trembling parched in their pots, often heard Professor Hendley call out, "Stiles!

Come in here, you have *got* to see this." From next door Lee would hear it as well: man-boy Hendley, curly-bearded and wire-spectacled like a John Lennon throwback, but in strange rubber sandals that closed with Velcro, and shirts you might see on a skateboarding freshman. Hendley was well known by his colleagues and students to have a girlfriend named Rachel who taught media studies, whatever that meant, and who flew back and forth as often as three times a month between San Francisco and the landlocked hamlet to which Hendley had moved, to lead the moldering world of scholarship into the digital age. So that in terms of the intangible, sexual taint of which nobody spoke, but which everyone feared, Hendley also was somehow immune, both further beyond suspicion than a hunchbacked, half-blind ninety-year-old might have been and uniquely privileged to be comfortable where no other professor dared tread. Hendley played Ultimate Frisbee with his male and female students and had parties at which he served beer. He seemed always to be in the company of a young person, as often a girl as a boy, in his office in the early evenings, where they tip-tapped and clicked and erupted with laughter in response to whatever they'd done. To be fair, Emma Stiles just as often made her way past an office door that was closed, a bright stripe of light from the low-hanging sun showing at the threshold. Hendley would be sitting behind the closed door, window blinds halfway down to take the glare off his screen; at this time of day, the sun was so low its light stretched the length of the floor, seeped beneath the closed door, made Emma's feet cast long, rubbery shadows on the opposite wall. In Lee's office the sun was allowed the full window, and Lee watched his own shadow stretch toward the opposite wall, the door on which nobody knocked. It was past six P.M., but the sun wouldn't go down until seven; the sounds of Hacky Sack and Frisbee and touch football sifted in from outdoors. The last wire cart of mail had been pushed down the hallway, its contents dispersed, around four. Often Hendley left his huge influx of mail, his complimentary gadgets and disks and slick trade publications, in the opaque white bins they arrived in, and the bins piled up on each other. Hendley joked that he was waiting for amnesty day at the post office, when he could return the white bins, which weren't for use by the public, without being arrested.

On the days Hendley did open mail, he opened the most recent mail first and worked backwards from there. Why not respond to a few things on time, rather than everything late? Hendley apparently wasn't much moved by degrees of lateness, an indifference with which Lee agreed. The box that held the bomb had arrived that same day and been handled by an unknowable number of people before being delivered to Hendley's office. It was designed to go off when opened, which meant it might have lain dormant forever in Hendley's unopened mail. The ambulances arrived first, and then the police and the bomb squad; it was the bomb squad that found Lee, sitting up by that time, with his back to his desk, his legs straight out on the cold tile floor, his gaze riveted forward, but empty. Later he would tell the police he had known, without doubt, that the bomb must have come in the mail. That rhythm, so deeply ingrained in Lee's being: the last mail of the day, the last light stretching shadows across the cold floor, the silence that grew deeper around him as the revelry in Hendley's office began. Loneliness, which Lee possessed in greater measure and finer grade than did his colleagues—of that he was sure—made men more discerning; it made their nerves like antennae that longingly groped in the air. Lee had known that the bomb had come in the mail because he had known that only an attack of mail-related scrupulosity would have kept Hendley in his office with the door shut on a spring day as warm and honey-scented as this day had been; Hendley was a lonely man, too, in his way. Their lonelinesses were different, but Lee saw the link. Hendley loved to be loved; there was never enough to put an end to his restless quest for it. While Lee had taken every impulse of love ever directed at him and destroyed it somehow. Because the neighboring office was quiet, Lee knew that Hendley must be alone; because Hendley was alone, he knew that Hendley was opening mail; because Hendley was opening mail, Lee knew it was that day's mail, freshly arrived. Then the bomb, and Lee's terrible gladness: that something was damaging Hendley, because Hendley made Lee feel even more obsolete and unloved. It had been the gross shock of realizing that he felt glad that had brought him to sitting, from being curled on the floor, and that had nailed his gaze emptily to the opposite wall. He was deep in disgusted reflection on his own pettiness when the bomb squad found him, but, unsurprisingly, they had assumed he was simply in shock.

2.

IT HAD BEEN SEVERAL YEARS SINCE LEE LAST HAD A
straightforward answer for the "next of kin" slot on a medical form,
but before that he had long been used to variation and doubt in this
realm of his life. His next of kin was his grown daughter, Esther, but
Esther frequently changed her address without letting him know and
only infrequently had a phone. It was also true that for these purposes,
the "next" referred less to blood tie than convenient proximity. Knowing this, Lee had always been relieved to give the name of a spouse,
when he had one. He had two marriages in his past, the one very different from the other, not just while they endured but in the way in
which each was inscribed in his mind once it ended. His marriage to
the second Mrs. Lee had lasted four years and had felt like a marriage
from beginning to end—his life had changed for her—but once it was
over, he didn't recognize himself in his memories of it. The man he
had been—admittedly happy, prone to impulsive travel, eager to embark on large projects and able to finish them—bore little resemblance
to the man he had been all his life. The second-marriage Lee seemed
like an idle daydream of himself, a projected ideal that was destined to
always recede, not a chapter of his past life, now closed. For a long
time, almost a year after that marriage ended, he had been paralyzed
by his unhappiness, because he suspected his second marriage to have
been the one time he'd realized his potential for human contentment.
But slowly, perhaps in self-defense, perhaps with genuine recognition,
he had been able to recategorize the marriage as an episode of dangerous delusion. In the course of those four years, he'd accomplished
almost no mathematical research, squandered great sums of money,
and allowed his already tenuous relationship with Esther to decline
even further. The happiness he had felt with the second Mrs. Lee had
resembled intoxication, a fraudulent loss of himself based on something as shallow, perhaps, as her relative youth and her beauty.

It was his first marriage that persisted, not as a shadow so much
as a ground; as if in the house of his life Lee had changed everything
but the carpet, which continued to underlie all his steps without his

consciously noticing. The second Mrs. Lee hadn't minded; Lee and his first wife, Aileen, had shared Esther. But more to the point, Aileen had been dead half a decade before the second Mrs. Lee came along. The second Mrs. Lee had no reason to suspect that Lee, in ways of which he was both conscious and unconscious, felt that his marriage to Aileen was in some way ongoing. She could not have known that Lee still thought of Aileen when he faced a crisis, so that when she, the second Mrs. Lee, left him, he'd been upset to realize he could not call Aileen for advice; and when the bomb squad found him and was lifting him onto a stretcher, he'd said senselessly, of Aileen, "I need to call up my wife."

At the hospital for once he wasn't bothered with medical forms. It was the only hospital their town had, the same hospital in which Esther had been born and in which Lee had undergone sundry minor procedures in the course of the decades. Lee arrived in his own ambulance, in Hendley's chaotic wake, but once there he neither saw Hendley nor heard anything about him. After the shocking, ghastly coincidence of having so closely felt the blast that had scorched and torn Hendley's body, and after the intensity of self-examination the blast had occasioned, this separation from Hendley felt imposed and mistaken; Lee felt Hendley's nonexistent presence like a phantom limb on the far side of the wall of his hospital room, and he wanted to go to Hendley, to speak to him, even speak for him. By the time the interminable battery of tests and observation periods and medical interrogations had ended and law-enforcement personnel were at last set upon him, Lee was bursting with unexpressed sympathy for Hendley, as if he and Hendley were one. He enthusiastically launched on his part of the story and as a result overtold it; it was true, he had to admit, that he could not be one hundred percent positive the package containing the bomb had been delivered that day, though he *felt* it had been. It was true he could not be one hundred percent positive Hendley had been alone in his office the whole afternoon. But he wanted everyone to understand that he overheard Hendley, that the sound track of Hendley's daily life underscored Lee's life, too. Hendley's frequent and lengthy and jovial phone calls, his loud visits from students, his bleeping and honking computers. Everything as it always was, day after day, until the thunderous boom.

"It was terrible," Lee said, his voice unexpectedly breaking. The re-telling of it had made his skin crawl. "It must be a mistake! Who would do this to him? Who would do this? Only sick people, animals—"

"Could it have been a mistake?" one of the policemen asked keenly. "Maybe there's someone else at the school you think might have been the real target for this?" This was before the FBI had arrived and brusquely shunted the locals onto the sidelines.

"Who would want to kill us?" Lee asked weakly. "We're only professors. We don't do anything."

Before the interrogation began, Lee had felt a raw force piling up in his gut—rage at the attempted murder of Hendley? belated fear for himself?—the pressure of which just increased as the questions wore on. Lee had thought that talking would help, but with the policemen he found himself under constant restraint, required to add qualifications to every assertion, so that by the time he was free to go home, he was quaking. "Are you sure you're all right?" said the doctor who'd come to discharge him. "I wonder if we ought to keep you another few hours."

"I'm all right!" Lee practically shouted. "I want to go home!"

Released at last, he floated down the hospital's hallways and through its main doors in surreal anonymity, but once he'd arrived on the sidewalk, he felt the atmosphere shifting. It was past nine o'clock; he realized he had not eaten dinner. The sidewalk approaching the hospital entrance met the curb in a T, and that T was outlined on both sides by crushed tufts of snake grass and recent tulips already losing their petals so that they looked like gapped teeth. Lee stared at the plants; they glowed a chill, livid white, as if blasted by rays of the moon. Their shadows were too long, and so crisp that their edges looked razored. He realized that the T was congested with people and lights, the harsh bluish white lights of news cameras. He stopped walking and squinted uncertainly.

"Professor Lee!" he heard someone cry then, in a voice like his daughter's. Lee swiveled his head in confusion. But before he could find her, the crowd surged toward him, stroboscopic with shadow and light.

"Professor Lee!" said a new, sharper voice. "Can we ask a few questions? You were there when the bomb went off, weren't you?"

"Yes," Lee said, on instinct pulling off his glasses, as he did when he lectured. "Yes, I was," he repeated.

Later on, many people—colleagues, students, his neighbors; Emma Stiles, whose voice he'd first heard calling him, from where she stood in the arms of her roommate, attempting to speak through her sobs to reporters—asked Lee with amazement if it was really his first time on TV, because he seemed born to it. Lee had had no trouble staring into the camera, his eyes blazing with rage. He had delivered his side of the story without pathos or exaggeration—in this way the questioning by policemen had been a useful preparation for him—but then he had launched into riveting, righteous invective. "Whoever did this," he said, "is a monster, a person—I don't even think you can call him a person—with no feeling for life!" His hand was clapped, fingers spread, at his heart, an indignant starfish. "Professor Hendley is one of the great thinking men of today. If he loses his life, we all lose—not just those of us who are his friends and colleagues, but this *country*." Lee almost spat at the revolting waste of it. "Here's a man who's the future, and this sonofabitch tries to bomb this man out of existence!"

Lee himself was surprised by his eloquence; the volcano within had erupted, and he'd hardly been conscious of the column of fire that poured out of his mouth. They used it all except the part with "this sonofabitch," and they had probably wished they could use that part, too. Of Emma Stiles's interview they used nothing, showing only a quick shot of her crying and being hugged by her roommate. When Lee had finished with the cameras, he'd walked over and hugged Emma tightly himself. And she'd come to him all in a rush, like Esther when she had been small and he'd had to awaken her from a nightmare. A gesture so natural to him, and yet so unexpected of him by the people who thought they knew him. Many of his younger colleagues weren't even aware that he had a daughter, although framed pictures of Esther—as a toddler, at six, at sixteen—always sat on his desk, as invariable as his green-shaded lamp or his fountain pen.

Stepping away, giving Emma with care to her roommate again, Lee had tried to forget what she'd said raggedly in his ear: *I SAW him—*

Lee watched himself that night on the eleven o'clock news, squirming with not entirely pleasureless discomfort at the strange sight of his own downturned mouth, his own vertical furrow like a knife wound between his eyebrows, betrayals of age he could hardly believe he possessed, and the messy white thatch that apparently passed for his hair. Seeing himself on TV was like seeing a stranger perform a harsh version of him, under the merciless lights, and then hearing his voice, the strong accent that still stained his English despite decades of rigor, was its own agony. Yet his words sounded good. The vain suspicion that had sustained him through unbroken disappointment at every stage of his career—that he was at least a good lecturer, charismatic and bracingly scary—now found new confirmation. He moved from the ottoman—where he'd been squatting like a true Oriental, elbows on his knees, focused motionlessly on the screen of his blizzard-prone Zenith—into the tattered La-Z-Boy, with his bowl of fried beef and green peppers and rice and his can of Bud Light. At least the second Mrs. Lee, in her rapacious divorce settlement, hadn't wanted this hideous chair, in which he'd probably spent twenty percent of the past twenty years. The chair's upholstery was some kind of supposedly wearproof, stainproof, punctureproof miracle fiber of the mid-1970s. He remembered the mentally unstable salesman at the La-Z-Boy store, leaping onto the chair like a hunter onto a felled elephant and stabbing it again and again with a silver nail file that he gripped in his fist. "See?" the salesman had shouted, panting with effort. "No . . . holes! No . . . holes. . . . The weave of the fiber just bounces right back!" "Oh, my God," Aileen had said, as Lee pulled Esther behind him protectively. But it had worked, hadn't it? They'd purchased the chair, on installment.

Now the chair was worn, and stained, and its hideous black-and-white plaid was dark gray overall. But there weren't any holes. Instead the coarse weave had grown less and less like a fabric and more and more like a net, barely restraining the chair's flesh of crumbling foam rubber. A chair after my own heart, Lee thought as he made it recline—and it still reclined effortlessly. Worn down so it looks like garbage, but at least no holes.

The next morning Lee read his remarks in the local paper, the *Herald,* and that afternoon, to his shock, also had them pointed out to him where they appeared in the *New York Times.* The *Times* story was small, from the Associated Press, but seeing himself in its pages gave Lee a more harrowing jolt than had seeing himself on TV. At least his newly discovered ill-feeling for Hendley was not just concealed but made to seem inconceivable by his eloquent outrage. And in truth, with the onrush of sympathy and admiration from colleagues and students and even strangers Lee was amazed to find lavished on him in the wake of the bombing—and with Hendley out of sight in the intensive-care ward—Lee was soon able to conceal from himself his own poor sentiments. He could even imagine he loved Hendley, and yearned for his recovery.

3.

JEALOUSY HAD STAINED MUCH OF LEE'S LIFE, YET HE'D never seen himself as prone to it, perhaps because he'd first become jealous surprisingly late. As a young man, before emigrating, he'd never experienced any of the circumstances that might have aroused that emotion. His had been, initially, an exceptionally privileged family. Then they had fallen, but no one had risen to usurp their place. The anguish of being a fallen aristocrat, or as much of a fallen aristocrat as your nation can muster, is a very different anguish from that of envying those better off. His family had only their past selves to envy, and envy was not what they felt; they mourned their past selves as if they'd been cut down by death. Lee felt fierce love for the naïve and arrogant young man he'd been, and sometimes, in his immigrant life, this love almost seemed to reanimate that former self, so that to outsiders he seemed both arrogant and remarkably blind to his own circumstances. They thought he believed in himself as an exception, whatever the case, but the truth was exactly the opposite: Lee knew that his exceptional status was irrecoverably lost. If he sometimes resembled the young man he'd been, it wasn't in defiance to new circumstance but from the painful awareness of how immutable the new circumstance was. He could never have guessed that his past self possessed him like a ghost, sometimes glaring out through his eyes or emitting harsh orders by way of his mouth. Had he known, he might have thought his past self could protect him from the gnawing sensation of inadequacy, and then he would have been disappointed in himself yet again.

But sometimes these seemingly incompatible sides of himself, his vestigial arrogance and his terrible envy, joined together to effect startling change. It had been in this hybridized manner that he'd won Aileen.

Aileen had been the wife of Lee's classmate and only real friend in graduate school, a pale, elongated wearer of tortoiseshell spectacles named Lewis Gaither. Like Lee, Gaither had arrived at the graduate level of mathematical study late by comparison with the other grad students. Lee had begun the program at the age of thirty-three, having been unable to start his undergraduate study in the United States until twenty-nine, on account of civil war and upheaval in his native country. Gaither had started the grad program at the even more wizened age of thirty-five, although for reasons very different from Lee's. After earning his B.A. in math at the standard age of twenty-one, for more than a decade Gaither had served his Lord Jesus Christ on a series of overseas missions, and had only returned to the United States at the behest of his parents, who had been waiting to marry him to a woman who shared his beliefs. Gaither was an evangelical Christian: a serene man whose unostentatious and absolute faith tended to have the most impact on those who had been nonbelievers all their lives until meeting him. Instead of hewing to one of the young women introduced by his parents, Gaither began spending time with the beautiful twenty-year-old who, despite privately professed atheism and reluctant public affiliation with her family's almost equally godless Unitarian church, sometimes filled in for the organist at the Gaither family's house of worship. Aileen's aversion to every sort of religion would survive her marriage to Gaither, by whose faith she was completely unmoved. Lee's own decade of marriage to Aileen never satisfactorily revealed to him why she'd married Gaither, or why Gaither had married Aileen. "It was something to do that summer," Aileen once said, opaquely. In any case, when Aileen's marriage to Gaither came apart, it did so like a garment that had been pinned by the seamstress and then never sewn. The rupture was ugly and loud, but afterward, in Lee's estimation, the two halves were just as they'd been before joined; neither took so much as a thread of the other into the next phase of life.

For the duration of his friendship with Gaither, Lee didn't like to think it was based on their age; once the friendship was over, he liked to think it had no basis beyond that. The other eight students in their year in the Ph.D. program—all men, all white and American-born except Lee—had seemed to Lee like lesser versions of their paragon, a mathematical prodigy if social oddball named Donald Whitehead. Like Whitehead, these eight all were goldenly handsome and brooding in the Byronic vein; all wore their hair distractedly untrimmed, their tweed jackets unmended, their ancient leather loafers unrepaired. All of them were young, well-bred, unapologetic introverts whose lack of cordiality and warmth was admired by professors and women alike as evidence of their genius; although Whitehead, as the acknowledged apotheosis of these qualities, tended to take them too far. Whitehead's dishabille left the realm of the romantic to verge on the incompetent. Whitehead's social disconnection from fellow students sometimes seemed less a proudly elected condition than an exile he was helpless to alter; his lesser, Byronic peers did socialize with each other, if in remote, haughty ways. Whitehead, Lee believed, was always left to himself. All of the ways in which Whitehead was distinct from his clutch of blond shadows both stoked Lee's desire to befriend him— only him—and led Lee to realize that this was impossible. Whitehead silently handed Lee class notes a few times on request and as silently—though Lee felt graciously, on what basis he couldn't have said—received them again with Lee's thanks, when he had copied them down. But the relationship did not progress, as it did not progress between Whitehead and anyone, and so Lee found himself pairing with Gaither, the other outcast.

Gaither made the first overtures, and here again there was much that Lee sought to revise once the friendship was over. Lee was canny enough to realize that Gaither's early, easy interest in him, Gaither's falling into step with him outside of class, the uncondescending manner in which Gaither filled in missing words, early on, when Lee's English still faltered, arose from a mixture of genuine kindness and the other strong motive of Gaither's religion. Lee was clear-eyed about his nonlofty status, enough aware that the depth of his loneliness exerted a force that repelled, no matter how hard he worked to conceal it. Lee modeled himself on the Byronic octet, not without some success; his ink-dark, almost mirrorlike hair grew to fall in a cowlick that hid his forehead; he found a battered calf briefcase, like a WASPy, neglected heirloom, in a secondhand store. He knew that the younger departmental secretaries saw him as an exotic prince of the Far East, a Yul Brynner with hair, and he would feel them staring after his tweed-covered back—the secondhand store again—as he left the office. But Gaither, perhaps because he was older, saw through to Lee's yearning; or was yearning, himself, for a friend; or was intent on a mission. Lee was aware of all three possibilities and stressed the second while the friendship endured and the third when it ended. Lee's mother, in the late and unhappiest years of her life, had been aggressively plied by a Protestant missionary and at long last turned into a Christian, and by contrast with that person Lee found Gaither admirably subtle. Their conversations scarcely touched upon religion; it was the friendship itself that would reel Lee in. But as aware as Lee felt of all this, he wasn't willing to admit what a prisoner he was of his loneliness and that he would have accepted Gaither's friendship even if it consisted entirely of the desire to make a new convert. Lee told himself, in his early encounters with Gaither, that he, too, was indulging one weaker; Gaither's need to convert was a flaw, toward which Lee could be kind.

It was in this spirit of wary but willing friendship with Gaither that Lee met Aileen. Lee knew that Aileen was Gaither's wife of less than a year; they had married the July before Gaither entered grad school, about six months after they'd met. Aileen had a secretarial job in another department and took the occasional class toward a B.A. degree; she and Gaither did not yet have children. Lee assumed, because Gaither had not said otherwise, that Aileen must be a Christian also, and he imagined her unremarkably, pinkishly pale and smooth-featured and plump. Perhaps she had lusterless, heavy brown hair in a matronly clip at the back of her neck and wore dowdy plaid skirts and support hose and practical shoes. Perhaps she was tranquilly faithful, like Gaither, but lacking his brains; though for the most part, until he met her, Lee did not think of Aileen at all.

One evening after their seminar, as they walked the flagstone quad path to the gate where they usually parted, Lee to his rooming house four blocks off campus, Gaither to the bus that took him several miles to wherever he lived with Aileen, Gaither said, "There's a shindig this weekend at the park outside town. A statewide church event. I know you're not in the market to pick up religion, but I'd like it if you met

my friends. My church friends. And Aileen. It would make a nice out-
ing. When's the last time you saw hills and trees? They must have had
those things back in your country." Gaither's peculiarly gentle, ironical
manner of speech was his most signal asset, the winking blade that allowed for his faith to be tolerable. His voice was slowed by a very
slight drawl from a boyhood in Texas, but this was entwined with pe-
dantic enunciativeness, which was then overlaid by self-mockery.
Gaither used words like "shindig" to acknowledge he was just the sort
of stay-at-home stick who should never say "shindig." And his reference to Lee's foreignness somehow worked as a reference to all those
who saw Lee that way, among whom Gaither wasn't included: their
peers in the program, who effortlessly shunned them both.

"Shindig?" Lee said, smiling wryly. This was one of many moments at which his awareness of Gaither's attempt to convert him was
outweighed by his pleasure at having the man as his friend.

"An evening cookout, in a tent, with some singing and talking and
milling around. You won't be preached at, I promise. The folks we
don't know will assume you're a Christian already, and my friends will
know better than to give you an earful. They already tried that with
Aileen. She got them trained pretty quick." This was the first indication Lee had that Aileen was not as he'd thought. Gaither winked, and
they parted, agreeing that Gaither would pick Lee up Friday evening
at six on that corner.

This had been early April, their first spring in graduate school. In
that part of the Midwest, April was even more variable than it is in
New England; the week of Gaither's invitation, the daffodils and the
tulips had started to open in the long, geometrical beds that outlined
campus buildings, but it happened almost every year and was endlessly discussed by the locals that after a week of exquisite, damp days
the temperature fell and brought with it several feet of spring snow.
That the statewide federation of Gaither's coreligionists had planned
their open-air shindig for this time of the year poignantly indicated
their faith, Lee reflected, as he turned up the collar of his thin black
suit jacket and pulled the lapels closed across his sternum. The afternoon was already cold, although it was perfectly clear; the declining
sun stained the drab campus buildings as if they'd been hosed down
with wine. The wind was increasingly strong; Lee watched the tulips,

already grown to full height and with their leaves raised like arms, flinging themselves supplicatingly onto the ground. It might have been his discomfort at the prospect of the evening ahead, but the wind-lashed flowers looked like penitents to him, prostrating themselves in abased ecstasy. Lee had inherited godlessness from his father, and it was one of his few characteristics about which he felt no concern. His discomfort arose not from suspicion that he did long for God but from the fragility of his belief that it was he and not Gaither who held the balance of power, that it was Gaither, in his desire for a convert, who was the real supplicant. By the time the car, a battered two-door sedan, pulled up at the bus stop with Gaither at the wheel, Lee felt his mood souring and detected in himself the first stirrings of resentment. Until now he and Gaither had never conducted their friendship entirely outside the classroom; even when they had sat in the campus tavern, where Gaither drank ginger ale or orange juice while Lee had a beer, their encounter had been framed by their status as equals within their department, both academically and socially. In meeting on a Friday night for reasons entirely unconnected to school, in driving together in Gaither's car to a meeting of Gaither's fellow Christians, in the company of Gaither's friends and Gaither's wife, Lee felt that Gaither had led him over a border on the far side of which they were vastly unequal. The front passenger door swung open, and Lee crossed his arms across his chest, as much in an unconscious effort to repel the car as because he was cold. A woman—small, brown-haired, with a stern, unremarkable, un-made-up face and in a brown blazer and long plaid skirt and loafers—got out of the car without so much as a glance at Lee, while Gaither leaned across the front seat and waved. "D'you mind riding in the back, Lee?" he called. "Ruth gets carsick." The small brown woman wrestled with the front seat until it hinged forward and then stood aside silently so that Lee could climb into the back. "It's my pleasure to meet you, Aileen," he said, holding out a stiff hand. He was aware of a feeling of triumph, on finding that Gaither's wife was as plain as he'd thought and, on top of that, rude.

"I'm not Aileen, I'm Ruth," the woman said, affronted. "Aileen's in the back because I get carsick."

Clambering, then, clumsily into the car, ducking his head underneath the low roof, feeling the too-long hair that hung over his forehead sticking into his eyes, hoping not to split the knees of his pants in the awkward position, because the pants were very old and overwashed and the knees had worn thin, Lee was doubly embarrassed, not merely because he had failed to hear Gaither name Ruth and had so made a gaffe. The woman in the backseat, whom he had not even noticed as the car had pulled up, seemed to exude such an air of intense disengagement, such a desire to be left alone, that Lee felt he'd been pushed through a window into her boudoir. As he struggled to insert himself into the seat beside her, she dropped a newspaper she'd been reading onto her lap and watched him, with indifference. She was shatteringly beautiful and as obviously bored.

"Hello," she said, when he'd settled himself. "I'm Aileen."

"It's my pleasure to meet you," he managed, in an unsteady sweat as if he'd sprinted to get into the car.

"Likewise," she said, without the slightest attempt at sincerity. She picked up her newspaper again.

However her carsickness manifested itself, Ruth was stoic about it. She sat motionless and erect in her seat, the mousy brown top of her head barely visible over the headrest. Lee guessed that her sickness was in part claustrophobia. She had rolled down her window all the way to the sill, and as they left town and pulled onto the country highway, a roar of cold wind filled the car and the air seemed to turn to a mass and pin them where they sat. Then it was too loud, and the cold was too numbing, to speak. Aileen's newspaper snapped angrily and was torn in so many directions she couldn't fold it; Lee held on to one edge, and together they tried until Aileen mashed it into a ball and put it under her feet. Then they went back to staring ahead in silence. Lee couldn't see Gaither's face in the narrow rearview, but Gaither drove through the howl of gelatinous wind in the dying daylight with the loose motions and confident shoulders of a man at the helm of his yacht. He seemed to smile beatifically with the back of his head. Lee twisted away and gazed out his window. He hadn't been outside the confines of their small college town since the late August afternoon eight months before when he'd arrived on a bus from the nearest big city, ninety minutes away—the same city to which Gaither and Ruth, he'd soon learn, commuted each Sunday by the same bus to go to their church.

The drive seemed to last hours, but when Gaither turned off the road into trees at a sign for the Corn Creek State Park, Lee was startled to see by his Seiko that it had not been even thirty minutes since they'd picked him up at the bus stop. The two-lane highway had left town for flat, stubbled cornfields that reached off endlessly; then the land had grown very slightly uneven, like a rumpled bedsheet, and unremarkable trees lined the sides of the road. Lee glimpsed a magnolia that had formed fuzzy buds; all the rest of the branches were still bare. Leaving the highway, they had dropped onto a drab gravel road that for no topographical reason pursued a meandering path through the scraggly woods; the occasional burnt-wood sign pointed on to a parking lot, picnic meadow, and lake. But the sun was now setting between the tops of the trees and the ground, pouring its blaze sideways into the car; in spite of the wind, Lee felt it hot against his cheek, and when he glanced at Aileen, he saw her skin illumined with reflected sunlight. The gathering had been planned, with permission from the park manager, to coincide with the park's closing time, so that the lakeside pavilion and its tables and barbecue grills could be had privately. Coming around a last bend, they could see, through the bare trees, the homely "pavilion," a sort of large shingled roof up on poles, already glowing blue underneath from its flyspecked fluorescents, and with a small stage set up. Lee thought he sensed Aileen recoil; perhaps she was embarrassed by the gathering's scrappy sincerity, its dowdy religiousness. And these were not even mainstream American Christians, they were marginal evangelicals—but as the car arrived in the parking lot, Lee saw that the lot was almost a third full and that men and women and children were ambling to greet each other on the blacktop, clasping hands beneath the afterglow sky. Gaither switched off the engine and turned around to the backseat. "We're here!" he said. The wind had matted his thinning brown hair, and Lee realized that in this context—in his shirtsleeves in the open air, outside a classroom, but most of all in the midst of his own beloved people—Gaither was a very handsome man. He had a strong-boned but delicate face, rangy arms, at least half a head's more height than Lee. Lee looked again at Aileen. She was pulling a comb through her hair, without vanity; he winced when he saw her yank hard on a tangle. For an instant the combing exposed shell-like ears and large metal triangular earrings that set off the finely sculpted planes of her face. They struck Lee as an admirably brazen choice for a church gathering. Aileen thrust her comb back in her purse, removed a lipstick, and retraced her mouth quickly in red. Lee realized he was staring, from a distance of inches. Ruth had climbed out of the car without waiting for Gaither, who was standing at the driver's side with the seat pulled forward, in readiness for his wife.

"You can get out now," Ruth told Lee. "The car's stopped."

As the four of them crossed the parking lot toward the pavilion in the waning twilight, Lee might have been afraid of Gaither's making him conspicuous, of Gaither with a proprietary arm around his shoulders, gently but firmly propelling him toward introductions, telegraphing Lee's vulnerable foreign godlessness to this church brother and that. But in the same way that Lee's preoccupations had altered radically once he'd climbed into the car, Gaither's manner toward Lee now was very different from what Lee had expected. As Gaither and Ruth encountered one group of comrades after another, their formation on foot, which had begun with Gaither and Aileen side by side, quickly reshuffled itself so that they were walking the same way they'd sat in the car. Gaither introduced Aileen to those church members she'd never met, let her exchange her wan greetings with those that she knew, but with the formality past she dropped slightly behind and gazed off at the distant horizon; and of course Ruth shared devout fellowship with each one of the people Aileen quietly snubbed. Soon Aileen and Lee had fallen so many paces behind that Gaither did not even attempt to include Aileen in his conversations; and the farther they penetrated the crowd, the less he seemed to recall she was there. Lee also had weathered an early round of brief introductions and also felt himself, to his relief, increasingly forgotten. Ahead of them Gaither seemed ever taller and lighter of step, while beside him stern, humorless Ruth also clasped hands and nodded intently and then spoke with great feeling, about what, Lee was too far to hear. By the time they had reached the pavilion, where, they now perceived, a little band was sawing away on banjo and fiddle without amplification, Lee almost dared to believe that Gaither had brought him not as fodder for proselytizers but to squire Aileen. Then suddenly Gaither was with them again, a large palm flat on each of their shoulders. "I hope you're both meeting people," he effused. "Are you hungry? Aileen?"

"I'm all right," Aileen said.

"Lee?"

"I'd take something," Lee said cautiously.

"Good! Come on over here. Where those lanterns are hanging there's a whole barbecue, with soft drinks and salads and pie. Our church is the nearest to here, so we're hosts for this evening. I can promise that the food committee will amaze with their efforts. We're hosting church members tonight from all over the region. There are even folks here from Ohio. Later on there will be just a few prayers and talks, and then we'll have some square dancing. Oh, come on now"—with a smile at Aileen—"it's not such an ordeal. George and Shirley are around here somewhere, you like dancing with them. Aileen claims she hates dancing," Gaither told Lee in tones of amazement.

"I don't do it either," Lee said.

They finally lost Gaither for good near the barbecue grills. There was, as promised, a tantalizing array of fruit and three-bean and potato salads, and pyramids of charred little burgers taken fresh off the coals and blown immediately cold by the late-April wind. Lee discovered he was ravenous, perhaps as ravenous as he'd been in his life. Forgetting caution and self-consciousness, emboldened by Aileen's presence to completely ignore the curious and encouraging smiles of the food-committee members with their barbecue tongs who were uttering platitudes at him—"Welcome!" "We're so glad to have you with us tonight!"—Lee piled his paper plate with the cold little burgers, with mayonnaised potatoes and cubed cantaloupe and peanut butter and oatmeal cookies. Aileen lagged along with him vaguely, but he could feel the precise contour of her presence, and he could tell that as much as she behaved like a stranger to the people around her, she was known to at least some of them. The food committee was composed of members of Gaither's congregation; there was an almost audible quality to the quiet that surrounded Aileen, amid a sea of gregariousness, as she followed Lee down the length of the food table, taking only a cookie. The barbecue grills were just outside the shelter of the pavilion's roof but still within the glare of its blinding fluorescence; when they left the food table and strode just a few paces farther away, the night returned startlingly, tall and cold and the color of blue ink in the bottle, not yet flat black as it would be in an hour. With the pavilion light at his back, out of his eyes, Lee was dazzled by stars; the smear of them was doubled in the round little lake, which in darkness, denoted only by what it reflected, possessed a mysterious dignified beauty entirely absent from the brown pond they'd glimpsed through the trees as they drove up. As his eyes adjusted, Lee made out the shapes of picnic tables like black nebulae against the shimmering lake, a few of them occupied by stargazing or less sociable Christians, but most of them empty. "You want to sit?" he asked Aileen, and his voice seemed awkward, and too loud. She led him to a table, both of them walking unsteadily although the ground was level, because of how little they saw. Then they sat down on the tabletop, with their feet on the bench to stay clear of the chill evening dew, facing back toward the pavilion, which glowed garishly like a UFO just touching down. Lee ate fiercely, almost vengefully, and as his plate emptied, he somehow grew more angry, more affronted, not less.

"So you and Lewis," Aileen began lamely, after moments of silence. Lee interrupted her.

"If you were my woman," he heard himself saying, "I wouldn't bring you to garbage like this."

"Oh, you wouldn't?" she said, as if she'd expected an outburst.

"And I wouldn't give a damn about God," he concluded, feeling suddenly dizzy.

"You don't give a damn about God anyway," she said. "Obviously."

"Neither do you."

"Again: obviously."

"Why are you married?" Lee said, with exasperation, and he never could have explained why he felt familiar enough with a woman he'd known barely an hour to ask such a thing.

Aileen laughed a compact, brittle laugh. "That's a pretty rude question."

"I don't care about being rude," Lee said, putting his empty plate down.

"That must be why he likes you."

"Who?"

"Who! That's terrific. My *husband.* Your friend. He must like you because you don't care if you're rude. I think that's why he likes me."

"Why do you like him?"

"Because he's a good man," she said vehemently, but her vehemence did not seem aimed at Lee. "You are rude. You're not much of a friend."

Lee didn't dispute this. It was a realization that would have pierced him if it had occurred just an hour before.

After a moment Aileen said, "I'm going to rudely suggest we go back to the shindig." There was finality to her statement, but there wasn't rebuke. Whether this was the end of that evening's conversation, or of all conversations, Lee couldn't have said, but the sense of finality was as absolute to him as it must have been to her; without another word they both stood and walked back to the pavilion, more quickly this time, because guided by its lights. They found Gaither backward on a folding chair, deep in conversation, but his face was unrestrainedly, unsuspiciously glad when he saw them approaching. Lee felt nothing at the sight of that face, no remorse whatsoever.

"Hello," Aileen said to her husband, and she bent down to kiss him. Then she stood behind him and held his hand, clasped against his large shoulder, as he continued to talk.

The drive back late that night was just as silent and even colder, but this time it seemed over in minutes. No one told Ruth to put up the window. The stars made white streaks in the sky. Aileen was a shadowed, unreachable presence on the seat beside him, a stone sunk in the depths of a lake. And there was something exquisite in this, in her distance from him, and in measuring it, and in weighing how little he needed to bridge it—and then all the newly strange familiarities of their small town, its still streets and empty porches and shuttered storefronts, were upon them, and the weak pinkish light of the streetlamps bled into the car. They dropped Ruth off first, at a plain wooden two-story boardinghouse that in its drabness resembled her, and then although Lee's boardinghouse was just a few blocks away Aileen got out of the backseat, requiring Gaither to leave the driver's seat and hold the seat forward for her, so she could sit in the front. Then they were at Lee's, and Aileen got out again, to release him. "I'll walk Mr. Lee up," she told Gaither, and Gaither, as he had done at the start of the evening, leaned across the front seat and waved.

"Good night, Lee," he said. "Thank you so much for coming along. I hope you had a fine time."

"I did," Lee said. "Thank you."

He and Aileen mounted the steps together, and although Lee was certain Gaither was gazing straight ahead out the windshield, his eyes dazzled with stars, his spirit sated by fellowship, Lee still felt a gaze of some kind, branding him. He already had his key in his hand, and there was nothing to wait for; Aileen offered her hand, and he shook it, hardly looking at her.

"Come over for coffee sometime," she said. He scarcely managed to answer; she was already turning away to go back down the steps.

"When?" he said.

"Sunday morning," she said. "At nine-thirty."

4.

LESS THAN A MONTH AFTER LEE BEGAN HIS AFFAIR WITH Aileen, she told him she was pregnant. "His, not yours," she said, before he'd been able to speak.

"How do you know?" he gasped then, feeling the words, with his breath, sucked from him too quickly, as if by a powerful vacuum.

"Because I'm almost ten weeks," she said. "And I was only sleeping with one of you ten weeks ago."

They would have been whispering, almost hissing at each other, in the drab, cluttered office of the professor of urban statistics whose papers it was one of Aileen's jobs to refile, while the professor was in Rome on a working sabbatical. The office was, apart from being drab and cluttered, cold both in temperature and in overall atmosphere. A single fluorescent panel hung from the ceiling, which they tried to leave off. The single window, which looked out on the building's parking lot from the height of only the third floor, was dressed with a dusty venetian blind, which they kept lowered and closed. The desk was university-issue gunmetal gray, as were the laden bookshelves. The absent professor's papers were kept for the most part in overtaxed cardboard boxes, splitting at their seams, squeezed precariously on the bookshelves or stacked three or four high on the floor; the stench of dust and dry mold filled the room. There was a broken couch, also covered with boxes, which squeaked, and an Amish rag rug on the black tile floor. Aileen had brought the rug from her home. It looked as out of place as it was, although for all its inappropriate implications of handcrafted domestic contentment, it wasn't comfortable either. It consisted entirely of knots; it was meant for shod feet, not bare flesh. Lee would feel the rug taking vengeance for Gaither as it bit harsh red dents in his elbows and knees and, he knew, as it steadily scoured Aileen's spine. In his feverish lust Lee would see, through the too-wide crack at the base of the door, the constant detached clicking shoe soles of passersby in the hallway outside. These were her co-workers, the heavyset, decades-married, full-time secretaries who snubbed Aileen for her part-timer status, her efforts to earn a degree, her superior mind—the department chair favored her and gave her special assignments and privileges, like the refiling project, and her key to this office—and for her handsome young husband, who picked her up at the end of the day when his schedule allowed and happily squired her home, with the nimbus of adulterous sex still swagged over her limbs like a fine length of scent-soaked chiffon.

It had been a three-week period during which Lee trysted with her almost daily, with the reckless bloodlust of a soldier in battle and the fastidiousness of a prodigy finally meeting his ideal instrument. She climaxed so crashingly, with such wails of remorseful abandon, she brought a towel to the office that Lee stuffed in her mouth when he felt her convulsions beginning. The rug's riot of colors had to increasingly hide the dried, crackling laminate stains they deposited on it. After the first time, he had never gone to her and Gaither's home again on a Sunday morning; they had left a rout of slime and semen and uprooted hair on her living-room floor to which, she said afterward, her lousy house-keeping skills were unequal, her voice shaking when she said it, though she'd attempted to joke. So that from then on, they met on her lunch hour, and again in the early evenings if Gaither had an undergraduate section to lead, and every Sunday morning, always in the office, the key of which Aileen copied for him, so that he could arrive early and, when the hallway was empty, let himself in to wait in the dark. And then after three weeks, or rather twenty-three days, she told him she was pregnant. "I should have known," she whispered, perched beside him, not touching him, on the squeaky couch, on which they scarcely dared breathe. "I've been so sick, so nauseated. That Sunday after you came to the house, I couldn't stop vomiting. I hardly eat anymore."

"You're never sick when I see you," he hissed. Her evidence seemed dishonest, contrived just to thwart him.

"I am, it's just other things . . . drown it out."

He stared at her, her face obscure to him in the darkened office. They had not touched each other at all; when she'd slipped through the door and he'd risen to meet her, she'd recoiled visibly. "No," she'd said. She was ruining him, perversely, with no regard for the consequences. He had an urge to strike her, to beat and kill Gaither; his body felt like a jar full of blood being violently shaken. The unprecedented complication of the situation, the terror of having come to feel so exclusively in possession of a body within which, all the while, another man's child lived, would not make itself felt until later. For now he only felt she was killing him, trivially. He hardly knew her; he was not even sure what her face would look like if he turned on the light.

"I can't believe I've wanted sex at all, all this time," she murmured.

"Get out of here," Lee said.

"It's my office."

"Get *out*."

After a moment she rose, and the couch groaned, letting go of her weight. He heard her crushing her keys in her hand. "You'll let yourself out without being seen," she said coldly. He didn't reply.

"I can't see you again," she said. "Ever."

He had not meant to speak. "You're a whore!" he spat.

"You're a coward," Aileen told him, much later. "You'll say anything to make yourself feel less weak."

Aileen also would later say to him, "If only I hadn't goddamn gotten pregnant. Our affair would have run through to its natural end, pretty quickly. Instead there had to be a big break, and that felt like romance. What a dummy I was." Aileen had a way of saying juvenile words like "dummy" with a chilling contempt that struck Lee to the quick. Her cruelty possessed a devastating stealth, while Lee's was obvious, clumsy.

He sat in the darkness a long time after she had gone. Grief had not begun yet. Finally, the hallway entirely silent, he let himself out and kicked his copy of the key back under the door. He also left the tawdry rug and the towel, for her housekeeping skills.

As finale, April unleashed tumultuous weather. Two days after Aileen broke with Lee, as the redbud blossoms erupted down the lengths of the boughs like tufts of purple piñata tissue, and bright yellow strings of forsythia hung in the yards, and the daffodils opened, a whistling spring blizzard left three feet of snow on the ground. Lee tried to read Mishima's *Spring Snow* while contemplating suicide, for the first time in earnest. It was the agonizing passage of time that made him want to die. He heard every slow tick of the second hand on his Seiko. He would will himself to read, read, read, to not look at his watch until eons had passed, and when he finally broke down and looked, it would be five, or just three, minutes later. He could hardly pull himself through the shoals from daybreak, when he woke from a jangled, unnourishing sleep, to sunset, when he let himself go back to bed. He broke with Gaither in turn because he couldn't maintain a façade. He tried, for a day, but when Gaither walked into their seminar, he felt himself redden to the roots of his hair. With his brown skin in that room of pale men, he must have blazed like a mythical savage. He felt the curious eyes of Whitehead and the Byrons on him, sensed their professor give him wide, baffled berth, but it was Gaither, seated beside him out of habit, who scorched him. Gaither leaned toward him and murmured a question when their professor had turned to write on the blackboard, and Lee sat transfixed, empty-lunged, not even able to shrug Gaither off. "Lee?" Gaither asked, in his siftingly soft southern voice. "Are you feeling all right?"

When class ended, Lee steamed from the room, but Gaither's long stride caught up easily. "What's bothering you?" he asked quickly. "I can see something's wrong."

"Leave me the hell alone," Lee said.

"Was it the church function? Because I thought that you had a good time, but if you didn't, that's fine. I never meant to offend you. I respect your beliefs, and I know you respect mine. I have no interest in making you share them. Aileen doesn't share my beliefs, and I'm married to her—"

"I don't respect your beliefs," Lee corrected him, stopping and looking at him finally—at his lean, handsome face and his long, rangy arms and his bulky, sincere spectacles. His stupidity and worthlessness were so glaring that Lee felt he could have been conversing with a talented mule or steer. "Your religion's a joke. If your wife doesn't believe in that"—and here he'd struggled for an erudite insult, something far more fatal than a mere expletive, but his excellent English, over which he'd so toiled, now completely failed him—"in that fairy-tale stuff, it's not because you haven't tried. I could feel you parade me around at that thing like your"—he'd struggled again, but recovered more quickly—"your *coolie.* Your little pagan whose lost soul you're going to save."

"That is unjust," Gaither said frigidly. Now he seemed as Lee had been only moments before, paralyzed by shock. But Lee had warmed to his task.

"You even fight like a preacher," Lee said. "I don't need your Christian handouts. Like I said, from now on leave me alone."

He might not have endured it if the academic year hadn't been almost over. Continuing to sit around a table in classes, to stand at colloquia with a teacup and a cookie, to walk out of their departmental building, always a few yards ahead of or in the wake of Gaither, Lee almost felt it was Gaither with whom he'd shared a passion that had now been destroyed. Gaither's humiliation and anger, and most of all his complete confusion as to the cause of the breach, roiled Lee with remorse and even with compassion. But this last feeling was so incompatible with the roots of his quandary, his desire for Aileen, that he shoved it away until he felt it transformed into rigid contempt. Above all, he shunned Gaither from fear. He was afraid not only of seeing Aileen but of the sound of her name or any other slim evidence she still existed. He wanted to think she'd dissolved from the face of the earth, that no one saw her finely drawn, cynical mouth or her thin, boyish shoulders or the place where her hips flared surprisingly from her small waist. Her pregnancy he completely erased from his mind, as only a man could, and only a man reared in an affluent household in which a pregnant wife and mother could be hidden away from her children and even her husband by a phalanx of servants until her condition had passed and her beauty returned. Lee knew nothing of pregnancy, Aileen's or anyone's, and so he banished the thought, simply wouldn't believe it.

In his homeland the ocean had never been more than an hour away, and although looking at it had involved a rattling bus ride and then standing on the land side of a chain-link fence topped with coils of razor wire, he had made the trip often for reasons he understood only now, in this spring of his American heartbreak. The pure texture of ocean ruined by the grid of the fence, and the rough, slimy beach out of reach, and watchtowers within sight in either direction with armed sentries inside, poised for signs of invasion, had not bothered him as much as the solitude and the noise of the ocean and the far horizon had solaced him. He recalled those days as always windy and gray, neither winter nor summer. He would cross his arms high on the fence, lean his forehead against them, and stare out through the links at the waves for as long as an hour. Once he had finally turned to walk back down the rutted dirt road to the regional highway, the fretfulness that had seemed to constrict him like vines, and his many-chambered anxieties, and his silted-up lungs, would all seem to dilate and collapse. He'd feel open and empty. Only when the ride home was over would he feel those pains rising to claim him again.

At the time it had felt like impoverished contemplation, if indispensable to him. Now, stranded in the Midwest, he was homesick for that route to the ocean, however grim it had been. The town was small, the campus even smaller, fitted snugly like a gift inside its box; the town existed to serve the school and held no dark pockets in which Lee could get lost. Seated tensely on a bench on the quad, he felt like a caged cat. The cherry trees had exploded like fireworks and left their pink litter all over the ground. The lilacs had bloomed and begun to wither, bunched in pendants like grapes, and their dizzy perfume, slightly tainted by vegetable rot, was still suspended in motionless patches like invisible fog; Lee would pass through one and involuntarily turn his head, seeking the source. Everywhere Lee went, he felt stripped and exposed to the flagrancy of the season, to its blunt smell of sex, as if he had never understood the raw basis for fertility legends and rites and agriculture's rhythms and poetry's worst clichés, and at the same time he felt uniquely dead to it, as if the sexual world, which he had just woken to, was defined by his absence from it. He was dangling, redundant.

His break with Gaither had not gone unnoticed by their fellow students, which made him realize that their brief friendship had been noticed as well. One afternoon he was sitting on what had become his usual bench, not because he was comfortable there but because, once he had managed to sit there a first time, he'd felt unable to pioneer another spot; it was the same paralysis that kept him from obtaining a map of the region, a bus schedule, from seeking any escape from the confines that made him so unhappy. It was almost five o'clock, an hour when friends sought each other out and the lonely wandered, looking for company; the air was the warmest it had been the whole month, and the quad's rich triangular patches of grass, outlined by flagstone footpaths, were crowded with small groups sitting and talking and smoking or lying on their coats with eyes closed and their faces turned up toward the sun. But Lee shared his bench with no one, and no one was near enough to him that he could hear conversation. The shadows of the large trees were long and exquisitely detailed in the intense slanting light; every once in a while, Lee would see a group shift, to escape a shadow's encroachment. Sunny days and sunny dispositions. Lee had met Aileen at the start of April, and the cruel month had only just ended. There was still one more week of classes; then exams, and release. Lee had one of his texts next to him but was not looking at it. The crystalline beauty of mathematics was no longer apparent to him. He had the unfinished Mishima, also of no interest, tented on his knee.

He was so detached, the field of his vision, despite the rich scene, so empty, that he did not notice Donald Whitehead walking toward him until he was only a few yards away. Whitehead was wearing a rumpled green and gold houndstooth jacket that was slightly too large but that somehow, for this flaw, was more flattering. And he'd gotten a haircut; his deep-set eyes were still shadowed beneath the shelf of his brow, but his square forehead and jaw and his strong nose stood out handsomely. He was shorter than Gaither, Lee's height, but more classically built, Lee decided; he entirely lacked Gaither's gentle effeminacy. His eyes sparked with an interest now that Lee had not seen before. "Mishima?" Whitehead said, coming to a halt just in front of him, so that their two afternoon shadows stretched out side by side, pointing east, toward the clock tower.

A few months before, Lee would have been flattered, even quietly excited, by this attention from Whitehead. Now he found it burdensome—not because it was Whitehead but because it was anyone. "I like him," Lee managed to say, tepidly.

"You're reading him in Japanese. That's impressive."

"Not really. I knew Japanese before I knew English. It's just easier for me."

"Wata kusimo sukosi hanasemasu," Whitehead offered, with a pretense at self-deprecation Lee could see was masked pride.

"Sukosi ja naide sho," Lee answered. "I didn't know that you spoke Japanese."

"Hardly. I've taken a semester or two, but I've probably just showed you all that I know. If you ever feel like more work, I could use a tutor. But it would have to be charitable, or we'd have to barter, and I doubt I've got anything that you'd want. I'm tragically impoverished this semester."

Lee doubted it, looking at the old but well-pedigreed jacket. He'd never found something like that at the secondhand store. The word "charitable" made him think of Gaither and the vile words he had spat at Gaither on the day of their break, and though he'd meant to tell Whitehead he'd be happy to tutor for free, a beat passed, and then another, in which he didn't speak at all. But Whitehead did not seem deterred. "All right if I sit for a minute?" he asked. Lee moved his textbook, and Whitehead sat down.

"Looks like you and Gaither had a falling-out," Whitehead said, as if reading Lee's mind. Lee's heart lurched in his chest, and he felt his palms tingle with mortification, but outwardly he was sure he showed nothing. So the rift had been noticed. He shouldn't feel surprised; theirs was a small, claustrophobic department in which little happened.

"I wouldn't say a falling-out. We're all busy this term. We just don't see each other so much."

"For a while there you seemed thick as thieves."

"I don't know about that." Lee was aware of a stirring of gratification, that Whitehead had observed this. Perhaps Whitehead had wished he were as thick with Lee. Or with Gaither.

"It's none of my business, but I couldn't help asking. I wondered if it had something to do with his saintliness. I can't tolerate religious men, personally. I can't tolerate religion. To me it's the most offensive form of so-called thinking there is. A pile of ludicrous irrationality that actually tries to dress itself up in rational arguments. Religion and mathematics shouldn't get within miles of each other. I'm not saying Gaither's not a mathematician, but I wonder about his work. I hope I'm not offending you. I've never had pretty manners."

"Not at all. I don't believe in any god."

"It's the rare mathematician who does."

After a while Whitehead added, in a musing tone, "So it was his religion. I'll admit I thought so. I wondered how long you'd be able to stand it."

Lee's gratification at Whitehead's abrupt interest in him was giving way, very slightly, to annoyance. There was something impersonal and condescending about Whitehead's observations, as if he were watching Lee not out of interest in Lee but out of interest in his own infallible deduction. Whitehead's manner was arrogant, even godly. Perhaps this was to be expected from a man who, like Lee, claimed he did not believe in God.

"His religion has nothing to do with it," Lee said, also arrogantly. "I'm in love with his wife."

As soon as he said this, he felt enormous relief, at the guarantee that his private misery would now be consequential. But Whitehead only laughed. "I think Gaither's married to Christ."

"No, he's married to Aileen," Lee said, and his tone must have made Whitehead realize he wasn't joking.

"And you've met this Aileen?"

Lee inadvertently paused, so that his reply took on excessive, almost comical gravity. "Yes," he said at last. Whitehead raised his eyebrows. All at once Lee felt frantically vulnerable. What had he done, confessing to this strange, golden-haired man? He envisioned Whitehead at the College Road Tavern, his beautiful jacket tossed carelessly over a chair, ankle propped on his knee, reenacting the scene for the Byrons as they convulsed with laughter. *And I asked if he'd met her, and he said*—and here Whitehead would mimic Lee's stern, downturned mouth, his "Oriental's" humorlessness—*"YES."* The absurd ostentation of it! The Byrons shriek, beg for mercy, pantingly lift their mugs when their laughter subsides. *Oh, my God, the Oriental*

Don Juan. Don Juan Lee. That's a gas. Lee pictured this humiliation so vividly he did not notice that Whitehead had flushed, as if he'd realized he'd entered a realm in which he was a stranger, where not even a Japanese phrase could reconfirm his authority. Whitehead sat back on the bench and pushed his natty blond cowlick away from his face, running his palm quickly over his skull.

"So—tell me about her," he said.

But Lee's sense that he was in danger had blinded him to the flush and deafened him to the tentative tone. He was already gathering his calf briefcase and his heavy math text and his paperback Mishima onto his lap. "I'm late," he said, although he had nowhere to go and Whitehead probably knew this.

Whitehead also stood up. "I'll walk with you."

"That's okay. I really need to get going. I'll see you sometime," Lee dismissed him, staring at the deepening blush on the other man's face. His rudeness might have embarrassed him equally, if his desire to escape hadn't shouldered past everything else.

"Don't forget about Japanese lessons," Whitehead said, almost meekly. "As I confessed, it would have to be barter, but I have decent German, if you're interested."

"I'll see," Lee said, turning away.

"Lee!" Whitehead called. Of course he had to have the last word—his persistence in the face of repulse was its own kind of rudeness. Lee looked at him with undisguised impatience.

"What is it?" he demanded.

"Love is even less rational than religion. You can't mix it with serious math. And you're serious, aren't you? You've always seemed so to me."

He'd had nothing to say to this. He couldn't guess what the comment implied: jealousy? condescension? He'd only known that in confessing his feelings for Aileen to Whitehead, he'd handed a stranger a powerful weapon. Departing brusquely, without a gesture of farewell, he'd felt Whitehead's gaze, whether contemptuous or baffled or longing, like a fire at his back. When he finally passed between the bell tower and the library, leaving the quad, he glanced over his shoulder, but Whitehead was no longer in sight.

5.

WHEN AILEEN HAD DIED, THE YEAR THAT ESTHER turned fourteen and that Aileen, given two more months, would have turned forty, Lee had imagined that it would be not just painful but perhaps impossible for him to ever revisit all those places indelibly hers. Then, as now, he'd still lived in the town of their domesticity and parenthood, if not their greatest happiness, and for a short time it seemed he could not set foot outside his home. Five minutes in the car and here was Klaussen's deli, looking seedy and dilapidated now, where she'd loyally shopped; once it had been the only place in town she could find decent lunch meat, sour pickles, and bread that had not been presliced. Turn a corner and there was the Y, where she'd insisted on teaching Esther to swim in a class for toddlers who couldn't even yet walk. To this day as uneasy in open water as at towering heights, Lee saluted her wisdom, although at the time he'd accused her of the callous desire to expose their child to certain death by drowning. The farmers' market in summer, the A&P all year round; Aileen had left Lee, and the town, years before she'd died, but only after her death did she threaten to haunt all those places she'd been while alive. And yet Lee instead found that his town's very smallness, which he'd feared would press unwanted memory on him, somehow gave him relief from the past at those very same sites where the past would seem most concentrated. This was the freedom of severe limitation, like passing a lifetime in one set of rooms; no single scent could remain in the air; no single occasion could claim the backdrop. The A&P was Aileen's at inexplicable moments, but for the most part it remained the drab store where Lee purchased his dinner.

It was the same with the shell-shocked campus, in the first days after Hendley was bombed. Lee knew that for many of those who'd spent less time on campus than he, the bomb blew a permanent hole in their sense of the place. The bomb had arrived just two days before the start of spring break, and the excuse to abscond had been seized with relief by everybody who could. But Lee felt he had long since grown used to his palimpsest world. Bomb or no, spring break or no, he drove to campus again, as was his decades-old habit.

Aileen's ghost had once made him want to avoid the old Mathematical Science Building, but now he enjoyed passing by it and even felt affection for its pebbled exterior and its rusting I-beams, considered avant-garde in 1972. Lee often missed his old ground-floor office in this building, with the slender floor-to-ceiling pane of glass by the door so that privacy was impossible, although at least then he'd been spared his current fastidiousness about the angle at which he propped open his door. That old office also had a floor-to-ceiling window in its rear wall, and because he had been on the ground floor, the grass seemed to grow right to the pane. Esther would sit cross-legged on the floor, staring out at the squirrels. There had been a time, when Esther was six or seven, that Lee had taught an evening class three times a week, and Aileen had bought a hot plate for his office, and then every evening at six she and Esther arrived with a pot of something, Irish stew or goulash, and after reheating they all ate together off Tupperware plates. That had been happiness, he knew now, the three of them cross-legged in an intimate circle, Esther in some sort of plaid jumper that Aileen had sewn and thick cable-knit tights, thoughtlessly talking away, thrilled to be in his office. As a younger child, she had even been happy to sit in his calculus class, in the back, with a coloring book. He had probably never thanked Aileen, perhaps never even noticed her tenacity in maintaining a family meal. At the time he had probably thought it was only her duty.

Now his old building housed the Department of Romance Languages; Mathematical Science had moved to its new building, or "facility," in 1987. The new building, called contemporary by the school administrators, to the naked eye shockingly cheap, with curved hallways in colors like "shell pink" and "mint green" and strange, unnecessary circular and triangular holes cut into second-story walls to look down on the cold "atrium" full of shivering, leaf-shedding ficuses, had been built around a vast computer center at its core and intended as the strongest manifestation of the school's new commitment to computer science. In truth the building had loomed like a folly, by the minute growing grimier and less used and more dated, until the fresh windfall of alumni funding that had enabled the triumphant hiring of Hendley, in 1993. Then the building's shabbiness and laborious whimsy had been reconstituted as the appropriate background tribute to Hendley's good-humored self-sacrifice, in consenting to join the department. Lee had never been comfortable in the building, beneath the incessant harsh whine of its arctic fluorescents, along its right-angleless halls, in which, at least for the first year, he was constantly lost. Doors to the outdoors and to restrooms opened only with the swipe of a magnetized card that Lee always forgot in his desk, as if the Mathematical Science Building were top secret, vulnerable to dark espionage. Lee's new office, where he eventually shared his left-hand wall with Hendley, had an untethered quality to it, each surface seeming not solid but more like the taut skin of a drum. When large delivery trucks passed the building, he would feel his floor tremble.

It startled him to see a policeman stationed at the door to Hendley's office, although he understood it must be to prevent any tampering with the crime scene. Now that he was inside his building, he felt less placid than he had while outdoors. As he passed down the pink hallway, an octagonal window at the far end framed the crown of a tree. Outdoors, spring had been sweetly indifferent to the disasters of man, but from this vantage the budding branches Lee saw appeared frozen in postures of horror. It must be the youth of this building, Lee thought; not enough had transpired here for the palimpsest theory to work. From its cold lobby tile to its dirty skylights, the place was all about Hendley.

Perhaps Lee would just check his mail and then return home. He let himself into the departmental mail room, that claustrophobically windowless chamber, barely more than a truncated hall, with a door at one end to the corridor and a door at the other to the cubicled space of the departmental office, today deserted, a graveyard of inert monitors and cold copy machines. He did not really expect to find anything; the usual ream of irrelevant memos would not have been issued in the two school days after the bomb. He was surprised, then, not just to find he had mail but to find that it was actual mail, an envelope stamped and postmarked and addressed to himself. Instinctively he tore the envelope open and read where he stood.

Dear Lee,

What a bittersweet pleasure to see your face after all of these years, even if through the mesh of newsprint. You are still a hand-

*some man. "Princely," I believe, was the word sometimes used
around campus for you. I know that you, like me, are rational, and
that you won't be offended when I say that the sight of my grad
school colleague almost seventy years (is that right?) from his start
in this life, was a bracing reminder to one of his peers as to how
many years of his own life have passed. Let me compensate for the
great gaffe of mentioning age by asserting you wear it admirably
well, a lot better than I do. I wonder if you would agree that there
is some relief, in becoming old men. What poet wrote "tender
youth, all a-bruise"? I can admit that you bruised me, that last time
we met.*

Lee's horror was intense and imprecise; like helpless prey, he felt
himself the narrow focus of amorphous scrutiny; he was the paralyzed
deer in the woods, hub to eyes and gun sights. He felt his bowels loosen.
"Jesus Christ," he murmured. He straightened and looked around himself quickly, his heart pounding away at the door of his ribs. Of course
he was alone. All morning he'd thought about ghosts, and yet here was
one to blindside him he had not even deigned to imagine.

The rest of the letter was absorbed in an unremembered instant,
during which he also burst out of the mail room and traveled back
down the hall toward his office, almost tripping over the feet of the
watchful policeman.

"Good morning," Lee exclaimed.

The policeman nodded to him with brusque courtesy. "How're
you feeling, Professor?"

"Just fine," Lee replied, attempting to sound stoic and warm and
forgetting all about going into his office. He hurried out of the building, back into the sun, and took a left down the concrete pathway, toward University Station.

The letter must have been delivered either yesterday—Monday—
or today. The postal service kept on implacably regardless of spring
breaks or of what deadly freight it might ferry. Its vast, branching, impersonal systematicity revolted him suddenly. Like a poisonous river,
it had brought Hendley that bomb, spewed it out on the banks of his
life without the least word of warning. Now it had brought Lee this
letter. He still held the single sheet of white typewriter paper, bent

against the twin folds that had thirded it by the surprising pressure of his hand, which had now left a rippled damp spot in the margin. This proof of his own physical contact with the letter made Lee feel somehow compromised. He refolded the letter quickly and slid it back into the envelope. The envelope was as characterless as the paper: white, business-size, cheap, with no watermark. It was addressed—snidely, Lee felt—to *Dr.* Lee. The italics were Lee's own, in angry echo of his correspondent. So Gaither had never finished his degree, as Lee had predicted he wouldn't—this was what the sour fastidiousness of *Dr.* Lee clearly betrayed, if unintentionally. Lee knew Gaither well enough to see through his fraudulent courtesies. The painful and intoxicating brew of shock and fear, of uncertainty and certainty, and of guilt, was now making room for plain anger as well. *Dr.* Lee, Department of Mathematics and Computer Science, all entirely correct down to the esoteric plus-four of the zip code. The return address was 14 Maple Lane, Woodmont, WA, but the letter was postmarked from Spokane. Gaither could as easily have put it in the mail during a layover between Bangkok and Boston.

Of course I was laughably innocent then, of the workings of human relations. But I am not a sentimental man—nor are you, I've long assumed and admired. I only press on the point (on the bruise!) to impress how I'd like to revive faded fellowship now. Now you are probably angry with me, as I once was with you. Please don't be. There's a reason my arrow grazed you. I can learn what my long-ago colleague has done in the long years since we last had contact.

My long-ago colleague. Long assumed and admired.

Long years.

There was only one kid in the mail room, a fidgety undergraduate with sticky black hair and a pierced ear, the kind of boy who prided himself on never going home to his parents, not even at Christmas. But he was anxious to leave now for his dorm; he'd probably taken the spring-break shifts in the building's mail room not for lack of friends or activities but to make extra money. "I'm about to take off," he told Lee. "There's no afternoon delivery today. All the mail that comes in now, they're keeping here extra time to go through it. Cops and stuff. So I'm sorry if you got something late, Professor, but I'm giving as fast as I'm getting."

"Nothing was late," Lee assured him, raking a hand over his scalp, which had gone slick with sweat. "I just wanted to know where this came from."

"Postmark says Washington."

"I mean . . . well, that's all right, that's all right," Lee said, gesturing in dismissal. What was he asking? This envelope had come to the departmental mail room from where he now stood, University Station; to University Station, via postal circuits unknown to Lee, from Spokane, Washington. And to the mailbox in Spokane from nowhere this boy, or anyone else on this campus, could tell him.

"Cops're screening everything now," the boy added, perhaps regretting his smart-aleck tone. "So you don't need to worry, Professor. I guess they've got a machine that can check mail for bombs."

"I'm not *worried*," Lee said. "Although I'm glad to hear that they're doing their job." The police might be able to screen mail for bombs, but not for insidious weapons like this.

> *I hope to hear from you soon. Until then I remain,*
>   *Your Old Colleague and Friend*

A slashed, crosshatched mark of some kind filled the rest of the page.

By the time he'd returned to his parking space, the letter was interred at the bottom of his ancient calf briefcase, which had grown spider-webbed with dry cracks in the course of the decades because he had never maintained it. *The sight of you a bracing reminder of years that have passed.* Lee's silver Nissan the opposite thing, a disposable tool. Lee's material world was made up of these two categories, the fleeting generic and the eternal and iconic. In the first category, his car and his plasterboard home in a suburb the name of which he had forgotten, a home several times too large for him now that the second Mrs. Lee had departed. In the latter category, his briefcase and the desk in his study, a gigantic oak treasure that had happened to live in his first rooming house in grad school; the green-shaded lamp in his office; the Montblanc pen, a gift from his undergraduate adviser, in the pocket of his cheap Penney's button-down shirt, a type of shirt he bought three to the package, like his briefs and his socks and his undershirts, like his food—cardboard cases of Bud Light, Valu-Saks of white rice, planks of beef framed on Styrofoam mattes. Gaither, he thought, was correct: he was not a sentimental man. He was pragmatic, and cheap. If he lost the Montblanc, he'd buy a Bic at the drugstore. But somehow he never had lost it, in almost forty years.

In the car he looked at his Seiko, still running, and thought about getting gradually, drowningly drunk on many cans of Bud Light in his La-Z-Boy chair. But he still hadn't started the engine. He took out the letter again and held it, by its edges: 14 Maple Lane. *Dr.* Lee. He felt a sob choke his throat, saw a single tear fall on the envelope, rippling it. Another mark that was his. Heat built up in the car from the struggling spring sunshine, but when he rolled down his window, the air came in cool. The most immediate source of his pain was his realization that once again he could not call Aileen. Of course he had thought of her first, when he'd opened the letter. Of calling and the instant she answered, declaring, *I've found him.*

He finally started the car, rolled the window tightly shut again, and pulled out of the parking lot. The letter was buried again in his suitcase. As he drove, his misery plagued him like a murderous passenger, blocking his airways and blurring his vision, but he blinked and took breaths and kept going, an undeterred stoic. Comporting himself admirably. This was precisely what Gaither must want, Lee's delayed dissolution, after all these long years. Vengeance not in spite of those years but because of them: it was far too late for every kind of reparation. It was too late for Aileen, and it was too late for Lee. Gaither must know this; Gaither always had seen the long view, a circumstance that had united Lee and Aileen in their absolute refusal to, or inability to, do the same. This must have been another gift of Gaither's religion: his grasp of their acts' future consequences, as if they lay before him sketched out on a map.

Lee had always treated his drinking as a casual thing, but at his core he knew that it was something more precious: a lofty plateau; a lush table above glowing desert, beneath pristine skies; a space in his life so defined that it was truly a *place,* and one he relied on returning to regularly. In three decades it had evolved, toward greater cheapness and ease: the twenty-four-can suitcase of Bud Light and the Almaden box. Almost home, he stopped off at the A&P and bought one of each, and broccoli for his dinner, and these mundane transactions almost let him forget about the letter in his briefcase, locked inside his Nissan, like its own kind of slow-acting bomb. The checkout clerk, a heavy, motherly white woman he probably saw every week, smiled sympathetically at him. As she returned his change, she burst out, "You're Professor Lee, aren't you? From the university."

"Yes," Lee said, trying to smile. He'd been recognized many times, at places like the gas station and in the aisles of this store, since his TV appearance, and he'd always responded with what he was starting to feel was his trademark calm dignity. But now that he'd gotten the letter, this recognition felt somehow menacing, though he knew that it was not.

"I'm so sorry to bother you. I recognized you from your being on TV. Of course you've shopped here for years."

"Yes," Lee said, feeling strain in his face where his cheeks remained lifted—gruesomely, he was sure—to bare his friendly white teeth.

"Is there any news of that poor man? The other professor?"

With relief, Lee let his face fall, back to its usual sternness. "Not yet," he said.

"We're all praying for him."

With alarm, Lee realized that the clerk was near tears.

"I never thought something like that could happen here," she said miserably.

"No one did—"

"You spoke so well on TV. Someone like me can't do much, but I'm praying. I pray that he'll live." She pulled a pawlike hand over her face, and it came away wet. "Oh, my goodness. And we've started a fund for his care, I don't know if you knew. On behalf of the store."

"I . . . didn't know," Lee stammered.

"It's in the jar by the door. Near the bulletin board. Of course you shouldn't contribute, Professor. You've already been through so much."

Lee left the store feeling sour acid at the back of his throat. He popped a beer the instant he turned into his driveway, drinking hungrily while he waited for the garage door to slowly grind open.

There was no longer much possibility of a message from Esther, brief and falsely cheerful: "Hi, Dad, it's me. I'm just calling to say that

I'm fine. I've been out a lot lately, but next week things should calm down a little, so I'll give you a call and catch up." These falsely dutiful messages, which had really been prophylactic, a firm barrier against substantive discourse, had never been followed by the promised catch-up, and in the six years since Esther had dropped out of college they'd trailed off into virtual silence. Esther now lived somewhere in the West, apparently as an unpaid volunteer for a group who were trying to save an endangered eagle of some kind by interfering—benignly, of course—with its reproduction. Esther was dropping shreds of raw meat through long tubes into the nests of eaglets, because the parent birds couldn't care for them, for some unknown reason. Esther lay all day pressed to the lip of a cliff overlooking a river, the tube's mouth near her hand, as the eaglets let out squeaks of distress in their wind-battered nest on the cliff face below. Or at least this was the incomprehensible image she herself had evoked, in a postcard of almost a year ago that represented the sum total of Lee's understanding of his only child's life.

Because there was no possibility of a message from Esther there was no reason to play the machine; with four messages, about four times as crowded as it usually was, it would only be more of the stock messages he'd received since the day of the bombing: from old colleagues who'd left town long ago with whom he hadn't kept up, from current neighbors in his beige subdivision with whom he'd only ever exchanged cordial nods or bits of news about septic-tank problems. There would be messages of concerned inquiry from these people, masking blunt nosiness; they'd want news, more than they got from TV and the papers, about the bombing of Hendley. Perhaps there would be a message from Associate Adjunct So-and-So, denied tenure a decade ago and now calling from the U of Paducah to share the school's distress. His concerned inquiry would mask schadenfreude. My God, that young Hendley, such an unequaled mind. An inspiration to colleagues, what a loss to us all if he died!

Lee thought of the clerk at the grocery store and her tears. He opened his second beer, pressing the tab into the top of the can with a *pop* like a gunshot. There was another reason he didn't want to push "play." The letter might have a telephoned counterpart, another arrow that would cleanly strike home.

Then he struck "play" anyway in defiance, and promised himself he would change his phone number the first thing in the morning. He would change it, and make it unlisted.

He started the rice cooker and boiled water for his broccoli while he listened. There was a message from Esther's second-grade teacher, who always asked after Esther—"One of my two or three best students ever"—on the rare occasions, every four or five years, she and Lee crossed paths in town. Lee took down her number, which he probably already had in a leather address book that dated from his years in grad school. Then, on second thought, he threw the number away. He didn't know how he would explain to Mrs. Frankford what Esther had chosen to do with herself.

But the second message and the third were from an old colleague of Lee's named Fasano, a man he'd liked enormously. He and Fasano had both been newly divorced, with young daughters, when Fasano had joined the department in the late 1970s. They had gotten into the habit of jogging the riverside trail together and then going to a nearby restaurant called something like the Corral, or perhaps it had been the Chuck Wagon, for steaks and beer afterward. Now this lost period of Lee's adult life seemed as remarkable and Arcadian to him as certain scenes from his childhood. When Fasano had been offered a much better job at Cornell and had left, Lee had felt the loss keenly. He and Fasano had only been friends—but the very simplicity of that formulation had been painful for Lee, for how rare he had realized it was. Fasano's two daughters had been two years apart, the younger just about Esther's age, and he had been an undisguisedly impatient and frustrated weekend father. He'd had a temper, like Lee. "Count your blessings," he'd said to Lee of Esther, who after the divorce had continued to be a watchful and reserved—perhaps too reserved—child. This had entirely changed in adolescence, but by that time Fasano was gone.

"Lee," barked Fasano's wonderfully familiar yet, through the machine, strangely abstracted voice. "I don't like it when the bullshit doings of sociopaths are responsible for getting me back in touch with my friends, but I don't deserve to complain. Neither do you, since I don't think you've been in touch either, so let's call it even and set the clock back to zero. I have to tell you, I could hardly believe it when I saw your face in the paper. First of all, I can hardly believe you're still stuck in that midwestern shithole. No, I'm honestly kidding. I actually miss it sometimes. But I can hardly believe you still have the same phone number. You're a sentimental fool, Lee. I'm kidding again, but seriously, be sentimental enough to call me. Obviously, I want to hear how you are and how Esther's doing, but there's a more immediate reason. I know you read the papers, too, so I won't insult you by recapitulating the whole thing, but I'm calling about the incident we had here in Los Angeles, about four years ago. Jesus, you probably think I'm still at Cornell. I'm not, I'm at U—"

Here Lee's machine had cut Fasano off, but after a beep and a click, Fasano resumed. "Sorry, Lee. These goddamn machines aren't designed for old Luddites like me who forget that they're not talking to a sympathetic human. As I was saying, I'm at UCLA. Been here since '90. And of course, as you must know by now, we had a bombing here in '91. I wasn't anywhere near it. Nothing like how near you were to this one. I'm goddamn glad you weren't closer. Anyway, give me a call and we'll chew it all over. It's good to hear your voice, though you sound like some terrified kid in elocution class on your outgoing message. Christ, I'm about to hang up without leaving my number." He did leave his number, and Lee, grinning, wrote it on his notepad and then drew a crisp rectangle around it and stared in amazement. Fasano.

The fourth message was from the mother of a girl who had briefly been a friend of Esther's in elementary school. Another tremulous, earnest voice; platitudes. Lee thought he remembered the woman, a famished, chain-smoking churchgoer. He hadn't cared for the daughter as a playmate for Esther; she'd struck him as stupid, as intellectually developed at nine as she'd be in her life. He was still gazing at Fasano's phone number; the churchgoing smoker left her number, but he ignored it.

He ate his dinner at his magnificent desk, the only thing of value in the house that Michiko—he winced hearing the name of the second Mrs. Lee in his mind—hadn't demanded and gotten. She had probably assumed she couldn't get it down the stairs. The desk had been the captive monarch of his first apartment in graduate school, the two cramped rooms with kitchenette on the second floor of an old widow's house a few miles from campus. Lee remembered mounting the precarious, jerry-rigged stairs to the apartment's improvised separate en-

trance and feeling the usual corrosive disappointment at how
diminished and shabby his American life seemed destined to be. He
was always ducking his head through too-short, crooked doorways,
shrugging his shoulders into undersize secondhand suits. Haughtily
carrying the calf briefcase of a man who had thrown it away as too old.
All his conditions were improvised, safety-pinned and rubber-banded
embarrassments—then he'd entered the low-ceilinged, drab little
room and seen that desk staring at him, an enormous, squat-legged
oak raja. *How did we, you and I, come to be in a hovel like this?* the desk
seemed to inquire. Lee had felt an immediate kinship with it. It was
his, a lost treasure, a diamond in the rough, a pearl cast among swine.
It was him.

"My husband's," the widow had told him, as he ran his hand
around the beveled perimeter. Lee hadn't even tried to conceal how
much he instantly coveted it. It was a desk that seemed to have a large
measure of throne in its bloodline, not to mention some grand piano.
"I don't know how he got it up here," the widow was saying. "That was
before we were married—this here is the house he grew up in. Anyone who can get the thing out, they can have it. I worry that one of
these days it'll fall through the floor."

"I'll take it," Lee had said.

"The desk or the apartment?"

"I'll take both."

When he worked, he used an old-fashioned blotter, to protect the
surface, and now he ate his beef and broccoli and rice with the blotter
as place mat. This room, with its wall-to-wall beige carpeting and its
gray baseboard heaters, a low ceiling of "textured" white plaster and
almost-bare walls except for his calendar, was as inappropriate a setting for his desk as the place where he'd found it, and every place he
had lived in since then. Always having to tap fresh reserves of ingenuity and underpaid labor, students and winches and rolling platforms
and foam rubber swaddling the legs, to uninstall and reinstall this
huge folly that housed his ego. Pulling open the top right-hand drawer,
the one most often used, a snooper would find it oddly empty: only a
handful of spare change, a few pen cartridges, and a single gray-scuffed
white baby shoe. Such a tiny, sturdy shoe! And so carefully made, the
cobbler's art in miniature. This was before the gaudy, Velcro-strapped

disposable shoes now secured to toddlers with no sense of ceremony, of the accomplishment of becoming a bipedal human. Esther had taken her first steps toward him, precipitately, her face lit up with wild delight, as if she had jumped off a cliff and found that she could fly. In the top left-hand drawer: a lopsided "dish" made of papier-mâché, on which Esther had drawn the rogue objects, always weighing holes in her father's pants pockets, which could now be securely deposited in the dish's confines. Spare change, house keys, paper clips, and a particular off-brand hard peppermint, football-shaped with a red and green stripe, Lee once favored above Starlight mints. Because earnestly used for years, the dish was now badly chipped and crumbling, and so empty. On the vast surface stood just a few lonely landmarks, the grain silos and windmills of Lee's Great desk Plain: a green-shaded lamp, the twin to the lamp in his office at school, and a photo of Esther at seven, in a faux-stained-glass frame she made from a kit. Lee remembered this project too well. The kit had come with the metal frame, divided into triangular sections, and packets of small plastic crystals that had looked like the sprinkles one used on cupcakes. The frame was placed flat on a cookie sheet and then the sprinkles poured into its separate triangular sections; when baked, the crystals melted and filled the triangles like "glass." That Aileen was allowing their daughter to melt plastic had almost reduced Lee to tears. Esther might eat the crystals and choke, and melting plastic released toxic chemicals that could stunt a child's growth, give her cancer, and what the hell kind of stupid bitch let her own child melt plastic? He'd shattered something, a bowl or a plate, hurling it at Aileen, but he had not confiscated the kit, and after he'd left the house for his office, the project had covertly gone forward. Esther had given it to him, with her photo in it, the next week for his birthday. "It was for you all along," Aileen hissed as he unwrapped the package.

This impulse of Esther's, to embellish the lives of her parents, had particularly moved and delighted Lee all of her childhood. Although for every embellishment Esther lavished on Lee, there were ten for Aileen. Lee had reasoned that this was because, as a woman, Aileen simply offered more opportunities for decoration. Esther fervently made Aileen bracelets and necklaces, wove her pot holders and trivets, transformed coffee cans and shoe boxes into shell-studded troves for her expanding collection of homemade jewelry. And while it was true that Aileen used the pot holders and trivets, wore a necklace or two on the rare occasions she had to go out, otherwise stored them in the elaborate boxes, which sat on her dresser, there was still something too casual in the way she received all these unequaled gifts from her daughter. Her surprise was only ever momentary, her praise insufficiently lavish. For his part, Lee extolled his far less frequent gifts; he would bring Esther's attention to his appreciation of them months and even years after they'd been bestowed. "I *like* this frame," he remembered reiterating, when Esther stepped into his study, perhaps a year later. "Look how pretty it is when the sun hits the glass!" But Esther had seemed to fidget at Lee's effusions, and at the same time she had never seemed injured by the way Aileen simply incorporated her gifts into everyday life.

Of course, although Lee had known there was no possibility Esther would call—even if the news of the bombing could have moved her to call, she lived in the middle of nowhere; the news had probably not even reached her; perhaps she had no idea—he'd still furtively hoped, as he'd hoped every day since the bomb but especially since he'd been in the newspapers.

He'd lost his appetite. Downstairs, he dropped his bowl in the sink and, before he could hesitate, picked up the phone. "I need directory assistance for Woodmont, Washington," he told the operator.

"I don't show a listing for a Lewis Gaither," the Washington operator told him a few moments later.

"No Gaither at that address?"

"No Gaither at all, sir. G-A-I-T-H-E-R?" she repeated. "No listing under that name at all, sir."

He returned to his desk and sat gripping the upper right hand of the four curved brass drawer pulls. He was almost relieved, to have this fresh proof of Gaither's duplicity. So Gaither had changed his name, or had an unlisted number, or had otherwise set up an obstacle, contrived to prod Lee with impunity. Lee should not be surprised; he was not. He found a clean legal pad in the drawer, uncapped his Montblanc, and started to write.

He discarded many vitriolic paragraphs before he was able to achieve the unruffled, arctic tone he desired: not falsely cordial and snide like his correspondent, and not shrill and defensive as he knew his correspondent assumed he would be. He felt he was channeling Aileen: her cold, smooth exterior, which he'd never been able to puncture, to demolish and step through, no matter how he had tried. *Dear Lewis,* he wrote, *as you yourself have pointed out, we are both old men now. I have no reason to make fresh wounds, and neither should you.*

Here Lee paused. Gaither wouldn't know that Aileen was dead. Was it Lee's job to tell him? He paused for such a long time that he finished his beer and went downstairs for another. Even referring to Aileen in this letter would be a defilement. On the way back up, Lee stopped in the bathroom to urinate, closing his eyes, an arm braced on the wall, as the long stream left him. Drink was merely a river, that passed through him. And time, too, was a river, with no beginning or end, passing through him. He was only a vessel. This idea was enormously comforting, suddenly.

> *I write back not from interest in you, but from my interest in the people who concern both of us. I think you know who I mean. I'd like to talk with you directly. I'm not interested in playing a game. The events of the last few days have brought many figures from out of my past. I am not surprised or dismayed by your appearance. Please send me your telephone number, immediately.*

He pondered how to close for a long time before he simply signed, *LEE.*

6.

CONFESSING HIS LOVE FOR AILEEN TO WHITEHEAD HAD been the urge of a desperate moment, a valve opened on awful pressure, and the reckless desire, the product of that pressure, to precipitate crisis. But once the confession was made, he'd recoiled in terror. He saw no reason that Whitehead, with his strange mix of brashness and social ineptitude, wouldn't casually comment to Gaither, "I hear Lee loves your wife." He imagined an alliance between Gaither and

Whitehead, based on hatred of him. But all three of them seemed to continue to be solitary. And the eerie, unhealthy limbo that pervades a campus during final exams, when students drift from one place to another in unwashed catatonia and the library stays open all night so its couches and floors become cluttered with splayed-open books and sprawled, unconscious bodies, extended itself into Lee's summer life, once exams had ended. The hot weather descended on him, and he began to pass days in the same dirty slacks and the same sweat-stained white undershirt, but otherwise he hardly noticed the shift in season. He slept at the height of the afternoon heat, as if ill, and then lay sleepless all night, hearing his Seiko tick on the nightstand. Sometimes he got dressed and went walking, at three or four in the morning. Sometimes he opened a soup can or book, but he had no recollection of eating or reading. He did drink: this might have been when the habit of drinking alone first came into his life. He didn't do it to be picturesque but just because he was thirsty, first for cheap cans of beer, then for cheap jugs of wine. Never much more than that—but a good deal of that, enough that he threw out the bottles himself, rolled them into newspaper and then into a bag and slid them into some other house's garbage on his nocturnal walks, so his old landlady wouldn't notice.

In the end it wasn't Whitehead who betrayed him, but Aileen. She had awoken one day in June without needing to vomit, had passed that day with the surreal sensation of the ground squarely under her feet—this after months of dizziness and nausea, as if she were a seasick sailor who'd finally gotten shore leave. She had grown so accustomed to the lurching of the world within its frame, to passing hours and even whole days in bed with her face to the wall, simply enduring the horrid sensation, that the vivid stillness of things now was almost too much for her. She dressed, stepped outside into a world that was stunning with color and light. It was June; her child at this point was fifteen weeks grown. She thought of negative numbers: now they were negative twenty-something. Fifteen weeks closer to zero.

Down the gangplank of her ship then, one step at a time. At the bottom she placed her hands on her hips and looked around herself keenly. In her absence everything had come up perfectly in her garden. Marigolds and snapdragons seething with bees, a dense carpet of phlox. Their backyard was almost no yard at all; it was the place where the twin concrete tracks ended up at a dangerously sagging garage in which their landlord stored piles of old furniture, although Gaither wouldn't have dared to park the car in that structure even if it was empty. He was afraid that the roof would fall in. Instead they kept the car parked outdoors, beside the bald patch of yard that spread out from the steps to the back door, and even if that small patch had appealed to Aileen as a garden, the nearness of the car dripping oil would have altered her plans. And so she'd spent much of the fall hacking beds where there had never been any, along the front of the house's old porch, and then, when she'd created a rubble of clods, planting tulip bulbs for the spring and a mishmash of things for the summer, whatever had looked gaudy and durable on the seed packet. She had never been a gardener in her life; her full education had been a few words exchanged with the man who ran the neighborhood nursery. But she had badly needed something when she and Gaither first arrived in this town, and she'd found that her initial investment in the gardener's tools—a narrow hand shovel and a heavy, sharp, three-fingered claw—had returned to her some small measure of the sense of self-control that since her marriage had otherwise left her. The hand shovel's shape had reminded her of a codpiece, or at least what she thought of when she heard the word "codpiece." The claw made her feel like a mad murderess, ripping innocent turf into shreds.

Looking more closely at the garden now, she could see the castrated stubs where Gaither had cut off the tulips' stems and leaves with scissors once the flowers had withered. He'd come into the bedroom to ask her, tenderly, one large palm on the small of her back, what he could do to keep her garden as perfect as she'd made it. She'd told him, "Just cut off whatever looks dead."

She wondered, without much real interest, whether tulip bulbs were supposed to be dug up and reused, and it was in that moment that she realized, in her brief contemplation of another full year in this house, the impossibility of it. The understanding was simply delivered to her, as if, like the garden and the summertime world, it had been patiently waiting for her to get up from her sickbed.

All this was linked to her child, and to her idea that its churning, inchoate potential had finally settled, begun to move in a single direction with quiet momentum. That it was also Gaither's child in no way confused her resolve, as if this distillation of Gaither within her had also distilled all her previously contrary feelings about him.

As she spoke, Lee saw clouds of dust whirling in space, asteroids coalescing, the hot lump of a planet accreting more mass. The unthinkable force of Creation. She was seated just inches from him on his room's threadbare secondhand couch. Arm extended, he might have touched her, but a chasm lay there. Was it the chasm of the summer, now ended, in the duration of which she had metamorphosed? It was early September; he'd last seen her five months before. Twenty weeks, when he had been her lover for only twenty-three days. The smaller number should be canceled by the larger. She should not even register to him. He couldn't look at her, at the distinct, compact slope of her belly beneath her sleeveless green dress. There was something unnervingly poignant about it, but also off-putting, almost offensive; he felt he had never seen her body before, so crude and exposing seemed the subtle convexity under her clothes.

If Aileen noticed his distress, the nervous darting-away of his gaze, she didn't indicate it. That day, she went on, she had stood on her front step awash in the newness of everything, agog at it, as if she'd been blind. The dogwood had passed her by, she could see that; the last time she had looked, it had just started pushing out buds, and now the blooms were long gone and it was glossy with great oval leaves. Across the street she could see where their neighbor's car had bumped off the driveway and onto the grass, a slight depression in the smooth coat of blades. She was still standing there, wasn't tired and couldn't imagine being tired; she wasn't showing yet, and her body felt like a spear some proud native had thrown down, stuck erect in the earth, and at the same time she felt like a skyward eruption of energy. She could have uprooted the trees and devoured them. None of these thoughts turned her indoors again; her new superhumanity had no interest in cleaning or ironing or otherwise putting right Gaither's hapless attempts at housekeeping while she'd lain in bed. She'd stood there, a proud spear, a fountain, and her loathed next-door neighbor, who had obviously seen her and put on shoes to take advantage of the rare occasion, came hastening out with her hands clasped theatrically. "Oh, Aileen!" she wailed. "Lewis told us your wonderful news. Oh, you darling," and here the woman's eyes actually filled with tears as she gazed on her neighbor, who had previously only snubbed her. Now Aileen faced this woman serenely and let her keep talking. "Lewis told us you'd been so very sick, you poor thing. But it's a good sign, you know. It means your body is doing its housekeeping, getting ready for baby. Out with the old, in with the new. And just look at you now! You look beautiful."

Aileen knew that this was true; she was suddenly more beautiful than she'd been in her life. "Out with the old," she repeated, smiling. "Won't you come in, Mrs. Cahill? I've been sick for so long, and I've missed company. Come inside and I'll make us some coffee."

For the rest of the summer, it had been this way: a remarkable serenity, patience, and even affection for all the aspects of life that she knew she was leaving, above all her husband. At that time she had not felt dishonest but attuned to a higher, or inner, tempo that proceeded apace. It advised her to no action, yet. Three weeks after the day she had coffee with Mrs. Cahill, she felt the baby's first movement, like a sly finger trailing an inner wall, beckoning her.

The July Fourth holiday they had spent with one of Aileen's older sisters in suburban Chicago, making the three-hour drive with Gaither's knuckles bone white on the wheel. His supreme confidence as a driver, which was one of the things about him she had once found attractive, had been shattered by the awesome new presence of his unborn first child. Now Gaither rode the brake, making the car stutter, and swerved away from imagined dangers. If Aileen hadn't emerged like the phoenix from her morning sickness, Gaither's driving would have made her throw up. She still found it unbearable, but he had stiffened with righteous horror when she'd offered to drive. "You can't *drive*," he had said. "The steering wheel pressing into your stomach!"

Since their marriage the summer before, Gaither had not spoken to or seen his parents. He wrote them regular letters, a single neatly penned sheet he composed at the kitchen table, the contents of which Aileen grasped easily as she passed from the sink to the stove. *Dear Mother and Dad, the weather here continues to be quite a challenge for Aileen and me. A snow shovel and snow tires are two of our more recent acquisitions.* As far as Aileen could gather, it took two or three of these letters to garner a response, very often a seasonal card merely signed beneath the preprinted message. The rare notes, as carefully anodyne as the letters to which they responded, Gaither read to Aileen as if they contained riveting news. *Dear Lewis, thank you for your letter. Dad's health continues to be very good, and he is planning a rearrangement of the trees in the yard. He would like to put in a magnolia.* Gaither's parents had failed to appear at the very small civil wedding she and Gaither had held, after not so much saying they'd come as not saying they wouldn't, and since then this cowardly, or perhaps she ought to think it was benevolent, policy of avoiding conflict by avoiding acknowledgment of the marriage had been as scrupulously pursued by the senior Gaithers as if it were a pillar of their religious practice. Gaither as scrupulously mentioned Aileen in each one of his letters, and it was probably only to do this that he wrote the letters at all, as he'd had little else to report.

But now that she was pregnant, the little dumb show, Gaither's penning of his letters in the kitchen where she would observe him and his cheerful reading of the paltry responses, had come to an end. It was true that she had mostly been in bed, and that Gaither had gotten the mail from the box when he came home from school, and heated chicken broth in the kitchen, and washed and dried the bowls afterward. But she could easily see him relocating his correspondence from the kitchen to the lamp table next to their bed, perhaps directing a superfluous inquiry to her prone form: "Aileen, what was the name of those beautiful flowers you planted? I'd like to tell Mother." She could easily see him having added the most recent card from his mother to the tray that he brought her each evening and expressively reading his mother's few words while she struggled to eat. But Gaither had done neither. She knew that for him estrangement from his parents was painful, both for how unwanted a condition it was for himself and for the distress he assumed it caused her. She couldn't disabuse him of this latter notion without insulting him further, but the truth was that his estrangement from his parents did not upset her at all. It was easier for her than she imagined the opposite would have been: their pious embrace of her as a daughter, correspondence duties of her own, treks to their sterile home on Christian holidays. All of it intensifying unimaginably after a child was born. Gaither had once compared her, with what had seemed to be uneasy admiration, to Athena sprung unsentimentally from Zeus's thigh, or maybe out of his head: neither of them could exactly remember the story. But Gaither's meaning had been clear, that even as a child Aileen was essentially parentless. Aileen's parents had been learned, mildly crusading, moderately well-off and extremely late-breeding; though when they finally had children, they somehow had six, of which Aileen was last. Aileen's childhood had taken place in the time after her parents had acquired housekeepers and assumed an emeritus status, so that passionate attachment to that primal relation of parents to child and measuring of all subsequent relations against it were foreign to her. What she had were her siblings, numerous enough that they comprised more a loose federation than a snug family. Some she had always shared an easy sympathy with, and others were so much older she'd hardly known them at all. With no one did she have an exceptional bond, as she might have if there had been fewer of them overall.

But the sister she and Gaither were visiting lay in the easy-sympathy category, and since Aileen's marriage to Gaither had brought her to the same part of the country in which this sister lived, they had seen much more of each other and grown closer than they had been before. Sitting in the kitchen while their husbands struggled to ignite a pyramid of charcoal in the yard, Nora said to Aileen, "I think that with the baby you'll find that sense of union with Lewis you don't feel now. That's almost the definition of a baby, isn't it? The union of two in one. It's what makes marriage real." Nora had two children, a seven-year-old boy and a three-year-old girl, and she was straightforward and commonsensical about them in a way Aileen was only now, just visibly pregnant, able to fully appreciate, as she constantly endured the unsolicited disquisitions of women who happened to have also experienced birth.

"That's what I'm afraid of," Aileen said. "The marriage being real."

"Oh, Aileen," Nora said, not chidingly but as if her worst fears for Aileen were confirmed. No one in Aileen's family had been particularly enthusiastic about her marriage to Gaither, although no one had been less than polite. They were not the kind of family to intervene forcefully in one another's affairs. But Aileen had been aware at the time that they all thought she was too young, that she was marrying Gaither out of a craving for direction, perhaps even constriction—that her rebelliousness was now taking the form of a precipitate rush toward conventional life. And now she was aware that this assessment had been largely correct.

"He's a good man," Nora said tepidly, gazing through the window. The pyramid of charcoal flared up, then went out.

"Oh, I *know*," Aileen snarled. "I know!"

The conversation hadn't gone any further; she hadn't told Nora then that her marriage to Gaither, for her part, was already over. She had only grown more certain of this since the day she'd walked out on her porch; every day the conviction gained strength, in a way she persistently linked to the wonderful, palpable increase in strength of her child. Perhaps it was for this reason—that the as-yet-unborn child already seemed to be not just an actor in the unfolding drama but the chief co-conspirator—that Lee began to feel coldness and even hostility for him. Yes, him: another fact of which Aileen was certain. In the kitchen with Nora, Aileen felt the child kick, pedal, brusquely invert himself searching for room; these outbursts were always sustained, they made her think of tantrums, and if she was alone when they happened, she yelped with laughter. She hoarded these movements from Gaither; she never mentioned them to him. She couldn't bear the idea of sharing them. But now she seized Nora's hand eagerly and pressed it hard to herself, and the two of them laughed together.

"It's wonderful, isn't it?" Nora said when the thrashing subsided.

"I never thought I'd say something like this, but I think it's the most wonderful thing in the world."

"A strong little critter," Nora said.

"A strong boy," Aileen corrected her.

"You're sure of that?"

"Yes. Weren't you?"

"Oh, I don't know. Both times I think I changed my mind every few days."

"Well, I'm sure," Aileen said.

That summer Gaither had been determined to solve a problem one of the department professors had presented in the spring, and once Aileen was on her feet again, she encouraged him to make up for time lost tending her, which he finally, reluctantly, started to do. He would rise very early, as had always been his habit, and by the time she herself rolled clumsily out of bed and zipped up her housedress, she would know he'd been in the library for almost two hours. Nights she packed him a sandwich to take the next day so that he wouldn't have to come home for his lunch; and when he came home in the evening for dinner, she had it ready for him and the table set and tumblers already full, so that he could sit down immediately and as quickly retreat upstairs afterward to his little home study. It interested her that these methods she'd found to minimize their contact coincided with those that seemed to make her an exemplary wife. The only fault of her system emerged when Gaither leaned toward her gratefully to wet her face with a kiss, and she would force herself to sit very still and receive it as the earth receives rain—she would tell herself this—with no outward show of resistance.

She thought of Lee more and more, as these everyday scenes from her marriage seemed to shift into frozen tableaux, memory dioramas she would view from a distant future. She missed him; sometimes thinking of him abruptly derailed her calm regime of housekeeping, and she would find herself sprawled on the couch, in the dusk of closed curtains, clumsily making love to herself, achieving at best an imperfect release that was more like implosion, because she felt truly depraved to be doing such things with the baby inside her. She swore it off and then found that both Lee and her own unpregnant, lascivious body had come to plague her in dreams. In her dreams she would climax and then suddenly wake to see Gaither's oblivious face on the pillow beside her. Just as after the times on the couch, her limbs would quiver and flop like rubber, unable to obey her. Struggling to get out of bed, to get away, she'd wake Gaither as she hadn't before. She could never believe that these dreams failed to wake him; they felt as real as if she and her lover were committing their wailing contortions only inches from where Gaither lay snoring in his pale blue pajamas. "Are you okay, Aileen?" Gaither would mumble as she fought with the sheets.

"I just have to use the bathroom." Immediately his breathing would deepen again.

Sometimes she sat up until dawn, in an old armchair in the small living room she almost never used during the day, as if the journey she was about to embark on demanded she first know—memorize—every aspect of the life she was leaving behind. This first and last home of her marriage to Gaither, at dawn. The geriatric couches and chairs and bookshelves it had come furnished with, mute witnesses to her sins. She wondered how many mundane revelations, humiliations to the pride we take in knowing ourselves, had occurred in these rooms. She was twenty-one years old, six months pregnant, the wife of a man she had wanted to save her from something. From her own indifference, perhaps, to herself, and to securing conditions for her own happiness. Gaither, when she met him, had exuded such ease, the confidence of a child of God. Now she watched as he made this impression on others, who didn't yet see the need this demeanor concealed. Though Lee saw it; he'd seen it that night at the church gathering, and he'd ruthlessly seized his advantage.

The fall semester always began late, the third week of September, and as August came to an end, a sense of meaningless limbo pervaded their house. She assumed that Gaither wasn't succeeding in solving the problem. "I'm sorry, Aileen," he said more than once. "I'm so absorbed in my work. I guess that's my way of feathering the nest. It would really help my career, and help us, if I could get my first real publication." She wondered if the extreme cordiality that marked all their relations had ever seemed fraudulent to him. To her they were both marking time, until the semester began and the separation of spheres was again ratified by Gaither's busy course schedule. She remembered this waiting from last year: they'd moved to town, at Gaither's insistence, in late July, "to get their bearings" and then had been left to wait—purposeless, scrupulously cordial with each other. They had bought the old car and new maps and driven the hushed country roads, stopping off at farm stands to load up on sweet corn and peaches. In the evenings Aileen would make pie, her hands quick, her mind fearfully empty, while Gaither pored over the department's course offerings as he'd done countless times. They must have seemed like any young married couple, to the farmers they approached with linked hands, to new neighbors like Mrs. Cahill, to Gaither himself, who had been a virgin when they'd first slept together. She had not. He hadn't known how to tell.

Then, she'd been waiting to feel it, too. The sweet solace of marriage. Always waiting: for school to start, for their real lives to start, for confidence in her marriage to start. A year later she was waiting again, but this waiting was different.

It was almost the last day of the month when, hearing the flag on their mailbox hinge down, she went out and found in place of the bills she had posted an envelope from Gaither's mother. It wasn't the out-size envelope of a card, those envelopes that for all their opacity exude inconsequence. This was a stationery envelope, rectangular and of heavy cream stock, and it seemed to contain more than one thickness of paper. Standing in the heat, on the baking sidewalk, she felt a thrill of cold sweat prickling over her skin. It was eleven o'clock in the morn-ing. Gaither wouldn't be home until six. Back inside, she propped the letter on the entranceway table and felt it like a beam of light cast on her movements the rest of the day.

When he got home that evening, Gaither didn't slice the envelope open with a disproportionate show of interest and then read the con-tents aloud while Aileen filled their plates. He sat sideways on his chair, his long legs crossed at the ankles, and read the letter in silence. Their cold tuna salad, their wedged tomatoes and hard-boiled eggs, all sat ready for him. When he was finished, he slid the letter half under his plate and began on his food.

"What does she say?" Aileen finally asked.

"She'd very much like us to visit for Labor Day weekend," Gaither said, as if the fact of an invitation, extended to them both, weren't completely unprecedented.

"That's just six days away," Aileen said stupidly. She was aware of the need to frame an objection that was calm, logical, but she felt herself flailing around in her mental closet, knocking things off the shelves.

"It is, but we can get there in five without having to rush. We could leave tomorrow. We haven't got any obligations until September nineteenth."

"Leave tomorrow and just drive across the country? What about your work?"

"I think I could use a breather from my work. And you could use one, too. Before the baby comes."

At this the rising heat of their conversation, the longest conversa-tion she felt they'd had in weeks, was snatched away, as if the sealed hothouse in which they'd thus far kept their marriage, urging it to sprout rootlets, to unfurl even one wrinkled leaf, had been swiftly unzippered. She felt the wash of cold sweat again, under her dress. "We just visited Nora," she pointed out, stalling.

"Aileen," he said, laying his fork carefully on his plate. "My parents have wronged you. We both know it. And perhaps you think I've wronged you, too, for not breaking with them. But what you have to understand is that I'd be giving you less of myself if I just cut them out of our lives. They're not disappointed in you, they're disappointed in me. They have a wrong idea about me I've been trying to change, for all of our sakes. It's the slow road to travel, but it's the right one. I have to ask you to accept this."

"Lewis," she began.

"No, I have to ask you to bear with me here. Please let me finish, Aileen. Many months ago I wrote my mother and father to tell them we were going to be blessed with a baby. Maybe you thought that I hadn't, because I hadn't yet mentioned it to you. Of course I told them. It's the most important event of my life, apart from marrying you. I knew I had to extend to my parents the opportunity to reconcile with us, before the baby is born. They're old, Aileen. And they're set in their ways. They have a lot of fears, about the modern world, about change—"

"Lewis," she broke in again. "I don't give a goddamn about your parents. I don't mean to waste an ounce of my energy in relations with them."

"You don't only marry a man," he said evenly, although he'd grown very pale. "You marry into a family."

"Oh, my God," she cried. "Listen to you! Do you even see me? Do you hear me? Do you have any idea who I am?"

"You're a woman who doesn't share my convictions about family. But you have to respect them."

"I'm not talking about *family,* I'm talking about us."

"We're a family, too," Gaither said.

"No, we're not."

She found she was standing away from the table, her fork in her hand. She threw it into the sink. The kitchen window was open, as were all their windows, because of the heat. She thought of Mrs. Cahill, as still as a statue, at her own kitchen window a few feet away. Mrs. Cahill would carefully stretch out an arm, turn the kitchen light off, then creep closer, one hand on the sill. Her excited breath trapped in her throat as she strained to listen. "I'm not your wife," Aileen said. It just came out like that, and then the truth of the statement amazed her. "I don't want to be married to you. And you shouldn't want to be married to me."

"And why is that?" Gaither said. He was still seated, but with a terrible gaze trained on her, like a biblical judge. So he did have a mean streak, which she'd always suspected. If only he'd shown it much sooner than now.

"Because I'm a whore." All at once his chair tumbled beneath him, and he'd crossed the short distance and slapped her hard into the wall. *Good,* she thought. *Good, it's real.*

Gaither had easily guessed it was Lee. Lee's strange, abrupt break from their friendship, the trumped-up insults about Gaither's religion. If not for the baby, Aileen thought, Gaither would have gone on beating her within an inch of her life. There was that much compressed anger, and knowledge, in him. All the gleamingly obvious facets of his wife's betrayal, which until then he'd kept airborne and separate, the same juggling act he'd applied to his parents, his faith, and his science, now fell like knives on a target. From here the story became cursory: everything that Lee felt concerned him, the disposition of actual persons in the physical world, Aileen glossed without interest. She was a scientist, too: obsessively interested in her own narrow field, the evolution and efflorescence of her will to leave Gaither. The rest was secondary, or inevitable, or fell outside her purview. Gaither had gone to stay somewhere, she didn't know where, until she had packed and been picked up by Nora. She would live with Nora until things were settled. "Things": Lee didn't understand precisely what this meant, though he could see that she'd brought herself to him, meant to give herself to him, this fierce and reckless young woman who still feared being left on her own. Or who'd never been on her own in her life and so perhaps didn't realize that it was an option.

"She's waiting in the car for me now," Aileen said, and Lee realized with a shock that cogs and gears were in motion, that a machine for disposing of fates was performing its work, and he was somehow inside it.

"You told Gaither without warning me first," he said, finally putting the thought into words that sounded frigid, efficient, which was not how he felt.

"He had to find out eventually! I didn't have time to warn you—"

"You should have warned me first," Lee repeated. "This doesn't just concern you."

She looked at him unflinchingly, but he could see she was frightened. "You dump your conscience, and then you get out of town!" Lee's arm had flown out from his side; a lamp crashed to the floor. "Why!" he shouted. "And now you leave, and we stay—"

"Why?" Aileen repeated. "What do you mean, why? I've told you why—"

"He's my colleague."

"You didn't seem to care about that when you came on to me." Belatedly, an urgent thumping arose from downstairs, chastisement for the lamp. The thought that they'd been overheard drained their anger from the room instantly, leaving them only cold and bewildered, as they stared at each other.

"What about the baby? His baby," Lee said finally, his throat feeling gummed with mucus.

"My baby," Aileen corrected, in a preliminary tone, but then she didn't say anything else. In the moment that followed, a moment of frankly terrified silence, Lee felt close to her for the first time since she had appeared at his door. Like him she was afraid, overwhelmed, and incapable; they stood side by side in the face of a rushing disaster that neither of them would know how to avert. He was stunned by pity; he wanted to fold this idea of her in his arms. But the actual woman beside him he wasn't able to touch.

She crossed the distance herself, tipping her face forward onto his shoulder. Then she remained very still, as if she were resting against a bench or a tree and didn't expect any gesture or word in return. Lee's hand fluttered tentatively; it settled on the back of her head. They held this pose, and Lee saw every object in his spare, squalid bachelor's apartment without turning his head and remembered the number of times he had daydreamed of pinioning her to this couch, the pale S of her body, her sharp gasps as he harshly erased her. Those visions, which had agonized him all the weeks of this summer, seemed like insane desecrations of the distant human lightly propped on him now. Three points of contact: her forehead on his shoulder, his palm on her crown, his left knee and her right pressed together. Almost all of this, bone against bone. Her swollen front, mercifully out of range of his vision, for the moment banished from the room. He only felt heat rising out of her hair. The summer heat in the room drowned out everything else. After some time, he did not know how long, they heard a distant car horn.

"I've kept Nora waiting too long," she said into his shoulder, and slowly sat up.

They stood at his desk and exchanged their addresses—Lee did not have a phone—he would have to call her from the pay phone booths at the library. And all too quickly she was back in the doorway, at the top of the improvised stairs to his floor of the house, with the intricate globe of the massive oak tree as her backdrop, as if she were floating twelve feet off the ground; this was how he had seen her when he'd opened the door to her knock, rising uncomprehendingly off his couch where he'd lain webbed in sweat-stained T-shirt, unwashed slacks, sour wine from the night before staining his tongue, dreams of her. Then he'd opened the door and she'd been there, clean and straight in her flared summer dress.

They kissed very briefly and chastely. The kiss seemed not empty but provisional, its meaning not yet clear. Then Lee stood inside the doorway and listened as she carefully went down the stairs. A beat later, the sound of a car driving off.

In the two weeks that remained before the start of the term, he had a haircut, bought a used summer suit, and then went to his adviser and lobbied aggressively for a semester off from classwork to pursue independent research. By every measure he was months too late to make such a request, but he persisted. He was a coward, he knew. "I'd like to take on the Dieckmann problem," he explained. "I've had an insight. I think I can solve it." Of course, this was a lie.

"Mr. Gaither has also been working on it," his adviser remarked. Lee absorbed this expressionlessly.

"Well, may the best mathematician prevail," his adviser said finally, signing the forms.

PART II

7.

LEE SPENT SPRING BREAK IMITATING SERENE SOLITUDE, mounting the stairs to his desk every morning and not going back down except for his meals, but finally accomplishing nothing, because his mind couldn't stop pawing over the letter from Gaither. The mailbox at the end of his driveway suggested a sequel, and so he didn't set foot out of doors. His desk had conspired in his shamefully feeble reply, and so he sat glaring angrily at it without reading or writing. The telephone commemorated his failure to get Gaither's address from the operator, and so day after day he did not even call back Fasano, the pleasure of whose conversation was coming to seem like an undeserved gift. But on the last Friday before spring break was over—nineteen days after the bomb—Lee had a respectably studious late afternoon and then sat with a beer while he watched the dusk deepening outside his kitchen. He was actually watching himself, for the more the sky faded, the more sharply emerged his reflection in the sliding glass door, a full-color man in his full-color home, layered over the looming black cones of the five Douglas firs in his yard. The five firs, planted along the property line between his backyard and that of his neighbor at what had once been quite wide intervals, had now grown so tremendously upward and outward that they formed a thick wall that blocked even his neighbor's house lights. Lee and the neighbor had divided the cost of the trees almost ten years ago, when they'd both bought their homes, and it was one of the very few schemes in his life that had actually worked. He felt a privacy and security in the rear-facing rooms of his house, where he left the curtains open for the sake of his plants, that he never felt in the front rooms or even up-stairs—from those vantages he was always aware of his neighbors, power-walking past his neglected front lawn with censure or perhaps even sadness for him in their eyes.

Now night had fallen completely; above the five great serrations of his Douglas-fir wall, he could see the pure blazing pinpoints of stars, and in contrast to them diffuse lamplight had spilled out his windows to spread raggedly over the grass. His stove's clock read 6:43; that meant 4:43 where Fasano was, in California. Lee was feeling authenti-cally tranquil for the first time in days, perhaps weeks, and this pleasure in being alone made him want conversation.

Fasano answered on the second ring—"Fasano," he said, nasally—and Lee was certain that Fasano's not answering on the first ring had been an act of self-restraint. Fasano, too, must spend his days and nights alone. When his phone rang, like Lee he forced himself to stay his hand until it rang again. When his office door opened, he forced himself not to leap to his feet.

"Frank?" Lee said, his voice sounding reluctant to him. But Fasano recognized him at once.

"Lee! Jesus Christ, I was starting to think the goddamn psycho *had* gotten you. How in the hell are you? Start with bodily harm, we'll get to intangibles later. Still got all your fingers and toes?"

"Yes, yes," Lee said, laughing.

"Thank God for life's little pleasures. And what about the other guy?" Now Fasano's voice changed. "He gonna make it?"

"They think so," Lee heard himself saying, realizing as he did that he actually had no idea how Hendley was doing.

"Thank God," Fasano repeated, but for all the joyous garrulity that had just been their reunion, they fell awkwardly silent. Lee was afraid that Fasano could sense Lee's neglect of his injured colleague. Lee could almost imagine Fasano, at the other end of the line, still in day-light, subsiding in disappointment.

But the awkward silence didn't last. It was soon over, and then Lee had the thought that he and Fasano had counted it out together, each instinctively holding his breath for a requisite number of beats, as if they were veterans of the same army and possessed all the same rituals. When Fasano started speaking again, he was audibly relieved to be past the formalities, and both Lee and Fasano were delighted, almost giddy, to be conversing again. Fasano, too, had remarried and redivorced; Fasano, too, invoked Zeno's paradox when explaining the never-quite-complete state of his book. Fasano, as Lee had guessed, lived alone now, was resisting retirement—"You hate teaching your whole lousy career, you just want to be alone with your books, and when you're finally old enough to cash in on the Double-A-Cref, you discover if you don't have a classroom, you die. Left alone with your books—it's like death"—but all the same was appalled by the state of his students. Couldn't read! Couldn't add! And why go on—but there were one or two great ones, two precisely, in fact, they were both foreign students, of course, and each was worth all the rest put together. "I tell them, 'When you go back to your countries, you're going to be, what? President? Chief justice? Head of whatever research institution you have over there? How're you going to choose?' And they're both like, 'What? Go back to our countries, no way!' "

"They want to stay here, of course," Lee put in, taking a sip of his beer. "What opportunity do they have where they come from?"

"Not so much, I suppose. They're both black Africans. One's from Ghana and one's from Nigeria. But they remind me of you, Lee. So bright they seem radioactive. Maybe they're Kryptonite People from Krypton. And yeah, they want to stay here, like a goddamn free gift to this country, and they're in danger of losing their visas. Feds treat them like hustlers who want a free ride. It's unbelievable, Lee. Another reason I haven't retired. I write letters, get mad. It won't help. It's not the same golden welcoming land that it was when you came."

"I don't know about that. There were problems then, too." But he was only dimly aware of having said this; it was a rote response that might have emerged at the touch of a button. His voice had dropped and grown thick, and he needed to swallow but couldn't—his throat walls were too stiff, or too dry. He wiped his eyes with the back of his hand. *They remind me of you, Lee. So bright.* That kindness of Fasano's had been so unexpected and at the same time so desperately craved; he was newly and unhappily aware of a longing for just such charitable donations to his dwindling self-regard, and for a panicked moment his gratitude to Fasano was erased by the suspicion that Fasano was pitying him. Fasano had left the department two decades earlier for a job at Cornell, had left there for UCLA; Lee had watched him disappear into the upper echelons of reputation as he'd watched every colleague he'd ever admired, while remaining, himself, where he was. And yet, even bearing the imprint of UCLA, Fasano now seemed to float at Lee's same unremarkable level, both of them neither the stars they'd aspired to be nor the failures they'd feared they'd become. And Fasano was still talking, as if his vision of Lee as *so bright* had not been charitably contrived. And just as important, Lee realized, Fasano was uninjured. Alive.

"Frank," he interrupted. Fasano had been cheerfully detailing the disappointments endured at the hands of his daughters—one was an aspiring-actress waitress and the other was gay and played drums in a band. "Our fault," said Fasano, "for being such high-minded, defensive elitists that we sent them to crap public schools."

"Frank," Lee repeated. "You said you'd had a bombing at UCLA like the one we had here. Who was it? Was it one person in particular targeted, like Hendley, or was it just one person who happened to get hurt?"

"It was one person hurt, but they don't know if it was one person targeted or, if it was, if it was *that* person targeted. Your guy's came in the mail, to him, right? This was different. The guy's name is Sorin Illich, a colleague of mine, but I don't even pretend I understand what he works on. He'd only been in the department a semester when this happened; we'd lured him with big money from MIT. He walks out to his car, which is parked in the faculty lot, and sees what he later described as a piece of wood lying behind his front tire, on the driver's side, where he'd have to roll over it when he backed out. I don't know what kind of piece of wood, how big, if it really was wood. Apparently it looked enough like any old piece of wood that he picks it up to toss it out of his way, and it explodes in his hand."

"And he's . . . dead?"

"No, no. This bomb was nothing like yours. It was a much smaller deal, if you can say that a bomb's a small deal. He's down three fingers and the thumb, wears a sort of robotic glove with prostheses that he invented himself. That's what was so strange, in the end, apart from the whole thing being psycho. Illich does some kind of hotshot research in robotics, and now he himself is part robot. You'd almost think he staged the bombing to help his career." Fasano gave a dry laugh. "You know I'm joking. I'm not that bad a bastard."

"But his career didn't need help," Lee pointed out. "He was a hotshot already."

"True enough. Like your Hendley."

"So whoever did this dislikes hotshots." Once he'd said this, they shared another comradely silence. He and Fasano weren't hotshots. When Fasano spoke again, Lee knew how mistaken he'd been to imagine even briefly that Fasano looked down on him. They were on the same level and of the same mind.

"It's never good to be the tall poppy," Fasano remarked. "You get your head snipped off first."

"Perhaps we should be kinder to our children," Lee joked. "They're just keeping their heads down."

"The short poppy can't help being short. The tall poppy who folds herself up to *look* short is contemptible. She's either lazy or neurotic or both. No offense meant to Esther. I'm talking about my own girls. But you and I, Lee: Are we short and can't help it? Or are we tall but somehow folded up?"

"I'm a mathematician, not a psychiatrist, Frank." That got a laugh from Fasano.

"Either way we'd please Darwin. We won't get our heads snipped. You know, Lee, it's hasn't only been Hendley and Illich. For a while after Illich's thing, I was researching this all the time, going through the old papers. It began to seem morbid, and I made myself quit. But I read about five or six other weird bombings. Sometimes in the mail, sometimes an object just sitting around. The guy who gets it is always a mathematician or computer scientist or a computer programmer. All relatively prominent in their fields. All guys. And all over. Another

one in California, two in the Midwest, one all the way out in Connecti-
cut, one I think in New Jersey. No one's died yet. They've all lost some
fingers, some vision, not that that isn't awful. But knock wood, so far no
one's dead."

"And you think they're connected."

"*I* don't think. I'm no sleuth. The cops think, the cops have theories.
But it always fades out of the news pretty soon, and then it's years before
another one happens. These ones that I've mentioned, the first happened
all the way back in the late seventies. Then it's years in between. If it's one
guy, he must keep on losing his nerve. Or he's not in a hurry."

Eventually Fasano's commute and Lee's hunger for dinner forced
them to say their reluctant good-byes. "Lee, the telephone is a wonderful instrument, easy to master and not even very expensive. Let's not
let it be another twenty years, all right?"

"All right," Lee agreed happily. "It's a deal."

"Give me a call next week sometime. Let me know how Hendley is
doing."

It was not quite the one note from their glad conversation Lee had
most wanted echoing in his bright kitchen once he'd hung up the
phone. Cooking his dinner and pouring himself a new beer, he tried to
determine whether it constituted a lapse and, if so, just how glaring a
one, that he hadn't yet been back to the hospital to pay a visit to
Hendley. It wasn't, he decided, that he was averse to expressing his
sympathy—after all, who had been more Hendley's comrade in the
disaster than he? It was perhaps that he'd assumed that he would only
be an unneeded addition to the crowd of well-wishers. There would be
the generically worshipful students and the exceptional Emma. There
would be Sondra, the departmental secretary and self-appointed den
mother, who had found in Hendley's vibrantly chaotic life the most
exalted arena so far for her tireless drive to perform the sorts of thank-
less, unnoticed, laborious tasks she performed for all the members of
the Department of Mathematics and Computer Science, all of them
incompetents in the science of everyday life. Moving briskly among
them, perhaps constantly shooing them out of the room, would be
Hendley's girlfriend, Rachel. Rachel was slender, urban, sardonic;
arrestingly beautiful in the severe, offhand way in which the very few

overtly sexual intellectual women Lee had known in his life always were. She had reminded him, when he'd first glimpsed her passing the door to his office on her way to Hendley's, of a sort of Aileen; a later edition, as if it had been possible to take Aileen, so out of sync with the frame of her life, and reissue her just a few decades later with far better results. Rachel had given Lee an unsettling shock, as briefly as she'd passed through his field of vision; the thought had entered his mind that he had possessed Aileen only as the result of a colossal temporal mistake, some cosmic snafu that had marooned her on the plane of existence ahead of her time. Now here she was again, or here was her close likeness. That day, about two years ago, Rachel passed Lee's doorway without even a flick of dismissal, he was so far beneath notice, entered Hendley's instead, and with the brusqueness of ownership banged the door shut.

Setting his usual place at the table, along the side nearest the stove, with his Corelle breakproof plate and his Tupperware tumbler—items Aileen had left when she'd left him—Lee relived that moment of Rachel's indifference as if she had meant to insult him, and all his doubts about a hospital visit were nicely resolved. If he went, he would be greeted with the same cool indifference. He wouldn't get from her the courtesy due to a senior colleague, let alone the warmth anybody might feel toward the bomb's almost-victim. Nevertheless, he would go anyway. Dignity required it. He would say he had been out of town on a spring-break vacation he'd planned long before and that in fact he'd arrived home just now, Friday night, around nine.

He was still so abstracted by his thoughts that his movements were rough as he spooned white rice onto his plate and poured beer into his tumbler, and when the telephone rang, he forgot about the menace of Gaither and snatched it up right away. "Hello!" he exclaimed.

"We lost him, Lee," he heard a woman say hoarsely. The emptiness of her voice was even worse than her tears might have been; he was left to imagine the violence of emotion that had emptied her out. It was Sondra.

"We lost him, Lee," she repeated.

"My God," Lee said, sitting down suddenly. He shoved his plate of rice far away from him. His message pad with Fasano's number still lay on the counter nearby; he saw *FASANO* printed on it and jauntily framed in a sharp-cornered box and remembered his shameful happiness of just minutes before, when he and Fasano had been reminiscing. Of course he should have been at the hospital weeks ago. And of course Rachel's slighting of him had been purely imagined, his own haughty self-justification to shake off his guilt. Because he was guilty: of profound self-absorption. Somehow, though Hendley's explosion was the force Lee still felt rumbling through his own body, though Hendley's impact crater—and the long-buried strata that it had exposed—was the landscape that Lee had been pacing for days, Hendley himself, torn asunder and fighting for life, had lain outside Lee's thoughts. It wasn't that Lee had forgotten about him. It was rather that, with so many of the artifacts of Lee's own life catapulted aloft, with the arbitrary detritus of this era and that, of chapters heretofore held apart, now suspended together in space and demanding Lee gaze on them—and with Gaither's letter the fiery star at their center—present time had not seemed to progress. Present time had not seemed to progress, let alone undergo deadly increase in speed, as it must have for Hendley. And now Hendley was dead.

They managed to discuss the details. The time of death, just an hour before. That it wouldn't be in the newspapers the next day, but on Sunday. The plans for a service and so on were all in progress. After Lee said good-bye, he pulled a sheet of Saran Wrap—like a shroud, he thought—over his plate of cold rice and put it into the fridge. Then he sat down again in his old wooden chair, sole survivor of the dining-room set he and Aileen had bought at the Salvation Army right after they'd married. The act of purchasing such a solemn species of domestic furniture, and the set itself, "mahogany" dark and with deep grooves and grim feet, had at that time felt very serious, almost pious. The set had already been wobbly then, aged and dry in the joints so that the chairs made rhomboid shapes with their legs if you pushed back too hard getting up from the table. This last chair Lee had wood-glued and bound with twine for drying again and again, like a veterinarian tenderly setting the joints of a completely lame dog, but to no avail; beneath weight the chair still creaked and tilted, refused to maintain its right-angularity, and even when Lee stood up from it—as he did now, restless—the chair groaned with reproach.

There was his reflection in the glass door again, as clearly cast against the night as it would be in a mirror. His lean face, his sharp jaw, his slight leathery jowls of age, not as if he had grown fleshier but as if his outlines had surrendered to gravity very abruptly. His mouth a little downturned at the corners, his eyes very remote, hiding fear. Every kind of death frightened him, whether of one he had loved or of one he had loathed. And it was that fear, anyone's fear of death, that now sat anxiously at his sternum, a pressuring fist—though it felt similar to remorse.

8.

LEE RETURNED IN DREAD TO CAMPUS THAT MONDAY, to launch those last downslope weeks of the term that in previous years he would have bounded ecstatically through, as if his sixty-five-year-old chest held the heart of a freshman. This time he had writhed without sleep the whole night before, and sliced into his face while attempting to shave, and then drunk a pot of coffee, a vice he'd given up several years earlier for the sake of his bladder, and though the coffee he'd brewed had been stale, it still burned in his gut as if he'd swallowed ammonia. He was going to be scrutinized—as the survivor, or as the hospital nonvisitor, or perhaps simply as the most senior member of the department who still foolishly taught and showed up for meetings. Whichever role had been pressed upon him, he was sure it was somehow ignoble. He pulled in to his space in the faculty lot doubled over his acid-gnawed stomach, shoulders hunched to his ears, his ragged margin of platinum hair prickling into his eyes. It was remarkable he didn't lock the keys in the car, that he'd remembered his briefcase; as he gathered these objects carefully, tremblingly, to himself, he seemed to watch from aloft, as if he were the dead man. He forgot that the last time he'd been in this space he'd been holding the letter, dotting it with his tears.

And so he felt, if not relief, at least a sense of reprieve when he arrived finally in his department and learned that the college was implementing a hastily drafted Grief Plan. It must have been the result of all-night, frantic effort, of committees swiftly cobbled together along the branches of the telephone tree, of the news relayed—no time for tears—Friday night, the plan drafted—no time for dissent—Saturday, its components amazingly hauled into place on Sunday, so that now, Monday morning, the campus was hushed and composed, like a church. Or perhaps it had been in the works for three weeks; perhaps only Lee had been naïve or selfish enough to make no preparations for Hendley's demise. In the course of his short drive to campus, Lee had struggled, with rising panic, to compose a few remarks appropriate to the disaster for his ten-thirty class; now he learned that all instructors were to preempt their original plans and instead read a brief text, imparting the news and directing the students to an unprecedented all-college assembly that afternoon in the stadium. In the meantime professional "grief counselors," scores of them, were holding casual "talk-outs" with students in groups, and meeting "one-on-one" with grieving students in private.

"Who did all this?" Lee murmured when he had finished the memo. He was only just managing audible words, in the same way that his knees were only just managing, with much wobbling and strain, to hold him upright. When he had inched into view in the department doorway, holding his briefcase by both ends as if he expected to need it as a shield, though in truth he'd forgotten in the course of his tunnel-like walk from his car that it had a handle, Sondra had rushed toward him from the place where she'd already been standing, beside her desk—she had not been sitting in her chair, a chair to which she'd been fused, in Lee's mind's eye, for the fifteen-odd years he'd known her. Sondra took the briefcase from his hands and tried to press him into the chair that sat under the bulletin board, for visitors waiting to see the head of the department, but he bullishly resisted her efforts. Little worms of light swarmed in his vision, from exhaustion. The department, he finally noticed, was silent and empty. All four secretarial desks were abandoned. Emma Stiles's computer, which in repose usually showed a continually morphing geometrical figure of colorful lines, was dead gray, not asleep but extinguished.

". . . emergency committee," Sondra was saying, in response to his question. "Lee, I'll say it again. Please sit down. You look the way we all feel, terrible."

"But why?" he said, looking into her face for the first time. Her eyes were horribly swollen—their rims were almost like pink lips—from weeping. "Why didn't anyone ask me to help? I could have helped, I could have helped make this plan—"

"Don't you think that you've been through enough? Sit down, Lee, I want to tell you—"

All this while, since rushing toward him and prying loose his briefcase and failing to seat him in the chair, she'd been holding his arm, attempting, through what she might have thought was a subtly constant application of downward pressure, to sneak him into the chair anyway. He knew she was in the grip of bereaved mania, that she'd been standing when he entered the department not because on the lookout for him but because she couldn't force her own body to sit, and that she was trying to force him to sit for the very same reason. But he was fevered as well. He shook her off, with surprising force and with a sound of anger that was almost a bark. "I'm the last person who deserves to be treated so kindly," he said, in the same barking voice, but which formed into words was for some reason uglier. They stared at each other a moment, Sondra frozen in an attitude of fright and Lee, he imagined, contorted like a madman. He sank into the chair, disgusted with himself. "I'm sorry, Sondra," he said.

After a moment's hesitation, Sondra said, in a tone not entirely certain, "You don't need to apologize to me."

"Yes, I do. I do because . . ." And here the spectacle of himself the past twenty-four hours—riven by insomnia, too tremored to shave, rehearsing phrases of wisdom and solace in an anxious whisper on his drive to the campus, as if any student would come to *him* seeking *his* help, when there were grief counselors and all-college assemblies and then of course all the Hendleys-in-waiting—rose up and smote him, with his deluded belief in his relevance. He knew he was about to grow maudlin, as if there were nothing to do in the face of his foolishness but to act like even more of a fool. "I do because I am ridiculous," he said.

"Lee."

"I am ridiculous," he repeated, with more conviction.

"All right. You are." Sondra went to her desk and returned pushing her own wheeled chair, which she settled on once she was opposite Lee. "You're also in shock. I know you and Hendley weren't the greatest of friends, but that doesn't mean you're not affected by this horrible thing." Sondra's voice, after she'd seated herself, had assumed a brisk, let's-get-down-to-it tone, but with "this horrible thing" her voice started to climb, and her swollen pink eyes filled again. "I mean, I know he could be an arrogant son of a you-know-what some of the time; who knows better than me? But that was just *him,* that was *Hendley.*"

"What do you mean, not the greatest of friends?"

It took Sondra a moment to be able to speak; she'd retrieved a hard, gray ball of Kleenex from inside her sleeve. "Just that you butted heads with him, thought he was full of himself—who didn't? He was a young Turk, and he knew it. But we loved him." She was crying again.

"I didn't butt heads with him," Lee protested. His gut was roiling again; he couldn't remember the last time he'd eaten. "My work hardly overlaps with his! What would we butt heads about?"

"Lee, it doesn't matter. What I've been trying to say is, even the kids here who never had him, who never *met* him, they need to talk to someone. *I* need to talk to someone. And you, you were right there—"

"I disagreed with him about Kalotay's tenure," Lee said. "Is that it? But I was right! Everyone sees now we should have denied it, even Hendley should see it." He realized he was repeatedly speaking of Hendley in the present tense, but Sondra did not seem to notice. "Everyone in this department argues!" Lee cried.

"What I've been trying to say is, they've gotten grief counselors for *us,* particularly for us, who aren't on that memo. For those of us who really . . . knew Hendley. And I've been waiting here. To see if you wanted to go."

"Waiting?"

"I'm nervous for some reason." Sondra scrubbed her eyes with the ball of Kleenex. "I just thought we'd walk there together."

"No," Lee said, abruptly standing up. The Grief Plan had let him briefly forget his dread of being scrutinized, so much so that he'd begun to feel oddly left out of the collegewide program for grieving and healing. But for the past several minutes, with Sondra, he'd felt increasingly under a lamp. He'd never gone to the hospital, and she certainly knew this, she who had probably been there every day for the maximum number of hours allowed. She was looking at him with concern, but he could almost have said she was using the look as a mask, from behind which she was judging him sternly, and finding him lacking.

"I really think," Sondra resumed carefully, "that you need to talk to someone."

"No," Lee said, "I need to teach class." Except that his class had been canceled, and replaced by the memo he held. He thrust it at Sondra, with its official grief text—*It is with enormous sadness that*—and picked up his briefcase. "Please, Sondra, make the announcement to my ten-thirty for me. I have to go home. I didn't sleep well. I have to go home."

"I'm going to call you later," she said—threatened?—as he rushed off. "I'm going to check in with you. . . ."

He encountered no one else down the length of the corridor back to the stairs, no one on the stairs, not even a sole wandering student on the first floor in the lobby, where the stairway emerged beside the elevator bank and a bulletin board whose rectangular shape was entirely lost beneath the countless aggressively colorful banners of undergraduate life. It was twenty past ten, a time of the morning at which this lobby was usually lively with students running to ten-thirty classes. But Lee's building belonged entirely to the kingdom of science; none of its four floors housed any branch of the arts or humanities, and it was the rare student of science, he reminded himself, who didn't begin the day with an eight-ten or a nine-twenty. By now only a radically out-of-touch straggler would be left to be notified of Hendley's death. Lee's flight from his class hadn't been necessary. Sondra was in his classroom upstairs adding layers of nasal lacquer to her ball of Kleenex, on the alert for footsteps, but there wouldn't be any.

He had left the department without having gone to his office; he hadn't even turned the corner of the corridor that led to his office, and which would have shown him whether crime tape still sealed Hendley's door and whether a policeman was still posted there, dozing

off in a chair. Lee suddenly felt something akin to the homeland longing of an exile for his office, with its impoverished décor that to the
outsider must bespeak lack of personal feeling, but which for Lee was
precisely the opposite. The very few objects Lee had placed in his office, the old lamp and the photos of Esther and her scuffed baby
shoe—partner of the shoe in his desk drawer at home—were personal
in the extreme, and the disproportion of their mass when compared to
the ranks of generic-looking, unadorned mathematical textbooks; the
gray metal utility shelves; the university-issue gray desk and bland
bulletin board with its very few bureaucratic reminders dutifully dis-
played, all four corners secured by pushpins, did not, for Lee, render
them atmospherically powerless but rather increased their potency
to the utmost degree. For Lee the ordered space of his office was
indelibly stamped with significance; what did it matter that Esther's
decades-discarded, heroic little white shoe was concealed in a drawer?
It was for no one but him. He yearned to be in his office right now,
with the door locked and that invisible atmosphere of his innermost
heart sitting calmly around him, and at the same time he was newly
aware of contamination. Hendley had been murdered next door. Lee
would have to move offices, and while he had never felt sentimental
about that particular junction of walls, floor, and ceiling—his office
was the lamp and the shoe and the outdated photos—he walked out of
the building almost overwhelmed by his feeling of loss.

Outdoors was, perversely, the sort of pulsing spring day that could
erase cluttered decades, pluck them out of his way and take him back,
not to Aileen or even his first years in this country but all the way to
boyhood, to that narrow collection of disjointed glimpses and pangs.
From his very early childhood, he recalled a pear orchard, and like
someone emerging again in a past incarnation, he could see, for a moment, the hills of white blossoms descending to a faraway sea. This
must have been the mid-1930s, before the arrival of war, even in its
first form as a distant event to which his father made occasional reference. Lee no longer remembered where that orchard had been, to
whom it had belonged, why he'd been there, alone, he feels, moving
resolutely on very small legs, and he no longer had any way to find
out. Nobody to ask. An ocean of blossoms, in humped waves and boiling with bees, and in the distance the line of the actual sea, like the rim

of his warm silver cup. Perhaps in recollection the orchard was vaster, the hills steeper, the sea's gleam more explicitly signaling *him*—in compensation for the plain diorama of American campus he'd occupied for the past three decades. The West Quad, which he crossed walking back to his car, was thinly scattered with students, but instead of walking or sprawling they stood huddled in small groups, as if holding councils. There was no trace of the immature, inappropriate, completely understandable attitude of celebration at classes' having been canceled that Lee had expected, and even hoped for, in minute quantities. They were teenagers, after all—they were children! What should they care about death? But they were solemn as priests, gathered into their secretive huddles, and Lee was reminded abruptly of a different day, in a different season, the November day when he'd emerged from his library carrel his first semester in graduate school to find the quad eerily dotted with just such small, motionless groups. Then he'd noticed a noise, the compound drone of numerous, widely spaced transistors, and realized that each group of hunched wool overcoats had formed around the small grain of a radio. Running up to the nearest, he'd heard low sobs as well and thought, *War.*

"What is it?" he'd cried.

"Kennedy's been shot," someone told him.

He'd taken off running again, still thinking, *There will be war. They've shot the president, there will be war.* But here today was only sun, delicious warmth to the breeze, and grave children—less traumatized, Lee decided as he passed them, than elevated by the sense of a drama in which they played roles. He recognized none of his department's students, the only students he felt would be justified in any real demonstrations of grief, and even then he was aware he was finding the prospect of such demonstrations distasteful. For Emma Stiles it might be warranted. She had idolized Hendley, unfortunately. But for the students of Hendley's persistently oversubscribed lecture, the hundreds of students who had watched him perform from a distance, who sat cross-legged and patient, a long line of them, in the hallway outside his office every week waiting for a bantering word with him, for the students who didn't even have their laborious papers evaluated by him, but instead by his lackeylike teaching assistants—were these students suffering genuine grief? Wasn't there something out of

proportion, not just about the stricken solemnity of the student population but about the official solemnizations of the college itself? The
collegewide assembly, the batteries of grief counselors, the suspension
of classes all began to strike Lee, now that he was free of the chastising
presence of Sondra, as sanctimonious and self-important, as if the single death of a popular professor of dubious talent, however inexplicable and unjust it was, was on the same level as the death of John F.
Kennedy. And he was not a victim of envy to think such a thing,
although he was a coward, because he knew he'd never say it aloud,
even to Fasano. It took moral courage to acknowledge that some humans merited more, were worth more alive—or more dead—than the
rest of their kind. Kennedy's life had been worth more than Hendley's
and would certainly be worth more than Lee's, whatever miracles Lee
might accomplish before the end of his days. And Hendley's life had
been worth more than Lee's; since he'd talked to Fasano, Lee understood that with calm clarity. Someone, whether with reason or not,
had found Hendley and Illich, and perhaps all the others Fasano had
mentioned, more substantial, and hence more threatening, than Lee
ever would be.

Somehow this self-diminishing acknowledgment helped him to
think of Gaither's letter, and his own swift reply, with some degree of
internal composure. After long consideration he had mailed the letter
to Gaither in a departmental envelope; though he had demanded
Gaither's telephone number, he hadn't reciprocated. This wasn't to
preserve an advantage, as Lee knew he had none. Gaither could find
Lee at home as easily as he'd found him at school; he probably already
had his number from the telephone book. But Gaither had initiated
the correspondence to Lee's school address, perhaps in sardonic hom-
age to their shared past as students. Whatever the case, Lee expected
Gaither's reply, if there was going to be one, to find him at school, the
way the first letter had.

By now he'd returned to the faculty lot again and caught sight of
his car, parked diagonally with its left front and right rear bumpers almost touching its neighbors. Lee hadn't been aware of this when he'd
left the car forty minutes ago. In its crookedness his generic Nissan
had been transformed into something extremely pathetic, like the
scarcely driven old-model Chevrolets and Lincoln Continentals plied

waveringly to the grocery store by nearly sightless and hunchbacked owners and left in the lot as haphazardly as boats washed onto land by a flood. Apart from the college, this town possessed nothing to set it apart from the rest of the Rust Belt and as a result had grown gray and enfeebled; all its young people had left or succumbed to drug use. Living on the gown side of the town/gown divide, though, Lee no more felt a kinship to these town geriatrics than he would have to horses or cows. Academic life demanded that reflexive belief in exemption from sorry surroundings, as if being a tenured professor at a second-rate school were like being an American diplomat in the Third World—unless you had luck, like Fasano, and got Cornell and UCLA, or unless you were actually brilliant, as none of Lee's immediate colleagues had been since Donald Whitehead in graduate school. But what if twenty-five years in the same place had filled with time's silt the dividing abyss, so that now Lee was less a grand Gownsman than another old Townsman who should give up his license? Approaching the car, he stopped short of the point at which any observer would see he was the owner and looked around anxiously, as if he'd run the car into someone's front yard. University Station lay on the far side of the lot, and it was as much to restore distance between himself and his car as to pursue his vague instinct of having a letter that he resumed walking, in that direction. First delivery to individual departments rarely occurred before noon, even later on Mondays because the weekend's backlog of mail took longer to sort. If the trundling mail cart, pushed along carelessly by a work-study student, were to emerge from the station right now, he could intercept it. He wouldn't set foot again in his department or its mail room today.

To his surprise, the same spiky-haired boy whom he'd questioned before was at the window again. "I'm beginning to think you and I are the last people alive on the planet," he said.

"Um, yeah," the boy said, scrubbing his hand through his hair in a gesture of defense against the baffling statement. The boy's scowling, suspicious expression was exactly like past expressions of Esther's at that same thorny age. Though Esther's had been a torment, this boy's prompted in Lee an upwelling of misty benevolence. And the dread he had felt earlier, when he'd thought he would have to teach class, was giving way to a truant's elation at the prospect of freedom. He felt able to back his car out of its space. If he did have a letter from Gaither, he wouldn't read it right now, or even today. After three decades, what was the rush? When he got home, he'd brew a pot of green tea and take a very long nap, and when he woke up, he'd drink a cold beer and make a strip steak for dinner. He would skip the all-college assembly, he would soak in the bath with the *Emperor* Concerto playing, then he'd sleep like a stone, for the first time in weeks, and in the morning—the perfumed light of Tuesday, with no class to teach—he would open the letter.

As he'd expected, the mail cart for Mathematics and Computer Science hadn't yet departed, although it was loaded and ready to go. "This'll be the only delivery today," the boy said as he wrestled the cart forward. "Second delivery's canceled so everyone can attend the assembly. Um, I need to see a photo ID if you want to take mail from here. It has to be a valid driver's license or, um, a passport or something like that."

"You do? Why?"

"It's just a new policy, for security."

"But," Lee said, smiling tolerantly at the boy, "my mailbox in the department doesn't have to show you my ID for you to give it my mail. Does it? So what sense does this make?"

"If you don't have ID with you now, we're just about to fire this cart off, Professor. Your mail'll be in your mailbox in about half an hour. Maybe forty-five minutes."

"But I don't have time to wait," Lee lied. His aversion to returning to his building had become absolute; he knew that it would ruin his miraculously restored mood.

"And you don't have ID? Because that's the only way. I don't know, you can talk to the guy in charge if you want. It's not like I make the rules."

Lee had almost imagined the entire mail-room apparatus under the desultory control of the spiky-haired boy, but of course there were full-time workers, actual United States postal workers, concealed somewhere behind the long wall of student mailboxes, each with its small window to show mail to someone looking in or, as one small aperture in a vast compound eye, to show the station's patrons, like Lee now, to someone looking out. "No, that's all right," he said. "Of course I have my driver's license. I only question this policy, because it seems very random to me." He wrested the license from his wallet with clumsy fingers and then proffered it haughtily, because now the boy was looking at him with another of Esther's former trademark expressions, the undisguised incredulity of a teenager forced to contend with a doddering parent. This time Lee did not feel as nostalgic in response.

"*Okay,*" the boy said, taking the license. "I'll be right back."

But the person who returned with Lee's license was not the boy, or even one of the thick-legged, dull-eyed, full-time uniformed postal workers. It was a middle-aged man, perhaps in his late forties, casually dressed in loafers and pleat-front khaki pants and a bomber jacket over a button-up shirt with no tie. He was not very much taller than Lee and not even, on close examination, very much heavier, but he somehow denoted a looming presence, seemed to refer to a previous hugeness, like certain aged football players Lee recalled from TV, earnestly endorsing deodorant. This man's earnestness seemed to arise not just from oversize shoulders, restrained and uncomfortable-looking in the snug bomber jacket, but from his face, which was even more paradoxically striking than his unaverage body. The face was appealingly ugly, sensitively crude, dominated by a shadow-casting shelf of a brow beneath which small yet bright eyes seemed to peer with particular keenness. Lee had the fleeting impression not of an unhandsome man but of an amazingly handsome gorilla, an impression deepened by the man's helmet of coarse black hair, going gray at the temples, and his matching eyebrows further darkening his shelf-shadowed face, and his arms, as powerful as the shoulders and perhaps very slightly too long; Lee was aware of their length because the man was extending both hands in what seemed an unusually warm show of welcome. The right hand was empty, and instinctively Lee reached to meet it, while his gaze was entranced by the left: it offered Lee what at first seemed to be a small billfold, held open, the interior busy with typescript of various sizes in varying shades of blue, teal, and gray: FEDERAL BUREAU OF INVESTIGATION *U.S. Department of Justice   By Order of the Attorney General the individual pictured herein* ... The small photo of the man who had now grasped Lee's hand failed entirely to capture its subject; it was clearly the same man, but at the same time it could have been anyone. An illegible signature climbed up one side, vertical to the rest of the text. "Special Agent Jim Morrison," he was saying. "Professor Lee? It's my pleasure to meet you. I have to correct our friend here: I'm not in charge, not at the post office. Your school's administration and the United States Postal Inspectors are working together to implement changes for all of your safety, and I'm doing my best to help out. Thank your Postal Service; they're watching out for your welfare. All right," he added over the bulk of his shoulder to the boy, who was gaping behind him.

"No way," the boy said. "Your name's Jim Morrison? Are you serious?"

"For the next little while, the post office will be screening your mail on arrival to ensure it contains nothing dangerous," the agent continued, ignoring the boy's interruption. "But they're also concerned no one tampers with your mail, once it's here. Let's say someone not you comes here claiming he's you, gets your mail on the strength of his word, and then tampers with it in a manner that's dangerous to you. But you're you, Professor: that's all we wanted to know. And let me add that I'm sorry for your loss."

For a moment Lee didn't know what loss was meant. He had flushed to the roots of his hair, and his overwrought gut had reactivated; the sensation he felt, inapt as he knew that it was, equally mixed apprehension with guilt. He had no reason to feel guilty apart from his being alive; but he'd long known that in the face of a cop, all grown people feel guilt, no matter how spotless their hearts.

By contrast, the boy showed no unease at all. After rooting through the bundles of mail in the cart, he handed one to the agent without a tremor: a large bundle, held together with two rubber bands, which the agent removed. The agent sorted through the bundle swiftly, was satisfied, resecured it, and gave it to Lee. Lee had watched this without seeing; he still did not know if the bundle contained a letter from Gaither. He dimly registered that it was the most mail he'd ever received in one day.

"So much," he murmured.

"The post office has been holding on to mail while departments install keyed mailboxes. You should have gotten some notification; I apologize on your department's behalf if you didn't. They've had to come into compliance with a lot of changes in not a whole lot of time, and of course the stresses in your department have been greater than anywhere else. Just to save you some time, Professor, as you're sorting through all of that mail, let me go ahead and tell you that one item will be a request that you make an appointment to come in and talk, either to me or to one of my colleagues, in the next couple days."

"About what?"

"We're speaking to everyone in the math/sci departments, as a matter of routine," the agent began soothingly, and from his tone Lee realized that his own had been shrill. His benevolent mood, his momentary truant's elation, had been misfired neurons, a glitch; he was the same trembling wreck he'd been when encountering Sondra. He struggled to master himself and wound up sounding brusque.

"Of course," he interrupted. "I'd be very glad to. I'd be very glad to help."

"Thank you, Professor. I look forward to speaking with you." And when the agent extended his hand once again, but with the left hand withheld in a pocket this time, Lee, like a marionette, extended his once again in response, so that they both felt, when their palms made contact, that Lee's was clammy with sweat.

9.

IT FELT IMPERATIVE TO HIM THAT HE GET HOME BEFORE encountering anyone else, that he get home, drink tea, nap, rise refreshed . . . but the sequence of restorative acts that had so logically presented itself a few minutes before was now incoherent. Bathe the *Emperor* Concerto, put beer to bed for a nap, strip steak like a stone— with the unlikely physical genius he otherwise only sometimes possessed after drinking too much, he had shot his car backward from its dangerous confines without any abrasions, and he exited the cramped parking lot as successfully. But once he'd left campus and merged into thin traffic, he knew he didn't want to go home, to the vaulted and drafty expanse of his "cathedral" front room, with its wall scuffs where the furniture Michiko had taken once stood, above the ghostly round furniture footprints still marking the carpet. The exposed picture hooks on finely penciled crosshairs and the soil-coated plates in the corners on which had stood potted plants made the décor complete. He avoided that room so assiduously that the cheap hollow-core front door with its faux brass knocker, which he never used and apparently never locked, had once somehow swung open and remained that way a whole day and night, showing his arid front room to anyone who drove by while he, in the back of the house, put another sweater on his body and then another blanket on his bed against the unprecedentedly powerful draft. He'd seen the door standing open only the following morning, backing out of his driveway, and almost hadn't bothered to shut it. If there were thieves, they had already seen he had nothing to lose—besides his desk, which he challenged the world to try to separate from him. Even Michiko, the shameless freebooter, had not dared ask for it. What a woman! From this distance, Lee was tempted to admire her, for having so thoroughly demolished one of his least examined and, as it developed, most unfounded beliefs, in the refinement and pure-heartedness of the Japanese woman. Of course she would turn out to be a dissembling, self-serving opportunist par excellence; she'd charmed Lee with her fears that by marrying him she might "cease to be Japanese," because he, Lee, was always insisting he was purely American. And so he was, Lee had acknowledged: he had been a United States citizen for twenty-eight years, a number, unlike his age, about which he was always precise. But he'd had no desire to remain what he'd been. She did: that was noble, and lovely. She need not fear losing her "Japaneseness"—she would always have that! So it had gone, Lee reassuring her all through the process of getting her green card, a process upon which she'd embarked with such apparent reluctance and which, as soon as it was concluded, inspired her to divorce him.

He was passing Mashtamowtahpa Park, a homely, tree-scattered scrubland centered on a small pond, which had once also featured a petting zoo, through which a little train wended its way. The train's miniaturized cars had been painted to replicate those of the freight trains that used to rumble through town, at so many points and so often that Lee suddenly had the sensation that Esther's whole childhood was comprised of their waiting together at a railroad crossing, the same moment repeated again and again like the train cars they'd counted. *Illinois Central. Union Pacific.* When had those freight trains stopped coming? The petting-zoo freight-train facsimile had in fact carried passengers, each open-topped car holding three tiny benches faced forward, each bench potentially holding two children or, more snugly, a child and an adult. The first time he and Esther had gone to the zoo, she had been as uneasy as he, although he'd tried to hide it: "Look, Esther, a sheep! Like the rhyme!" But Esther had seen no less clearly than Lee that the sheep's wool was dingy, and caked with sawdust, and stank, and that the sheep was quite stupid; only four years old, Esther had not run away or begun crying, but she had stood as if glued there, her brow dark with suspicion and blame. After this they had confined themselves to the train, which she loved. No matter that it struggled with much metal shrieking and trembling along a circuit that lasted barely ten minutes, even at minimal speed, and took in for sights the same sheep, the same unnerving goat, and the same pungent enclosure of chickens. Esther could not pass the park without riding it, could never ride only once, her small form warmly pressed to his rib cage, the glossy crown of her head very still as she gazed. They were sometimes the only ones riding, and when this was the case, the "conductor," a parks employee who remained at the "station" to turn the train on and off, would raise his eyebrows in question as the train reached the end of its circuit and, if Lee nodded back, would twirl his forefinger over his head in a "one more time" gesture and let them keep going.

Like the real freight trains, the petting-zoo train had vanished, and the petting zoo with it. The very half of the park that once housed zoo and train had passed out of existence. Beginning a few years earlier, after some small amount of outcry, the land had been converted into playing fields for John Adams High School. Lee remembered walking with Esther across tramped, dusty grass and beneath tall pines that left rust-colored needles thick under their feet; it had seemed like a poor excuse for a park to him then, and he'd regretted he had nothing better to share with his daughter. Now that abused grass, and the scent of those pines, and even the colorful American debris Esther loved to examine—the Bazooka Joe comics, the plastic charms from the gumball machines—were as potent in recollection as that orchard in bloom, rolling down to the sea. He'd once thought this was such a diminished landscape; he'd had no idea how far diminishment went. Even the trees were gone. The little plot of land, which had once seemed, if not expansive or beautiful, at least possessed of some texture and depth, was exposed to have been a mere lot where one might have parked cars. Instead the school had erected klieg lights and laid out Astroturf. As Lee passed the far side of the new playing fields, he saw that someone had put up a sign: SHAME ON YOU JOHN ADAMS HIGH SCHOOL FOR SHORTCHANGING OUR CHILDREN.

When had the freight trains stopped coming? Those trains that, he had explained to Esther, carried grain, like *amber waves of grain*, and fruits, like from the *fruited plain*, and anything else anybody might want, the whole sea-polished length of the country. He had wanted to teach her the wonder he felt, for Great Plains and grocery-store lettuce, for all the breathtaking grandeur and everyday comfort the unlikely conjunction of which was their life in this country. Had he only succeeded in making her realize how far she could run? Everywhere in this town, the streets rose over tracks or ducked under them, and wherever you crossed the town's river, an out-of-use railroad bridge ghosted your route, clamorous with graffiti. He remembered the first time he'd heard, from the mother of one of Esther's spurned friends, that Esther had begun hanging out on the river with townies, probably to do drugs. This in the year after Aileen had died. Fasano had left town by then, and Lee had felt terrorized by the prospect of Esther's delinquency and so had hidden from it and done nothing.

These thoughts had carried him over the river into a part of town he'd once feared he would never forget and that he now hadn't seen in a decade, though it was minutes from campus. This town was too small to spend four years in, let alone four decades, but Lee's habit of rigid habitualness, coupled with a habit of periodically smashing all habits and erecting new ones that are entirely different but equally rigid, had made of the small town several smaller ones, which shared almost no points in common. The town he'd just entered was the one where he'd lived after separating from Aileen. There was nothing here for him—except, he realized when he passed it, the gloomy western-themed restaurant/bar he'd once frequented, after riverside jogs, with Fasano. The Cowpoke or Horseshoe or Split Rail—the Wagon Wheel, as it turned out. He was amazed to see that it was no more or less dere-lict than he remembered. He pulled in to the small, cratered lot. It wasn't even noon, but the Black Label sign in the window was lit, and there were two other cars.

All this time the bundle of mail had remained out of sight in his briefcase, keeping company with the letter from Gaither and a half page of insomniac notes for his now-canceled class and a number of pens, some depleted and some leaking, which lived in the briefcase year-round. There was nothing else there, not even the semester's text-book, which he had years ago ceased to need and of which, in any case, he had multiple copies, kept at school and at home and—tossed there in a fit of car cleaning and now forgotten for years—in the trunk, be-neath the tire jack and shovel. On most days his briefcase hung from his hand virtually empty, but its purpose had never been as a means of conveyance. It was his keystone of self as projected by wardrobe, his version of the businessman's tie—though, unlike the tie, which denotes a whole species, that briefcase meant *Lee* and was as good as his double. So that when his colleagues at school saw the briefcase perched somewhere alone, looking back they would think they'd seen him. And so that Lee himself, having forced the mail down that unpro-testing throat, now felt the lump indigestibly in his own stomach. While driving he'd allowed himself only the thought that until the right moment presented itself, he would give no more thought to the mail. Now he hugged the briefcase with one arm as he approached the dim entrance—weathered boards, suggestive of a barn—feeling almost relieved at how promptly fate had made the appointment.

The dim entrance was no preparation for the interior darkness, which stopped Lee in his tracks, briefly blind from the lingering stain of the dazzling spring sunshine. When he and Fasano had come here, it had always been dusk, and he recalled the room gently aglow, lit by hearth or by candles, with a warm scent of steak in the air. It was noth-ing like that. The still air was colder than the stiff breeze outside, as if this air had been trapped in the room since the previous winter. And the smell, of cigarettes and concrete and mildew, underscored that impression. There was no hearth that Lee could make out, although there were candles, in squat globes the golden brown hue of day's first, darkest urine. He immediately wanted to leave, to be outdoors again, perhaps on one of the fragile, termite-ravaged benches still holding their ground in Mashtamowtahpa Park. But he could feel himself being examined by the bar's other patrons, the few miserable persons like him who had wanted to exile themselves from the first beautiful day of the year. He would drink one beer and leave, and he'd open the mail in Mashtamowtahpa Park. Unhappily, he felt his way onto a vinyl barstool that was chill to the touch and so tall his legs swung short of the metal footrest. Perhaps this wasn't the same place at all. The Barn Door? The Hayloft? At least it gave him a light opener for his call to Fasano. *I thought I was losing my mind. Could we have liked such a dump?* Then, after they'd laughed and resolved the enigma, he'd have to say that at the very same time they'd been talking last Friday, Hendley was already dead.

"Black Label," he said to the indistinct bartender who'd materialized from the gloom. When the beer appeared, it was not in the modern deplorable can but in the ancient brown bottle. Perhaps this was the same place.

"Professor Lee," he heard a woman's voice say.

He knew he couldn't blame the low illumination, or the one sip of beer, or even his insomnial night for the fact that he failed to see the young woman who had come to stand next to him, was not blind to her but rather misperceived her, drastically and to the point of conviction, *twice,* each misprision almost simultaneous to the other and to the final, correct apprehension, so that the woman herself would not realize that Lee had taken her first for his dead wife, raised healthy and young from the grave, and second for a heretofore-unencountered identical twin before realizing, finally, that she was neither Aileen nor an uncanny stranger, but Rachel. All Rachel saw in the seconds consumed by this turmoil was Lee staring at her in paralyzed horror and shock.

"I'm sorry. I didn't mean to startle you. You probably came here to be left alone. We met long ago at the college, at a function or something. I'm Rachel. I'm Rick Hendley's . . . I was—"

"Yes, I know," Lee said quickly, and in reward for having plucked her from that perilous branch he was graced by a smile, like the furnace door briefly thrown open to show the white suffering heat

trapped inside. That undid him; his first spontaneous words had somehow won her favor, and anything deliberate he tried to say now was
sure to blow the advantage. He had to get away. Now they had been
joined by two more ghosts, a couple akin enough to Hendley and
Rachel that, from behind, they might have been taken for them—or
for Hendley and the phantom Aileen. The young woman pale, slender,
severely melancholic in expression, with smooth classical hair tightly
pulled to the nape of her neck, clad in black or in a hue dark enough
to be taken for black in these murky surroundings. The young man as
carefully disheveled as the women were carefully groomed; by his
clothes he seemed to want to imply that he had just been performing
repairs to his mobile home before coming to have a drink in this bar.
All three had cigarettes pinned fastidiously between middle and index
fingers, and now that Lee's eyes had adjusted, he could see that the table from which they'd all risen to greet him, in the far corner, held an
overflowing ashtray and an impressive collection of glasses—short
glasses, for booze. Lee could also see now that apart from himself they
were the only patrons.

"... Natasha, and Gordon," Rachel was saying. "Natasha teaches in
the media studies department at Rochester. Gordon is at Santa Cruz.
Historiography of science. We've all known each other since graduate
school. Rick was our token hard scientist." She turned to Natasha and
Gordon. "Professor Lee is one of Rick's colleagues," she said. "Was."
Without warning, her face, which had been so composed, balled itself
like a fist, and she started to sob. "I'm sorry," she gasped, making no
effort to conceal her streaming eyes or phlegmy nose, to bend over or
turn or retreat. Gordon and Natasha watched solemnly, but apart from
Natasha's palm, which placed itself on Rachel's back, no further intrusion was made, as if, like Lee, Natasha and Gordon were too awestruck
by Rachel's grief to do anything except stare dumbly at her. But then
the bartender came down the bar to them, not at all alarmed—they
must have been doing this all morning—and in response to his questioning gaze Natasha said, "We'll have another round. And whatever
he's having. Please join us," she said to Lee, in a tone that suggested
not hospitality but an expectation of something: an overdue explanation, a reparation.

"You must be hiding out from that ludicrous college assembly, like us," Rachel said, as if her continued participation in the conversation were a given, despite her undiminished sobs. In her struggle to speak, she produced, drawing breath between words, a noise like a whinny. Lee's own larynx seemed to have closed. If he had gone to see Hendley even once, he would have also seen Rachel, spoken with her, perhaps come to know her as he never had in the two years that she had been Hendley's regular visitor from the West Coast. He longed to drench his parched mouth with his beer, but while Rachel sobbed, no one was drinking, although three new glasses, filled to their lips with dark liquor and ice cubes, had been neatly lined up on the bar, along with another Black Label bottle. Lee's first was still almost untouched.

"I'm afraid," he said, greeting the reemergence of his own voice with anxiety, as if it were an unreliable, half-domesticated beast, "I'm afraid I have to go. I do have to go, to this college assembly."

"But it's not until four," prosecuted Natasha. "You have hours. And we need to talk to someone who's senior in the department about what the hell's going on. The authorities won't tell Rachel anything; they won't even tell her *which* authorities won't tell her anything, in terms of who's in charge of this investigation. Because Rick and Rachel weren't married she's *beneath* their concern, it's not even no concern, it's a *negative* amount of concern that these assholes show her."

"Tasha," Rachel said.

"I'm serious!" Natasha cried. As if there were hysterical energy just for one person, Rachel grew calm as Natasha grew frantic. "Not to mention that even if you *had* married Rick you're still a woman, nothing's going to change that."

"Hey," Gordon said quickly. "Here's our drinks. Let's go back to our table. At least finish your beer with us," he tossed over his shoulder to Lee, already walking away and presuming that Lee would follow, as if they were peers, and not merely peers but unequal, Lee the lesser colleague who could make Gordon impatient. Gordon, the fake lumberjack and smug double for Hendley.

"Thank you, but I can't," Lee said, seizing his opening—they had taken their fresh drinks and were moving off. Rachel stopped when he spoke, then reversed direction, coming swiftly toward him, her drink splashing. "I can't," he repeated, seizing his briefcase with one arm and upsetting both bottles of beer. On impulse he took hold of her hand—that was how near she'd come, her crimson eyes imploring something of his. "I'm sorry!" he cried, and before she could speak, he had turned and rushed out of the bar. Back in the sun, he was blinded again, but he plunged to his car nonetheless and was most of the way to the park before his vision had cleared. Her hand had felt very cool and smooth, like a riverbed stone. At the park he dropped onto the first bench he found and sat a moment allowing the shapes of the Wagon Wheel's darkness and of his utter fatigue to swarm like petri-dish germs in his vision. Then, perhaps because it seemed the punishment that he deserved, he removed the bundle of mail from his briefcase, stripped off its rubber bands, and sorted through it as swiftly as Jim Morrison had. There was much junk, many departmental declamations—in other words, nothing unusual except for a white number-10 envelope, hand-addressed by a clearly meticulous person. It was his letter, to Gaither, *Returned to sender: addressee unknown.*

10.

NEITHER GAITHER NOR LEE SOLVED THE DIECKMANN problem; Lee hadn't expected either one of them would. The scholarly contest presented an elegant metaphor; it was a cryptic expression of the uglier, intimate struggle and at the same time that struggle's concealment; it was a genteel arena within which Lee could lay waste to Gaither without having to see him; and at the same time was no contest at all. Even if Lee had the talent, he now lacked the mental composure; he could not even read a newspaper. And even if Gaither was a sheer Christ of mental composure in the face of all woes, he still lacked the talent. Lee expected Gaither to continue earnestly, and himself to make a cynical start, and them both to eventually fail. What he didn't expect was for Whitehead to solve it, when no one had known that he meant to attempt it. Whitehead solved the Dieckmann problem and a second, celebrated enigma called the Gorence equation, completed and defended his dissertation three years ahead of the most optimistic prognosis and was offered and accepted the best job in the field to have appeared in anyone's memory, all by the end of October. Lee hadn't seen Whitehead since that day on the quad and never saw him again. He did see his picture—the fresh haircut and tight smile together producing an almost martial expression of triumph—in the campus newspaper.

By then, standing on the front porch of his rooming house receiving notification of his own obsolescence from the week-old broadside—he'd found it shucked to the floor in the foyer, another tenant's garbage—he almost could spare fellow feeling for his heretofore rival. He and Gaither had both been made fools of. Since taking his leave of absence, he had lived not like an independent scholar but like an exile, and now he felt this had been subtly encouraged by his department. He had heard nothing about Whitehead from his adviser, although his adviser must have known weeks ago; he had heard nothing from his adviser the entire semester. Though it was true that he had avoided his department and even the library since the beginning of classes, living like a monk in his room in the "town" part of town, far from the school's monarchical hill, he also knew that every graduate program was a Darwinian struggle. More doctoral students were admitted than would ever find jobs, and they were expected to winnow each other. He recalled the sensation he'd had long ago, before meeting Aileen, that he and Gaither were fated to be tied together—by their age, by their shared friendlessness. Now they weren't merely tied but entombed with each other. They both meant to possess the same woman, and in their fleshly struggles, in their thrashing and panting, they both seemed to have exiled themselves to the irrelevant margins of their shared discipline. There was a moment, standing on that sagging front porch, the paper flapping in his stunned and limp hand, his own sense of himself as a scholar—he might have once said "achiever"; he had traveled so far, hadn't he?—strewn at his feet as incoherently as his landlady's rubbish, that he felt a greater brotherhood to Lewis Gaither than he had ever been capable of at the height of their friendship. Lee's desire for Aileen had seduced him from scholarly work, the only marriage he'd ever purely desired, with his rational self. And so at that moment, with the prospect of failure before him, he was a brother to Gaither. He felt he could stave off that failure and give Aileen up. He could let Gaither have her.

Although it was the tenth of November, it was unusually warm; a front had blown in from the South, bringing not just the warmth but a strange, gusting wind whose combination of mildness and force felt to Lee somehow sinister. The wind had torn open the house's trash cans and was even now carrying their contents from place to place in the front yard; it was to remedy this that he'd come outside, at the request of his landlady. His discovery of Whitehead's triumph, his understanding that he would not be a failure but would give up Aileen and seize Whitehead's position as the dominant student now that Whitehead was gone, his condescension to Gaither—all this had taken him just a few moments, as the wind and a weird, eerie light surged and flickered around him. The light was eerie because it was winter light, dying at just four P.M., yet its sideways beams fell through a hurricane aura of August. He crumpled the campus newspaper into a ball with one hand and strode quickly down the porch steps to herd up the lost garbage. The past months of hiding and waiting, of furtive calls to Aileen and then strange nondiscussions, as if the telephone line were congested; of passing out at his desk in his clothes and then waking at noon to discover a blank notepad stained by saliva supporting his face; of anguish, and anger, and lust, and complete solitude; all dissolved now like the gauze of a dream that intrudes very slightly upon the fresh light of morning but is then blinked away. He began to gather the renegade garbage despite the ongoing work of the wind; dragging one of the metal cans after himself, he traced an endless, complicated pattern all over the lot as the surviving debris leaped and dodged him. It was a Sisyphean task, but he pursued it with a ruthless patience he was aware, beneath the blank of his mind, was unusual for him. He did not know how long he'd been working like this, sweating freely, the smell of last night's cheap bottle of wine steaming out of his skin, when his landlady called to him. She'd come out on the porch, and when Lee straightened to look at her, he saw the last lurid ember of sun slip beneath the horizon, and at the same instant the wind suddenly ceased, as if a switch had been thrown.

"Someone's on my telephone for you," his landlady repeated, now audible, even loud, in the twilight stillness. "I've told you not to give out my number for personal calls."

"I didn't," Lee said, shouldering past her. He left the can on the porch.

The wind seemed to have stayed in his ears; once he was inside his landlady's stale, tatted-lace rooms, his hearing felt muddled in spite of the silence. Holding the receiver, he smelled himself, pungent and sour. A fine grit had coated his skin.

"This is Nora," a woman was saying. "Aileen's sister."

"Yes," he heard himself say.

"Aileen gave birth a few hours ago. A beautiful baby boy. They're both healthy. She's very happy. She wanted me to tell you."

"Yes," he heard himself say.

His landlady came back in as he put down the phone. "Then how did this girl get my number if it wasn't from you?"

"I don't know," he said, shouldering past her again.

He finished collecting the trash as night fell. Having been scoured by the wind, the sky now teemed with stars; it was the sort of rare night on which he might have entertained himself with a wheel of the constellations and an astronomy guide, as he'd done in boyhood.

Instead he lay stretched on his sofa in his filthy clothes and gritty skin, drinking a bottle of the cheap wine he now bought by the case. The wine was dark as ink, and its acids were destroying his stomach; its label depicted a festivity of small woodland creatures imbibing together on a rotted tree stump. He could see, staring down the slack length of his body, the ribs of dead leaves clinging to him. The day's strange weather had left an evening so quiet he could hear, every once in a while, the rough and tremulous warble of his landlady's radio show, and this was another out-of-season sensation, that of barriers having dissolved, so that the most intimate sounds—a child's cough on the street, the creak of springs as his landlady shifted her hams— were carried without any diminishment to his second-floor room. The acoustics of winter, when the depth of the soundscape mirrors that of the landscape. When the trees drop their leaves, forcing buildings to look at each other, and the air drops its muffling warmth so a snapped twig resounds like a gunshot.

It came to him that he was so frightened he could not fill his lungs. It wasn't indolence that kept him stretched on the sofa, but terror. Terror of irreversible, unwanted change of the absolute kind, the kind separating existence from nonexistence, for which both "death" and "birth" are inadequate names.

He did not want that child to exist, and now the child existed.

As if the clarity of the idea had increased its reality, he leaped up now, away, seized his bathrobe and kit and strode down the hall to the shower. When he was clean and dressed, he left the house so quickly he forgot his watch and his jacket, but he didn't need a jacket. The night was still forebodingly warm, beneath its late-autumn sky. He walked with swift purpose but without direction, up one hushed street for blocks, a block over and back down its parallel neighbor, a block over and up, a block over and down, like the shuttle methodically making its way through the loom. This child, this boy child, had been conceived in the previous winter, when Lee lived in the same rooms he still lived in now, when he sat beside Gaither in classrooms and walked beside Gaither on walks and was even—Lee's face was wet now with anger—eager for that man's friendship. Lee had been unvigilant, and Gaither had made Aileen pregnant, on a night after which Lee had certainly seen him, tall and doltishly handsome and self-satisfied. Lee had known of Aileen's existence but then failed to meet her for weeks. But what he was doing was futile: it was not an equation he could meticulously unravel until the flaw was located and fixed, and the outcome transformed.

He must have walked this way for hours, his footfalls on the sidewalk like gasps interrupting the quiet. Despite the strange warmth, or perhaps because of it, because it made people uneasy, no one was out simply walking, like him. Even if there had been other people, he might not have seen them. He had walked these streets so many times they were no less a blank field for his thoughts than the lined yellow notepads he worked problems on. The sky was more present to him, as it gradually shifted its dome. He saw the long side of Boötes edge over the rooftops, like a whale's back breaking the surface, and knew it was late. He hadn't forgotten the resolution he'd made on the porch. If his footsteps grew even more rapid, it wasn't that the resolve was a thing that he hoped to outpace. His relinquishment now seemed ordained. (Not because of the child—the child tumbled away, a footnote, an irrelevancy.) Lee grasped how inevitable and awful the relinquishment was, and he pursued only a last glimpse of the sacrificed object. Then, in surprising response to his will, he felt something like exaltation and realized she'd appeared in his mind as she'd been at the start, with her unhappy beauty, gazing carelessly at him from the back of a car.

He had come to a stop on the sidewalk, just outside the pale nimbus of light from the nearest streetlamp. On the opposite side of the street was a drab wooden building he might not have noticed had he passed right in front of it, but from this slight distance he'd taken in its full outline, its three windows above, two below, and two steps to the porch. While Aileen, Aileen untouched by him, gazing out from the sphere of her utter aloneness and not dreaming she'd be less alone, and not seeking to be, because somehow at peace with her marriage, had appeared in his mind. He had loved her then, at that moment of seeing but not yet being seen, or desired or needed. His first time seeing her, he had loved her. The drab house told him this, resurrecting that day, because the house was where they'd dropped off Ruth at the end of that night.

As Lee stood there, the door opened and Gaither emerged, somehow taller, longer-limbed, more casually powerful in his physique than Lee remembered him being. Lee stood helplessly rooted in place, his body awash in hot sweat, his hands tingling primitively with the awareness of danger. He couldn't move. If he had, Gaither might have seen him. Instead Gaither passed quickly under the porch light and down the two steps, crossing the yard on long legs to his car, a colorless thing unobtrusively massed at the curb. Lee had only now noticed it. With the car before him, Aileen's vivid ghost disappeared. He could no more imagine her sealed behind those dark windows than he could imagine himself. Gaither had let the door to the house slam behind him with the heedless familiarity of an owner, not a late visitor. Now the car door squeaked open and slammed shut, and the car came to life and promptly drove away. Lee first perceived the extinguishing of the lights in the three upstairs windows as a slight alteration in his immediate atmosphere; it was only when he looked back at the house that he realized what had happened. Gaither had not seen him, but Ruth might have. Lee turned and walked swiftly the way he had come, without crossing beneath the streetlamp.

11.

GAITHER FIRST SET EYES ON HIS CHILD FIVE DAYS LATER, when the weather had resumed being typical for mid-November, and with Thanksgiving in less than a week. The first viewing coincided with the fourth attempt at a viewing. Although Gaither had been ideally absent throughout the last months of her pregnancy, so far as Aileen had known, the day after the birth he manifested at Nora's front door in a form suggesting that ten years, and not ten weeks, had passed. He was beautifully, if grimly, dressed, in a suit a successful executive or attorney might wear. His boyish cowlick, which at the top of his long, rangy frame and above his square glasses had given him almost a Beat poet's look, had been clipped. Also clipped, shaved away, were his southern ingratiations, his game lopsided smiles and deliberate speech. The loud, toneless, unmerciful blast that was Nora's front bell had not changed—Aileen abhorred it; it made the poor baby jerk with alarm—but it now seemed an extension of Gaither, when Nora found him implacably on her front porch. From such a historically pious and tenderhearted man—as Nora had characterized him in debates with her sister—Nora would have expected hangdog supplication, or hysterical fury, or even tear-softened saintly forgiveness. Instead she confronted a chill bureaucrat. His face, neither shadowed nor bearded, nevertheless seemed concealed. Just a few moments later, called upon to describe it, Nora found that she couldn't. She couldn't even remember it.

Aileen was unwell, the baby asleep, they had all just that instant returned from the hospital. . . . Having thus triply lied, Nora retreated in unusual panic and let her husband, Warren, escort Gaither to Warren's car. The two men drove away.

Now Nora had no choice but to explain to Aileen that Warren had telephoned Lewis when Aileen went into labor, and again seventeen hours later when John, the baby, was born.

"He's always hated me," Aileen remarked, of Warren. She said this with indifference. When the doorbell had sounded, when John had flung open his small chicken limbs and squawked at her with reproach, in her fear she'd felt strangely triumphant, her heart slamming and her skin streaming sweat as if she'd broken the tape in a race. She had known who it was. Yet her fear was snugly ensconced, infallibly fortressed, a sort of emotional luxury item unsullied by practical applications. Just as John, while still housed in her body, had lived imperviously in a sac, now transferred to her arms he seemed to have brought the sac with him, to swaddle them both. He was clamped to her breast, again nursing with the tirelessness of a tiny machine—she thought of train wheels busily turning. While he nursed, he wore a secretive smile on his face, a conspiring gleam in his eyes. She did not know what people meant when they groused that the eyes of newborns appeared blank, unfocused, unresponsive. Her newborn appeared the enthralled audience of some extraterrestrial plane; when she held him stretched on her forearms, his unpadded rear in the chair of her elbows and his tiny head cupped in her palms, she felt she could glimpse in his bottomless gaze the reflections of solar-furred galaxies' arms and billowing pink nebulae.

"He's John's father, Aileen," Nora said, by which she meant that Warren had notified Gaither not out of hostility to Aileen, although there was this, but in deference to a natural order of things. For Nora this order was unquestionable, and the conflict it presented with the equally nonnegotiable law of loyalty to a sibling was taking its toll. Of the two women, Nora could easily have been mistaken for the one who had just given birth. Her face was taut and gray with fatigue, and her hands, when attempting an everyday task, as now—she was folding diapers—shook and fumbled. In the heat of discussion, her clauses inverted themselves. Aileen knew that between caring for her own two small children and helping with John, Nora was getting even less sleep than she was, and she knew, though Nora thought she did not, that Nora had been fighting an ongoing battle with Warren over Aileen's, and now John's, tenancy in the house. But she also knew that the quandary supposedly at the heart of this warfare, that she and Gaither both had equal claim to their child, was false. Gaither's claims were not equal to hers; they were not even of the same nature as hers. She did not know what they were, exactly; to define them she would have to make use of that distinguished, desiccated library of abstract principle on which her parents had raised all their children, and of which Nora had always been such a gifted student and Aileen such a failure. She had never cared for that library, and she cared for it even less now that she possessed, for the first time in her life, a scrap of actual knowledge, as harrowing to her as any Old Testament revelation. The child, John, was neither Gaither's nor hers, but his own. He had only passed through her. Yet where there were no rights, such as Gaither sought now, there was responsibility, conferred by that passage, upon her alone. Until he was unthinkably grown up and gone, he was hers to guard fiercely, and she his sole sentinel.

It surprised her that Nora had forgotten this, for as much as the epiphany had shored Aileen up, making her seem almost arrogant with self-assurance, she never imagined that her situation was unique. It was the condition of being a mother. Nora must have known, at the moments at which each of her children was born and perhaps for years afterward. But now, with the younger child about to turn four, Nora had forgotten, as she had forgotten so many things Aileen needed to know. Some perhaps species-protecting amnesia seemed to afflict more experienced mothers: Nora had no idea when John might be expected to produce his first real bowel movement or support his own head, or how long he should sleep in a hat to protect against drafts, or how often Aileen should nurse. And so perhaps it wasn't an occasion for bafflement but for tender forbearance on Aileen's part that Nora felt herself trapped, between equal combatants, with the only solution imaginable an unimaginable reconciliation. It was for Nora alone that Aileen finally agreed to let Gaither see John, the fourth time he tried. The first time, Warren had returned alone to the house and shut himself up with Nora, and later Nora came red-eyed to plead with Aileen. The second time, the next day, Gaither reappeared, obviously instructed by Warren, according to Nora as impeccably dressed but not in the same suit, and Aileen and Warren shouted at each other across the back bedroom until John began keening. The third time, the day after that, it was finally Monday, and Warren was at work and the children at school; when the doorbell sounded, Aileen and Nora and John were in the back bedroom together, and Aileen pulled Nora's head to her shoulder and kissed her hair and stroked it, as if Nora were the one under siege. "I'm so sorry, Nonie," she whispered. The next day, the fourth day, she told Nora to let Gaither in. Whether it was a fourth brand-new suit or a third, they couldn't know, not having seen him the previous time, but in either case Aileen was struck by how much he had changed.

For all the revulsion and horror Aileen had experienced in predicting this moment, for all her feeling that Gaither was a gross violation of that natural order to which she felt so attuned—as distinct as it was from the order subscribed to by Nora—the meeting was eerily rote, as if there were a well-known protocol for such things after all. Gaither was standing at the parlor window, his back to the room, when Aileen entered with John in her arms. She had finished nursing in the bedroom, and had swaddled John in a fresh blanket, and even put on a fresh blouse herself, less from a vestigial instinct to look nice for her husband than in response to the strong sense of formality, of the absence of intimacy, that had entered the house with Gaither. He did not turn when she entered, and as she seated herself on the sofa she found herself studying the elongated triangular form of his back, the ruler-straight demarcation between his fresh haircut and his pale exposed nape, the plumb line of each pleat at the back of his slacks with the impassive yet careful attention she might pay to a commanding stranger. He aroused no feeling. She had forgotten their marriage—erased it—and if she was trying to recall the sensation of having had sex with that gravely clad body, it was not in hopes of salvaging something but because she found the void in her memory so fascinating. John was a bundle of surrender-limp limbs she held propped in the crook of one arm, and it was only as Nora moved toward her, a ferry crossing dark straits, that Aileen's mind grew turbulent. A hot kitchen smell steamed off John, the salt-and-butter scent of his sweat and her milk, and as she gave him to Nora, it died from her nostrils. Nora crossed the room and with instructive gestures, like a hospital nurse, placed John in Gaither's arms. Gaither turned again to the window, his head bent, his back eclipsing the small lump of blanket. It seemed to Aileen that not a sound had been made since the front bell had blasted many eons ago and she had looked at her sister and said, "All right." Even John's varied creakings and huffings were absent. In the five days since his birth, they had come to seem as much a part of the aural landscape as the oak's sighing or the mourning dove's falling notes outside the bedroom window. Now profound silence had spread like black ink through the rooms. For the first time, her son was out of sight and arm's reach; even when she slept, she kept a hand dipped in the warmth of his cradle.

Nora had seated herself on Gaither's side of the parlor, but a respectful distance from him; though she faced Aileen, she kept her gaze on the floor. Aileen's gaze had nailed itself to Gaither's back but was sightless. Gaither's gaze was presumably trained on his son. Where did John gaze? Were his dazzled eyes open, receiving his father, or—please, God, she thought—were they closed? She did not know how long the four humans remained in this state, like four planets stalled in their orbits. A feeling of acute panic, of having made in an instant the most fatal of errors, overtook her and was beaten back several times.

At last John let out a brief cry, and Gaither responsively, but without any show of discomfort or haste, handed him to Nora. "I'd like a word with you before I leave," he said. He turned again to the window.

As Nora crossed the room with John in her arms, Aileen found that her right hand had held her left wrist so tightly that she had made a deep print of her watch on her skin. She'd been wearing her watch all along, but she did not know when Gaither had come, so she did not know how long he had been here, although her sense of time was lately almost compulsive. She could know, for instance, that she had nursed John beginning at 10:04, and for twenty-three minutes. But now she could not remember when, after Gaither's arrival, she had last finished nursing and swaddled John in the blanket and brought him into this room. This lapse felt ominous, as if from now on, in spite of herself, she would increasingly be guilty of neglect.

She stood when Nora reached her, received her child—luminous eyes open, scrawny fist in the act of erupting oratorically from the blanket—and turned and strode out of the room, as if all had been smoothly choreographed from the start. But she was trembling so that she thought she'd drop John, and when they were shut in the bedroom, she quickly opened her blouse, as if in apology, although it was possible that barely fifteen minutes had passed since they'd last been in this room.

Finally she heard the front door swing shut and Gaither's car—her car also, she reminded herself—leave the driveway. The homely brown sedan would cancel the considerable effects of the upgraded wardrobe, but perhaps he'd upgraded the vehicle also. For the first time, she wondered how Gaither had paid for his clothes, and with this idle thought all the pragmatic realities of her impending divorce lit upon her at once. Until now she hadn't thought of the things that they shared—the brown car, a few sticks of Goodwill furniture—which were themselves almost worthless but which referred to the one thing that mattered, their money. When Aileen married Gaither, he had been almost literally penniless, while she'd had a small trust, about ten thousand dollars, that had come to her, as to Nora and their other siblings, when their parents had died. Whatever remained of this money now lived in a joint bank account, unless Gaither had used it for a new car and clothes. Even as she was starting to hope this was true, so that he might finally be guilty of something, she knew that Gaither was too morally fastidious. In all aspects of life, Gaither conformed to a rigorous set of precepts some of which coincided with law and some with his religion, but many of which he'd evolved on his own. It had discomfited him that Aileen brought more money to the marriage than he did, and although he had endorsed the joint checking account on the biblical principle that in marriage the two become one, in reality he had kept their standard of living artificially low, so that they never spent more than he earned. She could not imagine him freebooting now, however much he despised her. In fact, he was probably even more loath to make use of her money. As if something had snaked through the outermost edge of her vision, she had an instant's perception that there was some other agency working with Gaither, grooming and clothing and advising him. Then Nora came into the room, and the insight was lost; she wouldn't recollect it until much later.

"Did you see the car he came in?" she asked Nora.

"What?" Nora said, startled. "His car?"

"Was it our car? Our brown Dodge?"

"I don't know." Nora looked at her helplessly. "I don't remember. Is it important?"

John stopped sucking; he had fallen asleep. Aileen carefully closed her blouse and touched a finger to John's cheek. As if in response, his lower lip began working, a soft little pseudopod busily rushing somewhere, pursuing what had just sated him.

"You must want to know what he said," Nora offered, and there was something too-solicitous in her voice, as if Aileen were the hopeless supplicant, not Gaither.

"I doubt I could guess."

"He wants to take John for Thanksgiving. To see his grandparents."

Aileen looked up; Nora did not seem ready to laugh with her at the ludicrousness of the notion. "Thanksgiving is *Thursday*."

"I know. I told him it didn't seem . . . likely."

"And then what did he say?"

"He said he'd be back tomorrow for your answer, and if you say no, then he'll take John at Christmas—further from now, but for longer. He said if you say no to Thanksgiving weekend, he'll take John to see them at Christmas, but for a full week. The week between Christmas and New Year's."

"He won't take John at all, anywhere, but I'll tell him myself. When he comes here tomorrow, you stay with John in this room, and I'll tell him myself."

"I think maybe you shouldn't talk to him, Aileen. We can work out your message, and then I'll give it to him."

"That's all right. Speaking with him won't kill me. Don't think I haven't wanted to see him because I'm afraid of him." As she spoke, Aileen saw a movement of impatience, almost exasperation, mar Nora's face. Nora looked away, out the window. The oak tree was there, the only mature tree on the small property. When Nora had given Aileen this bedroom, the smallest one in the house, formerly home to the sewing machine, Aileen had swelled with a gratified greed she'd been careful to hide. It was the smallest bedroom in the house, but it was also the best, the only one with a view from the window of something other than the nude chain-link fence and Warren's nude, ailing saplings and the lopsided, rusting swing set. The doves roosted in the heights of the oak or waddled between its humped roots like tentative invalids, and for reasons Aileen did not yet understand, she connected this nature-made city of turned auburn leaves and fluttering susurrations and coos with herself and her son. She did not yet realize that John had transmuted the status of all of those things, material and intangible, monumental and trivial, that for the moment comprised her existence. She had always suffered from an aversion to taking the long view, from a reluctance to base her decisions on possible outcomes. Now the profound gravitational force exercised by her child seemed to confirm, finally, that one's life was best lived as an endless immediacy. Everything seemed to reflect this idea except Nora.

"What?" Aileen said, belatedly grasping that Nora had offered to act as a go-between for reasons other than sparing her feelings.

"That wasn't all he said, about Thanksgiving and Christmas. It wasn't even the main thing. He pretended it was, but I felt it was his way of testing the waters. I said I'd speak to you about Christmas, that's all. I didn't mean to let on what I thought you would say. But he must have seen more from my face. That's when he said this other thing. He didn't sound angry. He sounded very . . . calm. And cold. As if that was what he had come here to say all along."

"For God's sake, Nora."

"I just want to repeat it precisely as he said it! He made me feel like a stupid little child. As if I was supposed to repeat his words back so he'd know that I'd learned them. He said, 'I know Aileen is not concerned about the Bible's prohibition against what she has done. Perhaps it will make more of an impression on her to know that the courts take the same view of her kind as the Bible.' "

"Of her *kind*?" Aileen said, waking John. "Of her *kind*? What the hell does that mean, my *kind*?"

"Aileen, *don't*," Nora said, her face furious.

"He's an infant, Nora. He doesn't understand English, let alone filthy English."

"He understands tone."

"Then what does that mean," Aileen hissed, in a stage whisper, lifting John to her shoulder, where he continued to emit little yelps that were as evenly spaced as a siren's.

"I was hoping that you could tell me."

For a moment they sat quietly, letting John's hiccupped cries fill the room. As the cries grew in strength, Aileen undid her blouse again with her free hand, and in the same moment Nora brought a pillow from the bed and adjusted it beneath Aileen's elbow, in precisely the way that she wanted it, not only as if they had not just been hissing like snakes at each other but as if they peacefully shared the same mind.

Their silence lasted until well after they'd both heard, with satisfaction, the soft clicking noise that John made when he fed.

"Your friend Mr. Lee," Nora finally said.

"Lewis's friend," Aileen clarified automatically.

"When you told me he'd been so . . . understanding, when you and Lewis began having problems, and so helpful when you were upset, and such a good confidant . . ." Nora looked out the window again, as if she sought in the majestic old oak a few more anodyne formulations to do justice to the chaste and enlightened relationship she was describing. Aileen felt the heat of impending exposure and shame beating out of her skin, and because Nora was her sister, and because they shared the same opaquely pale complexion, which could magically burn like a furnace while showing almost no tint, Aileen knew that Nora was blushing as well, because Aileen had so brazenly lied to her.

". . . were you telling me everything?" Nora finally concluded.

"No," Aileen said.

"So you've been with him," Nora said, her face, still in profile, extremely immobile.

"Slept with him. Yes."

"This man whose house I drove you to, the day I helped you move out of your house."

"For God's sake, Nora, I didn't go to bed with him while you were waiting in the car."

"Don't," Nora said, wheeling to face her again, and as their eyes met, Aileen's lungs seemed to die in her chest.

"You just answer my questions," Nora said, after a moment.

"All right," Aileen murmured.

"Did you tell Lewis you'd been with this man?"

"Yes."

"You told him everything. You told him you'd slept with his friend."

"Would it have been better if I'd lied to him, too?"

"I wish you would shut up and answer my questions."

Aileen felt her eyes flood, humiliated, as if they were children again. "Yes, I told him. In no uncertain terms. Not how often or how long."

Nora held a hand up, reflexively warding off these embellishments, and Aileen felt an unfamiliar leap of hatred that left her almost dizzy. "And what about the note you left for Lewis, the day you left the house?"

"What about it?"

"Did it talk about Mr. Lee, too?"

"Only to tell Lewis to leave him alone."

"But that says it all, doesn't it," Nora said, in a tone of conclusion.

"Says *what* all?" Aileen mocked, thinking that Nora looked much older than a woman eight years and one child ahead of herself. She'd hoped the little flame of hatred was one of those idle experiments carried out for their lack of connection to everyday life, like romantic speculations about unpalatable men on the bus. Now she noticed a storehouse of tinder concealed in herself, as if against a long winter ahead; the little flame cracklingly multiplied.

"That Mr. Lee is your lover," Nora said very quickly, as if the words were indigestible objects she wanted out of her mouth.

"Lewis already knew, as I said at the start of this inquisition."

"Yes, he already knew, because you had to tell him. You just couldn't wait. You knew you were unhappy, that the two of you might be headed for trouble, and then you had to run ahead and rub his face in it, without it ever once crossing your mind—"

"Without being ashamed, you mean. Without showing adequate shame for my sins."

"Without being prudent, you little idiot."

"I would have thought of all people you'd understand that some shred of emotional honesty where there'd never been *any* was what we needed. *We* should have never existed, someone had to admit that—"

"Oh, please stop it. You've been dying for your moment on the soapbox, to wave around your 'honesty' banner and say 'someone had to admit' and 'at least I was honest,' and that's why you couldn't keep your mouth shut with Lewis, but don't do it with me. I don't *care*, Aileen. I might have last week or last month, but I don't anymore, and neither does Lewis. He's gone on to the next thing, can't you see that? *He wants John. He wants to take him from you.* And he will at this rate, with your mouth. With your *honesty*," this last almost spat, as if she'd said "*whorishness.*"

"He can't take him from me," Aileen said, reflexively clutching John so that he grunted in protest—but the foreignness of the idea, a cold steel sliding into the sac in which she'd nestled herself, somehow spread, making John feel strange in her arms. "I'm his mother," she said. Even this statement seemed suddenly tinged with bizarreness. As a corrective she thought of the moment she'd first seen the slick, brushstroked head bloodily inching forth from her crotch, but now the crazed luminosity of her condition at that time was gone, and, stripped of its fiery grandeur, the stark scene seemed remote and grotesque and unlikely.

"And you're Lewis's wife," Nora was saying, "no matter how you might feel, and he is John's father, no matter how you might feel."

"Children stay with the mother."

"Not if the court finds the mother unfit."

Now, thank God, the creeping sense of strangeness, of John as a mere lump of animate flesh in her arms, of the yawning abyss of her time as his sole guardian against infinite dangers—forever, forever—was scoured away, like a pestilent fog in the face of a strong, cleansing wind. "Get out," she said to Nora, the hateful flame having comfortably grown to the size of a coat, sealing her and John safely together.

"Get out?" Nora said, almost gently. "Of my spare bedroom, in my house?"

To her shame she was relieved when, unwilled and to her surprise, tears began pouring over her face. What am I turning into? she thought. What kind of manipulating, theatrical monster? But soon her relief, at having won back Nora's pity, and her shame, at having done it with a ploy, were both eclipsed by her alarm at the force of her tears. Without meaning or wanting to, she slipped into hysterics, sobbing so convulsively she couldn't catch her breath or govern her muscles. Her arms went slack as if they'd been anesthetized, and John, sobbing also, almost fell on the floor; Nora plucked him from danger and carried him from the room. A moment later Nora returned, John still sobbing into her shoulder, and handed Aileen a hot washcloth. Aileen pressed it to her face and heard a shriek come from herself—it was inexpressive, another attempt to gain control of her lungs, but it sent John to a new pitch of wailing, and it deepened her fear. Nora took John out of the room again. Aileen had the sensation of a subtle division interleaving itself between parts that had before been united, like metal sheets being dropped into place. Herself now and herself at the instant that John had been born. Herself now and her tears. This made her wonder what boxed cavity her mysterious "self" was confined to.

After a while she was breathing again with just a catch at the back of her throat. Beyond that soft rasping, she realized the house was silent. Her watch said four; Nora's children ought to be home by now. Warren would follow, at a quarter past five. John's bassinet would be moved to the kitchen, and they would all try to sit for a civilized dinner at six. She didn't think she could stand it, another day as an unwanted guest in this house, confined by her child's helplessness, which was now hers as well. But there was nowhere for them to go. Was there?

She found Nora reading in the front room, John asleep on her lap. As Aileen gazed down at him, this also seemed like a fresh possibility: that he would heedlessly sleep against some other body, his soft lower lip pedaling, in dreaming pursuit of her breast—or perhaps any breast.

Nora looked up at her, either questioningly—did she want her son back?—or invitingly—there was room on the couch. "He looks comfortable," Aileen murmured, and sat in the armchair Warren usually claimed to read the evening newspaper. The first time she had left John with Nora, her first day home from the hospital—so that she could bathe—she had been gripped by such a sense of coming danger, as if she'd stepped into the path of a train, that she'd almost cracked her skull in the tub, she'd been so clumsy and hasty. She had known that it was her body, installing John as an imperative, annexing him to her self-shielding instincts now that he was no longer housed inside her. Leaving him to walk around the block, as per Nora's orders, even leaving him to go to the toilet had made her tremble, an animal facing immediate threat. She had marveled that Nora could calmly shut her children's bedroom doors in the evenings, let alone watch them walk off to school each morning, yet at the same time she'd known that this crushing consciousness of danger would have to recede, if only for the sake of real safety. She couldn't protect John, or herself, so long as she quaked like a deer in the crosshairs of somebody's gun. And indeed the next day her terror had faded a little, and the next and the next, so that now, a mere five days into John's life, she could look at him from a distance of almost eight feet and feel utterly calm, almost empty.

"Do you think they could? Find me unfit," she asked quietly, as if their conversation had been civil all along, and uninterrupted.

"I can't imagine such a thing, but it seems that he can. That's what he meant when he said the courts take the same view."

"As the Bible. We don't live in a theocracy."

"I'm only repeating what he said, Nini."

"And I've given him his case. All the evidence he needs, and then some."

"That's what I'm afraid of. I know you were unhappy, but I'm so frightened now for our John." This time Nora's face shone with tears, but they streamed without bodily tremors, and John continued to sleep, his tiny form rising and falling with Nora's regular breath. Aileen briefly thought, *Let him do it.* It was an old habit of nihilistic bravado, for protecting herself. So she still wasn't in the firm habit of thinking for two. To atone, she moved onto the couch and wiped away Nora's tears. Then they both watched the baby together.

"Where are the children?" Aileen finally asked.

"I told them to go play at the Millers' after school, until dinner. I wasn't sure how long Lewis would stay."

"You're good to me, Nonie."

"I can't be forever."

Before Nora could repent of her outburst, Aileen said, "I know."

"It's not me, it's Warren," Nora said wretchedly. "I love you. I love little John." Her tears started anew.

"I know," Aileen said again.

That night while John slept, Aileen wrote out her letter—the letter that had been composing itself eloquently, sometimes ecstatically, always effortlessly, for almost a week, since her water had broken and she'd gone to the hospital. Everything that had happened to her, everything she had felt, had been slightly dilated by the echo of her internal narration, though she'd been too exhausted at the end of each day to commit it to paper. Now she was tireless, even strangely stimulated, as if she'd drunk coffee. She wrote with great speed, as if simply transcribing something already printed.

Dear Lee, she began, and then page after page of her pad of drug-store writing paper, the night passing not hourglass style, in a trickle, but with the intermittent force of a thaw. Great snowmasses of night giving way all at once to drop sighingly into the void. The clock said twenty minutes to midnight; the next instant—*sigh*—it said two-fifteen. She wrote without any idea of securing Lee's loyalty to her—his loyalty was the one thing she was certain she had. His love, his comradeship, his sympathy. She missed him as her only true ally—it was no painful revelation to her that Nora's duty to Warren came first, she had known this more easily than Nora had—and if her letter was unrestrained, it was not because she sought to make a certain impression, to a particular end, but because she felt the rushing relief of unself-consciousness—because she felt free.

When she was done, she was as exhilarated and drained as the traveler who's relived every inch of the trek in the chronicling of it. But there were many inches—those at the end—she left out. She did not mention Lewis's comment to Nora, about the courts and "her kind." She did not mention Thanksgiving and Christmas. Gaither's persistence in seeing his son, Aileen's finally relenting—this was the chain of events that seemed to end with Gaither's peaceful departure forever, as if the single glimpse was all he'd ever wanted.

That night was the beginning of a series of insomnial nights, as though the stimulation she'd felt while composing the letter were now trapped in her body, in the form of an antisleep toxin that only sleep would remove. She had never before been unable to sleep when exhausted. Now she responded to John's rhythmic subsidings with frantic attempts to accompany him; she would set him in his bassinet and then strip off her housedress and pull on a nightgown, raking her nails over her prickling skin and scalp as she climbed into bed and adjusted her pillow, her blanket, the sleeve hole of her nightgown that bit at her armpit, the hem of blanket that tickled her cheek, the sagging pillow that failed to cradle her skull, the teeming spot on her calf, her lower back, the nape of her neck, the tip of her nose, that now itched intolerably—she could not stop twitching and flicking as if sleep were flies, and then after twenty or seventy minutes John would whimper, and she'd vault from the bed like a jack-in-the-box. She had resolved to no longer allow Nora to help in the night when John was hard to console. It was as much for her sake as for Nora's; she knew that Warren had complained that Nora acted as though John were hers, disrupting Warren's sleep in the process with her comings and goings from midnight to dawn. In the first week of John's life, Aileen had scarcely seen past him to their shared situation, but now, even as she was somehow less able to meet her own and John's needs, she was increasingly aware of how much their dependence antagonized Warren. And so she sought to hide her fatigue from Nora, which was feeling less like fatigue than a form of madness. When John shat so wetly that it spilled from his diaper and onto her lap, her limbs were seized by the impulse to hurl him into the wall; she felt she'd fought to restrain them, and then she sat crying in fright, while John cried also, the two of them glued to each other by his mustardy feces. She had found the ceaseless physical awkwardness of caring for a baby almost entrancing in their first days together, like a puzzle to be constantly solved—place baby on changing table, but the diapers are still in clean laundry basket; lift baby, balance baby on forearm, squat to level of basket, snag diaper, return to the table, place baby on table, fold diaper, but where are the pins? lift baby again, locate pins, folded diaper somehow has been left on the far side of room where pins were; lift the baby, grab diaper, open pin with one hand, but the force of the metal tines coming apart makes the pin jump down onto the floor—but now any of the thousands of little rebellions the material world seemed inspired to stage in response to a helpless infant could reduce her to tears—or inflate her to rage. And she was surly to Nora and Warren, and even their children, and, worst of all, the almost rapturous state of contentment she'd felt with her son now seemed permanently out of reach, on the far side of the sort of renewal that she imagined, illogically, death might provide.

The answer she had given Gaither, via Nora, was that he could not take John on such short notice for Thanksgiving, but that she would be willing to discuss the matter of Christmas two weeks beforehand, on December 11. The rationale provided in both cases was that John was nursing; he couldn't be expected to learn to take a bottle overnight, but by December 11 he might have mastered it and so be ready for a first separation. He would be one month old, to Aileen an inconceivable milestone—but every possibility referred to in this message was for her equally fantastic. Her answer to Gaither would no more be yes on December 11 than on any other day for the rest of all time, even if by the age of one month John happened to have learned how to cook. It was Nora who had insisted on framing the answer this way. "It buys you time," she said, sealing the envelope that contained Aileen's answer—written out by Aileen after Nora's dictation. "There's no reason to give Lewis more ammunition."

"I don't need time. I certainly don't need time to train John to a bottle. I'm not going to do it."

"I think we've talked plenty about the things you're not going to do. You're not going to let Lewis see John. You're not going to let John take a bottle. You're not going to set foot in your old house so long as you live, which must mean that it's me who will go get the rest of your things. You're not going speak to your husband, so that I'm the one who gets to tell him about all the other things you won't do. That's wonderful, Aileen. It's so decisive and mature. I'm sure there's no reason to think about what you *are* going to do."

"I only said," Aileen said through her teeth, "that I'm not going to put John on a bottle. At least not by December eleventh."

"Good!" Nora said. "Don't! Don't do *any*thing, please!"

But in the week after Thanksgiving, John began to have colic—or at least that was what Nora called it for the first several days. He wept and screamed without pause, sometimes for three or four hours at a stretch, and though Aileen pushed her breast in his mouth, he wouldn't take it and nurse. His red face poured sweat, and his gaunt little limbs madly flapped—he seemed frailer when he screamed, though the noise that he made was astounding. Soon everyone in the house, the three adults and three children, seemed to be constantly screaming and crying. Aileen walked John endlessly in the hallway, his furious body draped over her shoulder, and was so tired she wove, and once knocked his head into the wall. The real winter had finally come, and it was too cold to take him outside. At night Warren and Nora also shrieked at each other, no longer trying to keep down their voices, and once, as Aileen trudged the hall like a pilgrim, she heard Nora's two children, clandestinely huddled in the older girl's room and tearfully trying to comfort each other.

When the doctor came, he confirmed what Aileen had been secretly fearing, as she changed John with obsessive attention and yearned for that overfilled diaper that had so recently fouled her lap. John had not just stopped gaining but starting losing again. He was only a few ounces over his birth weight. "He won't nurse," she said, helplessly crying as the dispassionate doctor—the apparently wonderful man on whom Nora relied—turned and prodded and pulled John as if preparing a chicken to roast. "It's his colic, he won't nurse, I've tried—"

"I don't like to blame colic," the doctor said, cutting her off. "Colic is a vague term, and it gets blamed for more than its share. My guess is your milk supply's down. He's not getting enough. You need to start him on bottles of formula. That way there's no guesswork. You know what he's getting, and you can give him enough."

"I do give him enough!"

"Well, apparently not," said the doctor.

Because the kitchen was the place to sterilize bottles and mix formula, and because the kitchen was Nora's realm, and most obviously because Nora had bottle-fed before, it was Nora who launched the new regimen, with brisk efficiency and even, Aileen thought, with some measure of poorly disguised cheerfulness. "You're glad, aren't you," she said. She didn't realize that her words were mumbled, almost slurred, as if she were drunk—she was aware only of the enormous effort to articulate her thoughts and to balance her head on her fist as she sat at the table. She wanted to lie on her bed, a damp cloth on her face. John had taken to the bottles with gusto, draining each dry in a fraction of the time he had needed to satisfy himself at the breast, and in the process ingesting so much air that he frequently vomited great arcs of white liquid that cleared whoever's lap he was sitting on and smacked splashingly onto the floor—but these events, the first of which made Aileen shriek with fear, did not seem to disturb him at all. He would emit a sated afterbelch and fall serenely to sleep, or to draining another full bottle. His hysterical crying disappeared without leaving a trace, as Aileen senselessly felt it should: some diminishing wail, to be heard in the hall at around four A.M. by the mother, now pacing alone. No, the crying was gone, as if the little body she'd held to herself had been some other baby. This baby, who took his milk from Nora—or *Warren,* for that matter—was a changeling, an impostor, although only Aileen felt this way. For the others it was the opposite story. It was the old baby, the one bound to Aileen by implacable grief, that had been inauthentic. Now when John happily belched, Nora cooed, "*There* he is!" as if John had emerged from a fog. "He's a strapping little man after all," Warren said in agreement.

Those first days, when Aileen had been unprecedentedly happy, adrift in the dazzling void with her child in her arms, seemed to belong to a prehistory everyone had forgotten. "It's not the end of the world," Nora had said to her sharply when, streaming tears, she finally came to observe the sterilizing process for the bottles and nipples. "With Nancy, I ran out of milk at twelve weeks and switched over to formula, and with Michael, I used formula from the start, and you can see for yourself they're both perfectly fine." Aileen was too heartbroken and tired to imagine that Nora was also a passionate mother and that she might take Aileen's attitude toward the bottles as a criticism of herself. Instead she saw Nora turning against her, like everyone else.

"You're *glad,*" she repeated wildly.

"Glad of what?"

"Glad I ran out of milk, and so quickly. It proves everyone right. I'm an unfit mother. Now Lewis can take John for all twelve days of Christmas. He can take John for a whole *year* of Christmas."

"For God's sake, Aileen. There's not a mother on earth who hasn't gone through a rough time like this. You're just tired. You've got to pull yourself together. You've got to sleep, for one thing."

"As if I don't want to sleep!"

"If you could stop, for one minute, believing that this is the world's greatest drama and that you are the star—" Nora's voice had not particularly altered, but a look of suppression came over her face, as if she'd been exposed to enormous temptation and had barely resisted. To slap me, Aileen thought.

"I can't wait to get out of here," she said, imitating Nora's calm, cruel tone, because she couldn't, she realized dizzily, find a tone of her own—because she couldn't find emotion of her own. Was she chastened or angry? Dependent on Nora or sick of her? "I can't wait to get away from your wonderful doctor, and your know-it-allness, and your wonderful competence. It makes you glad that I've turned out so awful! That I'm such a bad mother! It makes you glad, doesn't it?"

"Oh, Aileen!" Nora seized her on either side of her head, as if she did mean to slap her, or box her ears, or shake her until her neck snapped, but instead she pulled Aileen to her chest and held her sobbing face as if it were a treasure to be fiercely guarded. "You're a good mother," Nora whispered. "His only! And you love him, you love him. . . ."

"No I don't! No I'm not!" Aileen sobbed.

When Nora's doctor came back the next week to give John his checkup, he prescribed Valium for Aileen and suggested she see a psychiatrist. "It's often the case," he intoned, "that women postpartum experience some amount of depression. It's very little talked of, which is too bad, because it's really quite common. You shouldn't feel embarrassed about it. At the same time, you have to take it seriously and treat it like any illness. Nip it in the bud before it goes any farther." They were all sitting in the front room together, Nora, Aileen, and the doctor—John plumply asleep in his bassinet, having received the doctor's grunt of approval—as if they were at a funeral home, Aileen thought, engaged in a fake conversation while averting their eyes from the coffin.

"I'm not depressed," she said, hearing her voice tremble. "I'm very tired." Her eyes filled with tears. She cried constantly now, usually without a clear understanding of what was making her cry, although it was often the overwhelming complexity of everyday tasks.

"The Valium should help you with sleeping. And the sleeping should help you with everything else." Here he smiled encouragingly at her, and she was struck by how kindly he seemed—was he really a wonderful doctor, as Nora insisted, who had only appeared hostile to her because she was crazy?

"I'm surprised it's all right," she murmured. "All right to take pills, with the baby."

"It's perfectly all right," he assured her. "Now that you're no longer nursing."

She had forgotten; for more than six months, since learning she was pregnant, she had thought of her body so differently. Everything she'd ingested she'd first thoughtfully scrutinized, imagining what it would do to the cells that were building her child. She had even made Nora laugh at her. Nora, who of the two of them was so historically square, who nodded off after a half glass of wine, who'd turned purple and choked the one time she'd tried lighting a cigarette. Aileen all her life had been the careless sister, the one who acted with little regard for herself or the future. And then had come the day when she'd called Nora in terror because she'd drunk some weak tea—she had given up coffee—and had felt the baby flopping inside her. "I've made him have a heart attack, Nora!" she'd said frantically, and Nora—when she'd finally stopped laughing—had said, "You've only woken him up."

She'd never known such sweetness in her life. Her body, to its last molecule, had been the possession of somebody else.

She did begin taking the Valium, and though her ability to do so was a consequence, not a cause, of physical separation, in her mind this was the severing act. Something fragile was sliced, and destroyed.

12.

LEE RECEIVED AILEEN'S LETTER SOMETIME DURING THE week of Thanksgiving, by design forming only the vaguest recollection of when it had come. Immediately upon seeing it, thick with meaning in its barely adequate envelope, by far the most conspicuous item of mail that day on the console in his landlady's hall, his almost unconscious instinct was to treat it as though it were a bill, or a library notice, or a subscription renewal. Without examination he collected it into the papers and books in his arms, and upstairs in his room he left it, still interred in the pile, at the back of his desk. It wasn't destined to languish indefinitely; in the past couple weeks, since his rededication to research, his desk had ceased to be the fossilized archive from which he'd spent months averting his eyes. Once again a patient observer—or, better, a time-lapse camera—would be able to discern a dynamic, if very slow, process of change. Heaps inexorably crept toward the ceiling, came down, seeded new heaps or were thrown in the trash. Library books shifted position, according to due date. Outposts of new growth had appeared on the couch and the bed—half-used notepads and half-read abstracts. Aileen's letter would be gotten to, in its time.

Thanksgiving was the only American holiday that had ever captured Lee's imagination, and in previous years he had always spent it as a guest in the home of one of his professors or classmates. His interest in the holiday's historical underpinnings and his enormous enjoyment of the foods gratified all his hosts, and this along with the tradition of taking in strays had given him his choice of dinners for the past several years. But this year he'd been invited nowhere; he'd seen almost no one since the previous spring. And to his surprise, rather than feeling bereft, he fairly hummed with contentment. For the first time in recent memory, perhaps for the first time since meeting Aileen, he had purpose, and peace. He had always loved a university campus in summer, the mysterious abandonment of the medieval city, with just a skeleton crew of damned souls left to meet his few needs: a single heavy-eyed stamper of books, a single sleepwalking ladler of gruel in the one cafeteria. Now he found that the campus on a national holiday at the onset of winter was the purest distillation of that hush he'd first known in the summers. He drifted without constraint or anxiety through the math buildings, down the walkways of the quad beneath the ice-lacquered trees; he knew there was no chance he'd run into Gaither, the most pious of pilgrims, today. The library was not even on limited hours, but entirely closed, yet this setback failed to annoy him; it was another liberation. He walked downhill into town, the overdue book, which he had not finished reading, clasped to his chest, an unexpected reprieve. He would finish it now. He had gone out without a hat or gloves, and the lightless sky was bearing down with the weight of snow, but he didn't feel assaulted by the cold. It entered him, an energizing column, so that his lungs seemed to fully inflate for the very first time. He imagined them gleaming. In town he ate a sodden "Thanksgiving dinner with full trimmings," presumably surrounded by unloved solitary diners in the neighboring booths, but he didn't notice. He was absorbed in his book. He'd struggled with it before; now its fine grains of meaning seemed to pour themselves into his mind, like filings toward a magnet. When he was walking home again in the early darkness, he was happy.

He thought briefly of Aileen, understanding her to have entered an unknowable world of motherhood, as he had entered a world of scholarship. Their paths had diverged and would continue to do so, vectors obeying their laws. And he felt, as he had before on a very few, very precious occasions, an intelligence guiding his life. Not a God; he would never say this. But something blessedly Other than him, a calm orderliness, which had corrected and saved him.

And so it was with unease that he read Aileen's letter, some handful of days after getting it. His unease didn't arise from anything explicit; the letter hardly seemed to speak to him, and it never spoke of him. Apart from the very first line, the letter more closely resembled a diary, and after reading the first several pages Lee even flipped back—*Dear Lee*—to confirm that it *was* a letter, and a letter for him. He was disturbed, he realized, not by anything overt the letter stated but by everything it seemed to assume—by its implicit designation of Lee as the person not just entitled to but desirous of such disclosures. These were sentiments Lee wasn't convinced a wife would share with her husband; why would Aileen want to share them with him? And such outsize, almost lunatic fervor for her child by Gaither; had Lee not decided to give up Aileen, had he failed to arrive at his benignant position, he might have been spurred to a frenzy of rage by this stuff.

But Aileen didn't know she had been given up. Lee thought about this as he folded the letter; toward the end he'd been skimming, and he had no desire to read it again. The letter implied a remarkable intimacy—but the question remained, of what remarkable thing the intimacy implied in its turn. Nowhere was there mention of the future: Aileen's, Gaither's, Lee's, or the child's. Had Aileen articulated some clear expectation of him, Lee would have known to inform her of his decision to withdraw from her life. Instead there was this uncensored transcript of her most private thoughts, and now he wondered if this was her sign that she had withdrawn from him. Consuming ardor for her child by Gaither, no reference to a rearranged future. She didn't know she had been given up, but it no longer mattered, because she had released him.

And yet the letter was so unrestrained, so avidly confiding, as if describing one passion as a means of encoding another—but could she so love Gaither's child and also love Lee? Lee grew aware of a strain in his logic; to avoid thinking more about it, he forced the letter back into its envelope, and put it inside a textbook he almost never referred to, and put the book into one of the very deep drawers of his desk.

As November gave way to December, his existence achieved a complete transformation, as if the solitary peace of Thanksgiving had been the mere start of a growing alignment and amplification. Only musical terms seemed to capture this pleasant sensation. Everything from his morning oatmeal to the nib of his pen was caught up in symphonic concord, under the stirring control of a brilliant conductor. If it had ever crossed Lee's mind before now to describe his relation to his life circumstances, he might have attempted metaphors of storm-tossed vessels or mismatched wrestlers or frost-nipped blossoms as unoriginal and ineffectual and disjointed as the conditions themselves. Now both his life and his image of it were harmonically pure. He fell asleep at strange hours and woke up completely refreshed; he ate whatever he had in his cupboard and found it delicious. He made singing progress in his work. He read the way he ate, wrote the way he slept, never seemed to misplace so much as a thumbtack in an apartment that had given over all its limited floor space to squared stacks of paper. It helped that the term had ended the second week of December, so that the other habitués of his house—rarely seen, always heard—were now gone. No longer did he find the second-floor bathroom door closed when he went to take a long-deferred piss after hours of inspired mathematics and tea or beer drinking. No more cattlelike feet on the stairs, heedless voices through walls, doors slammed as if intended to shatter his thoughts. He generically hated all his fellow tenants for how oversize and unself-conscious they were, but now the house was abandoned, as if the earth had been cleared by a plague. He only sometimes heard his landlady's radio, as thin and querulous-sounding as she was, but her manifestations were so few and predictable he benignly absorbed them into his harmonized days.

The fact of Christmas came to his attention when his landlady surprised him with a knock at his door. Admitting her, after stuffing the tails of his shirt into his pants, he saw her swiftly assessing the state of the room: a fire hazard, but nothing she didn't expect, even probably hope for, from her student tenants. There was no woman and no dissipation; she was satisfied. "Mr. Lee," she announced, "I'm going to my sister's for Christmas. I'll be gone this whole week. I trust you to abide by house rules even while I'm not here." It was only now that Lee realized she was wearing a coat and a hat, and he belatedly identified a noise he'd been remotely aware of as an idling car. She must have been on the point of leaving before she'd remembered him.

"Of course, Mrs. Winnick. I hope you have a nice time."

"Do you celebrate Christmas, Mr. Lee?"

He knew better than to say that he didn't. As he spoke, he offered up a wry prayer that today wasn't Christmas already. "Yes I do, Mrs. Winnick. I'll be visiting friends."

"I hope you have a very merry Christmas, Mr. Lee." For the first time, he was aware of a flicker of curiosity, even of cautious fellow feeling, on her part—from one solitaire to another. But of course she wasn't truly alone; she had a sister to go to. Perhaps realizing this, she didn't take it any further. She didn't ask him, as she never had before, what faraway land he came from, where his family was. He was relieved.

"You, too, Mrs. Winnick. Merry Christmas."

When she was gone, he was finally interested in knowing what day it was, to keep track of the time he had until she came back. He had not minded her presence in the house because he'd never imagined her leaving. Now he felt a frank thrill, as if Christmas were a holiday for him after all.

Downstairs, he opened the door off the front hallway and entered her parlor, for only the third time in the year and a half he had lived here. The first time, he had been admitted to sign a tenants' agreement (it stipulated, among other things, that he was barred from her rooms of the house). The second time had been just last month, when he'd received Aileen's sister's phone call, about the birth of the child.

In her kitchen he saw she'd unplugged her toaster and left the faucet dripping in case of a freeze. He'd imagined the radio here, but it was back in the parlor, a decades-old Gothic hulk he hadn't even recognized as a radio his first time through the room. He turned it on and sat down in her old widow's armchair, with its antimacassars and its ruptures of stuffing, to wait. He was surprised by how easy it was to invade someone's home; he didn't feel the least out of place, or even curious, among all the strange objects. Still, he didn't consider retuning the radio to a more businesslike station; he didn't trust he would ever locate her station again. It played only big-band standards, the music speckled by static as if in some aural way moth-eaten; it seemed to be broadcasting not across space but from years in the past. Between songs an announcer barked out the titles too quickly; this was the human noise that from his room he'd mistaken for anger. Finally the date was referred to, in the same frantic tone: "It's Tuesday, December twenty-second—just three days until Christmas!!" It crossed Lee's mind that the voice might have spoken these words in 1945. Was it Tuesday, December 22, in 1964? Again perceiving belatedly, he stood up and returned to the kitchen: there was a calendar here. And here the temporal mystery was decisively solved. December 22 was indeed a Tuesday, and in its square Mrs. Winnick had shakily written, *To Elsie's.* In Sunday's square, the twenty-seventh, the same hand declared, *Home.*

Back upstairs, Lee was distracted from returning to his work by the fact that he didn't own a calendar, or a radio, or any other means by which he could keep himself tied to the passage of time. He didn't even want to be tied to the passage of time; he only wanted an alarm clock to go off Sunday morning, warning him that his sublime isolation had come to an end. He could make chicken marks on the wall like a prisoner, one a day for six days, but on any of those days he might forget to make the mark, or forget he had already made it. The absorbing triviality of the problem annoyed him more and more; the flawless peace he'd envisioned with Mrs. Winnick's departure already seemed tainted. He would simply have to leave his room once in a while to buy the newspaper, but he didn't want to leave his room and didn't want the newspaper. For weeks he'd lived perfectly balanced between desire and fulfillment. Now the petty obligation of timekeeping weighed on him, though he'd meant to keep time in the service of his own peace of mind.

He'd forcibly dismissed the issue more than once when the harsh bleat of the front bell startled him. He was doubly startled to realize that only he was there to answer the door. He sat very still, his heart banging, as if the downstairs caller might hear his quick breathing, scent the alarmed perspiration that had sprung up at his temples.

It was the postman, he told himself, a Christmas package from a Winnick relation, it would be left on the porch—but when the bell rang again, more importunate somehow, he jerked upright and went down the stairs. Through the center of the three small, high-set panels of glass in the door, he saw the crown of a head: a pale crescent of brow slightly fringed by the very fine hairs that could not be drawn back, and the drawn-back hair itself, just its uppermost gloss. This was Aileen; he would have known her by the pad of a finger, a kneecap. He didn't know if he realized this then or sometime afterward: that the peace of this autumn alone had been a fragile hiatus, not a new scheme of life. He felt it collapse as he opened the door, its almost noiseless downsifting, a weakness giving way, like the sighings of pulverized plaster within the walls of the house he heard on very late nights when only he was awake. There was wild combativeness in her expression, although she didn't say anything; but her eyes glittered, as if she were ill. And he noticed a change in her skin: around the line of her jaw, it had softened, gone slack, the throat skin of a much older woman. A stain of fatigue doubled each of her eyes. He was overwhelmed by his longing for her, whether in spite of or because of these changes, he didn't bother to wonder. Her pre-pregnancy slimness had not been restored but somehow overshot. She was severe in her thinness. Her hair was much longer. Behind her it had started to snow.

Gaither returned from his week of Christmas no less inexorable. He appeared not the least bit undone by his one-man encounter with the harrowing needs of a six-week-old child. The boy himself was apparently plumper, well rested, entirely clean, and encased head to toe in unfamiliar, ingeniously miniaturized winter gear that would have suited him fine in the arctic. The hand-me-down sleepers and buntings (from Nora's Michael), soft and pilled, with their arctically useless appliqué work of duckies and bunnies, had been laundered and dismissively packed in a brown grocery bag.

The custody arrangement that Gaither proposed was exhaustive and, like all legal documents, absurdly anticipatory, embracing contingencies it was hard to imagine someone having imagined. But at its core it consisted of one very simple exchange: sole custody of John Gaither for a discreet, uncontested divorce. Aileen would not be summoned to court, her distasteful infidelities would not be publicized, and the assets with which she had entered the marriage would be returned to her in their entirety. But perhaps the most compelling aspects of the arrangement had been those not translated into impenetrable legalese but conveyed to Aileen vocally, by Gaither and his lawyer, in those lengthy, unimaginable sessions from which Lee had been gladly excluded—and which Nora had not witnessed either, as she'd been caring for John. Those sessions—or rather "conversations"—Aileen had endured without her own lawyer present, because she didn't have one and wasn't sure how to get one, and in any case the conversations were supposed to be prefatory—Gaither's lawyer very nicely suggesting they simply "converse," in a noncombat setting, with the fine aim of maybe avoiding the combat completely. Aileen emerged from these conversations in the way the frilled, superfluous margin of a fresh-molded plastic object emerges from the pressure between the two plates: the actual thing remained hidden from view, and what could be seen revealed nothing of the shape the thing took. To Nora, Aileen wept hollowly and left her son sleeping across Nora's lap. To Lee she disclosed even less—but it was true that he hadn't pressed her, hadn't made the demands for disclosure that a real ally would.

Aileen also emerged from those sessions at the end of the process—not, as she'd thought, just a short way from the start. Gaither and his lawyer made it compellingly, doubtlessly clear that she stood a far worse chance in court. If she refused Gaither's offer and fought, of course Gaither would have to fight back, and it was likely Aileen would not even get visitation. Gaither offered her all the visitation she desired. This was not spelled out in the agreement; spelling out visitation would limit it, to what was spelled, to the literal letter: every other weekend and every fourth week, for example. Gaither had no desire to do that. Aileen was John's mother: that was a sacred condition that nothing would change. When she wanted to see John, she need merely call Gaither, and the thing would be done. If all went well, Aileen could have John overnight, even for many nights running, even for a week, for a month, for a summer—so long as she established a stable and wholesome domestic environment. Clearly such an environment was in Aileen's interest as well and would be no trouble at all to achieve with the significant funds that she stood to receive when she signed the agreement. Everyone knew that Aileen wanted to get back on her feet, to stop living with Warren and Nora, to perhaps find an interesting job at the university, which she'd do easily, as the ugly details of her affair and divorce would remain under wraps. Gaither insisted on full custody only to obtain full control of John's religious upbringing, and this was a point Gaither knew that Aileen wouldn't dispute. After all, she was an atheist, as she'd never hesitated to inform the other congregants at Gaither's church. And going to court for the right to impose atheism on a six-week-old child was a battle Aileen would certainly lose, with even worse repercussions.

What Aileen wasn't told, and what she wouldn't learn until after she had signed the agreement (her signature barely hers: the jagged EKG line of a faltering heart), was that Gaither's lawyer was a congregant, too, a church member from a neighboring state. And Gaither's new suits had been bought with church money, and little John's arctic gear, and every other thing Gaither required to start a new life. Aileen learned all this later: ten months later, in October 1965, after her divorce, uncontested and discreet, became final. After she and Lee, bristling like cats in their new too-close quarters, booked University Chapel for the first Saturday in December and then learned from one of the Byrons, all of whom Lee invited—they'd had almost no one to ask—that Gaither and Ruth had been married at their church, in a packed-to-the-rafters service, the very week the divorce was announced in the "notices" section at the back of the newspaper. After Aileen understood that it must have been Ruth who fed John his bottles for that week of Christmas. After Aileen married Lee without John in attendance, because Gaither and Ruth felt that Lee was an unwholesome element, and after Aileen realized that without visitation written formally into her agreement, in fact she was not guaranteed visitation at all. After Aileen's union with Lee, faltering even before its strained solemnization, began faltering more violently and after Aileen finally hired her own expensive attorney, with her own regained funds—not to get rid of Lee but to get back her son, no matter how little her new husband might want him.

Throughout all this, Lee had been at best passive, as if Aileen's loss of her son were the sort of arcane her-side-of-things situation, like a

great-aunt's estate, that a husband can comfortably view as no problem of his. At worst he'd been openly hostile. If he wanted a child at
all, it was a child of his own. How could she possibly think he should
raise Gaither's son? Gaither cherished the boy, and, what seemed no
less compelling, he paid for all the boy's needs; to Lee this was lucky,
for Aileen just as much as himself. He actually said this to her; for a
man who had never imagined himself married, let alone cherished
lofty illusions about the marital state, he was receiving a swift education in the effortless viciousness to which that state could give rise.
But for all that, he was no less amazed by the other dark fortune he'd
realized was his: Aileen actually loved him. He'd become indispensable to her. He had the power to force her to choose, between himself
and her son, and insofar as he declined to assist her, encourage her,
comfort her in her grief, he did this. Less with action than with the
absence of action.

Might he have risked an appearance of sympathy with her, had he
known that the stifled arrangement—Aileen three times a week per-
mitted into the house she'd once lived in herself, to kiss and dandle
her son, bottle-feed him and change him, shed her tears onto him
while he napped, while her former husband taught classes and his
homely new wife, the pious, self-righteous prig whom Aileen had so
scorned did the cleaning or yard work, or read a book in the kitchen,
but never left, *never left them alone*—was destined, as a result of her
efforts, to come to an end? Gaither and Ruth did not want Lee in contact with John, and this suited Lee fine. Gaither and Ruth seemed to
not trust Aileen; Lee didn't think it was business of his. His wife, the
woman he'd scolded for being married already, the first time they'd
met, hated him, saw his traitorousness in its component parts (selfish-
ness, cowardice) yet was still in love with him, and now also completely dependent—he was all she had left. And so he did not even
give her the comfort of mistakenly thinking he hoped she'd succeed.

She hired the lawyer, who deeply regretted her signature on the
agreement, as well as the year she'd let pass before she'd had "second
thoughts." But he was guardedly optimistic and sent a letter to Gaither's
lawyer stating that the agreement would now be contested. On her
usual Tuesday, Aileen drove to her son's, proud and frightened; the
letter had been put in the mail on the previous Friday. There was a

chance Gaither's lawyer hadn't gotten it yet or, if he had, hadn't yet informed Gaither. By what signs would she know? Would Ruth be different, as she let Aileen in, would she not as she always did open the door without words or eye contact, promptly turning her back, as if Aileen were the maid? Or would Gaither be there instead, having canceled his classes, so he could lash her with Yahweh-like fury for her awful transgression?

She must have mounted the two steps to the porch in her usual roil of anger and dread and deep longing, to see her baby, to hold him, all this heightened, made even more clamorous, by her new sense of coming combat. This time she was ready. She pressed the bell, and as it rang through the house, she remembered herself, her pregnancy just beginning, sunk like a secretive stone in the house's deep shadows, the drapes drawn against the blinding sunlight. If someone came to the door, she stayed still; no slit in the drapes for a caller to peer through, no danger that she might be discerned. The steps would retreat down the walk, and she'd again be alone.

Even before she'd noticed that the drapes were gone from the windows, she'd felt the tone of the bell hurtling somehow differently—unrestrained—through the house. She put her face to the window so quickly she smacked her brow on the glass. Inside was as dim as always, but she could see it was empty.

Lee had known then that the battle was won. Not because Gaither and Ruth had absconded with John, but because, once Aileen was back home and had sobbed several hours on the phone to Nora, she then sat in the kitchen for several more hours and sobbed all alone. She did not bring her grief to her husband. She had realized she shouldn't.

13.

ON HIS WAY BACK FROM THE PARK, LEE'S ENTRAILS churned with mortification. After having so easily vanished three decades ago, why would Gaither allow Lee to pounce on him now? The return address on Gaither's letter hadn't been the careless oversight of an old man finally losing his cunning. The only old man who was losing his cunning, if he'd ever had any, was Lee. He had the confused sense that his letter to Gaither had been opened and read and laughed at before being resealed and returned. At a stoplight he almost tore it open, as if by doing so very quickly he might glimpse the trailing edge of Gaither's tall, ambling body as it slipped once again out the door of the years, the face hidden, perhaps just the hem of a cardigan sweater or the beveled-down heel of a worn walking shoe indicating the vanishing owner, like the tip of a tail. But behind him an impatient car honked: the red light was somehow turning yellow again. He lurched through the intersection, the letter untouched on the seat beside him, and it was still there when he turned very slowly through the faux-pillared entrance into his subdivision and then off the winding main road and onto his street.

He had moved into this subdivision more than ten years before, his house one of the first to be built, although it looked more as if it had been dropped ready-made off the back of a truck. In the time since, for all the gasping labor he'd put in, a man deep in his sixties still stubbornly rolling out sod, hacking conical holes for frail shrubs, tipping wood chips from a forty-pound sack, his yard had never taken root in the earth, and his house had never taken root in his yard. There was a misbegotten, Frankensteinian quality to his failed landscaping that made his heart sink whenever he rounded the bland curve of Fearrington Way and his house came into view. His neighbors hired landscaping companies so that their houses were afloat amid clouds of forsythia or azalea or holly depending on the season of the year, but Lee had always loved caring for plants, with the contrary result that his yard appeared neglected and derelict because he continued to tend it himself. And after a decade he still knew none of his neighbors to invite them inside, where they would have seen his wildly thriving indoor plants, which were on the point of taking over his kitchen. He solaced himself with this thought as he rounded the curve and his yellow scrawny yard became visible, and with it an unfamiliar sedan sitting in his driveway.

It was considerately parked to one side, so that Lee was able to pull up beside it and, if he'd wanted to, push the button on his garage-door opener and continue inside. Instead he turned off the engine and emerged, aware of his letter to Gaither, left behind on the seat. Apart from the post-office ink, there should be nothing so different, as the result of its circular journey, about the thin envelope Lee had sealed with such grim resolution and put in the mail just a few days before. It was a feint in the dark that had failed to connect, and nobody—not even Gaither, Lee reminded himself—had seen Lee lose his balance from making the lunge. And yet he was trembling as if the envelope held Gaither's scalding riposte; his hands could hardly hold his keys, and his heart felt overworked in his chest. The strain of this noncon-frontation with his old nemesis wrecked his feeble defenses against last night's insomnia, and his vision was filled with fatigue spots again. Through their spreading stains, he could see that the driver of the other car, now emerging also with an overbroad smile like the work of an earthquake across the solemn landscape of his face, was the FBI agent from the mail room, Jim Morrison. There was a passenger, a woman, perhaps in her late thirties, wearing a belted shirtdress and sunglasses, which she pushed onto the top of her head as she also emerged. From the far side of both vehicles, she seemed to gaze at Lee in the chill, confirming manner of a doctor turning eyes on a patient after grimly perusing his chart, and Lee was startled into an awareness of how he must look, an old man stumbling forth from the tomb of regrets with their cobwebs all over his clothes. In the foreground Jim Morrison was amiably bearing down on Lee with a long arm extended again, as if their encounter a few hours before had made them old friends, and in the beat before their palms were reunited, Lee tried to will his unperspiring and steady. It didn't help that any conjunction of law enforcement with his home tended to bring out an obsequious, stammering side of himself, even if he had summoned the policemen himself. He could never seem to lay hold of the easy self-righteousness with which his neighbors demanded the arrests of teen Halloween egg throwers or drivers who sped past the Child at Play sign.

The handshake had taken place, but because Lee had so earnestly labored, fumbling through so many layers of enmeshed meditation, to bring it off carelessly, it had probably lasted too long or broken off too abruptly, and his palm had turned damp after all. "Go ahead and put your car away, Professor," Jim Morrison said, as if noticing nothing of Lee's disordered state. "And let me introduce my colleague, Special Agent Shenkman. We had a lunch hour to kill and thought we'd grab a chance to talk now, if it's all right with you. It would be very helpful. Of course we won't keep you long. I know the college is holding a memorial service at four."

"That's okay," Lee said. "I wasn't planning to go to the service. I'm not feeling well. I didn't sleep well last night."

"Would another time be better?" The commanding projection of Morrison's brow was surprisingly mobile; it formed a wrinkle of kindly concern. The woman's face hadn't changed.

"No, no," Lee protested. "Now is fine. Please. I hope I can help. . . ."

They filed into the house through the rarely used front door, Lee apologizing, as he had resolved he would not, for the absence of furniture in the front room. "Redecorating," he meant to say vaguely, but instead he said, fibbing only in terms of the time frame, "I've just been divorced."

"I'm sorry to hear that," Jim Morrison said. "No apologies are needed, Professor. This is a very nice house. We envy you, me and Agent Shenkman. Living out of hotels like we do half the time."

Something else was the matter now, too: a ball of dread in his gut, the body's urgent warning, an ache as piercingly narrow as the range of its causes was broad and diffuse. It was as easily the product of fatigue as of Gaither or Michiko, and yet as Lee closed the door, it took the form of the eyes of his neighbors, converging upon him like spokes, following him courtesy of the undraped front-room windows as he led the two agents past the sofa-leg holes in the living-room carpet and the pictureless hooks on the walls, through the untabled dining room into the kitchen, where the blinds were all open. Here were his indoor plants, almost dancing with health in the blazing sunlight. Lee had an impulse to lower the blinds, but doing so at the height of the glittering day was sure to make him seem strange. And so he put on the teapot, his neighbors' gazes perhaps slicing through him like alarm-system lasers, while Agent Morrison politely quizzed him on the local amenities. The agent imagined there had to be *some* decent place for a burger. The agent liked jogging, but not on concrete—were there any nice paths? Lee submitted to this interrogation eagerly, for the helpful distraction from the pain in his gut, but then found he was practically mute. Though he had lived here for twenty-five years and spent much of that time eating burgers alone with the paper, he now recalled none of the places he'd dined. Though only hours before, he'd been thinking of his old jogging days on the riverside path with Fasano, it now seemed he had not jogged a stride in his life. He groped blindly in the jumbled-up drawer of short-term memory, seared himself on the teapot, got the pot and the cups to the table with Agent Morrison's help. All this time Agent Shenkman said nothing.

"You probably know a good sushi place, too," Agent Morrison said, sitting back in his chair—it was the stiff-jointed one from the set Lee had bought with Aileen—with a satisfied exhalation, as if sinking into a plump-cushioned sofa. Agent Morrison held his teacup between both palms, in front of his face, clearly familiar with the cylindrical Japanese vessel that lacked handle and saucer. Lee knew there was nothing so strange about this. Everyone these days drank Japanese tea out of Japanese cups and ate sushi, even here in the landlocked Midwest. Except for Agent Shenkman, perhaps, who did not touch her tea. She had removed something like a hinged calculator or minuscule video game from her bag and was consulting it and poking it intently. "Not to suggest you're Japanese," Morrison continued. "You just seem like a man who knows how to eat well. Of course Lee's not a Japanese name. Or is it one of the rare ones?" Agent Morrison grinned: he was being facetious.

"It's impossible to get good sushi out here," Lee began. "We're so far from the coast, and the local airport—"

"My God, don't even tell me. When we were flying in here, I looked down at the airstrip and I thought, 'Is this really the States?' You've got your egg carton testing the wind, your little patch of concrete with some nice dandelions."

"I don't use the airport," Lee admitted. "I mostly drive—"

"But then there's a decent-looking Japanese place right on that road from the airport to town. Yokohama? Fujiwara?"

"Sakagura," Lee said. This was a windowless, dungeon-dark place, once the timid town's only and underused "gentlemen's club." Almost ten years before, it had been taken over by Koreans and relaunched on a Japanese theme. Lee had sought to avoid it, particularly while married to Michiko. The menu was limp, pallid, possibly dangerous sushi flown in secondhand from Chicago, and then a mishmash of

Korean-style barbecue, here termed "Asian grill," and Benihanaesque antics with cleavers performed by foreign-exchange students.

"*Sakagura.* That's right. Agent Shenkman and I went last night. A disappointing experience. Every sushi place I've ever been to hides the good stuff for the VIP customers, but either I didn't know how to ask or there was no good stuff. Both, most likely. It's possible I was rude; I'm no linguist. Tell me what you think, Professor. I said"—and then, in flawless, unhesitant Japanese—"*I'm sorry to be so much trouble, but is it possible there are additional items this evening? I'd be honored to try something new, and cost isn't important.* But my Japanese is lousy." The agent sighed, draining his cup and setting it on the table.

"Your Japanese is perfect," Lee said after a moment. "But they're not Japanese. They're Korean."

"I guessed that from the food, to be honest."

Now the conversation faltered. Normally Lee would have asked the other man where he'd learned his Japanese, but he was stymied by a new anxiety, that he couldn't completely attribute to his unsuccessful hospitality. He was actually relieved when Morrison said, accepting a file folder from Shenkman, "Should we get down to business? We don't want to take up your whole afternoon. And we have plenty of people to talk to before our day's done."

Once Morrison had opened the folder on his side of the table, after carefully moving his teacup, Lee was able to furtively read, upside down, UNITED STATES POSTAL INSPECTION SERVICE and beneath that a short letter beginning, *Pursuant to your request, please find attached for your review*— He felt Morrison's gaze on his face and looked up to meet it. "This shouldn't take more than a couple of minutes, Professor. We'd just like to review all the pieces of mail you've received at your school mailbox since the day of the bombing, just to have you confirm who the senders have been, if you would. In any case like this, where a lethal explosive is mailed to a certain location, we like to look at everything that came to that location, in the days just before and just after. So I have my list here of your mail, we'll just start at the top—"

"You have a list of my mail?" Lee exclaimed. He felt less intruded upon than astonished, as if this stranger had produced a complete inventory of the contents of his freezer and pantry. The generic lightweight envelopes, almost always impersonal communications from a professional association or a textbook publisher, that Lee received through the regular mail at his campus mailbox seemed both so inconsequential and so intimate—the very absence of personal letters was perhaps the most intimate thing—that he illogically felt that his mail was, to others, invisible.

"Not just your mail," Morrison was saying. "Professor, I have a full list of every item of mail that's arrived on your campus in the time span in question, indexed by date and recipient. So you can imagine how much work Agent Shenkman and I have to do!" Morrison exuded delight at his formidable task, so that it was Shenkman's immobile expression that made Lee realize he was being prodded, very gently, to help them get on with it.

"I'm sorry," Lee said, blushing. He seemed destined to blush every time he conversed with this FBI agent. "I just didn't realize they did that. Kept a list of my mail."

"They don't always do it, or they'd never do anything else. But in an investigation—"

"Of course," Lee said. But he couldn't help adding in spite of himself, "They don't look *in* the mail."

Morrison put down the printout he'd just taken up, in a gesture almost of reproach. "Looking inside your mail is illegal, Professor. We're law enforcers, not lawbreakers."

"Of course." Lee grinned wincingly in contrition and then flushed anew at the obsequiousness of the gesture. "Please, go ahead. You must have a lot of people to get through," he interrupted, just as Morrison started to read. "If you're doing everybody on campus."

"Quite a lot," Morrison said.

As was always the case with his mail, piece after piece was so impersonal and obvious that Lee found himself only confirming, again and again, what Morrison clearly saw for himself. "And this looks like the American Association of Mathematical Science. Some kind of newsletter." "Yes, that's right," "Here's a flyer from Wiley. That's a publisher, right? They bring out math textbooks?" "Yes, that's right." "This looks like something from a union. A teachers' union? Bill for dues?" "Yes, that's the union," Lee said as Morrison made another small check at the edge of his printout. "And here's—okay, there's no sender's name here, this is just from14 Maple Lane, Woodmont, Washington, and postmarked in Spokane. Who is this letter from?"

Somehow, in the immediate barrage of unfamiliar stimuli that comprised this encounter with FBI agents—in the consistently puzzling contrast between Morrison's warmth and the other one's chill, in the prefatory talk about sushi and the subsequent sudden unveiling of Lee's campus junk mail to the eyes of the law, in the three cups of tea now gone cold and the plain novelty of having guests in his home—the unbearable letter from Gaither, and his own in reply that had now been returned, had slipped out of his mind. For all that Gaither's letter had been prompted by the same incident—Hendley's bombing—that was the reason for this interview, it, and the unreceived answer, and the crisis of emotion that both had provoked, felt entirely separate, irretrievably lodged in the most wounded part of himself. When he realized that Morrison, reading off the computer printout in his genial way, was referring to this very soul sickness, this dart at the core of himself, Lee at first couldn't credit his ears. Then he blushed to the highest notch yet. Though he heard himself saying, with remarkable calm, "That's a letter from an old friend of mine. He was writing to see how I was. He'd read about the bombing."

"I'll bet." Morrison nodded with sympathy. "I'll bet anybody who knew you was very alarmed for your welfare."

"Yes, he was," Lee agreed helplessly. That he had characterized Gaither's letter as expressive of tender concern mortified him, not just because the idea was ludicrous but because he now found he had fibbed to an FBI agent. It couldn't matter, though; it was a personal letter, the only personal item of mail on the tedious list. He was so distracted he didn't hear Morrison's question until the agent had asked it again.

"What's his name? What's the name of this friend?"

"Why?" Lee said, startled.

"I'm just doing my job, Professor. There's no name on the envelope. Can you tell me the name of the sender?"

"Lewis Gaither," Lee said after a moment. At the agent's request, he spelled it, and Morrison wrote it down.

"I realize it's a personal letter, but would you mind if we took a look at it?"

"Why?" Lee burst out again, his heart galloping now. As if Gaither sat closely behind him, he heard again that elegant, perfidious voice, its sarcasm so skillfully pitched as to be felt only by its target. *What a bittersweet pleasure to see your face after all of these years. You are still a handsome man.* "Princely," I believe, was the word sometimes used around campus for you. "You": the malignant intruder, about whom "we"—*around campus*—all spoke. Lee was starting to feel he'd never been without the inflicted tattoo of this letter, inked onto his memory bank, beaten out word by word on his eardrum, and at the same time he was constantly grasping new shades of its meaning he had not seen before. *The word sometimes used around campus for you*: Gaither dared style himself as ensconced in some great campus "we" that had gazed upon Lee, at the best, with ironical scorn. *"Prince" Lee. What a gas! With that crappy old briefcase of his.* Lee didn't need to look at the letter to hear its interleaved insinuations, but he knew that anyone who did see it would know that he'd lied. It was no friendly letter. It expressed no authentic concern. He had lied because he was ashamed. Ashamed that his one piece of personal mail was an arrow of hate.

"You know," he resumed, his heart's wild locomotion almost tumbling his words, "I threw that letter away." He almost wept with relief that he'd thought of this.

Morrison cocked his head slightly, and then he closed the file folder, with the air of a man who has finished a tiresome duty. "That's it, then," he said. "I'd like to thank you, Professor."

"Not at all," Lee said. For the first time since the encounter began he could imagine himself left alone in his house, and he newly broke into a cold sweat of longing and rediscovered exhaustion.

And yet the agents still didn't seem ready to go. With an indistinct mutter and a toss of her head, Shenkman excused herself to the front steps to place a call from what Lee was now told was her cellular phone. "Not the best reception in these parts," Morrison apologized, after she had gone.

They sat another awkward moment until Lee compulsively reached for the teapot.

"I'm good, thanks," said Morrison, guarding his cup with his hand. Lee had clasped this hand twice, but only now that it was propped on the teacup, as if on a pedestal, was he presented with all its minutiae:

wiry black and gray hairs, gnarled veins, knuckles like smashed bits of boulder trapped under the skin. The hand was alarming; it had all the face's crudities with none of the ameliorations supplied by expressiveness. The hand pushed the cup a few inches farther away, a subtle gesture of dismissal that Lee felt, or hoped, was directed at him. Lee heard the indistinct drone of Agent Shenkman's voice drifting through the front door.

"Can I bother you for a restroom?" Agent Morrison asked.

"Please." Lee stood up, then sat again as Agent Morrison waved him away.

"I saw it as I came in," Agent Morrison said, disappearing.

Lee didn't know how many minutes he sat alone in his kitchen, confined by invisible tethers to his rickety chair. If he stood, Agent Morrison would hear the unburdened wood creak; Lee felt, senselessly, that he must remain glued to this spot so that when Agent Morrison returned, he would appear to be pleasantly adrift in his thoughts. The agent was experiencing no such restraint. Lee could hear him roaming the length, breadth, and height of the house. Every square foot of floor space, upstairs and down and in the finished basement, was muffled beneath thick beige carpeting, but Lee knew his house: it was cheaply constructed, or one might say sensitive to itself, so that near-silent footsteps at one end produced an odd squeaking sound at the other, and the basement door's being smoothly swung open unleashed a wave that, many feet from its source and close to where Lee was sitting, emerged with a soda can's *pop!* And yet amid all this, Lee had not heard the torrential, Pharaoh's-men-obliterated-by-God-in-the-trench-of-the-sea dissonant symphony that was unleashed every time any one of his house's three toilets was flushed. Agent Morrison seemed not to have gone to the bathroom at all. Lee sat motionless, translating small noises of structural strain into the agent's rambling trajectory, up, down, out the front door for a conference with Shenkman, by which time Lee was ready to confess, insanely, that the letter was not in the garbage but still in his briefcase—as if it possibly could have been this, and not the pathetic, impoverished state of Lee's home, that was propelling the curious agent. Of course the man wondered at Lee, even probably pitied him, this the most awful thought— not dispelled but confirmed when the agent returned to the kitchen and said, in an attempt to conceal his pity that was even more wounding than pity itself, "I like the layout of your house. It's very nice. Is this a recent development?"

"About ten years old," Lee said, lowering his mortified face to his teacup.

"Property taxes killing you?"

"They're not so bad," Lee managed.

When Agent Shenkman returned, her magical phone snapping shut in her palm like a squarish black bivalve, Agent Morrison removed a card from his pocket and gave it to Lee. "That's the number at which you can reach me, any time of day or night. I know it's very painful to talk about these things, with your colleague having so recently passed away, but if you can think of anything that might be of help to us—even something that seems very minor to you— please call me. As I said, any time of the day or night. I'll be glad to hear from you."

"I certainly will call if I think of something. I'm very happy to help."

"Anything at all, Professor. You might think of something and say to yourself, 'Oh, that can't be important.' Let us decide if it's important."

"I will," Lee affirmed.

Finally they were back in his doorway, Shenkman with her glacial expression, Morrison now exhibiting an encouraging one, like the face of the school's football coach, it remotely struck Lee: superficially robust and open, but beneath that brow somehow more narrow, determined, and grim. Lee didn't have a great deal of time to refine this impression; he and Morrison had shaken yet again and exchanged their good-byes.

His life in this country and his life in his native country had so few points of coincidence apart from himself—they had none, actually— that when Lee gazed on his past, it could seem as if he'd been young twice. First in his homeland, where his actual youth was spoiled for him prematurely, and then in his adopted United States, where as if in a grand compensation the uncoiling spring of his life had been rewound several turns. As a newly carefree man of twenty-nine, he'd been electrified by the greed the nineteen-year-old boy might have felt, so that at last came wolfish dealings with girls at the age, in his old life, he'd have long been patriarchically married; and at last there was scholastic pretension: unkempt wallowing in his self-declared genius, with shirttails untucked, hair uncombed, and books strewn on the floor. It was strange but true that university confines in democratic America had finally bestowed on him the vaguely aristocratic European young-manhood he'd expected since childhood. It had helped that he was not just exotic and handsome but in appearance quite young. No one had guessed he was nearer to thirty than he was to nineteen. But now that he was decades past both ages, the events of those times intermixed with each other—because while the break with his homeland should have been the clean epochal line, it was really his volatile heart that doled out the half-lives. Incidents could be psychically early but calendrically late; the young man of the East was in some ways more aged than his Western descendant. The appearance in his driveway of two FBI agents had resurrected for Lee not an episode postemigration, from his first several years in America, but an earlier one from his childhood, a primal scene in its way: he'd come home to find his mother and father submitting to questions from four uniformed army policemen, and as he'd rushed into the room, his lungs dying with dread, all four had wheeled upon him as one and barked at him to stop it or drop it or some such—even then their exact words escaped him—and his boy's burden of notebooks and textbooks and pencils had gone crashing like so many bricks to the floor.

But the soul of that boy had been battered and primed, and the incursion had long been expected, and the impression it left was of the sort that is never effaced by the subsequent siltings of life. That long-ago leap of fear had repeated itself many times, while any number of later events—from Lee's second, superior youth—had been completely forgotten, though they might have had equal significance. To Lee's own amazement it wasn't until almost two hours later, when he was finally stretched out in the tub, that he remembered that today's had not been his first encounter with the FBI but his second. He was listening to the *Brandenburg* Concertos—the *Emperor* Concerto in the end had felt too bombastic for midafternoon—and drinking a beer and nearly, finally, nodding off to blessed sleep as the bathwater cooled. Then the memory returned to him, and he set down his beer abruptly. He wished he could turn off the music without leaving the tub. It had been in the summer, perhaps his first summer in this country, although more likely his second. He had taken a long-distance bus trip to visit someone—a roommate? a girl?—and on arrival he'd been met by two men who had asked him to answer some questions. "WE TALKEE," one of them bellowed at him.

"You don't need to shoutee," he'd remarked. "I'm not deafee."

Which had prompted the other to ask him, perhaps a few minutes later, "Where did you learn your English, Mr. Lee?"—as if Lee's calm, assured grasp of that language were somehow even more suspect than the foreign appearance that had drawn them to him in the first place.

They had thought he was Chinese, and even after he'd convinced them he was not—a task remarkable both for the length of time it had taken and for the unoffended and unflagging patience that Lee had brought to it—they'd wanted to believe that he had numerous Chinese friends. "You're precisely the sort of fellow we need," one of the agents told him, in the confiding tone that overtook the proceedings once Lee's non-Chineseness was finally established, as if the two men were fraternity brothers trying to win a new pledge. "You certainly see it from our point of view, that we can't have Chinese in this country who are pledging allegiance to the Communist Party."

"I don't speak a word of Chinese," Lee had said. "I don't know any Chinese people, and I certainly don't know any Communists. Why would I know a Communist? Do you know what they did to my family? It's like saying a German Jew must have lots of good friends who are Nazis."

This had subdued the conversation. Finally one of the agents had asked Lee to please be in touch if he did ever meet Chinese Communists hatching plots in America. But Lee's memory of the incident was perhaps comprised less of the incident itself than of the way he'd described it to the few friends he'd made by that time in the days afterward. It had been a hilarious anecdote, scornfully told. Lee had enjoyed his immigrant's luxury of knowing what real danger felt like, while his listeners had enjoyed the American luxury of never having known danger at all.

But perhaps the encounter had excited real fear, which Lee had willfully purged—perhaps he had not been so witty and calm after all.

Was this possible? There was no telling now; almost forty years had gone by. Unlike the earlier moment, long buried but intact when unearthed, this had started dissolving the instant Lee stumbled upon it. Only one thing remained beyond doubt: Lee really had closed the door not just on native country and language and culture but on kin, all of them, said good-bye to all that and stepped over a threshold of ocean to never look back. There had never been a divided allegiance, a pang of nostalgia, not even a yen for the food, so that only months into his life in the States, when faced by two FBI agents in an American bus station, he could almost have laughed—not to be thought Chinese but anything whatsoever, apart from American.

He took a thoughtful pull from his beer can Now the sloshed inch of beer in its bottom and the delathered water in the tub were the same tepid temperature. With the absence of the carbonated cold on his tongue and the heat in his skin came a generalized clarification; all the dreary imperfections of the bathroom were revealed to him. The misaligned squares of linoleum, the ancient toilet-seat fissure, the mysterious discoloration on the edge of the tub. And the ephemeral blots: toothpaste spray on the mirror, and urine dashes and dots on the bowl, and shed hairs of all tones—translucent like fishing line, solid white, whitish gray, and the rare lengths of black that despite youthful hue had let go of the scalp anyway. This was Lee's private bath, accessed via his bedroom, not the "public" half bath—distinguished by the absence of dotted toothpaste and urine and the presence of dust   Agent Morrison had pretended to visit. Like Lee's bedroom, and kitchen, and study, the only rooms in the house that he used, the bathroom had reverted to its pre-Michiko state without any effort of Lee's. There had been no denuded hooks and square, picture-size fadings, no furniture-leg holes punched into the carpet. Michiko had reserved her considerable efforts for the public rooms of the house, where she had aggressively furnished and defurnished, hung and unhung, while in the bedroom she'd lived like a hotel guest, all her things in a couple of drawers and in a toiletry case, as if she expected to leave for the airport at a moment's notice; and in fact in their four years of marriage, she'd been back to Japan seven times. Lee had gone with her just once, although that he'd recrossed the Pacific at all, planning beforehand for months and reading numerous guidebooks and making copious notes, and then during the journey itself becoming almost insane with his desire to see everything while Michiko only wanted to have lunch with her friends, made this period seem like one of unending effort, of a great struggle all come to naught.

Lee stood slowly out of the tub, hunched with cold, and dislodged the plug with a toe as he reached for a towel; then he dressed in pajamas, though outside was still gleaming with sun. In decades of life with insomnia, he'd found that bedtime preparations at inappropriate hours sometimes slipped him under the radar; a long soak and pajamas at lunchtime, a too-heavy hot meal and several bottles of beer. Every miraculous once in a while, he'd drop hard out of consciousness and eerily wake more than eight hours later, then feel like the mighty conquistador of the night hush around him. On those occasions three A.M. wakefulness was a rare delectation. He would pad up to his study with a pot of green tea and work with a focused serenity he associated, perhaps wrongly, with youth. Now he performed his night ritual while trying, as was most effective, not to give it much thought, but once he was in bed with the phone off the hook and the blinds drawn, he felt even further from sleep. His bedside clock said 4:07; the memorial service for Hendley was just under way. He sat up abruptly, his pulse, amplified by his earplugs, like a tom-tom inside his skull. Was he supposed to have been there? By the time the clock read 4:19, he had churned his freshly made bed into the same strangling state he'd escaped from that morning. He got up and plugged the phone in again to call Sondra, but then the dial tone sounded wrong; it clicked once and seemed to yawn open, as if the call had been made, though he hadn't pressed numbers. And of course Sondra wasn't in the department. She would be at the service.

At five o'clock he turned on the television; as he'd expected, Hendley's service led the local newscast, although the service itself wasn't shown. "Newscenter 11 was asked, out of respect for the deceased professor, campus leader, and valued mentor to countless students, to refrain from broadcasting the service. At this hour the service is still going on, with a wide range of professors and students expected to speak. We asked a few students to share their feelings with us as they arrived at the stadium earlier this afternoon." Now the camera cut away from the Newscenter 11 anchor team to a sun-dappled stadium entrance, where a procession of students, clutching piles of books to their chests or backpacks by one strap to their shoulders, shared their distress with a young woman, dressed perhaps to "relate," in blue jeans and a windbreaker. Lee wondered if she was the same woman to whom he'd given his fiery statement the day of the bombing. That heady moment of near heroism now seemed very distant. Another student had been caught in the frame, the microphone tilted toward him; Lee experienced the oddly poignant, paternal feeling that sometimes overcame him when he spotted students from his advanced calculus or trig classes clowning down the aisles of his supermarket, loading up on bricks of ramen and frozen pizzas, before he realized the boy wasn't one of his students, but that same spike-haired, sloe-eyed student employee of University Station. "Do you think you'll be able to put this behind you?" the reporter asked gravely.

"Maybe if this was the end, but it's just the beginning," the boy said with composure, gazing, as many of his fellow students had not, directly into the camera, so that Lee almost felt he and the boy had locked eyes with each other.

"What do you mean, the beginning?"

"It was somebody here," the boy said. "I work in the mail room, so I just have some insights about how it happened."

"Could you share them with us?"

"Not really. But now that they've done it once, why wouldn't they do it again?"

"*Thank you,*" the reporter exclaimed.

"Yeah, no problem," the boy said.

Lee turned off the TV, and as if he'd drawn down a blind, the room felt newly lightless, though all the blinds had been drawn down already. He was surprised the newscast would air the groundless speculations of a young college student. *It was somebody here.* In the darkness of his shrouded room, Lee surprised himself by smiling and heard his chuckle make its minimal dent in the afternoon quiet. He'd been reminded of Esther again, and her keening complaint all her years as a teenager. "*Nothing* ever happens here!" she would wail, with an accusing glare at him—as if he could make something happen! It never solaced her, or brought them any closer, that he entirely agreed, even if he didn't share her displeasure. It was true, nothing ever did happen, apart from the seasonal swelling and ebbing of the town's population. Every May half the humans departed for eventful homelands, and every September like locusts they came back again. But for a disconsolate townie like Esther, the long studentless summer held none of the pleasures Lee savored himself, the deserted library and the drone of the lawn mower laboring over the quad. That irregular college-town heartbeat had been Lee's for so long that when Esther was born, he had assumed that registration and graduation and winter break in between would tranquilly mark out the wheel of her life, the same way they marked his.

He flinched with sadness and at the same time felt an opposite movement, a yearning forth from himself that reached searchingly for his daughter. He got up quickly and wrapped himself in a robe, as if he'd heard the doorbell, but he was only going as far as the kitchen for a fresh can of beer. It was just like a young person, he thought, drawing a dry hand over newly damp eyes, to relocate the drama so that the young person him- or herself occupied center stage. First the students had wept self-importantly for the professor the greater number of them hadn't known. Now they would quiver with thrilled indignation at the mysterious bomber who lurked in their midst. Lee took several long swallows of beer at his dining-room table. Even in the course of his talk with Fasano, he had still been so addled by the letter from Gaither he hadn't given much thought to who the bomber might actually be. He drew his message pad close to him, the same one that still said *FASANO* in an emphatic inked box, and wrote in the blank space beneath, recalling that conversation, *DOES NOT LIKE HOTSHOTS.* A few swallows later, he added, with an acknowledging smile, as if Fasano were with him, *OR TALL POPPIES.*

"Well, Frank, we can take it easy," he said, voicing the thought they had before left unspoken. "We never got very tall."

And what would have comprised height for Lee anyway? He remembered his twenty-sixth birthday, an occasion on which the idea of catching up with Einstein could still be entertained, if only by means of narcissistic delusion, or noble and ludicrous hope. Other young men might have hoped they could still be James Dean; Lee had entered his twenty-sixth year with a picture of Einstein taped over his desk in his family home, and the idea that mathematical genius might

appear in his brain like an unheralded tumor. If such a thing happened at all, it could certainly happen inside of twelve months ... and
then Lee had turned twenty-seven and let go of another small part of
his dream for himself. No Einsteinian *annus mirabilis*, no spearhead-
ing of revolution. Of course it had been laughable, at best childishly
naïve, for him ever to have harbored such outsize ambitions. As it
became laughable and naïve in later years, along the steadily cor-
roded downslope of the possible, that he might have at least been a
lesser-known Gödel if not an iconic Einstein; a respected professor at
Princeton, if not a singular Gödel; all right, at Harvard: his preference
for Princeton was sentimental; any ivy at all; Michigan or Chicago or
Berkeley; was it too much to simply want tenure someplace not too
awful? This at least he had gotten. He still stood a chance of seeing his
textbook adopted; he still published, every once in a while; he still attended the rare conference he could get to by car. And the truth was,
nowadays he was less prone to measure how far he fell short of his
wildest dreams than the tiny circumference in which even those
dreams were contained. Not how short a poppy he was but how small
the whole field. He had not been an Einstein, but neither had anyone
else, and much as he'd envied poor Hendley while Hendley still lived,
both Hendley and Fasano's Illich were tall poppies—hotshots—only
to a marginal, small group of people. The shorter poppies competing
for sun in the same little patch, like Fasano, Lee thought, and
himself.

   It felt peculiar to recognize, as he took a last draining sip of his
beer, that his mind, with these thoughts of poppies, was performing a
Holmesian act of deduction. Although Lee was a mathematician, logic
wasn't a habit ingrained into his daily life. Or at least this had been
Aileen's grievance, after her death taken up by their daughter. It was
true that Lee usually failed to discern the shortest route between points
A and B. Household storage was for the most part the same as irre-
trievable loss: he had no system either for the safeguard of critical
items or for the management of trivial clutter. In Aileen's time there
was always a place for rubber bands, twisty-ties, mason jar lids, spare
keys to the car and his office; there was a rigorous ordering of the lin-
ens and everyone's socks; but for all his (never-spoken) admiration of
her instinct for order, Lee did nothing but disorder that order, because

he didn't even slightly comprehend how it worked. That it was logical meant no more to him than if it were Hindi. But now he wrote *ONE OF US* and, beneath this, *MATHEMATICIAN/COMPUTER SCIENTIST*. He put the pen down. For the moment this felt like the end of concrete, concise points to set down in black ink. Yet his mind, parched from sleeplessness, drenched with beer, continued to glide along the tracks with remarkable ease. By "one of us," of course he meant not just a colleague in the field but a frustrated, unaccomplished colleague, a short poppy—yet not a short poppy like himself or Fasano. Fasano had admitted he scarcely understood Illich's work. Lee's relation to Hendley was similar. Certainly, he had envied Hendley's popularity with students, resented the toadying Hendley enjoyed from even senior colleagues, coveted his youth and vitality and publication record and, of course, his salary, and above all his Rachel—Lee surprised himself, realizing this. Yet why be surprised? The woman was a compact denotation of all of the rest. A man like Hendley stripped to his essence—an unremarkable physical presence and the abashed, gawking heart of a nerd—would never have won a woman like Rachel without all the rest. So yes, certainly Lee had envied. But his envy was idle and almost reflexive, the envy of all older for all younger men. It wasn't the combustible fury that could be sparked only in a peer.

He felt pleased, as if watching the train of his mind penetrating a new destination. The bomber was a mathematician or a computer scientist of around Hendley's and Illich's age. He was young enough to regard those men as his immediate rivals, and he was old enough to have seen his own chance for an Einsteinian *annus mirabilis* pass. Old enough to be bitter, young enough to do something about it. This man felt as Lee might have felt about Donald Whitehead, years ago, if Whitehead had continued on the meteoric rise that had first taken him out of Lee's sights. But Whitehead seemed to have been a mere flash in the pan; after Whitehead had gotten the plum job and left school midyear, Lee had never heard of him again. Another overestimated young scholar turned average old man. Whitehead was lost amid short poppies now, perhaps pondering just the same question of what made men kill as he shuffled to his grumbling fridge and got out a fresh beer.

14.

OFTEN SPRING BREAK WAS SPRINGLIKE IN NAME ONLY, but in the days after Hendley's memorial, spring secured such a foothold that some mornings felt more like summer. Lee as usual slept very little, but in the fragrant new atmosphere, with his heating turned off and his windows cranked open, he slept unusually well. Perhaps it was also because he'd decided to pretend to himself, as he had to the agents, that he really had thrown Gaither's letter away: by an arduous effort of will, he exiled it from thought. Along with the bombing of Hendley, it could almost be seen as the last overreachings of malevolent winter, which this past year had been cruel to Lee, inflicting constant illness. He last remembered a sense of well-being when he'd taken a walk in the local state park and there'd been crimson leaves on the trees. That had been in October. Now it was April, and the two magnolia trees on his block had erupted in huge fleshy blooms, and his neighbor's forsythia pulsed with a nuclear glow; in every other direction he looked, yesterday's lackluster branches and twigs had been transformed by a bright pointillism of just-visible buds.

The recollection that there was a state park to go to felt like divine revelation, and one morning after coming awake in the five A.M. twilight, he filled a travel mug with his tea and put a few slices of meat between of bread. Backing his car out of the garage, he saw that his two garbage cans, filled and placed at the curb for the pickup this morning, were already on their sides, empty. He felt light with amazement: when was the last time he'd slept through the garbage collection? Invariably it would find him still tensely in bed, straining for a morsel of postsunrise slumber to make up for a night of insomnia. The squeal of the garbage truck's brakes, the hoarse shouts of the workers, the truck's grinding jaws, and the thumps as his cans were tossed back—all seemed an external expression, as well as a mockery, of his unrested torment. But this morning he'd peacefully slept through the raucous event—and the event must have occurred earlier than it generally did. He'd never known the garbage to be collected before seven-thirty or eight. Getting out of his idling car to retrieve the empty cans, he noticed that his neighbors' cans were still sitting upright, expectantly plump, at the curb. But his subdivision consisted of unnecessarily tortuous streets, so that from the base of his driveway he easily saw only the ends of two other driveways, of the across-the-street house and the house to his right. Perhaps this morning his house had been the last on an incomplete round of collections; in a short time, the trucks would come back. It seemed strange, but once back in his car he'd forgotten about it.

At six in the morning, the park held just a few joggers pounding the trails; a few slow-moving old people in car coats were walking their dogs. Lee raised his hand at each encounter without making eye contact, as was the protocol in this park, by contrast with Mashtamow-tahpa Park, which was more like the grocery store. Even if Lee had run into someone he knew here, which had never yet happened, they would have just nodded briefly before leaving each other to fragile illusions of wilderness. But soon enough Lee was really alone on the path he had chosen. He walked briskly but unhurriedly, seeing the early bloomers here—the spindly unpruned forsythia and the rarer magnolia and a redbud or two, all a few sap beats behind their suburban yard cousins—bursting brightly like motionless fireworks amid the bare trees around them.

He ate his sandwich on the shore of the park's smaller pond, which had not been marred by a swimming beach or a boat launch or a picnic area, so that although there was nowhere to sit, it was almost possible, despite the faint path that led here and away, to feel like an intruder in an actual Eden. He supposed there was nothing remarkable about the pond or the trees ringing it except absence, but to him that was remarkable enough: The absence of wires slinging off from one electrical tower to another, for example. The absence, at this moment, of any airplane crawling through the sky and doubled on the pond's surface, like a metal-skinned insect. And when Lee stood in the right place and faced the right way, the absence of the path. He didn't even sit, but leaned against a nude maple with his feet on the snow-flattened corpses of last summer's ragweed. His sandwich was very dry, as he hadn't taken the time to add mustard, but he savored it gratefully; now he remembered that last night he hadn't had dinner.

In all the years he had lived here, he had never thought of communion with nature as a possible pastime; a few square miles of cornfield covered over with second-growth trees was not nature to him. But now he gazed into the eye of the pond and again thought of Esther, with her container of shreds of raw meat, and her eaglets, and her patience. He had rejected the notion of Esther's doing something like this—not just refused to embrace it but refused to believe it—because the angry, curt Esther of adolescence and young-womanhood eclipsed the previous Esther in his mind, invalidated her somehow. That had been a grave, patient child. Her attention exquisite and unwavering. He knew he saw Esther as not just divided in two but fragmented, into all the children she'd been—and that he considered the best, those who'd loved and revered him, as lost. But he could see her now, guarding her eaglets, patient and fierce like an eagle herself.

By the time he got back to his car, it was almost ten-thirty, and he was ravenous again. He would go home and scramble some eggs, and the hell with cholesterol. He realized that until this week he had been very tired, not just for days but for months. And fatigue shrank his mind to a single gapped track on which a single train faltered. . . . Now his thinking was vaulted and gleaming and lively with simultaneous movement. Despite his recent exhaustion, the idea he'd had about Hendley's killer had not evaporated. If anything, it had come to feel sounder, in his mind and, better yet, in his gut. It seemed to signal a general restoration of his life's functioning: the week of good sleep, the brisk walk, and now, as he was considering calling Agent Morrison to share his deduction, the convenient reappearance of that very man's car in his driveway. No less apt and unsurprising was the absence of the woman, whose name Lee had already forgotten, perhaps in self-defense: Shipman? Shankar? Lee parked beside Morrison and got out of his car feeling as glad as Morrison appeared to be at their meeting again. Beneath the late-morning light, the agent's smallish eyes achieved new prominence, and Lee noticed that they were not just interested but interesting in themselves: a lively color neither quite blue nor green. Lee could almost have thought Agent Morrison had also had his first sound night's sleep in a while. The agent bore down on Lee with a smile that seemed kindled from pure fellow feeling.

"It's funny," Lee said, as they clasped hands. "I was just about to call you."

"That *is* funny."

"I hope you haven't been waiting long?"

"I just drove up."

"Well, it's perfect timing! I've been up since dawn drinking nothing but tea. Would you have coffee if I made some?"

"Music to my ears," Morrison said, in the tone of a man who'd been waiting for just such an offer.

Inside, Lee opened the sliding glass door that led from the eating area of the kitchen to the backyard, and with that single act his winter-stale, uncomfortable home was transformed. Now the absence of furniture seemed deliberate—possibly, he thought with bemusement, *austerely Oriental.* The impersonal, as-delivered beige walls and beige carpet, which all winter long beneath the glare of the overhead fixtures had exhibited dingy smudges and scrapes, now presented a rich, creamy surface for shifting gold panels of sun. A mild breeze pulsed, freshening everything. Lee started the coffee and then stood filling a pitcher at the kitchen sink, to water his plants. "Can I offer you anything else?" he asked Morrison, who was studying the table of bonsai and jade trees. "I was thinking of making some eggs. I took a walk early this morning, and I'm hungry enough to have breakfast again."

"Just coffee's good for me, Professor, but please don't hold off on my account. I'm the one who intruded on you. Please do make yourself eggs."

"That's all right," Lee said, although he was so hungry he was afraid for a moment that Morrison would hear his stomach, which was yawning and grumbling with a vigor Lee hadn't experienced in at least a few decades. "And you're not intruding. Like I said, I was about to call you."

While they waited for the coffee, Lee watered his plants, tipping a small amount into each pot all the way down the row and then starting again from the top, and at the same time he told Morrison the conclusion he'd reached. Morrison listened attentively—as Lee worked, he could feel Morrison's gaze on his face—but he didn't interrupt with questions, nor did he take notes. Lee's notepad, he realized, was still on the countertop near where Morrison sat. When Lee was finished giving each plant a third splash of water, so that each drank its fill without overflowing—the pots had been almost dry, he'd been so absentminded—he was also done talking, and the coffee was brewed. "Milk or sugar, Agent?" he asked.

"Please call me Jim, Professor. I'll take it just like that, black."

"Then you must call me Lee, not Professor. I take it black, too." When they were seated at the table together with their twin coffee mugs, Lee went on, "I know it must sound imprecise to you. But here's where I can be of real help, like I said that I hoped I could be. What an outsider like you wouldn't realize is that our field is very small. It's true that I don't know everyone, especially the younger professors. But if you took me and a colleague of mine at another university and a colleague of *his* at a third university, between the three of us we probably are familiar with everyone working in the field, at least on a cursory level. At that level it's still very possible to assess for the presence of different factors. For example, lack of advancement, where advancement might have been expected. A bad publication record. Resentment of colleagues. Failure to get along on committees. You'd call it a profile, wouldn't you?" Morrison's expression was neutral, though not unfriendly, and it occurred to Lee that Morrison, like anyone in any field, was capable of feeling bested and threatened and that perhaps he, Lee, had stepped on Morrison's toes. "Of course, this is your field, not mine. I just mean to say that I know my field, and maybe that can help you, in yours."

"It's an interesting theory. Still, Professor Hendley wasn't just a professor. No offense, Lee, but you might be seeing things too strictly in terms of Hendley's professional life, since that was your relationship to him. It's possible that his killer was motivated by a side of Hendley's life that had nothing to do with his work."

"No offense taken at all. What you've said makes perfect sense. But I'm basing my theory of the killer not just on Hendley's murder. I'm thinking of the attempted murder of Sorin Illich also." For a strange moment, Morrison's complete unresponsiveness, the high-stakes-poker blankness behind which his face was so suddenly and uncharacteristically hidden, gave Lee the irrational sensation he'd somehow gone too far. But then Morrison's heavy black eyebrows belatedly jumped, as if he were surprised by an obvious point that had never occurred to him.

"You mean the bombing at UCLA. A few years ago now."

"I assumed you would know all about it—"

"I'm familiar with it. You think it's the same perpetrator?"

For the first time that morning, Lee felt a slipping of gears, a remote chance of error. "How could it not be?" he asked, hearing himself sound more plaintive than assertive.

"I don't know. You tell me." Morrison waited encouragingly.

"Well, Illich apparently is young—in the context of the academic world. You have to forgive us; our idea of youth is twenty years older than everyone else's." Lee tried a laugh, though he inwardly cringed at the way that it sounded.

But now Morrison seemed deeply engaged, as if Lee had been in the midst of a dazzling Holmesian monologue, instead of just clearing his throat. "Go on," Morrison said. "So he's young, about the same age as Professor Hendley."

"Yes, but that's not really the point. The point is his stature. His stature, relative to his age. In the context of our field, you could call him a hotshot." Lee pretended to coin the term casually and then flushed, realizing that the word was inked in large, deliberate letters on the notepad, which sat at the edge of his vision—and Agent Morrison's, he would guess.

"You said Illich is apparently young. Don't you know him?"

"Me? I'd never heard of him until just a short time ago." Lee immediately felt the lacuna in his own train of logic. "When I called him a hotshot, I meant he's a hotshot more to the younger generation. I'll admit it, at my age I have trouble keeping up with new work and the new applications, not just because I don't try hard enough but because some of it is honestly beyond me," and although these sentences could not have been more dismayingly true, Lee felt newly vulnerable, as if he'd been caught in a lie.

"How did you come to learn about Illich, then?"

"From an old colleague of mine who's now at UCLA. I mean, old in age, too. A guy my age. Frank Fasano."

"This guy," Morrison said, finally pulling the notepad from its unhidden, peripheral place so that it lay on the table between them.

"He got in touch with me after Hendley was bombed. He heard about it on the news."

"And he told you about the Illich bombing from a couple years back."

"Yes."

"And here I thought he must be your prime suspect."

"No!" Lee cried, horrified, at the same time as Morrison began laughing.

"I'm just kidding, Professor. You can't blame me, can you? I was hoping you had it all figured out, so I could take the month off."

"But what do you say to my theory, honestly?"

"Honestly? I think it's very interesting. I need to give it more thought."

"What is your theory?"

"I couldn't even say that I have one, Professor. We try to stick to the finding of facts for as long as we can, before we let loose with the theories."

"Please, just Lee," Lee reminded him. "That seems very reasonable."

Agent Morrison put down his empty coffee cup. "Do you mind if I revisit that restroom?"

This time Lee did hear the roar of his plumbing. His stomach growled as if in response, and he remembered his hunger, but while the bare fact of hunger remained, the urgent, sensual aura of well-earned appetite, so wonderfully unfamiliar these days, had somehow leached away. He no longer cared if he ate eggs or wheat bran. Waiting for Morrison to return, he revisited this same waiting moment from their previous meeting, but viewed minus his fatigue and confusion. He thought of Agent Morrison's footsteps, freely roaming the rooms of his house, and of the unflushed toilet, and of Shenkman—he remembered her name now—and her seeming hostility, in contrast, perhaps deliberate contrast, to Morrison's friendliness.

When Morrison came back into the room, Lee said, "What brought you here, Jim? I'm afraid I've been rude. You came here for a reason, and I've wasted your time with my Sherlock Holmes thoughts."

"Not at all, Lee. Your thoughts are interesting to me. And your house, I must say, is more pleasant than my motel room."

Lee let out a brief laugh, remembering the agent's similarly hollow compliment on his house's layout. "Please," he said. "You don't have to say that. I'm aware that my house is . . . unattractive."

"Not at all."

"I'm not normally so austere. My ex-wife took everything she could carry, as the saying goes. She only left the things that were worthless to her, like the chair that you're sitting in."

"How did she manage that?"

"How did she manage anything?" Lee demanded rhetorically, somehow forgetting, as his mind constricted to a single track again—because heartbroken rage and fatigue had many of the same debilitating effects—that he still hadn't learned why the agent was here to see him. "With utter shamelessness and greed. You can see that she took everything. Even things she didn't care about at all. Antique furniture, antique pictures. These old things I used to collect. Michiko didn't care about those things. She just took them to spite me." Lee noticed that Morrison, as if he were the host, had refilled both their cups; he took a long, acrid slug and was reminded of why he'd essentially given up coffee except for rare occasions on which he had guests. His heart was galloping again, perhaps a bit unevenly; a fresh sweat had come out on his temples, although the breeze in the room was quite cool.

"I'm very sorry to hear it," Morrison finally said.

"I'm very sorry to have bothered you about it," Lee said with embarrassment. The agent was the sort of man with whom conversation was almost too easy. "I got you off track again. You were telling me what brought you here."

"It's a very small thing. But the other day, when you said who that letter was from—who was it again? I'm not sure that I got the name right."

"Lewis Gaither," Lee said, and he was angry to feel, instantly, at the sound of the name on his tongue, a sensation like a very tight band wrapped around his rib cage.

"Spelling Lewis L-E-W?"

"Yes. Could it be so important? It's a personal letter. It has nothing to do with Hendley."

"Did you say you still had it?"

Lee almost faltered and forgot his white lie, but he rescued himself, without, he felt sure, betraying his moment's confusion. "I'm afraid that I threw it away, like I told you before."

"Oh, that's right. Forgive me. We're just chasing down so many things." Morrison reached inside his jacket and produced a pen and a notebook that in his hands appeared comically small. He hunched over it, writing. "And your friend Lewis lives in Woodmont."

Lee felt a tingle of warning, an alarm on his scalp. It was the false address Gaither had given—of course this was why they were asking. Yet he couldn't explain Gaither hated him and would do such a thing just to taunt him—he had already painted Gaither as a caring old friend. "Well, I suppose he does," Lee began carefully. A partial truth, he reasoned, was not inferior to a complete one, and perhaps it was actually better, because less confusing. Emboldened by this idea, he went on, "But I wrote to him at that address and my letter came back. So perhaps Lewis made some mistake on his own envelope."

"You wrote him and you got a 'returned to sender'? You didn't tell me about that the first time we talked."

"I assumed that you knew," Lee exclaimed, with all the force of resurgent anxiety as well as conviction—because in retrospect it seemed logical that the agent should have known this and not need to be told, although Lee knew in his heart that he hadn't thought this at the time.

But Morrison didn't seem suspicious, or dismayed; he was making more notes in his notebook. "Oh, I probably do have a record of that letter of yours, if it came back to you," he remarked as he wrote. "There's just so many things to chase down. I apologize if I'm belaboring points we've gone over before. It just would be such a great help if you'd quickly refresh me about that letter. I can finish these records and seal them up."

"But why is it so important?"

"You've said yourself the address doesn't work. Why wouldn't your friend use his actual address?"

"I don't know. I really have no idea."

"Can you tell me a little about him? And it is Gaither, yes? G-A-I—"

"Like what?" Lee felt himself giving way to inexplicable panic. He couldn't say that this caring old friend was his ex-wife's ex-husband. "I really don't know much about him."

"Didn't you say he was a very old friend?"

"I meant a friend from a long time ago. Not a friend that I've known a long time." At last Lee had stumbled upon a plain truth that might encompass all the previous statements he'd made. Relief poured through his veins. He and Gaither were very complex, it was true, but their tangles could still be summed up in a way that was simple.

"L-E-W-I-S G-A-I-T-H-E-R." Morrison was still toiling over his notebook. At last he sat up and smiled at Lee. "You met Special Agent Shenkman. She likes to have all the i's dotted and all the t's crossed. Far be it for me to criticize her work methods, because she's an outstanding colleague. But just between you and me, her tendency to leave no stone unturned can get a little extreme."

"I understand," Lee said, returning Morrison's smile gratefully. "Far be it *from* me," he added.

"Sorry?"

"Far be it *from* me. That's the phrase. It's a common mistake."

Morrison grinned. "Don't be insulted if I compliment your English, Lee. Clearly, it's better than mine." They both laughed, and when Morrison stood up from the table with his cup, he also reached for Lee's, which Lee surrendered without protest. Morrison rinsed both their cups at the sink.

"Looks like a great day to work in the yard," Morrison remarked when they were standing at the door. "Are you at home for the rest of the day?"

"Yes, I'm not going anywhere."

"Enjoy your afternoon."

They shook hands heartily. Morrison raised an arm out his car window while driving away.

That afternoon Lee changed into old slacks and a T-shirt and wrestled his ancient push mower out into the sun. He hated lawn mowing—it offered none of the pleasures of plant tending and ten times the toil. But he also hated to pay for it, and the infrequency with which he did it had long ago set the lawn on the path of dereliction, so that his reluctance to mow was complicated by guilt, which only made him stall further. Even after resolving to mow, he found much to derail him. There was, for a start, the disgraceful condition of his mower, with its deathbed repertoire of labored drones, its concealed set of loose-nut maracas, its juddering blade, and its dried algal scum of the dead sod of ages gone by. Add the clumsy lashing motion required to yank-start

the engine and the geriatric gasping unleashed . . . and, once the mowing began, the law of contrasts by which a shave for the lawn cast in
glaring relief the shagginess of the flowers and shrubs. At least there
were few witnesses. The generic children of his nearby neighbors
must all still be in school. No scuffed plastic Big Wheels or tasseled tri-
cycles or banana-seat training-wheeled bikes were being pedaled in
driveways. The elaborate cedar play fortress of his right-hand neighbor was abandoned, its turrets and drawbridges noiselessly soaking
up sun. At the moment no paired female walkers were huffing past,
with pert ponytailed hair and clenched fists. Lee sometimes was shown
the raised hand or quick smile of the walker whose habit it was to
greet all human beings this way. He didn't know names, nor did he
give much thought to these reflexive acknowledgments. They were
just part of the life of a smallish American town.

As he finished the very thin strip to the left of his driveway—
which he always did first for the quick, easy sense of accomplishment—the lone howl of his mower was joined by another commotion.
His across-the-street neighbor's small house, the same model as his—
just a little too much for an old man entirely alone and just barely
enough for a couple with a toddler and baby—briefly quaked, then
erupted, some restraint overcome. The resident toddler rushed out the
front door, shrieking and naked except for a diaper, and disappeared
around the side of the house with the mother and a hip-riding baby in
awkward pursuit. Lee did not know the name of the toddler or even its
sex, but now that he thought about it, plodding with his slight weight
pressed forward against the machine, he recalled that for the past several weeks there was scarcely a day this scene wasn't enacted. The
child must have just learned to walk, or to open the front door, or both.
What would that be—fourteen months? That was the age Esther had
been when she'd worn her first shoes. The three of them had lived on
Sawyer Street then, in a part of town now entirely different, for one
thing entirely black. Lee hadn't been there in years, not even to trawl
the now-broken streets for his best memories. But Sawyer Street existed without flaw in his mind: their very first house, their beachhead
as a new family. He and Aileen had been married four years, he'd had
his doctorate for one, Esther was going on one and a half. They'd had
a little metal stroller for Esther that compared with the strollers of

today was as crude as a Ford Model T, but Lee had approved of its un-gainly weight—perhaps because he was pushing a rolling thing now, leaned at such a sharp angle for progress that he might appear to be walking into a stiff wind, this recollection of pushing Esther overtook him completely. It fell onto him like a cloak, and now the breeze on his bare arms was balmy and sweet, and the sun had dropped off the ze-nith and blunted its rays—it was early morning—and his brown hands were wrapped confidently around the twin rubber handles, and he saw his smooth knees and his tan, slender shins and the toes of his leather sandals, always almost stubbed on the stroller's big wheels—with Esther he also leaned forward, pushed the thing with his body aslant to avoid this annoyance. A posture he dimly realized was in some way female—all the strollers were misdesigned in this way, though at the time no one called it a flaw, it was how strollers were, the handles rising straight from the rear wheels so that you had to lean forward to not stub your toes, and this was the profile of all the neigh-borhood's women and it was also Lee's profile, and he didn't mind this self-feminization, in fact he secretly liked it. Esther sitting very erect in her low-riding seat, often banging the palm of one hand on the metal restraint bar as if urging a horse to speed up. This gesture was very peremptory; it allowed of no doubt that the order would be promptly obeyed. And Lee always had his gaze trained on the crown of her head, on her very dark yet also wonderfully soft, wispy hair, which curled outward in all directions, in contradictory wavelets. Aileen's hair was wavy that way but entirely different in color, a very pale brown, while Lee's hair was typically Asian, the color of Esther's but straight as a broom, so that Esther's was a miracle blending of Lee and Aileen.

"It's not so astounding," Aileen once remarked. "All babies have very soft hair. Yours was probably like that." In other words, Esther's hair was like Lee's, and Aileen had no part in it. Why had she said this? And with the slight emphasis on *all* babies—which carried a meaning Lee chose to ignore.

Lee pushed harder, surged more powerfully through his forearms, and as if in response to the increase in speed, Esther raised an arm over her head. "Ya ya ya!" Esther yelled.

The asphalt was smooth, the street recent, all the aluminum-clad little houses proudly tended, still new. In this scene Lee is, as in every scene of his life prior and subsequent, a novelty, but the novelty of his novelty here is how well people like him. They might see him as an anomaly, a suburban Yul Brynner this time with his vague provenance and his careful English, but they also see a devoted father, and they embrace him. Both the women and men, though he sees women more. Lee is the most junior faculty member, the most recent hire, but nevertheless he's asked for a light load this semester, which means he's at home all day Tuesday and Thursday and home by three Monday, Wednesday, and Friday, while Aileen works from nine until five every day at the library. Either Lee picks up Esther from day care or Lee himself *is* day care, all day long, and this is one of those days, because they're having their walk in the morning. Encountering other mothers and children, all of whose names Lee knows, just as they all know his. He talks easily with these women, makes spontaneous plans, turns the stroller off its usual route to accompany Marge Morris and Mikey, Judy Krauss and Samantha and Wendy, to the school playground. His and Aileen's neighbors: the Boltons, the Strapinskis, the Yelvertons, the Tuttles, the Mieks. There are photographs, of baby birthday parties and joint barbecues, of the black Weber dome on its tripod, of the parched-looking grass and the failing saplings, overtethered with fat ropes and stakes as if they might burst their bonds and escape. No one on Sawyer Street has pretentious ideas about landscaping. Their fences are practical chain-link, with squeaky gates with squeaky horseshoe-shaped latches. Lee wears madras-print shorts, his hair long in the front, so it's almost obscuring his eyes. Big Beth Strapinski has the complexion of a ham and a stiff blond bouffant; all the various children have mouths gleefully stretched to show off sticky beards of ice cream. In these pictures Esther is a dazzling baby, brown as a nut in her puffy white diaper and sturdy white shoes. Unless it's actually cold, she can't stand to wear anything else. Lee, in his own clothing so modest as to risk being priggish, is delighted by Esther's barbaric disdain for wardrobe. Esther's perfect happiness at this age is confirmed on all sides: she sleeps soundly, eats like a wolf, and now walks on small, powerful legs. She isn't yet old enough to perceive the crosscurrents of tension, even of misery, that are already warping the walls of the Sawyer Street house. And maybe Lee isn't old enough either, though he's older than all of his neighbors by a decade or more: the father of a toddler, his first child, and he's already forty! Yet he feels fantastically young—or is it that for the first time in life he feels optimistic? One example: that Gaither and Ruth have absconded with John is to Lee not just apt, but a miracle. An as-good-as-divine intervention—to tip the hat to Gaither— and from the least likely source. Even before it had happened, Lee had tried to make clear to Aileen that their future had no room for John. He'd never said he would leave if Aileen pursued getting John back, but only because such a threat didn't seem necessary. To Lee, John was less than irrelevant, an unpleasant loose end from their tangled-up past that had been—*miraculously*—tied off.

Aileen generally said very little in these conversations. Lee felt she agreed; that she suffered some guilt over John needlessly, but that at her core she agreed.

It also went without saying that Lee wanted a son of his own, but when Esther was born, this desire for a son was forgotten. Esther, banging her palm on her stroller again—faster, faster! And Lee hurrying up in his gladness—

He yelped at a terrible noise, something violently hacked, as the handle leaped out of his hands. There was a double instant, Esther's small, compact weight torn from him. He was practically fainting on top of the mower, the blade fearsomely gnashing, but he'd only run over a branch.

Once the mower had been turned off and upended and the blade's path was clear, he was a long time stooped over the starter cord again without rousing the engine. It was almost as hot as a midsummer day. The hair at his temples was glued to his head, and his eyes stung where sweat rivulets reached them from his forehead. It was strange how the salt of sweat stung, while the salt of tears soothed. Or were these stinging tears? Was he crying?

Finally the mower was chugging again. Lee stood still at its helm a moment, rededicating his mind to the project. He felt a strange misery, very much like remorse, as if in running over the branch he had injured someone.

He started mowing again carefully, gazing down at his work. The resolute mower devoured; he heard the spray of cut grass in the bag. He wanted to reconjure Esther. He traced a shrinking rectangular spiral, at the same time retracing his thoughts. . . . Not long after Esther turned four, they had left Sawyer Street, at Lee's insistence. A new family had moved onto their block, with two girls seven and nine, and a shrill, angry dog Lee immediately hated that strained at a rope in the yard, snapping threateningly. Lee had forbidden Esther to play with those girls in their yard, let alone in their house, but the girls were like sirens to her: both very pale, dingily blond, with something slack and perhaps even mean in their otherwise vacuous eyes. They did strange things that Esther, wide-eyed, not yet capable of the least secretiveness, struggled to describe to her parents: they lit stalks of dried grass and pretended to smoke; they got under the covers together and pantomimed rough grunts and gasps. Lee had gone over to the house to speak sharply to the parents and found bedsheets tacked up for curtains, water glasses for ashtrays; a week later Esther, again disobeying, trotted hopefully into the yard in a little smocked halter and shorts and was knocked to the ground by the dog, somehow freed from its rope. The dog sank its teeth into her stomach, was kicked away like a football by Mr. Strapinski, just then passing by; the emergency room, rabies shots, and Lee storming the bedsheet-curtained house, screaming that he would carve up the dog with a cleaver. Then there had been no question but that Lee was on the side of righteousness. Mieks, Strapinski, and Yelverton had held him back as a show of solidarity with him, not to spare dog and owners. And from then on, the dog's family had been shunned by the whole neighborhood, the girls subtly and not-so-subtly excluded from neighborhood play.

Of course, Lee had had other reasons, other nascent dissatisfactions—the good but not excellent school—along with the imprecise sense that it was time for something bigger. But Aileen had accused him of reacting exclusively, and excessively, to the attack by the dog. "We have so many friends here," she wailed. "It's just a fucking dog!"

"You want to stay and let your daughter be bitten by dogs?"

"I don't *want* that. For Christ's sake! But there's things we can do besides *move*. All because of a dog!"

"The welfare of a child," Lee seethed, "is more important than anything else."

"I guess that depends on which child it is," Aileen said.

It also had to be admitted—with no small amount of irony, considering the jaundiced view Lee now took of the American suburb—that something in Lee had badly wanted not just a house of his own but a house built for *him;* not just a full kitchen but *his* choice of "avocado" or "chocolate" appliances; *his* choice of genuine wood floors or wall-to-wall shag; his choice of pedestal sink, of linoleum, of exterior brick, or of shingle; his 1.3 acres of churned clumps of dirt he would seed by himself, so that Esther could squeal when the blades first emerged, like a delicate aura of green. Three full bedrooms: one for Lee and Aileen, one for Esther, and one for Lee's desk, which on Sawyer had taken up half the front room—but there were also a den and a parlor, and Lee's desk could migrate to either location, he allowed, since he now had an office at school. It could migrate to either location whenever they felt that they might need that bedroom for some other reason.

Perhaps it had been Lee's failing that as he planted poplars at the property line, a dogwood and maple in front, Douglas fir at the sides, all the while fretting over his grass, feeding it fertilizer and watering it and despairing to see its thinness, its bald spots, its great delicacy like so many precise green brushstrokes—all the other homeowners had laid rolls of sod; *God, please make my grass grow!* he had moaned— perhaps it had been his failing that while doing these things he had never confessed to Aileen that the thought of a second child, just as much as the joy of the first, was what moved him. That the role of *father* was what made him a manic landscaper. Whether it was Lee's generalized Asianness or his particular prudishness or the long-standing glaciation of sex with Aileen, Lee couldn't help feeling that to discuss a second child, to "plan" for it, was to introduce something like agricultural method into the most—perhaps the only—sacred sphere of his life. A child wasn't schemed for or attempted—a child was bestowed. A child was the world's only magic, its only half-reasonable argument for the existence of God—Lee found himself thinking such outsize, out-of-character things while he watched Esther play, when he walked with her slim hand in his, when he tucked her in bed—yet somehow these thoughts never touched on the one other child that had impinged on his life, if briefly.

He was full of a wild optimism, a rising of sap—his grass did grow in, and because it was seed grass, it was that much more lush, a hand-knotted silk carpet to the other yards' department-store shag. "As thick as your hair," he told Esther, his palm on her shiny dark head—to celebrate they went and bought a lawn mower, glossy green with black licorice wheels, the same rusted and gasping contraption Lee now extinguished, his mowing complete.

15.

LEE WANTED TO FIND THAT THERE WAS SOMETHING even worse—more unnatural, more perverse—about the campus in its post-grieving phase, and the officially sanctioned romance with everyday campus life that was the next phase of the well-staged Grief Plan. And yet he was forced to admit that he too was glad to have his feelings directed, and to in essence be let off the hook. At clearly astronomical expense, the administration had printed up posters that read A NORMAL DAY IS OKAY, each reiteration of this placid idea underscored by a full-color photo: of students in a classroom, their eyes fixed on the chalkboard; of students walking the paths of West Lawn; of students playing Frisbee and jogging; of students slumped at study tables in the library, a few even blithely asleep. A NORMAL DAY IS OKAY, a pert, blond, Emma Stilesesque girl informed Lee from the door to his classroom when he arrived for his usual advanced calculus class that Wednesday, and though Lee, before he could stop himself, yanked down the poster and rolled it into a tube, he was already realizing that the message liberated him, too. He taught class, to a group short by only three students, and A NORMAL DAY IS OKAY seemed to hang in the air like a blessing, as if the nonutterance of Hendley's name in the building where he had been killed was not an oversight or an out-and-out crime but a rare act of courage. Apart from this quiet subtext, it did feel, strangely enough, like a regular day.

He had avoided the department office on his way to class, and he avoided it again on the way from class to his own office, thinking mainly of Sondra—and so absorbed by his unpleasant recollection of their last conversation that it was not until he'd unlocked his office door and shut himself inside that he realized it was the first time he'd been there since paramedics had carried him out on the day of the bombing. Had he walked the few feet farther down the hallway, he would have seen that Hendley's nameplate, with his name and office hours in English and braille, had been removed; the Grief Memo had tactfully warned that this change was impending. The office was slated to be fully renovated during summer vacation, though it was not likely to be occupied for a very long time. For now it was locked. Lee locked his door also, then thought better of it and reopened it, carefully cracking it one or two inches. But after this was done, he found he couldn't concentrate on anything; the slightest sound, from the far end of the hallway, pricked his ears as if he were a dog. And there was something wrong with every facet of his office to which he gave his attention. His books were disarranged. He remembered the bookcases rippling, and a few scattered tomes raining down, but now as he examined the spines from his chair, it appeared all the books must have fallen, then been reshelved randomly, he supposed by the janitorial staff. Normally Lee didn't like them to come into his office. *A normal day.* But Sondra had a key, and he was aware that every couple of months she let the janitors in for stealth dusting and mopping, while forbidding them, as his faithful proxy, to lay a hand on his papers.

Lee yanked open his desk drawers. Here things also seemed strangely churned up. His own organizational method was haphazard, but it was *his* haphazardness. He no longer discerned it.

He tossed aside the journal he'd been riffling and strode out of his office again. Of course his office must have been quietly cleaned, and ineptly restored to someone else's idea of the way it had been, prior to the disaster. Lee was less interested in reprimanding Sondra for overseeing this intrusion, as she must have, than in using the intrusion as his excuse to speak to her and so escape from the weird atmosphere that surrounded his desk. On normal days Sondra arranged cubes of Entenmann's coffee cake, or miniature powdered doughnuts, or no-brand pink-and-white sandwich cookies—the leavings of colloquia or her own home pantry—on a plate beside the coffee samovar in the department office, and though normally Lee avoided this watering hole, today he craved it. He would eat whatever stale thing she offered. Coming into the office, he saw Sondra and Jeanette, the lion-maned, overlipsticked, alphabetically challenged assistant administrator, and Susan Bloodhorn, an assistant adjunct professor of computer science so recently hired that Lee had never even sat on a committee with her, and a professor of statistics named George Marcus tightly huddled with their four heads together, not at the cookie plate, which was empty, but around Sondra's desk. As Lee entered, they sprang apart and stared at him.

"What?" Lee said.

Marcus was the first to move. "So I'll bring back the copy card when I'm done with it," he said loudly. "Thanks, Sondra. Lee," he acknowledged, with a nod, quickly leaving the office.

Jeanette was following him. "I'm going to the Coke machine," she bellowed. "Sondra? You want a Coke?"

Sondra's gaze was locked, somewhat helplessly, with Lee's.

"What?" Lee repeated.

"Coke? Sondra? Diet Coke? They've got Mountain Dew." Finally Jeanette left, hunched over a palmful of spare change and counting suspensefully. "I think I've got eighty-five," she called. "I'm sure I had a quarter! Oh, shoot."

Only Susan Bloodhorn, a tomboyish woman always seemingly dressed to go camping, had greeted Lee's arrival with no particular explosion of activity. But she was gazing at him as if he were a distant vista, something she had finally attained after a long, grueling hike.

"What?" Lee said. "Sondra?"

"I've got a quarter," Susan Bloodhorn said suddenly, leaving also.

When they were alone, Sondra said, "How was class?" as if there had been nothing strange about the abrupt exodus, but Lee saw unease and even something like misery in her expression.

"It was fine," he said after a moment. "A normal day is okay. But what's wrong? What's the matter with everyone?"

"People are just keyed up."

"Has something new happened?"

"Not really."

Lee gazed at her; she gazed back. Awkwardly, as if he were the single blind person on the entire campus who needed office nameplates to be printed in braille, he felt his way to the samovar and waggled the lever, belatedly remembering to rush a cup under the spigot. But nothing came out.

"Sorry," Sondra said. "Haven't had time today."

"That's okay." Had he been a paler man, she would have seen he was blushing, and this made him blush more. It was his absence from

the memorial service, he understood now—that on top of his failure
to ever show up at the hospital. Sondra, in her dumb loyalty, her ec-
static prostration before professors like Hendley—who'd had not
merely a full intellectual life but a lover, while Sondra had nothing,
just Hendley, his reflected glory, and his secondhand Xeroxing
needs—Sondra was shocked and disappointed with Lee, who might
have been all she had left, but she was done with him now. He was
heartless, a traitor.

He retreated to his office, feeling Sondra's strange gaze on his back.

He sat there a few minutes, intensely disliking his sense of a foreign disorder and staring into space as a way to avoid staring at concrete things, all of which, the more he thought about it, seemed to
have been picked up and set down again a few inches from where they
had been. He was remotely aware of the lengthening shadows from
the light slanting in through his blinds; at least this was the same.
There were still hours and hours of daylight, but his office window
was shadowed by the neighboring building such that any hour
after two felt like dusk. He could hear the calls of students playing
some elaborate game, maybe Ultimate Frisbee, out of sight on the
lawn. When the knock came, he cried out "Come in!" expecting someone from that day's advanced calculus, but it was Sondra. He felt a
surge of gratitude, as he sometimes did when Sondra rescued him
at the copier or surreptitiously moved the worst students to Kalotay's
section of trig. His taking of Sondra for granted was a constant, but
then so was the potential for moments like this, at which he could
repent.

"Hi," he said with emotion. "I didn't want coffee, Sondra. It's good
you hadn't made it. I'm supposed to have quit everything with caffeine."

Sondra gazed at him searchingly. The sadness that was always
implicit in her—the sadness of the heavyset, unmarried, childless,
middle-aged woman, the career secretary, the unthanked nurturer of
cats and plants and professors—seemed predominant now. "Lee," she
said. "I wanted to talk to you. Just you and me."

"Of course, Sondra. We're talking. Please, sit in the chair."

Instead she'd taken the back of the chair in both hands and kept
standing. "It's so weird," she resumed finally, with an obvious effort.
"There's these FBI people."

"Agent Morrison," Lee supplied. "He seems excellent."

"You've been talking to him?"

"Of course." Lee was glad for this chance to show Sondra that he, too, was involved in the effort to find Hendley's killer—it should more than make up for his absence from hospital and memorial. It also crossed his mind that she might not be angry at all; she might not even realize he'd skipped the memorial. The whole school had been there. Who would notice that he had been absent? "All of us have to tell him as much as we can. He needs to know about mail. Hasn't he talked to you?"

"I talked to a woman. Somebody he works with. But, Lee, it isn't just mail they've been asking about."

"I'm sure you talked to Agent Shenkman. So what else did they ask? Sondra, I wish you'd sit down."

She wasn't quite addressing his question when she said, with an air of confession, "Last week Peter gave them access to our files. Peter says that they told him they're looking for . . . maybe a student whose app we rejected or that flunked Hendley's class—"

"The lowest grade Hendley ever gave was A-minus," Lee pointed out.

"—but they also got minutes. Of department meetings. Like the ones about Kalotay's tenure—"

"Why would they care about that?"

"—and they've been asking about it," she persisted. "Asking people to try and remember if there was any . . . dispute, any really hard feelings—"

He was reminded again of her dramatic idea that he and Hendley had once "butted heads." "I've never known a tenure decision that wasn't divisive," he said, a bit testily.

"One thing everybody remembers is you and Hendley at each other's throats."

"What?" Lee said. "Now we were at each other's *throats*?"

"Well, you were. You were really in conflict."

"Everyone in this department argues!"

"Lee, all I'm trying to say is . . ." But she seemed to have misplaced that singular thing she had wanted to tell him. She turned her face toward his bookshelves, as if the thing had slipped between those spines. Lee was trying to remember, in detail, the fight over Kalotay's tenure, only the most recent in a series of similar squabbles in which he'd been forced to take part. He and Hendley had disagreed, sharply, but once the battle was over—Lee accepting defeat—by the gentlemanly protocols that to some extent still ruled their field, it had all been forgotten. Lee had once again listened to Hendley's long, smug monologues at the Thursday colloquia. Hendley had once again carelessly waved as he passed by Lee's door.

By that circular route—Hendley's ghost passing Lee's door—Lee was reminded of the irritating disarrangement of his office by the cleaning crew. And for nothing, he confirmed, gazing down at the dust and gray hairs evident on his floor. His office was just as dirty as it usually was. "Sondra," he said, breaking into her reverie, "I know you're just trying to help, but I wish you would tell me before you let the cleaning crew in. They've messed up my papers, and the office is not even clean."

"I didn't let in the cleaners. I haven't done that in years. I got tired of you yelling at me."

"I've never yelled at you," Lee protested.

But now she'd somehow recalled her objective. "Lee, all I want to say is—is it true you weren't at the memorial?" She didn't wait for his answer—his face must have told her. "You know, all of us in the department, we all sat together. And no one could find you."

"I was feeling sick," Lee began.

"Of course you were, and of course you should, it's just that . . . it didn't look right. And after you were on TV, speaking so well. And then not at the service at all. And these FBI people are asking about the department, and sometimes they just ask about you. And everybody remembers those fights you and Hendley would have—"

"Sondra, that is really ridiculous!" Lee shouted, banging his fist on his desk without quite meaning to, so that Sondra abruptly turned red—and Lee could feel flames in his own face and over his scalp. For a frightening instant, he thought Sondra might cry. But the flush of her face didn't melt into tears, as it usually would.

"Lee, last week when I asked you to go to the grief counselor, you said something to me. You were very upset, and you said something I thought was so strange. You said, 'I'm the last person you ought to be nice to,' or something like that. Why did you say that, Lee? What did you mean?"

He had no memory of the disordered comments he might have made on that day and felt almost insulted that she did—was she taking shorthand on every word that came out of his mouth? "How the hell should I know? I was very tired and upset then, and I'm very tired and upset now!"

Sondra's lips flattened into a line, perhaps to control their trembling. "All I meant to say was, sometimes you don't make the ideal impression. You should have gone to Ricky's memorial—"

"Sondra, leave me alone!" he burst out, and as she turned away, slamming his door, he remembered to shout, "And don't let the goddamn cleaning crew in my office again!"

At home that afternoon, every object seemed to have struck up a posture of combat. The lunch meat in his fridge was rancid. He had used up his tea. He stubbed an untrimmed toe on the leg of a dining-room chair, and the yellowed nail tore; he swore from the pain and knocked everything out of his medicine cabinet while his hands agitatedly groped for the toenail clipper. Upstairs in his study—where he hoped to rise above hunger and thirst, above toenail pain, and most of all above his recollection of what Sondra had said—something was terribly wrong with his desk. The same malevolent interference he had sensed in his office also seemed present here. The whole room was so spare, and the desk's surface so bare, that a stranger might think no attention had ever been paid to the relative sites of the very few objects involved. But to the person who maintained that desk as a Buddhist priest maintains an altar, one slight alteration could have an enormous effect. Lee sat gripping the arms of his chair and bending a furious gaze on the objects he cherished, as if they'd betrayed him. The picture of Esther in the faux-stained-glass frame, the disintegrating papier-mâché dish for spare change and candy. Had they moved? Traded places? He abruptly yanked open his right-hand desk drawer, as if the disordering poltergeist might be caught in the act—but Esther's scuffed baby shoe was still there, in the drawer that was otherwise empty.

Only in the heat of his quarrel with Sondra had he forgotten her claim that she'd never let in the cleaners. Once back in his car driving home, he'd remembered this clearly, and even though he was furious with her for her irrational, hurtful remarks, which made the less sense the more closely he tried to dissect them, he still couldn't find any reason to think she'd been lying. And even if she had brought in cleaners, and lied to his face, she wouldn't also bring them to his home.

Nor pick up his garbage, before that of anyone else on his block.

A cracked laugh escaped him, of fear and contempt—contempt not just for the notion that had formed in his mind but for his *mind*, which he once had so cherished and which now was as senseless as Sondra's, for being able to form such contemptible notions at all.

He'd imagined that someone was spying on him.

In the same spastic manner in which he'd opened his desk drawer, he now twisted to look at his carpet, as if, like fresh snow, it might show the intruder's footprint. It showed him nothing but the faint gray path of his own travel, through several years of indifference to carpet shampoo, between his desk chair and the door. Even so, he pushed back the chair and retraced his habitual route out of the study, across the landing, down the stairs to just inside his front door, where he was standing, unsure of what he sought, when the now-familiar car of Agents Morrison and Shenkman pulled up.

"Lee," Morrison acknowledged in his genial way when Lee opened the door. "You remember my colleague, Special Agent Shenkman? Is this a good time for you? Would you mind if we came in a minute?"

"Please," Lee said as he moved to make way for them, almost falling backward off the short step at which his "foyer," really just an interior ledge for a welcome mat, turned into his living room. He was a mathematician, he reminded himself. He attached no mystique to coincidence. And yet the coincidence of his ludicrous thought with the agents' arrival had robbed him of whatever composure he might have called up. If he was right, he was childishly scared, if wrong, deeply embarrassed, despite the fact that the ludicrous thought went unspoken. He couldn't possibly say to the man he'd been told to call Jim, "Are you spying on me?"

"Whoa!" Morrison said with a laugh, reaching out for Lee's elbow. "Take it easy there, Lee. Did you turn your ankle?" Shenkman closed the door behind them, pulled a file from her bag, and without waiting strode past Lee toward his kitchen, as if toward her own office.

Soon they were seated around his kitchen table again, although this time Lee didn't make tea. His consciousness of something wrong—particularly, inexplicably wrong, in their eyes, with him—warred bewilderingly with his consciousness that *he* might be wrong, ridiculously mistaken, no better than a paranoid patient in a mental asylum. In this state of internal division, he could no more meet their eyes than perform hostly gestures. He could barely sit still. But Morrison was as cheerfully calm as he'd been when he came to see Lee on his own, while Shenkman was as cold and withdrawn as the first time Lee had met her.

"Lee, I'm glad you were home, because I think we can straighten this out very quickly," Morrison had begun. "Remember when you and I were talking just the other day, we went over that letter. That letter that says it's from 14 Maple Lane in Woodmont, Washington."

The interior battle had been decided; he was not deluded, which perhaps was a comfort. But he was mortifyingly foolish. Lee cursed his vanity, his exquisitely bruisable ego—it had landed him where he would otherwise never have been. "Agent," he interrupted Morrison, and he deliberately chose not to be familiar, not to use "Jim," to signal that if he'd proceeded in a fuzzy way before—if he'd committed the sin of omission—he would not any longer. "I think I know what this confusion is about. I want to tell you something more about that letter. I didn't tell you about it before, because I honestly thought it would not interest you, and also, it embarrasses me. But I should have told you everything, to prevent this confusion."

Now even Shenkman had set down her magical phone.

"Go on," Morrison said.

"I told you before that my friend must have made a mistake when he wrote his address. But the truth is, I don't think he made a mistake at all. I think he wrote a false address on purpose, so that I couldn't find him. Because the truth is also that this person, Lewis Gaither, is not my friend. He would probably tell you that I am his worst enemy. We were friends long ago. That I said, and that's true. But our friendship had a very bad ending. And I think . . . well, he would have every reason to despise me, and I don't care for him. So I think he wrote that fake address to taunt me. I know this must sound ridiculous, an old grudge between very old men. I hope you can see why I didn't go into the whole thing before." Even in his limited experience with Shenkman, Lee knew better than to search for a lifting of clouds, a frank smile of relief, in her face. Instead he focused on Morrison—but the other man seemed only to be carefully taking in what had been said.

"So this individual, the person who wrote you this letter, he considers you an enemy. He intensely dislikes you. Is that what you're saying, Professor?"

Lee noticed that Morrison, too, had returned to a more formal mode of address. "Yes," he answered.

"Can you explain why that is?"

Now his desire to have it all straightened out, which already was daring to feel like relief, came up short against an upsurge of loathing, that he had to disclose such an intimate thing to these strangers. Especially Shenkman. But he girded himself and, hoping it would suffice, said at last, "It was over a woman."

Morrison seemed to weigh, for a moment, whether this would suffice or not. Then he said, "Of course, it wouldn't be possible for us to look at the letter. You've thrown it away."

"No," Lee said, feeling real relief here—this small misjudgment could be cleared up, too. "No, I didn't, in fact. I was just feeling embarrassed that you would see that this man is not actually friendly to me. I didn't want to go into these personal things. But I shouldn't have caused this confusion and wasted your time. I know you have to confirm all these pieces of mail. I'll just get it for you." And lighter already from the purgative of his confession, Lee sprang up to retrieve his briefcase and the letter within, while the two agents waited in silence. It was interesting, Lee thought, how the act of handing the dread correspondence to Morrison seemed to transmute it into something else—it was leached free of its sad history, folded into a bland inventory of envelopes mailed and received, so that Lee could almost forget that Gaither ever had touched it. He should have given it to the two agents the first time they asked.

Morrison took the envelope by its edges and, seeming scarcely to touch it, extracted the single sheet, gingerly unfolded, and regarded the typewritten contents. His face had grown strangely opaque. Lee watched Morrison's eyes linger over *Dear Lee;* he urged the agent on the unpleasant journey to *a bracing reminder to one of his peers as to how many years of his own life have passed.* Without another glance at the writing himself, Lee could easily accompany the agent, through the haughty understatement of *I can admit that you bruised me, that last time we met;* past the fraudulent camaraderie of *I am not a sentimental man—nor are you, I've long assumed and admired.* By the time they had finally reached *Now you are probably angry with me, as I once was with you,* Lee was mentally dragging the laggardly agent toward the blessed conclusion of the illegible bramble that passed as a signature. All his mortification and fury, all the pains he had suffered since Gaither had sent him this dart threatened to reemerge, but he held strong against them by riveting his attention on Morrison's face. Morrison, for his part, was still riveted to the letter. Abruptly he refolded it and, without returning it to the envelope, handed both pieces of paper to Shenkman, who dropped them into a clear plastic bag, stood up from the table, and walked out of the room—the entire transaction seemed contained between serial beats of Lee's heart. Lee heard his front door being opened and shut. "You're keeping it?" he belatedly said.

"Lee," Morrison said, looking up at him again, and instead of the warmth Lee expected, as thanks for his clarifications, Morrison's face had grown yet more opaque and a little bit harder, like wax that had cooled. "There's nothing on that sheet of paper that tells me a man named Lewis Gaither, spelling 'Lewis' E-W and 'Gaither' A-I, is the author. That signature at the bottom could say anything. Why should I believe that this letter is from Lewis Gaither?"

"Why should you believe it?" For all the brevity of their acquaintanceship and all the formality of the past several minutes, Lee felt as ambushed and stung as he'd felt with Sondra. "Why wouldn't you believe it? It's my letter. I'm telling you who it comes from. I can't help that he has bad handwriting."

"You're telling me," Morrison mused. "You're telling me, and I should believe you, and last week you told me you'd thrown it away, and you still had it in your briefcase."

"Jim," Lee said, in his rising confusion laying hold once again of the other man's name. "I'm very sorry I said that. I was just so embarrassed. It doesn't mean that I'm lying to you."

"You must see why it's hard to believe that. Lee, it's hard to believe that you're being completely forthcoming, when you've just changed your story since the last time we met."

"Changed my story?" Lee repeated, amazed. "But it's only a personal letter. It's just so you can dot all your i's and cross all your t's, as you said," and with a sideways glance in the direction in which Agent Shenkman had vanished, he tried to recapture his and Morrison's camaraderie of a few days before. "It's not important—"

"Lee," Morrison interrupted, "let's start over, all right? Let's do this all over again, as if this is the very first time that we've talked about it. Did you receive a letter with the return address on it of 14 Maple Lane, Woodmont, Washington?"

"Yes, you know that I did—"

"Starting all over, Lee. Turn back the clock. And were you aware that this address was false, that it doesn't exist?"

"I realized it must be, after getting my letter—"

"And who sent you this letter?"

"Lewis Gaither—"

"Write it down," Morrison said, pushing a pen and his small notebook, turned to a blank page, across the table.

Lee did, in his careful block letters: L-E-W-I-S G-A-I-T-H-E-R. Morrison took back the notebook and scrutinized it with what looked like displeasure. "And who is this person?" Morrison recommended. "The other day you said he's an old friend, very worried about you. Then you said he's somebody you hardly know, you haven't seen him in years. Now you say he hates you, that you've had issues over a woman. So which is it?"

"Jim," Lee implored. "I'm not being dishonest. I just don't see why it's important—"

"Please let me decide what's important. Who is Lewis Gaither? What can you tell me about him?"

Agent Shenkman had still not returned. "He was my wife's husband," Lee managed. He felt his gorge rising—it was a panic reaction, he knew, but he was suddenly sure he would vomit. Morrison rose and took a glass from the cupboard, filled it at the tap, and set it near Lee on the table. Lee drank. "I stole his wife," Lee whispered, looking up gratefully. "We were friends. Then his wife left him for me."

"Where did you meet?"

"We were classmates. In graduate school."

After this they both sat in silence, as if by these very few words Lee had unfurled around them the full tapestry of his past. Lee felt certain he had. Sadness pierced him. His eyes had grown damp.

Lee did not know how many minutes had passed when Morrison finally spoke. "I'd really like to believe, at this point, that you're disclosing everything that there is to disclose, about this piece of mail."

"I am," Lee said passionately.

"But it's hard," Morrison continued, "given that, in effect, you've lied to us. About the nature of your relationship with this person, Lewis Gaither. About having disposed of the letter."

"I wasn't lying!" Lee cried, bewailing the inadvertent confusion he'd caused.

"Lee, you have to understand what it looks like to me. I really want to believe you."

"You should!"

"As far as Agent Shenkman is concerned, while I can't speak for her, I wouldn't be far off base if I said that she wouldn't be sorry to find that you're lying. But I would be. I like you, Lee, and I'd like to believe you."

"You both should believe me!" Lee was only remotely aware that his temples were streaming with sweat—his mind was cornered and panicked, as it had sometimes been in the worst of his fights with Aileen, when, after an originating spark he could never recall and a swift escalation he could hardly perceive, he found himself howling with her on a precipice, hearing that she would leave him and he declaring the same. He no longer knew how he'd gotten here or what sense it made, only that his survival relied on persuading this obdurate man. "I'm telling you the truth—"

"If that's the case, then would you like to take a polygraph?" Morrison said.

The howl in Lee's ears ebbed away, like the tide rushing out. He wasn't sure he had heard correctly. "A lie detector test?" he asked tentatively, afraid Morrison might burst out laughing.

But the other man's face showed no tending toward humor. "At this point, if you're disclosing everything, the polygraph can only serve you well."

"A lie-detector test implies the person being tested is suspect," Lee said after a moment. Despite being on the defensive, he spoke to Morrison admonishingly. He felt offended to his core. At the same time, he still was a prisoner of panic. The panic interfered with his indignation: it would soon deplete it.

"The test itself implies nothing. Only the results are meaningful. If you're telling me the truth, the polygraph shouldn't be any problem for you."

"It isn't," Lee heard himself saying. "Of course it's no problem."

"You consent?"

"If it will resolve this confusion, yes, of course," Lee said, with what he hoped was calm dignity, but as he rose from the table, he was aware he was trembling—he never had eaten lunch nor, for that matter, breakfast this morning, and he found himself, like a frightened child longing for bed, picturing the warm meal he would make for himself, then the bath he would take and the beer he would drink, and the sated, self-confident man he would be when the test, which he assumed would be scheduled, like a cholesterol test at the doctor's, was in some hazy future administered—

"If you'll follow us, then, unless you'd rather not bring your own car. But you're free to, of course." And with that the remote, swift-moving, palpably malcontent man who had only a few days before begged to just be called "Jim" was replacing his notebook and pen in his pocket and departing, while Lee stumbled half blind in his wake.

16.

FOLLOWING THE FAMILIAR SEDAN, HE HAD TO STRUGGLE to keep up when Agent Shenkman exceeded the speed limit, but even as his car plodded, his heart was a riot. He'd absorbed from somewhere that polygraphs measured heart rate and breathing, but he lacked all concrete sense of how that might work. Surely the accelerated heartbeat of a man in the grip of confusion and fear, if subjected to polygraph measurement, wouldn't point to that man as a liar? Most racing hearts, ardent or fearful, were entirely innocent hearts. The machine would know that, wouldn't it? By the time he was trying to follow the sedan into the parking lot of a Motel 6 he had never noticed at the intersection of old Route 19 with the interstate highway, Lee had difficulty turning the wheel with his petrified hands. Could the machine tell the wild pulse of terror apart from mendacity? Morrison waved him into a space, and then he was following the two agents through a tiny generic lobby, past tall plastic sentinel plants, down a dim, Windex-smelling hallway lined with black numbered doors.

He didn't notice the number of the door that swung open to Morrison's knock, and once shuffled into the cramped entry space between the room's closet and the door to its bathroom, he felt scarcely able to digest his surroundings, although at the same time he saw it was just a motel room, squalid in its stark, hygienic cheapness, its mustard-toned drapes drawn to shut out the sun, a suitcase frankly open trailing trousers and socks on the nearer of two made-up beds, and a sprouting apparatus on the other, seemingly just escaped from its box, probing the motel bedspread with a half dozen suction cups.

The chair to the small writing desk had been pulled out and ro-tated to face the farther bed, but apart from this innovation, and the presence of suitcase and machine, the room showed no traces of occu-pancy, as if they had all—Lee, Morrison, Shenkman, the pale balding man who had opened the door and who looked like an insurance ad-juster or an uncharismatic shoe salesman—tumbled into the room at that moment. The pale man might have been interrupted in changing his clothes after arduous travel. A pair of loafers were kicked off near the window. "Right now?" he inquired. He went padding to the ma-chine, in his socks, and bent down to heft it from the bed to the writ-ing desk. Tendrils trailed and were almost tripped over.

"Need a hand?" Morrison asked.

"No, no." Once the machine had been heaved onto the desk, the pale man stood with his back to them, disentangling its many extru-sions. "As discussed?" he asked over his shoulder.

"As discussed. Give a knock on the wall when you're finished. I'll be right next door."

"You're not staying?" Lee exclaimed, turning back toward the door. Morrison was departing; Agent Shenkman was already gone. "How will you know . . . How can I tell you I'm telling the truth—"

"Gerry knows what to ask. And I'll follow up, if necessary." Morrison closed the door.

Lee felt his heart bounding and shuddering. After they'd been alone for an agonizing moment, Gerry tweaking and tuning, Lee could not stop himself from asking, "Are you doing this to lots of people?"

"You should probably leave all the questions to me," Gerry said, although not unkindly.

Once Gerry had made his adjustments, he ushered Lee into the desk chair. "And untuck your shirt, please, and undo the buttons. . . ."

The machine had a sort of large bladder appendage that Gerry fitted around Lee's torso like an oversize blood-pressure cuff. With deft, impassive fingers, Gerry affixed suction cups, wire ends, indescribable chill antennae to Lee's skin with first-aid tape. The room was stuffy, but Lee felt himself goose-pimpling, his surface recoiling in fear and revulsion; the same defensive mental absence he employed whenever at the doctor's office tried to armor him now, but it was interfered with by rogue cogitations, almost all in the key of self-justification. He had misrepresented the letter from Gaither only to save Morrison time; why would Morrison want to meander through Lee's sordid past? And he'd pretended he'd thrown out the letter only to cover the fact that he'd misdescribed it; and once he had seen that it mattered, he'd told the whole truth. And, come to think of it, skipping Hendley's memorial didn't mean he was happy that Hendley was dead. He wasn't so self-dramatizing as to engage in hysterics like Sondra, but he was certainly sorry, and startled, and he condemned senseless murder— who didn't? He was an honest man, honest to a fault, in fact: witness his skipping the service because he just couldn't stomach the pageant. His perpetual crime was the failure to keep up appearances, to even notice the masks he'd do better to don; he should have gone to the service and wrung a few tears. Maybe he should have praised the "self-knowledge" that helped Esther drop out of college. Should have raised Aileen's son by Gaither and said things like, "You're no less my child than Esther!" He certainly should have hired professional landscapers to deal with his lawn, should have replaced the antiques Michiko took with cheap pieces from Macy's, should have learned, at the very least, how not to wear his every failing and humiliation embroidered and badged on his sleeve, and certainly shouldn't be sitting in a cheap motel room, sleeves pushed up as if donating blood, to allow the suspicious machine to encoil his arms. And yet he'd consented to do this precisely to keep up appearances, to show, with serene dignity, he had nothing to hide. Why then did he feel shamefaced and degraded already?

He thought again of the letter from Gaither, now surrendered to Morrison. Gaither was the only human being who had ever moved Lee to duplicity: witness not only Lee's affair with Aileen but his absurd fibs to Morrison three decades later, when he couldn't admit that Gaither's arrow had been dipped in hate. "An inquiring letter from a caring old friend": more like a sop to his own tender ego. And a rare veer from blunt honesty, although it was more honest to say he had spent his life not so much in pursuit of occasions for honesty as in wincing avoidance of lies that might get him in trouble. Perhaps it was the immigrant's sense of hopeless illegitimacy and impending exposure, but he probably would have been the same man had he never left home: less fastidious than loath to be faulted, even by people he didn't respect. The one time he'd been spurred to deceive, in pursuit of Aileen, he had still been a faltering liar, who had blushed, and felt burned by his secret, so that he fled Gaither's gaze. Another man might have used passion to lay claim to righteousness, but Lee had been ashamed of the passion as well, startled by its animal strength and its adverse relation to scholarship. He had given in to it as he imagined an addict must give in to a drug, and even after Gaither had married Ruth, and engineered custody of the child, and then snatched the child away, Lee had been hampered in his response by the sense that he'd stained his own character. Who was he, with his lust and poor discipline, to harp on another man's faults? It might have even been true that Lee's difficulty in condemning Gaither's acts was aggravated by Gaither's piousness, despite Lee's own stark atheism. Lee had mocked that piousness, but because he feared it, as any person who entertains doubts has to fear the undoubting. All of which meant that Lee was never able to muster quite as much solidarity with his new wife, against her old husband, as that new wife required. It was only once she had left him also that he became positively outraged, yet by then Gaither had been gone for years. There was nothing to do but hate him, aimlessly, to maintain dormant heat without planning to tap it—that wasn't required. His hatred of Gaither became a form of fidelity, to himself just as much as Aileen, and until the surprise of the letter this had been satisfying and in fact inexplicably peaceful.

"The test will take place in two parts," Gerry was explaining. "The first part isn't part of the actual test, it's preliminary, and I won't be recording responses. During this part I'll explain what my questions will be, and if you have any questions about them, you'll ask, so we both understand what we're talking about. The second part is the actual test. During this part your only response to my questions should be yes or no. For example, I'm going to ask you about a letter. I will say, for example, 'Did you receive a letter in your campus mailbox with a return address of 14 Maple Lane in Woodmont, Washington?' And you'll—"

"Yes," Lee broke in.

"—and you'll either say yes or no, depending on which is your answer. Or, for example, I'll say, 'Is your birth date March ninth, 1930? And you'll either say—"

"Yes," Lee repeated. He knew he should not be surprised that they had his birth date.

"Then I'll ask, 'Was the author of the letter from 14 Maple Lane an individual named Lewis Gaither?' And you'll either say yes . . ."

His train of thought about Gaither had absorbed him so deeply that despite its undiminished woundingness, its status as worst episode of his life, beside which the debacle with Michiko was a mere triviality, Lee experienced a sedative effect, as if he'd finally outflanked his emotions. For a moment he savored the sense of self-mastery and felt complacent and even slightly heroic in the machine's rubber clutches. He was doing his duty for justice. He was not merely seeking to prove he was honest. He was seeking to free Morrison, from the pointless distraction he himself had become. He was helping a good man fight evil, the one way he could.

"And now, if you understand fully, we're going to begin. I'll ask the questions I've already mentioned. Please only respond yes or no. Is your birth date March ninth, 1930?"

"Yes," Lee said. Somewhere a needle, delicate as a hair, traced a river of calm on a rotating roll of paper.

It was like this for the first several minutes: factual, straightforward statements Lee was not merely willing but surprisingly happy to affirm.

It was a relief, to feel himself verified by a machine. He eagerly confirmed his name, his position at the college, his whereabouts on the day of the bombing, the year of his emigration, the triumphantly dull history of his citizenship. His college routine was rehashed. Did he hold office hours for his students in the afternoon three days a week? Yes. Was one such afternoon the same day that the bomb had gone off? Yes. Did Lee feel lucky to have escaped injury, Gerry asked, in a sudden departure from the tone of the rest of the questions? The query seemed so spontaneous, so artlessly revealing of Gerry's own gladness that Lee hadn't been hurt, Lee felt the further surprise of tears filling his eyes.

"Yes," he said feelingly. "Yes."

The questions about the letter had been so rehearsed beforehand that when Gerry reached them, they were comfortingly catechistic. Lee felt the certitude, almost the joy, of repeating a credo. "Did you receive a letter addressed to yourself, with a return address of 14 Maple Lane, in Woodmont, Washington?"

"Yes."

"Was the author of this letter an acquaintance of yours named Lewis Gaither?"

"Yes."

"Is this the only such letter or communication you've received from this person in the past thirty years?"

"Yes."

"Do you know where this person resides currently?"

"No."

"Lee, please listen to this question very carefully. Have you ever been aware of terroristic or violent tendencies in this man, Lewis Gaither?"

Lee was just able to stop himself blurting out, "What?" Not only had this question not been rehearsed, it was completely fantastical— and yet it also conformed to Lee's most puerile ideas of Gaither. Since stealing Aileen, Lee had preferred to think of Gaither as an obsessed religious nut, the man who had stolen a child from its mother (so much worse than the theft of a wife!). Sometimes Lee was obliged to admit that Gaither had been a gentle enough proselytizer, at least while they were friends. But even this gentleness could take on a sinister character, with decades' retrospect. A wild idea, that Gaither had killed Hendley by accident, aiming for Lee, flashed past with a glitter of scales, and a hysterical disturbance escaped Lee, a shocked gasp of laughter. "No," he said, recovering himself. And then remembering the format of the test, he repeated even more firmly, "No."

He was startled by Gerry's crisp knock, on the wall against which the desk sat. "We're all finished, Professor," Gerry said. "If you can just lift your arms, I'll detach you."

"I did all right, didn't I?" Lee asked eagerly, knowing he must have. He felt entirely different than he had when he'd entered this room. Adrenaline had drained out of his limbs; he felt clean and reborn.

Before Gerry could answer, Morrison had returned, and Lee thought he saw mirrored in Morrison's face the same eager desire for clarity Lee also felt. "Was it as we discussed, Gerry?" Morrison asked. "You can leave him there, I'll finish unsticking him once I've done follow-up. I'll take over from here."

"Actually, I've had no problem," said Gerry, leaving off disentangling Lee. He reached over Lee's shoulder to tear off a tail of paper that hung from the machine. Lee craned around to look at it.

"I passed, didn't I?" Lee said. "You see, Jim?"

Both men had their backs to him now. "I don't have a problem with these charts at all," Lee heard Gerry remarking. "There's no evidence here of deception."

"You see, Jim," Lee exclaimed with relief, and so happy he started to laugh. "Can I . . . how do I undo these things—"

"Please go out to the lobby," said Morrison curtly as Gerry bent down to release him. "Please wait for me out in the lobby, Professor, if you'd be so kind." Lee had scarcely tucked his shirt into his pants when the door slammed behind him.

Returning down the hallway alone, he took a chair in the lobby, like a dentist's waiting room in its cramped size and cheap, ugly furnishings. He was so anxious for Morrison to return and perform absolution that the few minutes he waited seemed static and endless, but at last he saw the agent approaching him down the hallway and stood quickly to meet him.

"I passed, didn't I, Jim?" he repeated. The elation of just a few moments before had been swallowed again by anxiety. Too late he realized that the question itself might cast doubt on his honesty.

Morrison was regarding him not with the resumed friendliness Lee had hoped for, nor with the waxen remoteness of an hour before. He seemed wary, uneasily neutral.

"We don't actually say 'pass' or 'fail,' the way you might in school," Morrison said at last. "Your test showed no evidence of deception."

"And that means I passed," Lee persisted.

"No evidence of deception," Morrison repeated, and then put out his hand. The gesture held no renewed warmth; it was only cordial, the least gesture required for good-bye.

17.

DESPITE PASSING THE POLYGRAPH TEST—HE STUBBORNLY clung to that familiar, unambiguous verb—soon every glad feeling he'd had somehow dwindled away. He could feel he was avoided at school. The department was strangely deserted whenever he came to teach class, and while his students seemed mesmerized by him, none of them could respond to his questions. He told himself that this was normal, the way they fixed him with glittering stares, the same way he told himself it was only coincidence that Sondra managed not to be at her desk every morning at precisely that hour when, for all the years they'd worked together, Lee had faithfully come to greet her. The very night of the polygraph test, he had called her, hoping to mend things between them, but she'd hardly allowed him to speak. "This is a bad time," she'd interrupted. "This isn't a good time, okay? Let me call you back later."

"I just wanted—"

"It's not a good time! Let me call you back later." But she hadn't called back, and so Lee stood unhappily in the departmental office each morning, amid silence that was disturbed only by the coffee urn's comfortable gurgle, as if it were boasting of having been tended by Sondra just moments before she had vanished.

The contrary torment of the polygraph test was that while it had blessed Lee and sent him away, he couldn't boast of the test's affirmation to anyone else. He could never reveal that the FBI agents had asked him to do such a thing. An inexplicable sensation of shame had attached itself to the very process that was supposed to have proved his virtue. And, even more strange and frustrating, the one person in whose estimation Lee could assume he'd been raised by the polygraph's verdict was the same person from whom the verdict now seemed to have severed him. Now that Lee had been proved "not deceptive," Agent Morrison had no more reason to spend time with him and had brusquely dismissed him.

So he was feeling uneasy and anxious, and unthinkingly sprang for the phone when it rang—and then was delighted to realize that it was Fasano. "I've just read it," Fasano began, without any preamble, as if the conversation they'd ended the previous week had sustained only a brief pause. "Time difference, out-of-the-loopness, whatever. I didn't have the faintest idea until a colleague here called me, and then it was the goddamn 1849 gold rush to get my own copy. I had to drive to Venice Beach. They sleep late there, I guess. What did you think? Murderous jerk has the world on a string—they ought to get me to write the headlines. Lee? What did you think?"

"About what?" Lee managed, groping behind him, while uncurling the telephone cord to its limit, to locate the teapot. He hadn't slept well the previous night, or the night before that—or any of the nights since his polygraph triumph had started to curdle.

Fasano was sputtering, asking and answering in the same breath. "About *wha*— The manifesto, our guy's manifesto! 'The Technology Class and the Fate of the Earth' or some shit— 'Cut the rotten parts out of the flesh'? 'Sentimental fixation on lives at the expense of all life'? 'Innovation is regress, not progress'? 'Collaboration of the ignorant masses in their own enslavement by the techno-elite'?"

"Where does this come from?" said Lee, stopping short in his search for the teapot. Since his boyhood he'd abhorred every species of fist-shaking speech. But the zeal of these words filled him less with his lifelong disdain than with a sense of foreboding.

"From our tall-poppy hater," Fasano was saying. "From whoever took Illich's fingers and your guy Hendley's life."

Of course Fasano had heard without Lee's telling him; it had been in the papers. Lee sat down on his rickety chair, the receiver unsteadily pinned between ear and shoulder. The teapot was now in his hands;

he gazed down in surprise, not remembering how it had gotten there.

"He thinks he's the messiah," Fasano went on. "A reluctant messiah! He didn't *want* to be savior, you know. It's just that no other 'sufficiently intelligent, capable person' came forward. What a stuck-up shit-for-brains. Here's small justice: the tabloids have started to call him the Brain Bomber. As noms de guerre go, he was probably hoping for something a little more suave. He says if he'd been around to kill Einstein, we would never have figured out nuclear war."

"Kill Einstein!" Lee said, the teapot falling to the floor.

He and Fasano kept talking, or rather Fasano kept talking while Lee went on struggling to listen. There was an unfortunate coherence of reason to the mad savior's rantings, Fasano complained, which meant that, of course, overnight there were jaded and self-righteous students swanning into the classroom in BRAIN BOMBER FOR PRESIDENT T-shirts. They never would have dreamed of it four years ago when Sorin Illich had just been dismembered—they were too busy holding candlelight vigils and expressing themselves—but Lee knew as well as Fasano that four years was a full generation in undergraduate life, and this current crop ruthlessly cheered for their anarchic hero. "Who doesn't hate computers sometimes? Who doesn't hate the hydrogen bomb all the time? It doesn't mean you start serial-killing the best minds in the country." But even the lunatic's manifesto was a model of clear argument when compared to the specious self-justifications for publishing it that the newspapers gave. "The *L.A. Times* and the *New York Times*," Fasano said. "Apparently this thing lands in both of their mail rooms sometime last week—typescript, both copies, of course the messiah won't Xerox—with a note that says if they don't publish the whole thing by Monday, someone else gets blown up. So they do! The whole thing! In a *supplement*, Lee, like it's the State of the Union Address. And here's their explanation for why this is ethically fine, giving the greatest public platform in the world to a homicidal maniac: *because lives might hang in the balance.* As if his word is good as gold that he really won't kill if they print it. And besides that, they say, 'We cannot discount the chance that the publication of this work might lead to the apprehension of its author.' Yeah, or maybe just the formation of Brain Bomber Fan Clubs. Oh, and before I forget: 'The

Times condemns terrorism in every form.' Except the form that sells papers. They act like they're heroes, for turning this creep into some kind of hero himself. . . ."

For all the decades Lee had lived in this town, there had been just one place where the *New York Times* could be bought on the day it came out: Klaussen's Delicatessen, the same deli Aileen had discovered the first year of their marriage. But even if one of the five or six copies of the *Times* that Klaussen's carried each day still remained at this hour, Lee found himself failing to get into the car. He could have called, but he refrained from this also. After talking so long to Fasano, he ought to leave the line open, in case Morrison called. It was only after having this thought that Lee grew aware of his pitiful urge to converse with the agent, as if, having heard about the Brain Bomber's manifesto from Fasano, who'd read it in that day's newspaper, Lee finally had exclusive information that might crack the case.

By five that evening, Lee understood that Klaussen's was closed. He didn't turn on the television evening news, as he usually did, while preparing his dinner. He had the sense of a respite, a featureless pause, that seemed somehow endangered. It was nothing so precious as tranquillity, yet he still felt provisional peace, and he went to bed early, as if to conserve it. A few times Gaither's letter flashed the length of his mind, like a bat slicing arcs through the dusk. *I wonder if you would agree that there is some relief, in becoming old men. What poet wrote "tender youth, all a-bruise"?* He could still see it perfectly clearly, as if it remained in his hands and was not in a clear plastic bag in the FBI's files. For some reason Lee thought of its typescript, each letter a minuscule brand on the skin of the page.

Shuttling to and from campus the next several days to teach class to his hypnotized students, and avoiding the departmental office to avoid the sensation that *he* was avoided, Lee sensed the manifesto's having thickened the air like a pollen. The students huddled on the quad, who went silent upon his approach, must be buzzing about it. The vans from Newscenter 11, sometimes brazenly parked in the handicapped spots, must be egging them on. But Lee found that because he saw no one—because he avoided or was being avoided, whichever it was—the fragile sensation of respite remained like a cloak. The unpurchased newspaper from Klaussen's drifted further and further away, became garbage, perhaps was already interred at the dump. Lee arrived at the conclusion, which now seemed so simple, that not only did he not want to read the vile words of the man who'd killed Hendley but, more important, he had no obligation to read them. Perhaps his obligation was *not* to—why should he honor the thoughts of a killer? This conclusion seemed less a conclusion than the discovery of a sound principle that had always been his, and it lifted his mood. He wondered whether Morrison was under tremendous new pressure to get a break in the case. Lee felt anxious on the agent's behalf, and hoped for his success. For his own part, he wanted to further discover the best way to savor the precious respite. Every other day he had no class at all, no office hours until two and even then they were really for him, to give him someplace to go; and lately there was nothing to grade, as in tacit recognition of Hendley's death for three weeks in a row he had given no tests. Somehow, in the course of the most recent decade, all the extra pursuits he'd once had—the jogging and the furniture fixing and the light carpentry, the occasional drives to the city to wander museums, the subscriptions to newsmagazines and the viewings of films—one by one had slipped out of rotation, become foreign, even onerous. He was finally left with his work as his sole consolation. He had abandoned those other diversions, but because he could not recall quite when or why, he instead felt abandoned by them. He dreaded a similar loss of his work, though in fact with tenure he could never be forced to retire. He could teach trig to bored freshmen until he dropped dead with the chalk in his hand. That was the one luxury he had earned.

And so when his phone finally rang early one morning, more than a week since Fasano's last call, Lee leaped on it again eagerly, with no preconception of who it might be: Sondra at last, or Fasano again, or, most unlikely, Morrison. But it was Peter Littell, the uncomfortable chairman of their department. "Could you drop by my office? As soon as you can? I know you don't have class today, but my schedule, my own schedule . . . ," he apologized, trailing off tensely.

"I have office hours starting at two," Lee began.

". . . right," Littell said unencouragingly.

"But I can come now. I was on my way there," Lee decided. He would work in his office; he ought to be spending more time there, not less. He shouldn't seem to be shirking his duties, as he'd shirked the memorial.

On the drive to campus, Lee kept having the sense that the car behind him wanted to pass, but the more he slowed down to let it, the more it slowed down, too. He lost track of it navigating the entrance to the MathSci Building's lot, congested, as it was every morning, with wild-driving students running late to their classes and this morning additionally with more news vans, not only Newscenter 11's but several others painted loudly with numbers and logos, all with a sort of a periscope unit on top. The vans were trying to depart the parking lot, or perhaps they were just arriving; Lee sat several minutes in the unusual bottleneck before he could get to his space. Inside his building, once again Sondra wasn't behind her desk, though the coffee samovar was emitting its tendril of steam, the sign of Sondra's stewardship. Jeanette was filing her nails at her desk in the corner; she glanced up at Lee, colored deeply, and swiveled toward her computer.

Littell was waiting behind his desk, seeming very pale, even slightly ill. His reddish beard clashed with his grayish complexion. Lee still thought of Littell as one of the young faculty members, though Littell had been in the department for more than ten years. He was in his late forties, a computer scientist like Hendley but otherwise nothing like Hendley. Lee had always assumed that Littell, colorless even on good days, found Hendley mortifyingly charismatic and enragingly overvalued. Littell had been saddled with the department's chairmanship for a record six years, in large part because he had never resisted what to everyone else was a burden to be passed off as quickly as possible, or even totally dodged. Lee, for example, had served only one semester as department chairman, in the Bicentennial Year 1976, after which he had never been approached for the duty again. Hendley had also never served. While Lee had gotten off due to administrative incompetence, Hendley, by contrast, had gotten off due to scholarly brilliance. The deans of the college had felt that Hendley's time should be all for his research, and Hendley had sainted himself by insisting on teaching even more than they'd asked, for the sheer love of it. Lee was sure all of this had scorched Peter Littell to the same degree it had scorched Lee, but they had never discussed it, being cool with each other, and now never would.

"It's been a hard month," Littell said when Lee had sat down.

"The students seem to be doing okay," Lee offered, having finally learned after decades that in faltering chat with his colleagues, expressing concern for the welfare of students was always a good thing to do.

"Well, that's exactly what I want to talk about. How the students are doing. If you can try to think of this in . . . that light, I think that'll be helpful."

Littell was gazing at him with a mix of distaste and uncertainty, as if searching for confirmation of something he also dreaded to find. Under that gaze Lee felt his hand closing more tightly around the cracked leather handle of his briefcase, now unburdened of the letter from Gaither and transporting solely a book on a French numbers theorist Lee had hoped to peruse in his office. "Think of what?" he asked Littell, although he already felt his gut tumbling. It was the same crime again, his failure to mourn publicly. Compounded, if Sondra was right, by ancient memories of antagonisms over Kalotay's tenure. Either this had reminded his colleagues of that, or that had left them less tolerant of this; either way Lee felt barely able to discuss it again.

"This is very hard for me, Lee," Littell said.

"I wanted to attend the memorial," Lee rescued him wearily. "But I was very sick that afternoon."

After a moment Littell said, "So you really weren't there? I thought you might have wound up with some other department. It was packed. It was sort of a madhouse. In a way they're two sides of a coin."

"What are?" Lee said, now entirely lost.

Littell seemed to be fighting a twitch or an oncoming sneeze, not a rare expression for a man whose most colorful trait to his colleagues was his ceaseless discomfort, but Lee suddenly wondered if Littell had played truant to Hendley's memorial also—if that was the real origin of his squirmish distaste. Even a slavish bureaucrat like Littell must find it absurd to chastise another man for his own misdemeanor, and "packed . . . a madhouse" was a tellingly vague depiction. But instead Littell said, "That outpouring at the memorial and now these . . . rumors. Some hysteria fueling both. They're very wild rumors, I know. Lee—" He interrupted himself, as if Lee had interrupted and needed to be quieted, but Lee was still straining to catch Littell's meaning.

"What you have to understand," Littell went on, "is that it doesn't matter if the rumors are wild. It doesn't matter if they're just so much . . . playacting," he compromised, though he seemed to have sought a more harrowing term. "I don't have any interest in acting on rumors, but it looks like I don't have any choice but to act on the rumors' effects, and it's gotten to where I've had the TV news people all over the campus this morning. Which brings it all back to student welfare."

"There are rumors about me," Lee said into the uncertain silence that followed this outburst. Of course this was what Sondra had already told him, and what he'd tried not to hear. His misunderstanding with Morrison and Shenkman, the most minor and private of things, had somehow tunneled out of his intimate sphere and embarked on a new life as gossip. While his polygraph test—absolute and official and exhibiting no evidence of deception—would remain his own secret. Through undeceived eyes he saw anew Sondra's constant elusiveness, and the students he passed on the quad, and, worst of all, his class— short, as it had been every day since the first "normal" day, by a third of his students. He'd benignly forgiven the absentees' above-average grief for Hendley. And he'd noted as well the keen gaze the remaining ones pinioned him with, their almost sentrylike attention to his blackboard performance, their dead silence when he'd asked for their questions. He had thought, in a small skip of hope, they finally understood calculus.

"One of our students was on TV the day of the memorial, giving his brilliant opinion. No one at the time treated him as an expert. You'd think that no one ever would. But now our story is national news again with this 'manifesto.' " Lee didn't respond, because the belated dawn of humiliation, humiliation he was not sure for what, had advanced another dumb increment, so that his body seemed suffused from its core to its dermis with unpleasant, prickling heat. Littell added, clearly hoping to be told not to bother, "I guess I should tell you what's going around. Or rather the upshot, since I don't really know what they're saying. It's like the Telephone Game that Sophia plays," twitching one hand at a framed photograph of an ugly, pale, redheaded girl of about nine or ten. "Who knows where it starts, then it travels with rapid mutations, and lo and behold I have people who've heard you're an FBI suspect."

Lee's mortified heat had evolved into visions of Gaither's letter, and the moment he'd finally handed it over to Morrison, and his own disappointment that Morrison wasn't relieved, as Lee was, but angry. The word "obstruction" sounded in his mind, gleaned from movies. Had a rumor gotten out that he'd been an obstruction to Morrison's work? Lee blinked. "Suspect for what?" he asked cautiously.

"For the bombing." Littell blinked back at him.

"For the bombing!" Lee said.

There didn't seem to be any joke, although Lee, feeling almost concerned for Littell, probed with his gaze at the other man's face, as if this might uncover an uncharacteristic, but explanatory, glint of mischief. "The students think I did the bombing?" Lee said. "Do they also think I wrote this manifesto? This thing that . . . well, I don't even know what it says! I still haven't read it. Something about getting rid of computers?" Lee saw that Littell wasn't in on the joke—with his floury consumptive's complexion, poor Littell didn't even know what a joke was. But Lee did; it was not the first time he'd been darkly amused by the students' rich, if cruel, fantasy lives. "That's *much* crazier than me thinking the bomber is Gaither."

"Gaither?" Littell asked warily.

"But the students are capable of thinking anything," Lee went on, relieved that the rumor was so fantastic, so distinguishable from a possible truth—for example, that Lee hadn't gone to the service because he disliked the dead man or that he had told some white lies to an FBI agent. Whereas something like this, so flamboyant, so *youthful*, was clearly absurd. Lee did feel a passing sadness—he knew it was because he was not only Asian but old, an easy target for juvenile rumors as much as for egg throwing on Halloween. "Well, that's outlandish, even as rumors among students go," he went on. "I remember the student who spoke on TV, by the way. He must be annoyed because I asked him to give me my mail when we were still on spring break."

"You don't seem that concerned."

"Should I be concerned about something so ludicrous? No one over the age of eighteen could believe it. And even with the students, it will pass. Things like this always do."

"I hope you're right," Littell said. He seemed coldly surprised, perhaps at Lee's greater wealth of experience—Littell was still, Lee reflected, a young faculty member when compared with himself. Littell seemed to realize this and by visible effort to take up a cajoling, acknowledging tone. "Of course you're right," Littell said. "It'll pass. So the best thing to do in the meantime, I think, is not give anyone any more to get worked up about. My thought is that you take the rest of term off. Take it easy. Get off campus and avoid all this nonsense."

It felt like the moment when Morrison mentioned the polygraph test—Lee was sure his interpretation was so flawed it would make Littell laugh. "You want me to stop teaching class?" he essayed, more uncertain than incredulous.

"Just for the rest of this term. And for the summer, perhaps, if you were going to do summer session."

"I do every year."

"In that case, for this term and this summer, you could take the time off. Kalotay's already offered to cover your classes and give your exams, and I think he'd be happy to cover your summer also, I can just double-check—" Littell riffled his desk as if to secure Kalotay's assistance that instant, to oblige Lee's concerns. At the mention of Kalotay, Lee's astonishment was eclipsed by a darker emotion; he was very near saying something to Littell from which, tenure or not, he might never recover.

"It is just the students, isn't it?" he asked tightly. "Who are thinking these things?"

"And the TV reporters, unfortunately," Littell said, with comradely academic disparagement for the rabble of popular culture, now that he seemed to have won Lee's compliance.

"The TV news can't report lies," Lee observed, but Littell seemed disinclined to view as less than very grave a situation he had himself just a moment before called "hysterical." Lee felt the need to escape Littell's office. He had a vertiginous sense of reversal he recognized only from dreams, so that everything it crossed his mind to say seemed at once too severe and too frivolous; he couldn't read the temperature of this encounter any longer, and he'd never been friendly enough with Littell to appeal for help. He heard himself saying, in a veer toward the too-severe end of the spectrum, "I have tenure," as if, with his decade-old scoff at retirement—a trait he had always assumed endeared him to his colleagues—there were anyone, let alone Peter Littell, unaware of this fact.

"Lee," Littell said very coldly, as if Lee's hysteria were the one species he couldn't bear, "I'm not suggesting you give up your job. I'm just letting you take some time off until all this blows over. We'll all be glad to start fresh in the fall."

It wasn't until Lee had left the building, his office unvisited, the French numbers theorist still cached in his briefcase, that it occurred to him that Littell probably welcomed the rumor; it gave him a noble excuse to push Lee into quasi retirement, no doubt with the hope that Lee might then retire for good. He knew that Littell would prefer he recede to emeritus status and give up his classes to a new junior hire who could be paid less than half what Lee got. Lee couldn't be disposed of, but he could be marginalized, so that his long memory of the way things were done no longer embarrassed Littell's inexperience, and his centrally located office—though it had a bad view—could be conferred on obsequious Kalotay. Or had he in fact been disposed of already?

He'd come to a shocked halt on the sidewalk, baking beneath the high sun. The day was another taste of midsummer in April, and he was aware of being over- and shabbily dressed, despite having meant to appear very august, in his teaching khakis and an old not-quite-houndstooth jacket he'd purchased years ago, in an unsuccessful effort to fulfill some ideal of academic élan he no longer remembered. The jacket was not one of those that look better with age. As he stood paralyzed just outside the shadow of the MathSci Building, not even taking the few steps backward that would allow him the shadow's blue refuge, a pair of female students came conversing around the corner, their heads inclined toward each other. Seeing him, they stopped short and stopped talking, and it was less their approach than its sudden arrest that drew Lee from his thoughts. For a moment the ponytailed blonde, in frayed shorts and T-shirt, and the more elegant, sober brunette, with short hair sleeked close to her skull and in a slim navy skirt and white blouse, confounded Lee in their sisterly union, though he would have known both instantly if he'd seen them apart. The blonde was Emma Stiles, who'd last sobbed on his shoulder, and the brunette was not a student but Hendley's girlfriend, Rachel, whom he'd last seen in the crepuscular light of the Wagon Wheel bar.

"Hello!" Lee cried out in confusion.

Emma Stiles, already very fair, seemed to blanch; she gaped at Lee with incredulity, then rushed past, leaving Rachel. Emma tore open the MathSci Building's entrance and vanished inside.

He turned back to Rachel, his supplication for Emma, which would have resembled a father's to a furious daughter, still taking form on his tongue. Rachel met his gaze for an instant, then moved quickly the same way Emma had gone. "Excuse me," she threw over her shoulder, without looking back.

There was Morrison's car in Lee's driveway and Morrison himself in the front seat, speaking into a portable phone. Lee's armpits prickled, his bandaged heart labored, his ugly jacket's unraveling collar abraded the back of his neck. He had actually hoped for a friendly encounter with this very person, and it had even crossed his mind on the drive home from campus that Morrison might rebuke Littell on his behalf, for giving a legitimate cast to such juvenile rumors. But now that he saw the agent, he felt stirrings of dread. Morrison looked displeased, even angry, a notch down again from the wary neutrality with which he'd parted from Lee on the day of the test.

"Put your car in your garage," Morrison said. "TV people have been here. I sent them off to a briefing that Shenkman is bullshitting up, but I'm sure they'll be back."

"TV people were *here*? Why?"

"I'd love dearly to know. It's the last fucking thing that I need. Come on, Lee. Get inside." Lee clumsily rushed to obey. The alarming idea that the TV news people had been to his home was overshadowed, briefly, by the even more proximate shock of the other man's speech. Lee had never heard Morrison swear.

Inside, Lee began banging his way through the process for tea. His hands were shaking. "I don't need tea," Morrison told him, pacing the kitchen from the sliding glass door to the telephone table, openly examining the stack of Lee's bills, the memo pad, the recipe box that had once been Aileen's and that Lee kept for exactly two recipes, shrimp jambalaya and strip steak with peppers, though the rest of the yellowed, stained cards were still there, necessary if never consulted. "Lee, be still. Please sit down and be still." Lee dropped into a chair, although Morrison kept up his restless movements. "Your polygraph was sent to FBI headquarters, and they've reclassified it. They find the results inconclusive."

"Inconclusive? But I passed. Gerry said so. You said so. I passed!"

"I did not say you passed. I told you what Gerry told me, which is that he saw no evidence of deception. That was Gerry's conclusion. Headquarters arrived at a different conclusion. Their conclusion is that the test wasn't conclusive."

"But what does that *mean*?"

"Lee, I can't say it five different ways. It means just what I said. It means that the test does not yield a clear meaning. Is that clear enough?"

"But that doesn't make *sense*—"

"Lee, I need you to shut up, as if you were one of your students and I'm the professor. I need you to shut up and listen to me. Can you do that a minute?"

Lee was too stung by this to do anything other than color while making a quick, scornful gesture with one hand, as if to say, *Be my guest.*

"I've been doing what I do a very long time," Morrison recommenced, "and I've always believed, and always had that belief reconfirmed, that you never get if you don't give. And so, with you, I've given. I've given you respect—I think you're an extremely intelligent man. I've given you patience. I've given you the benefit of the doubt, when I could tell you weren't being completely forthcoming. And in return, I have gotten. I got the letter, after you'd said that you'd thrown it away. But the balance is very unequal. I have not gotten, in anything like the proportion in which I have given. You're a mathematician. You grasp what I'm saying. Yet in spite of all that, I am going to give yet again." Here Morrison paused, as if to underscore his generosity. "Lee, I'm going to tell you something that very few people are privileged to know. In my business, which is the business of law enforcement at the federal level, there is a general belief—by this I mean it is generally shared, Lee, and there are very few who strongly disagree—that certain persons, of certain racial and cultural backgrounds, are immune to the polygraph test. The polygraph test is astoundingly accurate otherwise—but with these groups it's worse than useless. It produces false negatives, always. It can never detect deception. No one really knows why; maybe these people don't have the base ethical orientation of our mainstream Judeo-Christians. Maybe they have a relative notion of truth, or they're lacking in guilt. Whatever the reason, we can't use the polygraph on them. Who are they? I told you no one outside law enforcement is aware of this problem. That's because it's not something we walk around talking about. We can't polygraph Asians. The Chinese, Japanese, the Malaysians, the Indonesians. The Taiwanese are a maybe. Can't do Koreans, it doesn't matter which side. Can't do Pakistanis, Indians, Bangladeshis, and can't do any of the people of the region some call Western Asia and most people call Middle East. None of the Arabs, which is a very big problem, and for some funny reason Hasidic Jews also don't work, although once again, no one knows why."

"That is ridiculous," Lee broke in. "And despicable. The entire idea."

"It would be if it wasn't a plain fact, empirically verified all of the time. But I don't tell you this because I think you are an Asian immune to the polygraph test; if I thought that, I wouldn't have wasted my time and yours giving you one. You've lived in this country four decades, you're completely assimilated, and besides that, you seem like a person of conscience who's not unfamiliar with guilt. I tell you all this to give you some sense of the atmosphere, of the mode of thinking about you going on at headquarters."

"But why are they thinking about me at all? I haven't done anything wrong!"

"And I'm telling you this," Morrison continued, ignoring the disruption, "to help you understand that although you might think I'm your biggest antagonist, in fact in this situation, which you may not see clearly, I'm at this point your sole advocate. I'm the person who thought it was worth it to polygraph you. I'm the person who's giving and giving, but I just don't get anything back. So I'll give yet again. Lee, the letter you gave me, the letter you got in your box from 14 Maple Lane, was mailed by the same human being who sent Hendley the bomb. What it looks like to me is, you've been aware of that fact all along but weren't sure that I was. You lost the letter, oops, you found it. It's from your good friend, no, your worst enemy. You've been saying these things, and you've even said them to the polygraph, and you haven't been nabbed. So how does it change the equation if I let you know that I know? I *know* your letter came from the bomber, Lee. How do I know? I have plenty of ways. That I know is just one more thing I've given you, and it's really time, now, that you gave something useful to me."

"Lewis is the bomber?" Lee said. "Oh, my God, is that possible?" Morrison's foul, shocking speech had fermented in him righteous indignation he'd been bracing himself to unleash, but this articulation, in actual words, by an actual person, of the wicked idea he'd had in the polygraph chair, wrenched his anger away. He was left spent and breathless, trembling.

"Given what I know about Lewis Gaither," Agent Morrison said, with sarcasm, "it's highly unlikely."

"What do you know?" Lee exclaimed.

"Oh, no," Morrison warned him, and now Lee saw, through the blur of his shock, that the other man was watching him with the same indignation Lee had felt only moments before, as if Morrison had absorbed Lee's own rage. But Morrison wasn't angry about racist notions; he was angry at Lee. "I'm not *giving* anymore, remember? I'm still waiting to *get*."

"Lewis can't be the bomber," Lee said. "Jim, you've made a mistake."

"Lewis sent you that letter?"

"Of course. I told you."

"I think it's you who has made the mistake," Morrison said at last, standing. "When you have more to tell me, and I hope that you will, you know how to reach me."

"There are people at my school who think *I'm* the bomber," Lee replied quietly as he trailed Morrison to the door. "I don't know how it is, but everyone seems to be wrong."

Morrison turned around. "It's all in your hands to correct them. Isn't that what your job is, Professor? To correct and enlighten? To broadcast the truth?" Morrison pulled a photograph out of his pocket and flashed it at Lee.

"Oh, God!" Lee said, cringing away. It was torn limbs, charred skin, and splashed blood.

"That's what the cops and the EMTs found in the office that's right next to yours."

Lee remembered when Esther had flung herself into his arms. . . .
No, that had been Emma Stiles. She had sobbed on his chest and then
whispered the terrible words in his ear.

I saw him.

"That's what your old pal did," Morrison added, before letting
himself out the door.

18.

AFTER MORRISON HAD GONE LEE SAT AT THE KITCHEN
table pressing the heels of his hands in his eye sockets, but this only
made the image Morrison had shown him return more vividly. Like an
invalid, Lee pulled himself by the edge of the countertop island to the
sink and hung over it, coughing and gagging, but wasn't able to vomit.
The kitchen was so still he could hear the minute hand on his electric
wall clock when it jerked itself forward a notch, with a sound like a
faraway arrow released from a bow.

When the telephone rang, he seized it. "Jim?" he said huskily. That
man's vengeful anger, and his own need to cease being its object,
whatever the cost, were all he could think of—apart from that nightmare image of a mangled but just-recognizable man.

"Dr. Lee?" asked a voice with alacrity. "I'm so glad to find you at
home. This is Sheila Klegg from the *Examiner*, and I'd like to ask you
for your comment—"

Lee automatically hung up the phone.

He took it up again quickly, before it could unleash another assault,
and dialed a number his mind had not realized his fingers remembered. When the familiar voice answered, it took him a moment to
understand what he had done.

"Jeff," he said. "This is Lee."

Jeff Trulli was the young, inexpensive lawyer who had handled
Lee's divorce from Michiko. His faintly shiny suits, and plainly shiny
ties, were more memorable to Lee now than his face; he must have
descended from immigrants who had traded their Mediterranean
traits for the outlines and palette of soft, snowier peoples with whom

they had bred. Lee was only sure now that Jeff had a weak chin, for which he compensated by knotting his ties very high. He was the only lawyer Lee knew, apart from the real-estate lawyer who'd refinanced his mortgage.

"Hey, Dr. Lee, wow, I'm so sorry about this catastrophe up at the school, I've been meaning to call you and see how you were—you were close to it, right? Jesus Christ, goddamn loonies, it's a miracle that you're alive, that poor other guy, friend of yours, right? God, I'm sorry, I've been meaning to call." The inelegant, genuine speech, with its effect of a radio broadcast from an innocent era long past, almost left Lee unable to scrape forth the words of his story.

Jeff was audibly discomfited once Lee had finished, or at least once Lee managed to pause so that Jeff could cut in. "The first thing I'm going to say, before I say anything else, is that I think that you want someone else."

"I don't know anyone else—"

"If you give me a couple of days, I'll chase down a few names."

"I don't have a few days," Lee insisted, although he did not really know what he had. He understood nothing: stark panic had wiped his mind clean.

As if seeing this void for himself, Jeff was saying, "I don't quite understand what the trouble is here. They haven't charged you with anything, with harboring a fugitive, or acting as an accessory, or whatever it is you think they think—it's not my corner of the law, Lee, but even if it was, you don't seem to have any legal problem here that a lawyer could deal with."

"They think I'm lying. They think I'm a liar."

"About what? They think you know something about this you're not telling them? That sounds to me like they don't really have anything, and they're grasping at straws."

"But my letter—"

"They say your letter comes from the same person who mailed the bomb. So they're saying your ex friend is the bomber. I agree, that's shocking. But is it totally outside the realm of the possible?"

"I suppose it's not," Lee said in confusion. A debilitating sadness came over him, though he wasn't sure why. Perhaps it was the sadness of his own death, having so closely approached him and then passed him by. . . . "But I told them from the very beginning who the letter was from, and they're not satisfied."

"If your ex-friend has gone into business as a serial bomber, he'd be pretty stupid to have the same name," Jeff remarked. "But, Lee, like I said, this doesn't sound like a legal problem, it sounds like cops getting tough. That's unpleasant, but you have to just keep doing what you've been doing, keep telling the truth, and you're going to be fine. If you want, I can still call some people, try to line up some names."

"Call *them*, Jeff. Tell them what you told me! He must have changed his name, of course he's changed it, and how could I know what it is—"

"I hardly think the FBI wants to hear a divorce lawyer's theories."

"Jeff, I'm begging you. Call this man Morrison, just ask him what he wants me to do. I don't know what to do! I'll *pay* you." And whether persuaded by this or shamed by it, Jeff said that he would.

The phone rang again the instant Lee hung up. He gasped and jumped back, as if it had not rung but spoken to him, or stung him. The *Examiner* again. He would say "No comment!" as he'd seen on TV. Or he simply would not pick it up, he would unplug the phone, never answer again. . . . But what if the call was from Esther? The leading edge of the past weeks of news might have reached her at last, the way all the planet's transmissions reached ceaselessly out to the stars. Somewhere all the old stories were revealing themselves for the very first time, and somewhere Lee was still an admirable, eloquent, almost-victim of a terrible act—not a liar, sullied and suspicious. Esther would finally call; Lee never had changed his phone number to make it unlisted, as he'd resolved to after getting Gaither's letter. Because he'd had the same phone number all these years, as Fasano had noticed, for her.

The telephone was still ringing. He picked it up, ready to declare "No comment!" if he had to, and then he grew still with amazement, because the voice on the line saying "Hello . . .?" with great caution was not the sharp, avid voice of the newspaperwoman but a young woman's voice that he knew. "Is this . . . Dr. Lee?"

"Yes," he said, crushingly disappointed.

"This is Rachel."

"Yes," he murmured.

"I saw you today."

"Yes."

"I was rude. I want to apologize."

It was a tremendous mental effort, to remember what this was about, the encounter less than two hours ago in the sun on campus. Lee found himself laboring to bring her face into his mind—her face that had once made him think of Aileen.

"This is going to seem weird, but I want to talk to you. I mean"—and this was almost to herself—"the worst anybody could say is I believed the best of human nature. And I want to. You know? I need to."

"Yes," Lee said again. He could barely make sense of her words.

"I don't know if you'd be willing to meet at the Wagon Wheel. Say, six o'clock. I have to talk to these TV news people beforehand. It's disgusting. But I can be there by six."

"Yes," he heard himself saying. "Okay."

"Thank you. I'll see you there."

"Okay. Thank you," he added stupidly, before hanging up.

Then he did unplug the phone, yanking the cord angrily. If Esther had not called before, there was really no reason to think she'd call now.

He remained several minutes at his telephone table, his hand still at rest in the posture of ending the call, the thunderbolt of Rachel's voice vestiged by warmth in his palm. The yellow legal pad on which he had written *does not like hotshots or tall poppies . . . one of us: mathematician/computer scientist* still lay within sight. Gaither was not even a "short poppy" in the field like Fasano and Lee; he had failed to work his way onto the field at all. A talentless mathematical aspirant and a grad-school dropout, a Christian zealot who never had what it took to do science . . . Lee was reminded of the condescending verdict Donald Whitehead had once passed on Gaither. *I can't tolerate religious men, personally. I'm not saying Gaither's not a mathematician, but I wonder about his work.*

He was still reverberating from the shock of Rachel's summons, but now that shock seemed to dislodge him from the vault of immediate pressures, so that he could examine this thing that until now had obstructed all view of itself. Not merely the letter, which he saw had always been Morrison's object: the "inventory" of all Lee's mail, of *everyone's* mail, had been a ruse, a smoke screen. And yet, Lee realized, Morrison had been ensnared in another man's ruse all along. The letter had forced Morrison to investigate Lee, the same way that the bomb had forced the agents to come to the school where Lee taught. Hendley's awful death, for all its shock waves, was not even the primary thing; it was only a means, the first step of a much larger scheme.

Until this moment Lee had not really known if he would go to meet Rachel. The imperative to see her was no less overwhelming than all the obstacles, the Sheila Kleggs and news vans, he might encounter on the way. But at the same time, the momentum of revelation was dictating its own harsh demands. He must find a listener, if not an ally. His fear was so great now it functioned the same way he assumed courage must: he was able to think very clearly, pressed against his own possible ruin. The proximity of the bomb to himself had been no accident. Gaither had mailed the bomb, to Lee's very close colleague; and then Gaither had waited a short interval and had mailed the letter, to Lee; and then, just as Gaither had known that Lee would, Lee had pounced on the bait and replied. And by now, just as Gaither had planned, the FBI was the avid observer of this postal exchange: Gaither's first letter, and Lee's letter back, and that letter's instant rebound stamped *Addressee unknown* and delivered to Lee by no less than an FBI agent.

In the polygraph chair, Lee had glimpsed just the tail of this truth, something flashing and fleet through the dark underbrush of cognition. Then he'd wondered if Gaither had meant not to kill Hendley but him, with a poorly aimed bomb. Now he cringed at his slowness, almost optimistic in its miscomprehensions. Gaither didn't mean to end Lee's life: he meant to destroy it. He meant to spatter with spots until stained. He meant to scorch with the beam of suspicion. He meant to bring ruin.

He felt certain the white car was following him. He'd first noticed it after turning off Fearrington Way onto the main artery of his subdivision, though whether it had also come out of his street he couldn't say; he'd always been too scrupulous a driver to find consulting the mirrors instinctive, since even such momentary glances took him from what lay before him, sometimes causing an involuntary swerve that Esther, in her teenage years, had always answered with a gasp of dismay or disgust. But coming to a stop at the "fieldstone" gates that marked his subdivision's entrance, and waiting patiently with his left-turn signal on to join the sparse, steady traffic along Route 19, he was able to consult his rearview and see the white car behind him. Often, at this precise intersection, and despite the unhurried prudence of most mid-western drivers, a car caught behind Lee might honk after Lee had passed up several chances to dart into traffic in favor of a clear road both ways almost to the horizon. Now Lee made a point of being even more cautious than usual, but the white car was as patient as he was. Though he squinted, the late-afternoon glare blocked his view of the driver. Finally he made the turn, the white car coming with him as if they were shackled together.

The car stayed with him all the way to the Wagon Wheel. A few of the times he managed the increasingly spasmodic flicking of his eyes to the rearview—he would feel his Nissan twitch to the right in tandem—it seemed to have gone, but then, the next time he looked, it was back, unless it was replaced by another white car that was almost the same. He couldn't tell what the make was. It only looked very generic, and new. Then he pulled into the Wagon Wheel parking lot, at five o'clock occupied by just two other cars, and the white car continued, whispering out of sight down the riverside road.

Lee felt he could hear—as if it had quavered a note upon being drawn taut—the thread linking that car to the letter from Gaither.

He'd arrived at the bar with an hour to spare, meaning to translate his thoughts into the briefest and clearest and calmest speech possible, but he had no idea where to start. He thought of the way Gaither had changed, all those decades ago, how the mild, plainly handsome young man, whose feelings Lee had feared he might injure by rebuffing the church invitations, had abruptly shape-shifted into a grim-jawed patriarch of revenge. The ruthless campaign he had waged for his child, his sanctimonious, cold condemnation of his wife and her lover . . . This didn't help Lee to make his thoughts calm. While he sat there gripping his keys and staring out the windshield, a heavy man emerged from the bar, climbed into one of the two other cars, and drove off; a young man arrived on foot, passing Lee's car very quickly and heading inside as if late; and a new car pulled in. It was Rachel. Lee saw her turn off her engine and sit, gazing forward at nothing. Then she raked one hand through her short hair, checked herself in her mirror, and got out. Seeing Lee brought her up short, visibly dismayed, and Lee understood that she had come to have a drink ahead of him, to be established, even fortressed, in the bar as he arrived. In a sense this had been his intention, too.

He got out also. "We're both early," Rachel said, resuming her approach. He saw that she was striving for courteous lightness, as if the occasion of their meeting were no stranger than the weekly colloquium, but he could no more emulate her tone than he could stop himself saying,

"I know who killed Hendley."

She recoiled, clearly horrified; she managed mostly to conceal her reaction, but it registered as anger in her face. "Really," she said, as if unveiling the murderer were somehow as foul an act as the murder itself.

"We should go in," he said, and though her face hadn't recovered—it was the face she had shown him that morning—she let him lead her inside.

The only patron was the young man who'd arrived on foot. He sat at the center of the bar, nursing a beer, and didn't look up at them. Nevertheless, Lee chose the most remote booth, and it was only after he was seated in it, hunched by instinct away from the bar and the door, urgently poised to unravel his story, that he remembered it was the same booth Rachel had sat in the day of Hendley's memorial.

"Don't you want something?" she interrupted, as he drew breath to speak. She seemed less solicitous than suspicious of him, for not hewing to the conventions.

When they were seated together again in front of his Black Label and her glittering tumbler of syrup—he guessed it was bourbon—he told her, as clearly and as simply as he could, who Gaither was, how and when he had known him, and why he imagined that Gaither had turned to violence. She didn't interpose any comments or questions, only sometimes pushed her chin forward, with her head slightly turned, which he belatedly realized was her way of telling him to speak up. Even so, he spoke just above a whisper. The young man at the bar still had his back to them, but to Lee it seemed almost a conspicuous show of noninterest.

"Why haven't you told the investigators?" Rachel asked when he was finished.

"I did. I told them 'Lewis Gaither,' but they weren't satisfied. They think I'm not telling them the right person. Now I realize this can't be his name anymore. He wouldn't contact me if he knew I could just point a finger and say 'Lewis Gaither.' He can get me, but I can't get him. He's cast a shadow on me, and I can't even see where he is."

"Are you saying he's done this on purpose, to hurt you?"

"Yes."

"He's done this—killed Rick—to hurt you."

"Yes," he repeated, with even more emphasis, feeling only the gladness of gears meshed at last, of sharing with Rachel his terrible realizations. He saw something pass through her, like bad weather under the skin. Only then did he understand that to her there might be something unwelcome in the idea of her lover's death as a mere utensil, the vehicle for a vendetta between other men.

A little of her drink had splashed onto the table. "I'm sorry," she said, snatching her hands toward herself in a gesture of withdrawal that continued, in clumsy extension, until she was suddenly standing up out of the booth. "I'm not up for this. I'm very sorry. I need to go."

It was one more bewildering snag, perhaps no worse than the voracious student gossip, which had clearly found its echo among faculty, and no worse than Littell's opportunism or the "reclassification" of his polygraph test, but because just a moment before he had felt forward movement, the fresh setback affected him powerfully. "Wait!" he cried, lunging after. "You have to help me. Help me!"

He'd forgotten all about the bartender, whoever that was, and about the young man who'd been hunched at the bar, seeing only the young woman's back as she tried to escape him, and in any case now they were outside again, Rachel gripping her car keys as if she thought Lee might attack her. "You're trying to tell me that you're being framed?" she said, turning abruptly. "So this Gaither person wrote the manifesto. He wrote this screed of irrational, cowardly hatred for computers and the people who work on them. It doesn't quite suggest that applied mathematicians like Rick or Neal Kalotay shouldn't get tenure, but it might as well have."

Lee couldn't follow this sudden barrage; he remembered the day she'd erupted with tears, the day she'd seemed to fling open the door to her soul, in the very same bar they'd just left. "Gaither always was a fanatic. He failed at mathematics, he never got his degree, and this must enrage him. But I'm not sure what he says in this manifesto. I haven't read it myself—"

"Oh, you don't have a copy?" she sneered.

He could see, from the irrelevant comment, that her passions had scattered her thoughts. All his past combat with Esther rushed to counsel him now. The moment's unmerciful pressure seemed to unlock his brain, and he understood several facts simultaneously: that Rachel was hardly older than Esther, not yet thirty; that the death of Hendley was the first tragedy of her life; and that for both reasons she disliked what she took as a shift in attention, from her situation to Lee's. She was failing to grasp that Lee could help her to justice and vengeance, if she could help him to thwart Gaither's game—the diabolical efficiency of which had been webbing his movements for weeks; he felt the confines of the trap only now that he'd begun thrashing. Panic threatened to stampede over all his deductive achievements. "The FBI can't see the truth, Gaither's made sure of that. Yes! You're right to say he's framing me," the simple word for what was happening to him solidifying now that she'd said it, like the crystal whose hard edges and facets surprisingly spring from a cloudy solution. For a moment his heart jerked with hope; she would be his ally after all.

A cross between pity and horror distorted her face. "You're scared, aren't you," she said. "Now that everyone thinks it was you."

Again she'd swept aside all the murk and delivered a verdict, but this time Lee was so shocked by the world she revealed, the unthinkable process already elapsed, he could not even speak. He might have been shot and wound up somehow stuck to the line marking life off from death. He was still there a long time after Rachel had driven away.

19.

A FEW MINUTES PAST SEVEN THE NEXT MORNING, HE grew aware of a gathering, cars arriving, doors opening, indistinct voices joining together. He hadn't slept at all that he was aware of, had not even moved from the armchair to bed. As if at a primal signal, he stood up from the chair, his blood surging, and locked himself in his downstairs bathroom. He showered rapidly, scattering soap gobbets onto the walls. He slashed his razor over his face. He stubbed his toe but didn't feel it, roughly yanked on clean clothes. The tableau of himself and Rachel in the booth at the Wagon Wheel some twelve hours before floated past, isolated and unexplainable. The doorbell rang, and in the action of answering it he had the sense of producing, himself, the procession that bore down on him, the way a magician pulls a colorful handkerchief chain from a hat.

It was Agent Morrison who served him the search warrant. "Professor, for your own privacy I would suggest that you sit in the back of your house, in your bedroom or kitchen, with the blinds drawn, until we're all finished. Members of the media have accompanied us here, unfortunately." Morrison's tone of voice suggested he and Lee had never met except perhaps on the most bureaucratic occasions. A small herd of purposeful adjuncts, in zipped jackets and gloves, were pouring through the door. Lee had the detached, uncertain thought that there were far more purposeful adjuncts than there were household objects, even if they counted his forks and separated his laundry. Outside, he saw his neighbors clustered excitedly at the edge of his lawn, a few of them nodding as they spoke to those reporters who weren't otherwise preoccupied with shifting and positioning their cameras. So here at last were the TV reporters. It had only been weeks since he'd spoken to them with such facility and passion outside the hospital in which Hendley lay dying, and yet he felt he had never seen anything like them before. Burly, potbellied men looking slightly cycloptic with the lenses of cameras hitched onto their shoulders, and other men probing the air with long poles baited with microphones, and still other men, and a woman, microphone-poking their ways to and fro, trailed by people unfurling long cords, as Lee did every once in a while when he vacuumed his carpet. Lee found himself transfixed in his doorway, his just-showered body a fountain of sweat.

"What are we looking for, Agent?" a reporter was shouting.

"Professor, please get out of the way," Agent Morrison said from behind him. "I would really suggest you get out of the doorway and sit in your kitchen."

Lee stared at the cycloptic eyes, which stared patiently back. Several people were asking him questions. He shook his head, stumbling over himself as he groped his way back through his front door and into the living room. When he reached his picture window, he pulled aside the curtain, as if this view might be different.

The cameras seemed to content themselves with his oddly forgotten form, sweating and blinking on the far side of the window screen and otherwise utterly still as behind him the drawers to his telephone table were emptied, then the few shoe boxes of recent miscellanea— disputed bills, replacement batteries not yet replaced—then the single bookshelf on the staircase landing, then even his desk—from his spot he could only have heard this, but he seemed to float upward so that he could see, as the searchers swarmed into that room, their movements eclipsing and revealing and eclipsing the sparse little tableau on the desk's leather surface, the papier-mâché candy dish and the photograph of Esther in the faux-stained-glass frame. Another photograph of Esther, from a year later, hung on the wall. They were small windows onto the last year before Aileen left. The two Esthers, only slightly different from each other, seemed to gaze at Lee expectantly, and he seemed to gaze back, as the jacketed forms crisscrossed in the foreground, though he still hadn't moved from his spot in the living-room window.

"Get out of that window and sit in the kitchen; you'll be more comfortable," Agent Morrison said, passing by.

There was so little; he could sense them thinking that, pawing over it impatiently like dogs. For a man in his seventh decade, where was all the stuff? Had he hidden it? Driven it out to the country and buried it? The dull truth was, he'd been a thrower-away all his life, and if he hadn't pitched it, then someone had taken it from him. Everything that most mattered to him could fit in his briefcase. Esther's pictures and her shoes, and a handful of papers. He had a single, two-drawer filing cabinet in the corner of his study, gray and ugly and almost entirely full of transient items, household records that apart from those concerning his mortgage he'd throw away in a couple of years, bank statements and paid bills and tax stuff, but in the back there was a slim clutch of items concerning Aileen. Their divorce papers, and the letter she'd written, from before they were married.

Time seemed to have stuttered. He had remembered those things, and then, without meaning to, he'd burrowed deep into himself, and now he resurfaced, to see the two-drawer filing cabinet as it was borne downstairs and out the front door.

"Wait—" he said.

He had also been remembering, somewhere in the midst of that temporal glitch, the first of Aileen's collapses, when they hadn't had any idea what was gathering in her. The paramedic had been shouting out her blood pressure as it nosedove, numbers plummeting second by second, and Lee had been screaming incoherent imprecations and wrenching Aileen's bloodless hands, and all around them had been the sort of pandemonium no sane person associates with the salvation of life. It had looked like life's utter unraveling, as this present scene did: the very last things roughly yanked from their moorings, Aileen falling from him, white as ash, while syringes and tubes flew around. But Aileen shuddered suddenly, and the oxygen mask dropped off her face, and she said to Lee, with a sort of amazement, "I'm not scared at all." It hadn't been the beatific acceptance of death; later she'd told him it was just that the worst had arrived, and she wasn't afraid. "You know: 'the only thing to fear is fear itself.' " *I'm not scared at all.* For his part, Lee had been so terrorized it was surprising his heart hadn't stopped. Yet now he thought he might understand, as he watched his house being dismantled: when disaster's thumb bears down on *you,* there's a peace to that pressure. The worst isn't coming, it's here. And there's nothing left to fear.

Except this loss. *"Wait,"* he cried, plunging out the front door in pursuit. He felt a hand grip his wrist, like a cuff.

"Professor," Morrison said. "I really think you'd be more comfortable if you sat in the kitchen."

It disappeared, that downpressing thumb, Aileen's fearless peace—why couldn't he keep hold of the least goddamned thing?— "I need something out of there," he gasped, making for the cabinet as it was borne across his freshly mowed lawn. His free arm pinwheeled ridiculously—Morrison had him firmly by the other wrist. "Get your hands off me!" Lee shrieked.

Herky-jerky they danced with each other on Lee's welcome mat for the avid cameras, straying perhaps five steps from where they had started before moving back, the big agent with the filing cabinet having turned to give a glance to the scuffle, turned away, resumed his steady, laden steps toward a truck at the curb like a professional mover; he paused again at a fresh cry from Lee and met Morrison's eyes, so that now the three of them stood on the lawn in an oval of news cameramen, the fish-eyes of the lenses turned on them and the long fishing poles—the booms, Lee would learn—following with their microphone bait, while at the same time the petty procession of old-bill-filled shoe boxes and calculus textbooks and much of the basement—cardboard evidence boxes into which had been whatever-way hastily dumped crescent wrenches and pliers and hammers and drill bits and C-clamps and random scrap ends of lumber from a shelf-building project of ten years ago and slivers of balsa and dowel from a dollhouse-building project of twenty years ago and coffee cans of loose nails and a four-fifths-full sack of lawn fertilizer and countless other things he never could never have named, staring at the stripped space, until he read the newspapers—continued, the steady annoyance of the box-bearing agents and the steady obstructiveness of the unmoving newspeople a happy symbiosis despite the pro forma shouts of, "Please *move*, you are on private property, move to the curb," despite the stubborn evasive response of, "What are we looking for, Agent? Is this what we're looking for?" A gray filing cabinet of telephone bills and the voice of a woman long dead?

Lee's previous TV appearance had been on its surface entirely different, but perhaps at some more basic level exactly the same. The first time he'd been a Hendley-envying, rattled bomb victim transformed into selfless and eloquent hero. This second time he was even more simply himself, and turned into a criminal.

Restrained by Jim Morrison's hands, he watched the gray filing cabinet vanish into the truck. The cameras watched it also, as they'd watched other items, although when the breaking news aired in a couple of hours, the clearly mundane things—the school textbooks, the can opener—would be edited in favor of the opaque evidence boxes, the opaque filing cabinet. Also not to be shown was Lee shaking his head very slightly, in acquiescence, so that Morrison unhanded him. Lee walked back into his house, and then into his bedroom, where the agents were done, and observed the tawdry appearance of his ungarnished bed, a mattress and box spring on bare metal frame with four scuffed plastic casters clawed into the carpet. His armchair appeared to have been reupholstered with threadbare dish rags. His dark wood dresser and his antique floor lamp did not elevate the generic cheapness of the room so much as suggest they'd been burglarized from more tasteful surroundings. The dresser's drawers were yanked out, dripping unfolded clothes. A basket of laundry was dumped on the floor. A dizzying shame overwhelmed him, that so many strangers had seen the squalor of his bathroom.

Lee closed the door and crept onto his bed. He hadn't pressed the button of the lock; he was afraid he might be reprimanded. He heard the thump of feet and the shifting of objects. No one pursued him, to put a camera and microphone close to his face. No one needed to, having already captured him lunging and twisting in Morrison's grasp and then crazily yelling, "It's none of your goddamned business!"

The ceiling of this room, like the ceilings of all the rooms, was done in that same textured plaster that resembled acne. Lee stared at the irregular bumps as if he might find a pattern.

Through the thin walls, he heard Agent Morrison say, "Dr. Lee is a Person of Interest to this investigation. He is not a suspect. It's as simple as that. We have never said he's a suspect. If we ever do say it, you'll know."

"But what exactly do you mean by that, Agent? Is there some legal difference between the two terms?"

"Dr. Lee is a Person we've been talking to and who's fully cooperating—"

"Is he going to face charges?"

"Look, this isn't a briefing. You people aren't even supposed to be here."

"Can we expect him to be upgraded from a Person of Interest into a suspect pretty soon?"

Lee rolled his head back and forth, almost writhed in torment. In the kitchen his phone began ringing. He had been so swiftly dispossessed he felt a moment of childlike dismay that no one of the agents or TV reporters took the trouble to answer it for him. Who was calling? Was it Esther? He gasped, writhed, clenched into motionlessness suddenly. From where he lay, when he looked to his right, into the dresser's mirror, he saw reflected the fissure between the edge of the blinds and the frame of the window that lay to his left. The two slivers of view, reflected and real, were entirely different; of course, this was the simplest geometry, the angles of incidence and reflection, but while the leftward view muffled itself in the bosk of a pine Lee had planted for privacy a few years before, the rightward just managed to escape the pine's boughs and run clear to the street. There a knot of spectators stood talking, one of whom, as Lee watched, suddenly turned and strode straight toward the pine, as if he'd realized, as had Lee at that instant, that the pine tree was protective only in concert with the basic respect neighbors grant to each other, and that today the respect had been breached with remarkable speed, perhaps permanently.

"I saw him out in the yard once," he called over his shoulder to his less-bold companions. "I don't know what the hell he was doing, digging holes in the middle of the night. Maybe burying things."

In fact he'd been planting a Japanese maple, at the start of a summer that had been such a hell that he'd waited to dig until sunset. The delicate maple had scorched and expired within days, and then its slight skeleton, almost invisible from a few yards away, had remained memorializing itself for almost a year because Lee couldn't bear to acknowledge his failure enough to uproot it; and the following spring he'd accidentally run into it with the lawn mower. But he was thinking of none of this now, as in a rush of pure instinct he twisted off the bed and fell hard on the side farthest from the window. Sore and gasping, he crouched out of sight on the carpet as the man crackled past the fat pine—unlike the maple, it had thrived—and presumably pressed his face onto the glass. "Naw, nothing," the man called toward the street, in a tone of apology. Lee heard the man's movement in the direction of the backyard but remained where he was, his heart clogging his throat. He'd lain stunned and still when the force of the bomb had thrown him. As if the mnemonic conditions were ideal for the first time in weeks, Lee remembered anew and with unsentimental precision the impact of the floor like a swollen heartbeat in the bones of his face, and the warm tongue of blood sliding over his own, and the inaccurate, passionless thought that he'd lost all his teeth. He had knotted himself automatically, like a fetus, he'd supposed then because he'd been bombed in his youth, and you never forget. But perhaps it was not a learned reflex but a species instinct—every animal curls into a ball when God's fist thunders down.

It came to him that he'd been hearing engines departing, the dense babble of voices deflating. Now there was silence. He didn't know how long he'd been on the floor. He got to all fours with effort and lingered there before standing up, with the feeling of baring his stomach to rows of sharpshooters. His hand lay for a while on the knob before somehow exerting the force that swung open the door.

He hadn't imagined that his house, with its bare picture hooks, could look emptier. It looked roughed up and shaken down, raped. Bits of sod were mashed onto the stair treads.

The front door had been left standing open. When he went to close it, he found his across-the-street neighbor, the young mother of the toddler and hip baby, standing on his stoop, her face recklessly flushed.

"I just want you to know," she said, as if they were lines she had practiced, "that I have two little children, and if you so much as *think* about them, I will make you regret it."

He gazed at her a moment. Another young woman around the same age as Esther, and Rachel. Twenty-five, twenty-six. She was alone: she'd found someone to tend the two children while she accomplished this mission.

It was possible to take a step backward, and close the door in her face.

He stayed in the house just as long as it took him to reach Jeff Trulli at his office, which turned out to be more than an hour, because, first, Jeff had not yet arrived, and then, second, Lee's phone began ringing. The sound nailed his feet to the floor; he couldn't brew tea or pour cereal or even go to the toilet but only stand as if being electrocuted;

when it stopped, it was just for a beat, as if catching its breath. Finally, in one of these pauses, he lunged for his chance and called Jeff again. "Christ, Lee, why aren't you picking up? I've been calling your place for an hour," Jeff said. "I think you should come by my office."

"I can't—"

"When's a good time for you, then?"

"I can't leave my house, Jeff!"

"If the press is still there, they're still there, Lee. Just walk past them and get in your car."

As the garage door rose up, he shrank into his seat; he expected to see his across-the-street neighbor and her children, and the man who'd peeped into his bedroom window and his less-bold companions, and all the other unfamiliar persons among whom he apparently lived waving pitchforks on the edge of his lawn, but there was only a slight alteration in the smothering tension he already felt, the cause of which he understood once approaching the end of his driveway. There were five cars parked fender to fender on Fearrington Way, where cars were never parked, except perhaps for a holiday party, because every house had a two-car garage. As he moved off, all five smoothly detached from the curb and fell into formation behind him.

Yesterday had been a bright day, but today was overcast, heavy and humid, the sun suffocated, so that now Lee could easily see the young man at the wheel of the forwardmost car, wearing a baseball cap and sunglasses, resembling any one of Lee's students, or perhaps the solitary drinker Lee felt sure had eavesdropped on the meeting with Rachel at the Wagon Wheel bar.

Lee drove achingly slowly, almost at a walk, and the five cars, respectful as a funeral procession, drove slowly also. He increased his speed, and the baseball-cap car jumped magnetically forward, and its fellows jumped with it. Lee could hear his car making a terrible sound, like a handful of marbles thrown onto the engine, which he somehow realized was the sound of his chattering teeth.

At Jeff Trulli's office, the five cars assembled themselves on the far side of the street, in a no-parking zone. Lee stumbled into the building with his eyes fixed in front of him, as if avoiding eye contact would make him invisible, but once safely inside he couldn't tear himself away from Jeff's window. He cranked closed the blinds and then scissored the tiniest fissure, through which he gazed dizzily, hardly able to breathe, like a furtive voyeur. "I have to urge you," Jeff Trulli was saying, "especially in light of what's going on now, that you talk to another attorney. Someone who actually works on this turf." Lee was staring down at the cars as if he could memorize them, though they were almost aggressively generic—he seared himself with their rounded corners, their rubber bumpers, their unblemished exteriors, then closed his eyes and they melted away. It was with difficulty that he detached his gaze, to accept the neatly rectangularized sheet of newspaper Jeff Trulli had been trying for the last several moments to give him. Jeff remained there, pointing; Lee followed the line of Jeff's blue polyester suit jacket, traversed fabric creases that marked the elbow, acknowledged the pale cuff of the shirt and a sprinkling of masculine hairs on the back of Jeff's hand, picked his way down the forefinger and finally arrived at its base, the flesh pad and the stubby, square nail planted onto the sheet as if the least relaxation of pressure might permit its escape. Lee was reminded, gazing down at the coarse printed surface of his local newspaper, which he hadn't subscribed to in years, of an ardor of Esther's from remote childhood. She could not have been older than seven. She had fallen in love—that was the only phrase for it—with a mediocre television actress, a young woman barely out of her teens who starred in some sort of mystery series, forever toting a flashlight into derelict houses and shrinking gaspingly into the walls as some malevolent thing leaped at her. Lee hadn't thought it was appropriate, but Esther had been smitten, had responded to attempts to limit her viewing with extraordinary intransigence, a startling preview of the storms that would come in her teens. The other six days of the week, when the show wasn't on, she had to comb through the paper for any mention of the actress's name, and these, when located, were painstakingly cut out with blunt-ended scissors, the slenderest slivers of paper, almost always from the television schedule; the young actress was not otherwise very newsworthy, but Esther wasn't deterred. The tiny slivers of paper, each just barely touched with a glue stick, went into an album—she was such a meticulous child! Could any grown person have performed such a fine, useless task without tearing the slivers of newsprint, or letting them mash up like so many hairs on the end of the glue stick? The Name, lifted out of its meager context and accreted on the clean album page, so that the page came to look like the work of a stalking obsessive. The Name The Name The Name The Name The Name (and just once, a PHOTO-GRAPH of the actress, with caption, an explosive surprise in the album's landscape like an earthly appearance by Christ)—it was ironic, of course, that Lee couldn't remember the girl's name now. And where was the album, that chronicle of obsession, of heartbreaking self-abnegation? And why was this the sluiceway of his thoughts, so that he just barely glimpsed the ink stain of The Name, saw the image, an imprint from a dream, but could not read the words, before having been carried along, or returned, to his own name, beating faintly at him from the page, a trapped moth beneath Jeff Trulli's finger?

FBI Questions Local Professor. FBI officials in charge of the investigation into the bombing death of Dr. Richard Hendley earlier this month confirm that they have questioned Hendley's colleague

Lee's name occurred on the page as a thin stripe of superreality, as if the ink had been mixed from a dense interstellar material and then finely tattooed with a needle:

"Dr. Lee is a Person of Interest to this investigation. We've had discussions with him and expect to continue to do so. This is a routine aspect of the investigation, and it is ongoing," an FBI source confirmed. At the time of the bombing, Dr. Lee was working in a room right next door to the room where the bombing occurred

"You haven't seen this yet?" Jeff Trulli said.

Lee failed to register the question; he heard words and could have repeated them, but only to the depth of penetration at which he saw the words of the brief article, and could have repeated them, but still had not managed to read them, as if his mind were a phonograph needle that kept slipping out of the groove, so that a snatch of the music was heard here and there while the melody never cohered. *Dr. Lee is a Person of Interest.*

"You didn't know this was in today's paper?" Jeff Trulli persisted.

It seemed a strange lapse to fix on, and Lee ignored it, his mind for the moment still pawing the words. *A Person of Interest.* He leaped at a vague reminiscence, as if this might prove that the strange label was something familiar, a normal if infrequent part of his life. Then he realized he'd heard it before, just an hour ago, as the FBI ransacked his home.

Dr. Lee is a Person of Interest to this investigation.

When his gaze stumbled back to *was working in a room right next door to the room,* the contrast was jarring. If the *Person of Interest* was an alien notion he strove to draw into the realm of the known, *working in a room right next door* was a sad, well-worn fact that now seemed to recede toward exotic frontiers of insinuation. Even he felt a sick-making upsurge of doubt; he *had* been in a room right next door, and the merciless truth of these words seemed to press on him lurid ideas that were not true at all. Was he a sleepwalking bomber? A servant of Satan? Why was his own innocence not a plain fact for him, but elusive and fragile, a condition requiring caretaking he couldn't provide? "He knew all this would happen," he said as Jeff looked at him blankly. "He planned everything!" His voice climbed, but his mind had stalled out. His voice was scaling, ascending, barely corresponding any longer to an inner condition. Inwardly he was strangely inert. He was aware of the theatricality of his voice and in this awareness had his first intimation of the theatricality of innocence in general: all the protestations and endurances its enactment required. Write a letter to the paper, confront Jim Morrison, ask for meetings with Peter Littell and the dean, finish landscaping his yard, perhaps finally put in azalea bushes, whistling all the while, make daily visits to the grocery store, be friendly to neighbors who had already decided to hate him while he'd still never found out their names, because until now there had not been the need, another advantage of living an invisible life—there were drawbacks to adoration, he had told himself back in the days he'd been pained by his envy of Hendley: all the maintainance, the handshaking and smiling and small-talking and dinner-party attending and squiring of Rachel and laughing with students, a grown man playing Ultimate Frisbee, wowing over the wicked new software, the line of waiting students in the hallway outside his door at all hours, not just office hours, while Lee's door, cracked invitingly open, was never approached. And now Hendley was dead, and Gaither somehow had made the world think Lee had done it.

Jeff Trulli was saying, "In a way this is better, to have it in print, this is really concrete, but it adds to my point that you really do need someone else. This is out of my league."

"You won't help me," Lee said, but he was barely listening, and at least in regard to this aspect of things—how badly Jeff Trulli wanted him gone—he did not feel surprised.

"I'm helping you by telling you I'm not the right lawyer. I'm a divorce lawyer, Lee. I've made some phone calls for you, there's a few names you might want to try, but if you really want to retain someone, I'd drive up to the city. I'd look for someone who's familiar with this kind of thing."

"I can't go to the city," Lee said angrily. "I'm being followed, Jeff. Look. Look outside!"

"In terms of your movements, I'm assured you can still go wherever you want. I called that guy Morrison and told him a white lie, I said you're my client. Listen: You're not facing any charges, Lee. You're not a suspect. You're just a Person of Interest. It's two different things. What he said to me is, you should just go about your business. Do what they ask you to do when they ask you to do it, and for the rest of it lead your everyday life. What I think is, and I say this as a friend, not as a lawyer, but what I think is, these people are just being thorough. They're covering their butts. And if you have nothing to hide—I mean, given that you have nothing to hide, you should cooperate with them. Breathe easy, and this will blow over."

"How can I cooperate more than I have? I talked to them, I told them everything I knew. Then they come and tear apart my house—"

"I know that must not have felt good, but what you have to realize is, you didn't *look* good. The way you reacted, in front of the cameras. You've got to try to let it slide off."

Lee had not thought he could be shocked again. "You saw me?"

"You're big news, Lee. They cut into the morning talk shows." This attempt at a humorous tone was a failure. Jeff Trulli's expression now bore relation to Rachel's, in the Wagon Wheel lot: uneasy with pity, but crimped by imperfectly hidden disgust. After a moment Jeff went on, as if he and Lee were discussing meter maids, "These are people just doing their job. Do *your* job. Go to school, teach your classes. What is it, advanced calc? I mean: yikes! I never made it past circles and squares." Jeff Trulli laughed nervously.

"They've asked me not to come back," Lee said. "Until this is resolved."

"I'm sorry to hear that." When this brought no immediate response, Jeff added, but without eagerness, "If you're saying this was an unlawful dismissal, then that's something you should talk to someone about."

"I don't know if it's that. I don't know if I'm . . . dismissed," Lee said, blindly struggling into his jacket, feeling he couldn't leave the office too quickly, even with the five cars keeping vigil outside. Now it was close to noon, and, amazing as it was, all the self-satisfied bustle of a normal weekday was in progress throughout the few modest blocks of downtown where Jeff Trulli kept his office, not far from Penney's and Sears and the rest of the town's somehow changeless attractions, which persevered despite two shopping malls and the strips of cheap commerce along the highway. The five cars, if they were still there, were camouflaged now amid identical cars parked the length of the street, and the traffic was as congested as it ever got, without losing any of its Sunday gentility, and as he groped his way into its lazy current, Lee dared to wonder if the five cars were actually gone. Almost as soon as he'd parted from Jeff, his eyes had sprung a leak, and he wiped at them with alternate hands, impatiently and ineffectively, smearing wet down his cheeks. Despite the gray weather, old people and young mothers with strollers were ambling through the crosswalks. He compulsively rechecked his mirrors, glimpsing drivers who might have gasped and jumped out of their cars if they'd seen him, the day's breaking news, in return. He emerged from the small traffic snarl into the emptier streets on the edge of downtown. Then he saw, in the heartbeat between his quick glances, the car with the baseball-cap man reappear behind him.

Now it was the streetscape in front, not behind, that came to him in disconnected tableaux, while the nose of the baseball-cap car was an ongoing presence. The baseball-cap man betrayed nothing, his eyes hidden behind sunglasses, his jaw clean and impassive. When they stopped at a light, Lee's eyes darted and his head jerked the same half rotation again and again, to confirm what the mirror told him. He remembered the day he had gotten the letter, and the tears he had shed, driving home.

"You goddamned lousy sonofabitch!" Lee cried out suddenly. "Sonofabitch murderer! So you got what you wanted! You got it!" The light changed, and he stamped on the gas in his rage, as a phantom form passed by his hood—could Gaither have managed this, too? Conjured a mother and baby, or a little old lady, or a Boy Scout and his dog, in the path of Lee's car? But before Lee had seen that it was just an illusion, he braked, with an inhale of horror, and felt the baseball-cap car hitting him.

He sat stunned, while an echo of impact seemed to pulse from the back of his neck. He had already shifted to park, but he only noticed when he found himself trying to grind the gearshift further into that notch. Perhaps it was the feeling in his neck that made him unable to look behind him; he was even afraid to look into the mirror. His Nissan was running through its repertoire of ill noises while idling, and each gurgle and wheeze sounded slightly more dire than it had in the past. A police car appeared, as if magically summoned. "License and registration?" the policeman asked when Lee had tremblingly rolled down his window.

"He hit me," Lee said.

"I can see something happened," the policeman said amiably. "License and registration. Let's just do first things first."

The baseball-cap man still had not left his car. Seeking his wallet with trembling fingers, Lee saw, finally daring to look at his mirror, the baseball-cap man with one elbow propped in his car's window, speaking into the same sort of portable phone Agent Shenkman had used.

An older woman had appeared, lumpy and slow in an aqua sweatsuit. "I saw everything," Lee heard her say to the policeman. "That first car pulled out, and then all of a sudden it stopped. It's that car's fault for sure."

The baseball-cap man now got out of his car, in the same motion snapping the little phone shut. "My car's fine if yours is," he remarked to Lee casually. His gaze captured Lee's like a snare; Lee couldn't look away from it. Baseball Cap stared at Lee blankly yet confidently, as if he knew every contour of Lee that there was and at the same time could never have told him apart from the world's countless other small, brown-skinned old men for whom he did not give a damn.

"That's him!" the woman said suddenly, following Baseball Cap's gaze. "That's the man that they showed on TV!"

"I don't know," the agreeable, stupid policeman was saying. "I may have to file a report. This lady says he was braking to create a hazard, and that merits a ticket."

"It's him!" the woman repeated, pointing. Lee shrank back in his seat, his laboriously located wallet now clenched in his fist; the rush of detestation he felt for her struck him like nausea. How had he lived in this town, with these people, for so many years?

"Stop pointing at me!" Lee shrieked at her. The policeman looked up in surprise.

"Can I just have a word with you, Officer Patchett?" Baseball Cap said with easy authority, leaning forward to read the man's badge as he reached toward his own rear pants pocket for something his gesture implied would be a similar object.

In the next moment Lee found himself speeding away.

He'd never broken the speed limit—he'd never broken any law— in all the time he'd lived in this country, and for some reason it was this ghastly perversion, and none of the others, that obsessed him as he raced along in the protesting Nissan. *Never in my life,* his mind kept dumbly blurting. Never, never in my life! Before he realized where he was he had turned through the entranceway to the state park, where the accelerated onset of spring gave substance to his sense that the last time he'd been here was eons ago, when in fact it was a week ago Tuesday, the day that he'd had his first idiot's notion about what kind of person the Brain Bomber was. A week of unfurling green leaves and the thorough unraveling of his own life. He parked at the farther side of the empty lot and turned on his car radio, expecting reports of his flight, but no stations had news, only agonized popular music of the kind Esther might have once liked. More than anything he wanted to sleep, to slip free of the waking nightmare by becoming unconscious. The familiar symptoms of insomnial hangover underlay all his panicked attempts at clear thinking. He could not go home, where the five cars had no doubt reassembled, with reinforcements, to pick up his trail. He couldn't go to the department; he thought of Peter Littell and Emma Stiles and Rachel and even Sondra and their disgusted condemnation of him. He couldn't go to a pay phone, or anywhere else where a townsperson might recognize him. He did not know Fasano's address; this deficiency seemed the only obstacle, if an insurmountable one, to driving the two thousand miles to California. He had no idea where Esther was living. But was it possible Esther had heard what was happening to him? Was she on her way here?

It was difficult to distinguish his longings from his practical needs, and both from likelihoods. He knew it was not really likely that Esther was racing to save him, but his chest still kept leaping out hopefully toward that idea. And he knew he should now regard Morrison as his enemy, but he also saw him as a singular arbiter. If his cravings for sleep and for the company of his estranged only child weren't exactly useful, at least his craving to beg Morrison for mercy touched directly on one of the principal elements of this disaster. He thought resentfully of young Baseball Cap and his portable phone; if he possessed such a thing, he could call Morrison from right here! Now it was the top of the hour, and the music had paused for a news break: *"FBI officials this morning searched the Farmfield Estates home of the math professor who was working next door to Dr. Richard Hendley at the time of the bombing that claimed Hendley's life. FBI officials describe Dr. Lee as a Person of Interest to their investigation. No charges have been filed yet in the case. In local sports news—"*

Lee snapped off the radio in horror, not just at what he heard but from the illogical sense that by receiving the radio transmission he was somehow broadcasting his location. In the silence that followed, his tinnitus, a condition he'd temporarily suffered after Michiko's departure, returned in the form of a low-level shriek in his ears. Across the empty expanse of the parking lot, he saw another car entering, and because there was nowhere to run he sat staring at it, hardly breathing, as it parked far from him, and the young woman driver got out and liberated a huge wolflike dog from the hatchback, clipped the dog to a leash, and strode off with her bounding companion. Lee longed to go walking himself, almost as much as he longed to sleep, but because he was afraid to leave the car, he instead reclined his seat and closed his eyes by an effort of will. Little bugs seemed to jump and squirm under his eyelids. He had to sleep; it would help him to think, and it would make the time pass.

He pressed his hands to his eyes, removed them, and stared up at the lint-colored cloth that lined the roof of his car. He consulted his Seiko and the Nissan's clock hundreds of times and reconfirmed every time that the two disagreed by just under three minutes. He could hear, beyond his tinnitus shriek, the satisfied chirring of newborn insects in the depths of the park, and a few times, at the ends of long struggles to empty his mind, he felt himself sweetly subsiding in imagining crawling among them, like a primitive man, and lying down on the ground. . . . Then he startled awake, terrified by the lapse in alertness that at the same time he'd been trying so hard to accomplish. Finally he must have succumbed. When he startled again, the sky was purple and dim, and his wristwatch and clock had skipped forward. And he had a plan, now, for evading the five cars and reaching his phone.

20.

IT WAS DARK BY THE TIME HE WAS NAVIGATING THE asphalt margin of the Street, or Lane, or Way, or Circle—although not circular, but this wouldn't have mattered—whose proper name he had never learned in ten years of proximate residency. His subdivision, all oversize beige and blue houses on unfenced sod lawns pierced by spindly saplings, backed onto another development that predated it by around twenty years. This neighborhood was split-levels and ranch-styles in heavy earth tones, on more generous lawns with back fences and even some dignified, columnar trees. A twin of the neighborhood Lee and Aileen and Esther had lived in and that Lee had loathed for its generic cheapness, though the twin neighborhood now was strangely enriched in appearance, perhaps by the passage of time, or by comparison with what had come after. Lee had discovered the connection, the secret seam between worlds, back when he had still jogged and had wanted to get in his run without having to drive. Out his door, left three times to pass the house of his back-facing neighbor, with whom he'd bought the pine trees, then past endless iterations of that house and his house and two other models of house, distinguished by just a few variations in color and siding, until the road dipped and crossed the pasture boundary of a previous era, a line of old, vigilant oaks stretching in both directions. From here, dappled shade and deep lawns and six or eight different models of dwelling instead of just four, and even more in the way of the surface distinctions, the shutters and porches and claddings of brick or wood shingle. It still hadn't been enough for Lee not to feel crushed by its sameness, whether its sameness to itself or its sameness to that other farm tract–become– suburb he'd lived in with Aileen and Esther, he couldn't have said. After just a few tries, he'd stopped jogging those streets, and his own, and returned to the twenty-minute drive to the riverside path, so that on this night, in this darkness, he hadn't been here in years.

He almost missed the entrance, a modest pair of stone walls, bracket-shaped, each adorned with a lantern and barely discernible curving black letters: Mashtamowtahpa Trails Estates. A single miles- across square of once-farmland contained Mashtamowtahpa Trails and Farmfield, Mashtamowtahpa's gate on the square's western side, State Road 28, while Farmfield's (ostentatiously huge and floodlit) gateway lay on the north, along Route 19. This meant that the mem- brane dividing the two neighborhoods was somewhere to Lee's left, now that he'd cautiously passed through the brackets. He advanced the car slowly, scarcely touched the gas pedal, almost noiselessly rolled through the waxing and waning of widely spaced streetlamps, each sifting its light down like pale orange snow; he was struck by the depth of the darkness in which the neighborhood lay. Single porch lights and even wide panes of curtained house glow seemed to snuff out as soon as he saw them. His own headlights a weak stain just ahead that was always retreating. He turned and turned along the dim involutions, found himself in a cul-de-sac, ringed by six houses, and felt his panic returning, as if the houses together would sense his intrusion and tighten on him like a noose. . . . He quickly rotated the Nissan and retraced himself. A left turn off the cul-de-sac street and he was mounting a crest and then dipping, and he remembered the attenuated version of that quick rise and fall, the signal it beat in his calves, his footfalls on the road, the unremarkable conjunction of place and sensation he'd possessed perhaps three times in all, although it came to him powerfully now, as a precious lost thing. Against an opening of night sky, he sensed the shapes of the oaks, black on black, angling off from the road. He had entered his own neighborhood. He turned the Nissan sharply and bumped off the asphalt and into the weeds. No one seemed to own the oaks or the ribbon of land that they stood on. There was a drainage ditch here and some mounds of dead leaves that had clearly been dumped. The nearest house was a half lot away. Lee turned off his lights and his engine and got out of the car, realizing he was standing lined up with the oaks, when he had always passed through them. For all their superior height, he had an uneasy notion of subterranean passage, as if on this spring night he'd smelled the chill, damp-earth breath of a cave.

The Nissan wasn't hidden, but in the narrow no-man's-land beneath the oaks, far from the streetlights of either development, it would be inconspicuous, at least while it was night.

It took him far longer to get home than it had in the days when he'd jogged, though he was half jogging now, huffing clumsily, the loose gravel at the margin of the road skidding under the flat leather soles of his shoes. So the briefcase wouldn't bang against his thigh, he held it pressed to his ribs. He hardly realized until the handle cuffed him under his chin, but he'd tucked his head low, to evade recognition. Luckily there was no one. He skirted zones of cold light and stark shadow where his neighbors had floodlit their shrubs. And he stumbled with alarm when he heard a strange, ascending gurgle and a then a long, hissing sigh, before he realized it was an automated sprinkler, a premature sign of summer.

He had passed his back-facing neighbor's, hypnotized by the scrape of his shoes, before realizing he was starting to make the hairpin, take the two curving rights, that would have landed him in his front yard. He felt suddenly frail with his own carelessness and almost dropped his briefcase. His back-facing neighbor's, as always, showed a huge SUV in the driveway, a basketball-size azalea floodlit like the tomb of a king, a light on the front steps and at the base of the drive, blinds down, lights on deep in the house. Looking over the roofline, toward his own house, Lee couldn't see anything strange, and this was even more awful, that the curtain of night had been hung in its usual way.

From a distance he heard a car approaching, and without further hesitation plunged across his back-facing neighbor's front lawn, skirting the SUV and the garage, his feet silent on a trampoline of sod. Past the garage and into the backyard, with its cedar deck and deck furniture, its aboveground swimming pool still covered and trussed like a tom-tom, light spreading from the back eaves but guttering and failing before reaching the pine sentinels. Lee pushed through them, felt their needles graze over his arms and their boreal scent shock his nostrils, confuse him a moment with pleasure, and then he was in his own yard, with its absence of floodlights and even house lights—his house was utterly dark in and out, clearly empty, as if abandoned.

The sliding glass door that led from his kitchen to his back patio— or to the slab of concrete that could have been the foundation for a back patio, if Lee had bothered to build one—had been open for days, since Lee had first been beguiled by the fragrance of spring. The screen door was closed and locked, pointlessly. Lee put the heel of his hand against the screen and pressed hard, and the screen broke, simply zippered away from its frame in precisely the way Lee had often imagined it might. Reaching in, he pushed the cheap plastic lever that locked the screen door, slid it open, and stepped into his house.

The digital clock on his stove read 9:40. He slid the glass door shut, and the noise of the pines slightly ruffling their needles, and the almost inaudible sigh of the sprinkler, and the rasps of the newborn insects—the conglomerate whisper of night, comforting and impervious—died away with the click of the latch, and he felt his chest tighten.

But the windows at the front of the house were still open, and with the sounds of the backyard removed he now heard something else: idling engines. And a murmur of voices. Baseball Cap and his colleagues, waiting.

Very slowly, as if its small metal feet might thunder on contact with the floor, Lee set down his briefcase, and his emptied arms, which had been clutching the briefcase so tightly, seemed to float into the air from the loss of their burden. He pulled his shoes off, wrenching impatiently, without undoing the laces.

Because his blinds were still raised, as he'd left them that morning when he'd rushed out to Jeff Trulli's office, he had to crawl and slink, hewing to the core of the house, and even then he imagined himself visible from outside, though his rooms were so dark he could scarcely see where he was going. He felt his way down the brief corridor, closely rounded the corner so that he was glued to the flank of the staircase, then followed it forward—steps invisibly descending beside him—until the banister had come to his level and his hand closed around it. A fat upright dowel, like the bar of a cage made of wood. The engine noise had unbraided itself into layers, and at the same time the murmur resolved into snatches of words. The foot of Lee's staircase delivered itself to a point just inside his front door; the house was so poorly designed that if the front door stood open when someone descended the stairs, that person had to first shut the door to step off the staircase. The door was shut now, and locked. Lee got himself to its threshold as if leaving dry land for a small, pitching boat and pressed himself against the door's surface. His eye found the tiny peephole, and then a cone of night opened before him.

It wasn't the five cars, but the news vans, each with its periscope neck straining up as if trying to see past his roof. Had he rounded the hairpin after passing his back-facing neighbor's front yard, he would have run squarely into their headlights—an old man in the "nice" outfit he'd been wearing since meeting with Rachel, cheap blue oxford now soaked through with sweat, baggy slacks belted somewhat too high, the shabby briefcase clutched to his chest as if he thought it stopped bullets, half-white ragged hair—when had he last had a haircut? his hair looked as bad as his house—standing shocked off his forehead. His eyes bright with terror, his trotting feet stalled in their tracks. He felt his bowels soften, a spongy sensation as if the floor of his gut might fall out. He saw that other Lee, his almost-self, as clearly as the rest of the moonlit tableau: two men sitting and smoking in the drivers' seats of two of the vans, and then a small, milling crowd of as many as twelve, moving in and out of view from where they stood indistinctly conversing, on the far side of the wall of three vans, in the middle of the street. For all their numerousness, the scene was strangely hushed and lethargic. Several people paced, their ears pressed to portable phones. One man said, *I did already, you know?*

Yeah, we are. We're set up. Lee's neighbors had gathered again; they stood deep in conversation on the lawn of the mother and toddler and hip baby. Then as Lee watched, the young mother herself made her entrance, scarcely dressed in a tank top and shorts and flip-flops, with the baby weeping loudly on her hip, but with an air of authority over the scene despite her dishevelment. She walked up to a woman in jeans who'd come to stand at the end of Lee's driveway.

Someone doesn't feel like sleeping.

WHO could sleep with soo much excitement? Could you, mister? I don't THINK soo. Nooo. Oh, he's darling. How old?

This little guy is four months.

Oh, he's precious. Mine are seven and five.

So where were we? I'm sorry.

I was thinking you could just go on camera with what you were saying. About how he's always unfriendly, and slammed the door in your face.

On camera? Right now?

In ten minutes. For the ten o'clock news.

Oh, gosh. I mean, looking like this?

He's always home by this time, a woman from the lawn group volunteered, coming over. Lee strained at the tiny porthole, trying to recognize her—his right-hand neighbor? *I mean, this is really unusual. No lights or anything.*

Like, maybe he's there, because it looks like he's not? asked the woman in jeans.

I'm not saying I saw him come home, but he's just always home by this time.

Brendon? the jeans wearer called. *Could you please try again?*

Do it yourself. You saw me do it ten minutes ago. You think he dug a tunnel?

He could have come through the back.

What'd he do with his car? He just made it go poof?

He might have been asleep before.

I've come over and rung his bell, continued the woman Lee could not recognize, *and I've known he was there, and he just didn't come to the door. One time when we were going to put up the play set we have for the kids, I just wanted to apologize in advance for the noise, and he let me stand there on the porch like a fool. I could hear his TV.*

A man was suddenly striding toward Lee's door, was approaching so quickly Lee found himself looking in the man's eyes—gasping, Lee dropped to his haunches, as if the man, peering in the wrong end of the peephole, might still somehow see the black O of a pupil, an iris cranked open as wide as it went. Fresh beads of sweat itchily writhed on Lee's skin. Lee felt the man's feet landing on the front step, and though he tried to brace himself, he still jerked in alarm when the dissonant chimes of the bell sounded through the dark house.

Dr. Lee? the man shouted. *Hello?*

The slab of the door jumped against him as the man began pounding on it with his fist. Each blow touched Lee at the base of his spine, where he sat curled with his back to the door, staring into the dark.

Dr. Lee? If you're there, we'd just like to talk a few minutes, okay? Dr. Lee? Then a scuffing as the man turned around. *Dana, there was no one here ten minutes ago, and there's no one here now.*

Could you just walk around to the back, please? Just try the back door?

Lee heard the man curse, his feet leave the front step, and as the man started his circuit, Lee flew up the stairs.

Morrison's card was where Lee had left it, dropped into the top right-hand drawer of his desk. Less locatable were the upstairs phone jack and phone. Lee had only ever put a phone upstairs for Michiko's convenience, and after she'd left, he had yanked the cord out of the wall and trussed the handset to the cradle and tossed the entire assemblage somewhere—on all fours he crawled the perimeter of his study, where books and notepads and other detritus were stacked on the carpet, pushed close to the wall. He held his breath and opened the accordion door to the room's only closet, and though he did it exquisitely slowly, the door still faintly squealed in its track. From downstairs he heard rapping on his sliding glass door, and the man's voice again.

Dr. Lee? Anybody in there? Dr. Lee?

The phone lay in the corner of the nearly empty closet; Lee's hand closed around it and squeezed tightly, and he felt the wrapping of cord biting into his palm. He backed out of the closet, the phone held to his chest, and with one hand resumed clumsily crawling the rim of his study, his free hand patting and fluttering, unexpectedly loosing a *ping* from the baseboard heater on the room's eastern wall. The carpet

was abrading his kneecaps through his thin classroom khakis. He suddenly remembered that the phone jack was for some reason out in the
hall; the knowledge came to him in the form of an image, the cord
snaking out of its notch and across his unvacuumed hall carpet and
under the door of the extra bedroom in which he kept a twin bed in
case Esther should visit. The voice faintly leaking beneath the closed
door in this flash recollection belonged not to Esther but Michiko, her
Japanese unmistakably outraged and yet also confidingly hushed so
that Lee couldn't make out her words as he stood with his hand reaching for the doorknob—as if now making up for that moment of cowardly hesitancy, he charged for the hallway, still scuffing along on his
knees, and lost his balance and pitched forward onto his face.

He lay there a moment, the hard shape of the phone carving into
his sternum, and the dusty smell of the carpet winding into his lungs.

Helloooo! Dr. Leeee! Bangbangbang.

Let's do the stand-up right here in the driveway.

Like this? Could I put on some blush?

Once the phone was plugged in, he could actually see by the fun-
gal green glow of its keypad. He punched the number with such haste
he misdialed, hung up, flattened his ear on the handset in search of the
restored dial tone, and instead heard the strange hollow click he had
noticed before; he rattled the receiver until at last the steady, flat tone
emerged, and then he forced himself to try again very slowly, with utter precision, as if reassembling the chain of a complex equation.

"There you are," Agent Morrison said.

At the sound of that man's voice, so unsurprised, even slightly
admonitory, as if Lee had arrived late for lunch, Lee's mouth was
leached of all juices, and speech suddenly seemed like a muscular
impossibility.

"Lee, you're going to have to speak up. I can barely hear you."

His mouth was pressed so intimately to the mouthpiece he felt its
plastic perforations on his lips and tasted its sour, used smell—
Michiko's left-behind breath and spit. He had the impression that
apart from his hot, flattened ear and his mouth, his body had vanished. "I can't speak up," he said.

"Where are you?"

"You tell me," Lee said, after a moment.

"Don't be paranoid."

"There are television trucks at my house."

"I can see for myself. Is that where you are? In the house?"

"Why even ask?"

"Lee, I don't know where you are. I'm not sitting in some big control room with a Lucite map that shows your current coordinates in blinking red lights. That's Hollywood stuff. I'm sitting in my crummy motel room, talking to you on my cellular phone and watching the front of your house on the ten o'clock news. If you're in there, you're going to have to tell me."

"I'm not in there."

"Well, good. I don't like the thought of you sitting in the dark listening to your neighbors call you a sociopath on TV."

Lee said nothing a moment, staring into the grainy obscurity that began where the weak phosphorescence that was shed by the telephone ended. The unseen hubbub in his front yard was obscurity also, the incoherent admixture of three live news broadcasts occurring at once. "Why have you done this to me, Jim?" he finally said.

"Why have I done this to you? I might ask you the same question. First of all, who is Jeff Trulli? You never told me you'd hired a lawyer. That seems very combative."

"Combative? You tore up my house! And you're having me followed!"

"I've taken that tail off you, Lee. Behavioral Science thought it might be a good thing to rattle your cage, but I didn't care for it. Happily, I'm even starting to think I might no longer need it."

"You expect me to believe that? You expect me to believe that you're so nice you told those men to stop following me?"

"Lee, in the short time I've known you, I've made it a policy not to have any firm expectations about you at all." This was said almost with the same geniality Lee remembered from their first conversations. Lee felt his chest tighten with longing—to be spoken to kindly again, to be highly regarded, again. . . . "Please excuse me a minute," said Morrison, and Lee heard a sound in the background, and then Morrison saying, indistinctly, "Is it here? Yeah, I'm coming right out. Sorry, Lee," he resumed. "My cab's here. I can keep talking if you'll pardon some bumps."

"Your cab? Where are you going?"

"How about, since I don't have unlimited time, instead of me telling you where I'm going, you try telling me why you called?"

He might have been trying to keep up with Morrison's taxi, on foot, he felt that breathless suddenly, with how urgent it was that he finally be understood. "Please, Jim, listen to me. The man you want really is Lewis Gaither. I know you haven't been satisfied with this answer, and I understand now! He must have changed his name years ago. Why else would he write to me? Why else would he expose himself to me? I told you this man is my enemy, Jim. He's hated me for thirty years, since I was a young man like you and you were just a little boy. And he is—let me tell you some more about him—he is a religious fanatic; he does not believe he is capable of anything wrong, even of *thinking* something that's wrong. I've been thinking about it, my God, I've been thinking about nothing else: How could this happen? Why should Lewis change in this way? But the truth is that it's not such a change. Jim, we get older. And the parts of ourselves that are the most rigid, the most extreme, the most difficult, sometimes these are the parts that come more and more to the top. When we're young, they're just an aspect, but if we're unlucky, they grow and expand and crowd out everything else. And this is what's happened . . . this is what's happened to Lewis. . . ." He had been speaking urgently, passionately, unfettered by any restraints of protest from his listener, and in the course of his speech he knew, from the awful elation he felt, that these were right ideas, true ideas, that had been long assembling like the dust in the voids between stars, awaiting the confluence needed to join in a mass. But the awful elation he felt was also the effect of another void, lying inside the phone line. His voice had poured forth, uncollected—the phone must have gone dead.

Just as he'd been on the point of whispering anxiously, *Jim?,* Agent Morrison sighed. "Maybe you really are the great actor, and I'm the big sucker."

"Jim, I'm no actor."

"So tell me the rest of this story. You want to tell me, don't you? About how he's trying to frame you and ruin your life."

"And he's done it," Lee said. "Even you think I'm guilty. You gave my name to the newspaper!"

"No, I did not. I'm going to tell you something right now, and I want you to listen to me. I did not leak your name to Eager Beaver at your piece-of-crap newspaper. Nor do I know who, on this little town's little police force or on your little school's little administration, might have done it. But let me explain it to you, the same way I explained it to Trulli. The Bureau has acknowledged that you are a Person of Interest. No one's calling you a suspect, except maybe your idiot neighbors. A *Person of Interest,* Lee, is all you have been called. It shouldn't be news to you, or to anyone, really. A Person of Interest is a person we think may know something of interest to us. A suspect is a suspect. You're a Person of Interest, and you'll stop being that if you'll stop being so interesting."

"But I've explained everything." Lee was trembling, his voice guttering as if he'd just been on a jog. "I've explained everything about Gaither."

Morrison let the slightest pause follow this return to the subject of Gaither. "Lewis Gaither never changed his name, Lee. He was born Lewis Gaither and died Lewis Gaither, and he's been dead for almost ten years."

These words hung in the air with a weird singularity. In the course of their whispered and hissed conversation, and outside Lee's notice, the dense percolation of engines and voices had diminished by steady degrees. Now all that remained was a last van door slamming, and then a last acceleration receding down Fearrington Way.

"It can't be true," Lee whispered, almost to himself.

Morrison let the shocked murmur pass by, a featherweight rag carried off on the breeze the night slipped through Lee's open windows. Like a seer Morrison said, in the same musing tone, "Now they'll leave you alone until morning. They've done their stand-ups, wagged their tongues. No one wants to lose sleep on you yet. But in the morning maybe they're here from the twenty-four-hour cable news. And from the regional bureau of the *Times.* A big break in the Brain Bomber story. And don't forget Eager Beaver from your local newspaper. He'll be back, with a sleeping bag this time, unless he's already bunking with one of your neighbors. They seemed pretty happy to help."

"He can't be dead, Jim," Lee whispered. "He wrote me that letter."

"But you'll go on and do what you do every day. Eat your break-fast. Teach class. Go about your business. You're an innocent man, aren't you, Lee?"

"*Yes*," Lee said, the phone seeming to slip from his hand.

"I can only tell you the facts, Lee. Your Gaither is dead. Is this re-ally a big shock to you? Most of my colleagues don't think so. They think that you're toying with us. But, happily, it now seems there's an-other old friend of your friend, who's more willing to talk. So if things go my way, I'll soon know what you know. Perhaps more." Their con-versation had become strangely languid, dreamlike, a hushed game with no purpose beyond killing time. From downstairs came the roar of an engine and a loud, compact crack, as of an ax striking wood or a gun going off, and then a more diffuse noise of scattered explosion. Voices, the engine departing again, Lee's body abruptly returned to him, crouched in the dark pouring sweat, the handset of the phone wetly pressed to his face, magnifying his terrified pulse as it beat in his temple. Agent Morrison sharply said, "What was that? Somebody toss a brick through your front window?"

Too late Lee remembered his frayed camouflage. "I told you I wasn't at home!"

Lee hung up and snatched the cord out of the wall.

He knew that his neighbors were at their windows, in the dark, as he inched his way back down the stairs, leaning hard on the banister to make up for his buckling legs. In the ambient light from outdoors, he could easily see the disorderly blades of glass glinting at him from the carpet. His thin curtains stirred. The temperature had gone down; he felt gooseflesh come up on his neck and his arms. At his front door, he peered through the peephole and saw his mailbox beheaded, its post angled from impact and the black box itself in the street, mouth flung open. Some distance beyond, almost to the lawn of the vengeful young mother, lay an envelope, a long white rectangle, reflecting the light from the streetlamp so that it was starkly aglow, almost blue, like a small sheet of ice.

It felt less like courage than a yielding, an almost grateful surren-der, when he opened the door and stepped onto the cool concrete stoop in his socks. The news vans were gone; all was eerily still; yet he would not have been surprised or dismayed to be cut down by bullets. Leaving the stoop, his feet sank into his freshly cut grass, and he felt the night dew instantly soak his socks to the skin. He walked toward the bludgeoned mailbox as if on a high wire. He felt almost pierced by how intently he was watched, and somehow this certainty, the needle pricks of eyes in a loose ring around him, was impelling. He must keep moving. He reached the mailbox, bent down, and picked it up by its door. It was empty. He closed it and put it under his arm. Then, squarely beneath the streetlight, he stopped and surveyed the stillness around him, made a hurried inventory with his eyes even as his head and limbs seemed suspended, motionless as a statue's; he had the idea that he must limit his actions as much as was possible, that he couldn't be seen dithering, that this would deplete him, make him more vulnerable. From a distance he must appear calm and resolved. He saw an advertising circular from the grocery store rustling slightly on the young mother's lawn. This would have been from his mailbox, too, but he didn't retrieve it. Otherwise he saw nothing but the stark white rectangle. Delivered as the mail always was sometime late in the morning, probably while he'd been leading the five cars to Jeff Trulli's office.

He went to the envelope and plucked it up quickly and before he could hesitate tore the thing open so that he was ambushed, overpowered, the past's etherized handkerchief snuffing his face; though he stooped shiveringly in the streetlamp, his nostrils had filled with a fragrance of days when he'd been a young man, the magnolia tree in full bloom and the mustified heap of old books overdue from the library. . . .

He turned quickly and recrossed his lawn, willing himself not to run, the lawn doubling and redoubling in depth. This was what felt like death, these falsely courageous deliberate steps across dew-drenched grass, his socks wetly sucking the soles of his feet, as he gazed at the face of his house, with its ruptured front window and its deserted darkness and no one in her bathrobe waiting on the front step, arms crossed over her chest, mortified but defiant, let the neighbors think what they want, fuck them, the hell with them all.

It was Aileen that he saw there, not Michiko. For an instant the lights flared on, bright little flames springing up on the eaves and the porch and behind the windows, all intact. Then the vision blinked out. He was back on his dark stoop alone, on a pair of wet footprints.

He had slippers in the front coat closet. He stowed the dead mailbox, peeled off his wet socks, put on the slippers, and crunched carefully across the living-room carpet to the back of the house. He still gripped the shredded envelope and its contents. In the kitchen he dropped them into his briefcase, where Gaither's first letter once lay. He removed the French numbers theorist and carried the briefcase into his bedroom. He packed by the light from his digital clock. It said 11:01 as he left the house the way he'd come in, by the sliding glass door.

His pines touched him again as he left his backyard, their needles clinging a bit in farewell to his bulkier outline—a suitcase added to the briefcase. He encountered no cars on the streets as he hurried. He'd changed the thin-soled loafers for his old running shoes, and he jogged a few steps but was slowed by his cumbersome bags. His car was where he'd left it.

He didn't stop to examine the new missive again, because it required no further analysis. Its origin was no less certain than its sender, and the implicit instruction it gave him enraged him not because he was doubtful about it but because of how promptly he moved to obey. The envelope was like its predecessor, a plain business-size 10, neatly typed, except this time it addressed Dr. Lee at his home and claimed to have traveled from "12 Ailanthus Circle, Lumberton, Idaho," though it was postmarked Pocatello. The address was a fresh fakeness that clearly succeeded "14 Maple Lane, Woodmont, Washington." The contents comprised just one sheet, creased in thirds. It had been the cavalier violence of those knife folds as much as the scent of the paper that had almost undone him. The page was all dense hieroglyphs of obscure mathematics. Because it was page twenty-four of a typescript, the author's name didn't appear, and there were just a few people on earth who might have known, as Lee did, that the author was Lee and the page from Lee's dissertation.

One was Aileen, who had typed all those pages of baffling symbols herself, but of course she was dead. One was Gaither, who'd never finished his own dissertation, who'd let the loss of Aileen end his grad-school career; Lee's dissertation must especially gall him and the chance to deface it provide an especial pleasure. As Lee had told Morrison, Gaither couldn't be dead. He was clearly alive.

It was just after four in the morning when Lee entered the town, and though he could see almost nothing of it, he felt abrupt gravitational loss, as if he and the car, any second, were about to be airborne. It had to belong to the past, to the lost and unsalvageable, yet once he'd come through the loose rind of outlying strip malls, just the same as the strip malls he lived among now, the old town, at its core, was the same: the same stalwart frame houses on companionable little lawns and the same brick storefronts and then the same abrupt intake of air, of surprising grandeur, as the campus first came into view. Great temples of limestone and blood-colored brick and the acres of lawn and the wide flagstone walkways. There had always been an all-night diner on the corner of Campus and Church, and it was still there, the diner he'd once gone to for Thanksgiving dinner and into which he crawled now, like a child into bed; he was served harsh black coffee and not bothered again, even after he woke with a start and saw dawn in the windows and the early-bird townies, white and thick and reserved and unchanged by the passage of decades, coming in on their ways to their jobs, at the school and elsewhere.

Adrenalized by exhaustion, he walked the quad, its perimeter and its dividing diagonals. He sat briefly on a bench as he'd once sat for hours on end, head bent over a book. When the library opened, he went in beneath THE TRUTH SHALL SET YOU FREE.

Not once in the twenty-six years since he'd submitted it for binding had it ever crossed his mind to seek out the library copy of his dissertation, which lived here and had a permanent address in the card catalog, memorializing a time of his life when it had seemed possible it would be sought by others, his own follower scholars, although by the time he'd defended, he'd known it was far from a Dieckmann solution and himself no Whitehead, let alone an Einstein. It caused him a particularly many-sided pain to conclude that apart from the attending librarian's, only one set of hands had likely touched this work in the decades it had sat on this shelf. Gaither's: they might have been grubbing the pages mere days ago. The image repelled him; he stood before his book unable to touch it himself, as if it might have been dusted with some fatal spore. The timed light at the end of the shelf row clicked off, and he was left in the dimness of the aisle fluorescents. He hurried down the row to reignite and, coming back, mittened his hands in his windbreaker pockets and pulled the book off the shelf that way. The pages had turned a sour yellow at their edges but were still white inside. With his fingers groping through windbreaker fabric, he had to make a few clumsy attempts to reach page twenty-four. It was still surprising to see that it was missing, despite the fact that it lay in his briefcase.

He stared at the broken page sequence, twenty-three, twenty-five, an upwelling of steam from his scalp forming worms of cold sweat down his neck. A much smaller sheet, from a notepad, occupied twenty-four's former place. This bore a message in English, not math.

The row light again turned itself off. With one hand Lee unclasped his briefcase and edged the intruder sheet toward its dark mouth. Catching the air, the sheet bucked very slightly, fell in. Lee shut his dissertation and returned it to its notch. He closed his briefcase, clasped it to his chest, and made his way back down the darkened row.

PART III

21.

MARK'S FATHER'S DEATH HAD BEEN SUDDEN, BUT IT
had been anticipated ever since the British doctor in Calcutta had
made the diagnosis of congenital heart-valve defect and told them that
death was not just impending but long overdue. In the end, the
impending event took another six years to occur—perhaps, as some
in the household maintained, due to divine intervention; perhaps, as
others (well . . . just Mark) theorized, because the doctor had been a
sadistic, fearmongering jerk. Either way, Mark and his mother had
each grown exhausted by waiting, and as a result both were caught by
surprise. Mark's mother had no longer been armored by stoic acceptance. Mark himself had no longer even shared with his parents the
same hemisphere. Because Mark's parents had called every materially
and spiritually undernourished corner of the planet—and so no
place—their home, and because Mark had been a two days' journey
from his father's body even after the three days it took his mother to
reach him by phone, his father had been cremated. It would have been
arbitrary to bury him in Indonesia, sentimental and expensive to fly
him to the States, just as expensive and perhaps as arbitrary to take
him to Sri Lanka—where he'd seemed happiest, but that was only a
guess: who really knew? not his son; did his wife?—and the weather
had been very hot, and the electrical grid overstrained, and the
morgue's refrigeration undergoing occasional brown-out. The decision to cremate had been unavoidable and yet completely haphazardly

made, and it showed how little all the years of expectation had as-
sisted in preparing for the actual event. Mark knew that his father
would have wanted his body intact in the earth, against a nearing day
of resurrection. Of their trio it was only Mark's mother who shared the
convictions that underlay this desire, but Mark felt his father's desire
as importunately. When he arrived in Jakarta, where his father had
been pronounced dead in the Catholic hospital five days earlier of the
heart failure that had finally struck as he walked with a young Christian convert to inspect the bore hole for a well that was under construction, Mark had scarcely been able to look at his mother. She
hadn't been able to look at him, either. All the painful, cleaving differ-
ences between them, the fruits of two decades of quarrels on every
subject from peeling bananas to thrice-daily prayer, seemed as nothing compared to the severing power possessed by that moment of perfect agreement. Mark and Ruth had both known that the box of gray
ash represented an inexpiable blunder. If relations between mother
and son had not improved, as Mark had hoped they would, when he
left home to live on his own, their sensation of shared failure showed
signs of providing the final rupture. After Mark left Jakarta, he and
Ruth did not speak for a year.

That had been nine years ago, the summer before Mark had turned
twenty-one. Since then he and Ruth, after the one-year hiatus, had in
fact seen each other four times—more than often enough, considering
the distances involved, to let Mark conclude that the death of his father had not provided the final rupture after all, but the beginning of
a gentle, and surprising, and to him desperately needed—that had
been the main surprise—rapprochement. His father's death, at the
time, had appeared as a climactic catastrophe perhaps because it had
come at the end of a period of Mark's life that had been exceptionally
eventful and, as he saw it now, miserable. Mark's difficulties with his
parents had at last driven him out of their house, then in Ghana, at the
age of nineteen. The time between then and Mark's reunion with his
mother and his father's dead body had been the most tumultuous and
lonely of a short life that, up to then, had consisted mostly of tumult
and loneliness. In the States, Mark had lived largely as he'd been
taught, like a penniless vagabond, but without the ennobling purpose
of service to God. He had lived with a series of girls, some actually

girls, even younger than he, still in the homes of their spaced-out or drug-dealing parents; some more accurately women, who were parents themselves, of children nearer Mark's age than was Mark to the woman with whom he was sleeping. One girl had taught Mark to cook heroin and then watched him turn blue on her living-room floor because she thought if she called for an ambulance, she would wind up in prison; and Mark had been saved by her neighbor, who was allergic to peanuts, and who came and stabbed Mark with her Adrenalin auto-injector, so that Mark came to life in convulsions, with his teeth chattering and his frozen blood screaming the length of his veins; later he'd prayed, secretly, and phoned his mother in Ghana. And there had been sufficient moments like that, of a helpless and harrowing sadness while lost in the wilds of his childhood's end (which he mistakenly thought was the start of his life as a man), when he had needed his mother, and called her, and so put in her hands a crumb trail of his wide wanderings, though it still was a small miracle (not that Mark liked this word) that she had managed to find him at all when the heart attack happened.

There had been the year of silence, then, and then the start of the slow rapprochement, which Mark only dared see in these terms as he crept close to thirty. His life after his father's death had not changed abruptly, but it had incrementally steadied itself. It had moved the balance toward legality, threadbare solvency, and monklike isolation. Mark was still, in his essence, a chaotic, disorderly person; he didn't know why it was so, but he recognized the fact now, which he felt was the fragile beginning of authentic self-knowledge. By twenty-five he had sworn off all drugs, cigarettes, and hard liquor, though he drank microbrewed beer with the obsessive connoisseurship of the sublimating addict. He suspected he might enjoy wine but did not feel educated enough to try to buy a nice bottle. He grew chary in his encounters with women to the point of seeming strange and virginal, so that though he still drew attention in bars, where he would nurse a beer and read, the women who spoke to him always grew uneasy and eventually sidled away.

Ruth had broken the silence, by visiting Mark, while he was living in Ashland, Oregon, and working on a flower farm, hauling hoses and hefting bags of fertilizer. Their encounter had been awkward and brief and unexceptional until Mark realized, once she was gone, that her stated reason for coming—a conference of Christian NGOs being held in Portland—must have been a pride-preserving subterfuge. Ruth had always scorned conferences, rooms of self-loving people who spent their time talking instead of just doing. The following year Mark went back to Jakarta to see her. After having spent more than two decades, Mark's entire lifetime, moving annually—if not even more often—from one benighted locale to another, Ruth had remained in Jakarta for almost four years. Mark suddenly felt that he understood why: The box of his father's ashes sat alone on a shelf in Ruth's small, barren room, in the home for impoverished and mentally ill women at which Ruth now worked. She had neither housed the ashes in a crypt nor scattered them; she had made one mistake and did not want to make another; and so she remained in Jakarta, Mark was sure, to be in the place where her husband had last taken breath, in the hope of some guidance from him. Seeing the box there pierced Mark. Ruth must have gazed on it all her nonworking hours. Perhaps she chastened herself before it, begged forgiveness from it, solaced it as she could. Mark had been an unpeaceful child, angry at he knew not what, wayward toward he knew not what, rebellious against God, he had claimed, but this had just been, in his family, the most incendiary thing to seize on. Yet he had never suffered parents who did not love each other; he had never known anything less than their flawless devotion. At the time he'd only seen it as another force ranged against him, a unified front he could not hope to conquer. He'd had to go far from them and live too close to—and sometimes inside of—some of the most miserable unions ever forged, to understand the rarity of their marriage, within which they'd tried so hard to shelter him, with so little success.

By the time Ruth reciprocated his visit, to join him for his twenty-sixth birthday, Mark had found something he liked, even loved. He'd found hiking. He had also been thinking, since the last time he'd been to Jakarta, of where his father's ashes should rest. The mortifying fact of the ashes themselves had been blunted by time. Mark could take them as a given fact now, and work forward from there. He had moved again, from West Coast to East, and when his mother came, he took her on a two-and-a-half-hour hike he had specifically reconnoitered for a woman of fifty-five, forgetting, somehow, that his mother, for all that her stride was very short against his, was as hardy and quick as a goat and could easily have hiked four times as long on a grade twice as steep. But he'd had another reason for choosing this hike. Though seemingly tucked in unremarkable central New York, amid nameless hills and generically pretty farmland, the trail, after gently ascending through fern beds and second-growth woods, emerged suddenly at the top of a thousand-foot drop at the bottom of which was a lake that appeared to be perfectly round. The hills rose straight out of the lakeshore on three sides, like a horseshoe-shaped fortress, but the fourth wall was open and gave a view of the quilted farmland, rolling into infinity. It was a kettle lake, formed when a glacier had pushed its load of scraped boulders and dirt to this site and no farther—this was the horseshoe-shaped rampart—and then started melting. A great chunk had sunk into the ground, like an ice cube in sand, and once melted became the round lake, a strange eye gazing into the sky.

Mark knew that for all his mother's devout Christianity, she was no science-denying zealot who disavowed the Ice Age. She was, in fact, a practical-minded woman who over the years in the course of her work had taken a keen interest in meteorology, geology, agricultural method, and even electrical engineering. This again had been a point of agreement between herself and her husband: the compatibility of Christian theology with scientific progress. She listened to Mark with clear pleasure. He knew that it had been a long time since he'd shown the sort of ardent interest in the workings of nature that had possessed him when he'd been a young boy. After they had taken in the view and Mark had shown her the direction in which Syracuse, where the airport was, lay—although, thankfully, it was not visible—Mark said, feeling his pulse quicken in trepidation, though he'd been trying to work up to it for the whole of the hike, "Sometimes I think about Dad resting someplace like this."

She didn't reply for so long that he began to feel claustrophobic, at the top of the dazzling cliff, with an hour's worth of walking back down before they'd be in his van and driving quickly away from the place where he'd made this mistake. But when she did speak, he was startled by how well she'd understood him.

"Because it's a beautiful place, and any beautiful place on this earth would be an equally right place for him."

"Yes," he said.

"You know," she went on, as if it were a topic they'd discussed on and off for the past half decade, "I think the difficulty I've had in deciding what to do with his ashes has to do with just that. With beauty. Because all the places your father and I lived, all the places in which we were so grateful to be able to do God's work—"

"I know, Mom," he said, because he could never abide being preached to by her. But she didn't bristle in return, which was another surprise.

"All those places were our homes, but they're not . . ." She paused, caught between truth and conviction.

"They're not restful places," Mark said.

She looked up at him, surprised also. He was much taller than she, on top of all the other ways in which he failed to resemble her, both physically and temperamentally, but he could see that he'd spoken her thoughts. "They aren't," she admitted.

Of course they'd made no decision just then, and Mark had even shrunk back from his own idea, perhaps because of how readily Ruth had agreed. If choosing any one of the two dozen places where Mark's father had lived as his last resting place felt too random, how much more random to choose a place to which he had no connection at all, just because it was pretty? But still, the idea persisted, not as a project requiring completion so much as a prism through which Mark now saw each new place he set foot. He had the sense, sometimes, of hiking alongside his father. There was nothing so certain as a voice in his ear or a second long stride ghosting his on the path. But he felt companioned, if not quite by his father then by a frail sense of purpose regarding his father, and his unhoused remains.

Meanwhile the odd jobs came and went, the apartments and towns were tried out and discarded, seven pairs of high-quality boots were worn out and replaced. One summer the derelict fire tower on Little Blue Peak, seven miles from his house, was rebuilt with state money, and on a warm day in April when the snow had been thawing for over a week, Mark packed tent and bedroll and three days' worth of food and made camp at the summit. He surveyed it, as usual, for everlasting sublimity of the sort that would suit Lewis Gaither Senior, and found it lacking, as most places were. It was still a fine place to spend three days alone, eating freeze-dried stew out of a bag and sleeping under the stars. He'd turn thirty this fall and was surprised to realize that in careerless subsistence survival, in apparently purposeless wandering, his twenties had almost expired and he didn't feel older but lighter. Part of some burden was gone. He still looked twenty-one, perhaps more than he had at the time. He still felt women, and sometimes furtive men, staring at him on the very rare occasions that he still ventured, battered paperback under one arm, into bars, slumping to distort his long-limbed, feline body, wearing a beard to conceal his face. But most men, the sorts of places he lived, far from desiring him, found him too pretty to supply his own woodstove, as he did, and felt compelled to be rude, and most women wanted to devour and mother him; so that, for the past half decade, since he'd given up serious drinking, it felt easiest to have few friends, no lovers, and certainly no one to whom he gave out his address. At the end of three days, he hiked home in the same deeply abstracted, unself-conscious trance by which he was always enveloped coming down from a mountain, scarcely aware of the smell of himself, or the raw spots his boots had chafed onto his feet, or the exhausted but pleasant vibration he felt in his calves. As his house came into view, it took a beat for him to fully perceive the two men, in a brand-new Ford Bronco, parked on the sprinkling of gravel that served as his driveway. He lived at the dead end of a very poor road that needled as far as it could into state-preserve land before giving up at a ROAD ENDS barricade, and people never happened onto his house unless they were lost, in which case they reversed in his yard and drove quickly away.

The Bronco, however, was waiting. He felt his rib cage constrict in alarm. He had to remind himself, as he approached, that he was now a law-abiding citizen. He possessed no narcotics. He paid his bills working construction and had taxes withheld. Even his van's registration was current. "Help you gentlemen with something?" he called as the driver's-side window scrolled down. He had a vanishing glimpse of himself in its glass, his dirty beard and long hair, his tall pack with his bedroll on top and his drinking cup dangling from one of the straps. The two men were clean-shaven and short-haired and dressed as if going to play golf, although there was nowhere to do such a thing in the region.

"Lewis Gaither?" the driver asked.

After a moment he said, "That's my legal name. I go by Mark."

"Your middle name," the passenger said, which was a statement of fact, not a question.

Both men emerged from the car, holding out their credentials. It wasn't the first time that Mark had faced cops—but the first in a long time. "I'd like to take off my pack," he murmured, making clear he was docile. When they nodded approval, he lifted the weight from himself—tenderly, tremblingly—and then set it, his only true home, on his steps, before leading them into his house.

In fact he had faced cops all over the world. At ten months of age, so the story was endlessly told—its repetition by Ruth her failed effort to seem merely amused by the startling event—he had vaulted from his crib and not walked for the first time but *run* through the house (Tanzania), out the front door, and into the bush, from which local police and search dogs had been required to extract him. At six years of age, he'd first run away purposefully. That had been while they lived in Sri Lanka, so he hadn't gotten far. He still remembered being led down a hallway, a khaki-clad Sri Lankan policeman to each side, each resting a palm on his shoulder. His waiting parents coming into view, his father's face wrung with mortified anger and Ruth for once actually crying, a startling sight because rare. After that he'd run away from almost every domicile in which they had tried to install him, been retrieved and returned by grim cops of all colors and flags. He'd run away for no reason he knew—was he searching already? He'd held nothing against them, hadn't even disliked them, let alone hated them, as they often theatrically claimed. He'd only felt separate from them, from the very beginning. Uncompelled by their faith, which was the whole of their lives, and so unable to connect himself to them. They had loved him, he knew, but he'd felt like a caged animal, restricted by all sorts of conventions that were contrary to him—and so misconstrued, and extremely alone. And perhaps this was why, though he felt he would like a companion, even after he'd forged his own life, the aloneness remained. Now he was forced to assume he must simply prefer it.

The conversation took place in his living room, the two special agents from the FBI perched uncomfortably on the block of upholstered foam that served as his sofa and pretending, Mark could see, not to absorb every detail of the thoughtless improvisation that was his house, which had been built—not by him—with components so shoddy that although Mark possessed all the requisite skills, he felt there was no point in ever replacing them. The Wonderboard in the bathroom was a soft mash of mold, the floor a spongy mélange of carpet scraps and plywood, the rest of the house an array of fire hazards, as if to offset the triumph of moisture. It was a house that rented for an almost token sum, even by the depressed standards of the local economy. No one had ever seemed to like living here, not because of the tangible defects but perhaps due to something more generally wrong, a misbegotten and mistaken sensation that applied to the entire site the house sat upon, and maybe even to the road that led here. There shouldn't be a house or a lot or a road; it all sat in the shade of the unfriendly mountain, in fact butted heads with it, and lost. All of which had made it, in Mark's view, the ideal habitation. The thing he'd grasped about the house at first sight was that if he lived there, he could walk out his front door and onto the mountain, which meant he hardly need live there at all. He had only ever cared for apartments or houses as places where he could store his equipment and park his car without getting a ticket. In his wandering youth, he'd once chosen the wrong place to live in his car while unemployed and without any money, and had wound up with tickets in excess of six hundred dollars, and a brief stay in jail, and a year on probation until the debt was resolved.

It had been a long time ago, although the emotions the episode provoked in him remained stormy and self-castigating. Even so, he was unprepared when the agents referred to the lapse. He'd been thinking they must be pursuing the methamphetamine labs that were now everywhere in his area and wondering if they could possibly think he had something to do with them, when the first agent, from the driver's seat, said, taking out a small notebook and examining it, "Lewis Gaither, formerly of Morro Bay, California, is that right?" Morro Bay was the town in which Mark had incurred the six hundred dollars in parking tickets, almost eight years before, not long after his father had died.

"I realize you said that it's Mark," the agent went on politely. "But I'm working here from your arrest record."

"Yes, that's me," Mark said after a moment, while within the constriction of his boots his feet suddenly boiled with pain, and within the darkness of his torso his guts somersaulted. He could not imagine in what way that incident was going to resurface now.

"Thank you," the agent said with surprising simplicity, making a note in his notebook and closing it. "Special Agent Schoonmaker and I don't want to take up too much of your time."

"Would you like to take your boots off?" the second man, Schoonmaker, asked. "You must be beat, just back from a hike."

"No, thanks," Mark said, flushing at the unexpected solicitousness. "I'm fine, really."

"If we could take one more minute," the first agent resumed. Mark had forgotten his name already. "We may be looking for another Lewis Gaither, who shares the same spelling you use."

"My father," Mark said.

Both agents nodded, unsurprised. "And he's currently residing . . .?"

"He's dead."

"I'm sorry for your loss. When did he die?"

"In 1986."

This seemed to cause some slight surprise. "Where's the death recorded?"

"Jakarta, Indonesia. He was a missionary there," Mark added, though this last was in answer to a question that hadn't been asked. On the inexplicable introduction of his father's name into this inexplicable conversation, Mark was aware of a rising rigidity, of a feeling of affront so powerful as to overwhelm any sense of caution on his own behalf, and even any politeness. "What do you want with my father?" he said. "My father never did anything but work for the church and for poor people. Are you sure you're not looking for me?"

The first agent said, "Unless you've gotten a new set of hands since you left Morro Bay, I don't think we're looking for you. We're looking for past acquaintances of a man named Lee. A mathematics professor."

"I didn't go to college," Mark said brusquely. "What does that man have to do with my father?"

"We think there's some possibility your father knew Professor Lee. Does that seem possible? Did he ever mention this person to you?"

"No," Mark said, his voice sounding thin to him, almost shrill, with impatience. "Can you tell me what this is about?"

It was about, apparently, the fact that the person called Professor Lee had gone to some midwestern school with Mark's father, where both were doctoral students in math. "That's not my father," Mark broke in, overwhelmed—almost weak—with relief, as if there could have been any chance that his father—so pious and remote and resented and insufficiently known, but not the least unpredictable—might in fact have had some other life, some dark secret, no hint of which Mark had discerned. "My father was never a doctoral student, and he never lived in the Midwest. He got a B.A. degree somewhere in Texas, Southern Christian Men's College or something like that, and then he went overseas to do work with his church, and he stayed overseas for the rest of his life. You must have the wrong person."

Both agents paused, to assimilate this. "Your father, to your knowledge, was never a student at the U of I?" Schoonmaker said.

"I think I would have known about that. He was interested in science—in reconciling science with religion—and I think it was his dream I'd pursue something similar, but obviously I didn't," Mark said, the unpremeditated, unsolicited, inexplicable, and far-too-intimate disclosure giving him the sensation of hurtling downhill too quickly, so that his center of gravity outstripped his feet, and it was all he could do to catch up, before painfully falling.

The encounter concluded in empty pleasantries about the region and thanks for his time that Mark barely heard, except for the final reiterating words of the agent who had driven, as the two men were preparing to resume their places in the Bronco: "Jakarta, you said? That's where your father was buried?" Mark had the sense, far less pressing than other current emotions but still irritating, that this was the critical point for some reason, and that he was not quite believed. But they could check for themselves, and he was sure that they would.

"Cremated, not buried. Jakarta. Nineteen eighty-six." They thanked him a last time and left.

It was only a moment before the sound of their engine had died in the distance and the sounds of his hills had reclaimed their dominion: a catbird in his backyard complaining; the breeze registering in the hemlock grove's faint susurrations; and almost drowning these out, the machinelike emissions from some ubiquitous insect that had hatched in that week's rising heat. Yet Mark was agitated, so much so that despite his exhaustion he could not sit still to perform the deferred liberation of his feet from their boots. It wasn't only the intrusion of his father's cremation into this brush with the FBI agents, as if the entire bizarre episode had been staged to reopen that barely healed wound. Mark had also felt a startled discomfort—which, rather than diminishing now that the agents had gone, was growing more acute— at the agents' suggestion, completely mistaken, that his father might have once studied math at a graduate school. The idea *was* completely mistaken—but it struck far too close to a true fact, repeated by Mark's mother as often and as tiresomely as the Tanzanian crib-escape story: that his father had dreamed of becoming a great mathematician. In fact, Ruth would say, he'd shown real mathematical talent. But he'd sacrificed all such ambition to serve church and God.

When Mark had moved into his house the year before, its mildewed basement had presented him with an ugly shock, if no surprise: it had been crammed with the leavings of a disordered life, if not several, and Mark had almost felt he saw the phantoms of those vagabonds as they'd been when they'd made their untidy retreat. No concrete idea of where they were going, no new pad yet; some fragile connection to somebody staying behind. *I'll be back for this stuff in a month or so, man. You're totally welcome to play the records, just make sure they get back in their sleeves. There's some good stuff in there.* Then a year would have passed, and then five, the caretaker long gone. . . . Mark had been able to learn nothing from the rental agent. And so, after a few months of uneasy struggle with the ethics of it, he'd borrowed a small Dumpster from a construction contractor he knew and set to cleaning out the basement himself, not entirely free of the feeling that he was chucking some alternate past of his own. Most of what he'd found had been worthless. The records, sliding heaps upon heaps of them, American rock he supposed might have been his own sound track if he'd grown up in this country, all the jackets and even many of the plastic disks themselves now grown over with bright-colored cushions of mold. He'd found a ghastly box of women's clothing, almost transubstantiated into a single webby fungus; milk crates of newspapery pulp, some of which he recognized as songbooks and some of which he couldn't recognize at all. And he'd grown sadder and angrier, in equal and increasing amounts, though why either and not just irritated he couldn't have said. What had happened to this music enthusiast, to his perhaps-girlfriend, to their whole sloppy circle of gypsies? Boxes of hostile, indestructible jumble: a filthy metal ashtray in the shape of a crab, a baffling sculpture of a figure wielding comedy/ tragedy masks, all the components being hardware, like nuts and bolts, welded together. Himself pitchforking it like so much rotten hay.

Only two items had resisted disposal. They were two saxophones— *two* of them. In almost identical mildewed black cases, the velvet within two identical horrors of mold. But the instruments themselves, once Mark cleaned them and applied metal polish and buffed with difficulty around all the little levers and doors, were dazzling, a pair of gold dolphins. They seemed to have rocketed out of the muck. Mark had no desire to keep them, yet something about the whole episode began to feel ordained, the dolphin saxophones leading him some-where. . . . Aggravated by this illogical, God's-hand-in-it-all strain of thinking, which could have been Ruth's, he wrapped the saxophones in towels and drove to Albany to pawn them, and there, in the pawn-shop, found himself irresistibly drawn to an old Canon camera, though he'd never had the slightest interest in photography. He made a trade and left the store with a camera: God's hand in it all after all.

Now it was hard to dismiss the aptness of the fact that out of the ruins of another life's archive his own life had a record of sorts for the very first time. With their ascetic and wandering lifestyle, his parents had never kept anything. Not just sentimental ephemera—photo al-bums and scrapbooks, baby clothes, toys, and drawings—but even such basic documentation as Mark's birth certificate were entirely missing. These lacunae had not bothered Mark. (Except, briefly, for the one where the birth certificate ought to have been. At age nine Mark had become determined to have his name changed and, being told by some helpful adult that he would need his birth certificate, had asked his mother for it and learned it was lost. "So you can't even prove Lewis Junior's my name?" he had said and, impelled by how clearly she'd blanched, "You can't even prove you're my parents? Or that I'm nine and not ten? Or that I even exist?") This was because

Mark's own habits were identically monkish. He had always disliked household accumulation so much that even when he'd lived in his car, he had felt too weighed down. This was why he'd experienced such recognition when he'd first bought and outfitted a backpack: his every need anticipated and ingeniously jigsaw-compacted, a whole elegant homestead that barely topped thirty-five pounds. Yet, whether paradoxically or not, it was his hiking that first made him want to accumulate—not objects but a record of things. More and more often, he found himself holding his breath at the sight of a black bear plumped on its bottom pawing blueberries into its mouth, or a beaver pair churning their pond with the whacks of their tails, or a pileated woodpecker drilling a tree while its manic eye twinkled at Mark, as if to suggest it could do the same job on his skull. Mark knew he was just passing through, that the woods were not his, but he wanted these things to remember. He wanted some proof for himself. He wanted to formalize memory—he had the sense he'd begun reconstructing himself, so that these encounters, and not his childhood tempest, were the touchstones he harked back to when he asked how he'd gotten to where he was now. He was no writer; the self-conscious, hunched labor of keeping a journal was foreign to him. But the old Canon settled itself in his hands as if it had never been anywhere else.

Of course, no sooner did he carry the camera into the woods than the bears withdrew up-mountain, the beavers ducked underwater, the pileated cackled from an unseeable height in the canopy. Mark found himself photographing those things that could not run away. The scarlet fallen leaves of maples beneath a first skin of ice. Sunfish Pond frozen solid and purple. And then, after the thaw, waterfalls to which no trail led, multistepped cataracts beneath shawls of hemlock seen by just a few people, if that many, in any one year.

He was miserly with film and took a long time to use up a roll; he also kept his library books past their due dates; and he grocery-shopped only rarely, and then extensively, for shelf-stable food. Those traits had in common, besides him, only their effect: that he drove to town very infrequently. Yet now, without showering or eating or even changing out of his boots, Mark backed his car down his driveway, with his library books, his shopping list, and even the Canon, though his current roll was only half shot, on the seat beside him. He felt he needed not just one but several excuses for going to town—as if the two agents were watching his movements.

At the general store, he bought neither groceries nor film but a one-hour phone card, which translated, if he recalled correctly, to just under ten minutes when calling Jakarta. He hadn't had a phone since the second time a bear pulled down his box and then sharpened its claws on the pole; by a tacit understanding, Mark now called Ruth from the pay phone in town every couple of months, while she wrote him brief, factual letters. When she picked up, she said sharply, "What's happened?" It was the middle of her night, and she'd last heard from him so recently that he knew she'd assume an emergency.

"I'm all right. It's just . . . something's been strange."

He told her, as concisely as he could, about the FBI's visit and then was surprised by how long she was silent. It could not have been more than five beats of his heart, but that was a long time if you knew, as they both did, how expensive the call was and how finite his card.

When she finally did speak, the focus of her interest seemed entirely wrong. "What did they say that this man Lee had done?"

"Him? They never said."

"They didn't give you any reason for their questions?" She sounded annoyed, less with the incomprehensible manifestation of FBI agents than with Mark, the typically disorganized narrator. "You didn't ask?"

"I might have, but it wasn't my focus. I thought it was a total mix-up. Are you saying Dad did know this guy?"

"No. I don't think so. Not unless it was long before I met your father."

"Then how can you explain the coincidence?"

"What coincidence, Mark?"

"The one I've been talking about. That they thought Dad had gone to a grad school for math. Didn't you say he always wanted to do that?"

"Mathematics was one of his interests. You know that."

"But he never actually went to a grad school for it. That's true, right? He never actually went?"

"Not so far as I know. No, he didn't. He would have liked to, I think, but he didn't."

There was something very tepid in these answers. "Then don't you think it's kind of strange, that these FBI agents seem to think that he did go to grad school? They even named the school. U of I—"

"I think the whole thing is very strange," she concurred, her tone no longer tepid but interruptingly final. "It's obviously a mistake. Your father never broke a law in his life."

He knew she hadn't meant to imply a comparison, yet her comment still triggered an ache of remorse, and for a moment he thought not of his father's strange past but of his own. "I thought it was me they were after—because of that thing." Although she knew all about it, he still couldn't say the word "jail." It seemed crude and aggressive, although on some level he was aware it was more his own feelings he needed to spare.

"All that's behind you now, Mark," she said gently, and there in her voice was her tenderness, that it surprised him to realize he still craved: that beam of enfolding compassion, which as a child he had constantly fought to divert toward himself and which, when he succeeded, was an unstinting dazzlement, like the mercy of God. His father's attention, by contrast, had pawed over him constantly, but in a spirit of dissatisfaction, which sapped Mark instead of succoring him. "It's behind you," she assured him again.

Then his phone card ran out.

Everything had bloomed late in the mountains this year. Even the mountain laurel, which every spring startled Mark with its instant appearance—the white froth of its blooms boiling over, the same way in the fall the tree line would abruptly ignite—seemed impeded, the usual process unfolding in syrup. While the buds formed, Mark had time to debate if the laurel would look best from far off, in its froth, or close up, as distinct little stars, and then he still had time left over to feel impatient. He'd often thought, in the spring and the fall, that he must be overly emotional, because of how intolerable he found the change of season—he couldn't bear to see it start, nor could he bear to see it end. Stalking those ephemeral blooms with his Canon seemed like a fine way to rob them of their power, to assuage his aching heart with the complacent sentiment of possession, as he imagined the lepidopterist meant to in pinning his catch. But he was also aware that all this thinking about his emotions was an emotional smoke screen he'd blown for himself. Behind it squatted the increasingly unpleasant form of his actual preoccupation: the unsettling, unfinished conversation with Ruth.

April gave way to May. The mountain laurel bloomed and submitted to Mark's Canon, and to his somehow diminished interest in its beauty and brevity. Mark took a job on a small crew erecting a modern-style house, very cheap and enormous with a vaulted living room that would require a fortune to heat. His days became purposeful and repetitive in the way they always were when he was working, and he felt the preoccupation recede from his mind, even as he felt himself scanning the streets of his town for the FBI agents, and scanning his empty mailbox, and passing with an accelerated step the town's telephone booth. The agents did not return, and he never, in his terse lunch hours with the rest of his crew, heard them mentioned by anyone else. He felt that his rolls of film shooting the laurel had been thoroughly wasted; he knew that the pictures were worthless.

The Tuesday he drove to town meaning to drop off the film for development, he left the rolls in the glove box instead, where the heat would destroy them, and went to the library. The town library, a minute institution of two rooms, was open just two days a week, on Tuesdays and Saturdays, because the librarian was an unpaid volunteer, who spent Wednesdays and Sundays in a neighboring town, helming their equally unfunded collection. Mark also knew how Dorothy spent her Mondays, Thursdays, and Fridays, doing accounting for a few local businesses, and driving for Meals on Wheels, and striving to inspire her retired husband to a level of activity more like her own. Mark was a favorite of hers, in the way that autodidacts are always beloved by the librarians whose labors they justify. Dorothy often signed books out for Mark from the other library and waved away his fines when he was late, which was often, because apart from funny fiction, which was very hard to find, his taste ran to overlong nonfiction books that took more than two weeks to read. He'd had *The Discoverers* by Daniel Boorstin for two months and was not even carrying it now, but instead a history of oil called *The Prize*, which he'd had even longer.

"There he is!" she said when he came through the door. "And he's got—oh, it's hard to see without my glasses, but I think he must have

The Discoverers tucked under his cap. No? What's that big square thing up there, just your brain?" Dorothy was not a librarian on the model of a delicate powdery granny with glasses on a long silver chain. She was a large, robust woman who more often served as a ranger for visiting backpackers, distributing maps and advising on weather conditions.

"If I needed to find out some things about somebody, how would I do it?"

"What somebody? Have you finally got a girl?"

"I'm looking at her."

"Shut up, you." As always when he came to the library, she indicated a small stack of books. "New arrivals. I hit a library sale in Ellenville over the weekend."

Mark sat down at the room's one small table, while Dorothy shuffled trail maps and newspapers out of his way. He knew she must spend her own money, not just on used library copies but on new books she read about in magazines and newspapers and then ordered by mail, many of which captured her interest solely because she imagined they might capture his—she was a careful student of his tastes, though she tried to conceal this. "Funny Englishmen?" he asked hopefully.

"Misters Wodehouse and Waugh. I hear they're funny. I haven't tried them myself."

"You're too good to me, Dorothy."

"I'm just trying to soften you up to get Boorstin. I've actually persuaded a patron at the other library to put down the *Time-Life Book of Home Electrical Repairs* and try Boorstin instead. Help out a curious mind in its first little efforts, Mark. Maybe you'll raise up another book lover. You don't want to be Professor of Pine Hill with nobody to talk to."

Mark abruptly put down *Vile Bodies*. "What made you say that?"

"What?"

"'Professor of Pine Hill.' You've never said that before."

"I didn't mean anything by it. I just meant for all the reading you do, you ought to get a degree."

"It's just strange. The somebody I want to know about is a professor, but that's all I know. And that he's called Professor Lee."

"The one they think is the bomber," Dorothy said easily, as if this were another of their ongoing discussions, warmly but intermittently pursued, for example their debate on the books of Tom Clancy, which Dorothy was "hooked on" and Mark found despicable. "The *Brain* Bomber," she supplied helpfully. "The guy who says he's going to kill the Great Minds to save the world from war? Earth to Mark? Come on now, don't be looking so pale. I don't think you're on his hit list just yet."

"The *Brain* Bomber? What the hell is the Brain Bomber?"

"You can't be serious, Mark."

"I don't read *People,* Dorothy."

"It's not in *People.* It's in *Time* and *Newsweek* and *USA Today.* He sends bombs in the mail to brilliant professors on the argument that it's better to kill them before they invent something that kills all of us." Dorothy riffled through the piles on her desk and then through the pages of a copy of *Time* before handing it to him. "Now the police seem to think it's this Oriental fellow named Lee, but he says that he's not, and very frankly I don't see it myself. He just looks like a little old Chinaman."

Mark winced at her comment; he never could get over how narrow even the best-intentioned Americans were. Yet the man did, as she'd said, appear little, and old. Narrow-shouldered, a slight stoop from age that perhaps only Mark would have noticed, with his keen hiker's interest in posture and gait. A complicated, weathered brown face, eyes concealed beneath the bill of an old baseball cap that appeared to have gone through the wash. A professor of math. Mark closed the magazine and returned it to Dorothy. "You want to know about him, but you've never heard of him," she said.

"I just . . . I thought he might have known my father, a long time ago."

"What would make you think that?"

Dorothy was the only person Mark could have called a friend in this town, yet he found he did not want to tell her about the FBI's visit, though he wasn't sure why. "My mother. She just mentioned this person, like he's someone I'd heard of before."

"Is she here for a visit?" Dorothy harbored a keen and poorly hidden curiosity about Mark's life before he'd come to Pine Hill. She'd once said, "You never *tell* me about yourself, Mark."

"No, Dorothy. She's in Indonesia."

"Well, excuse me. There are *airplanes,* Mark."

"And there also are *telephones,* Dorothy."

"There wouldn't be either if the Brain Bomber had his way. He's against all technology's marvels." Dorothy was filling a brown bag with *Newsweek* and *Time.* "If your dad really knew that man Lee, I want to hear all about it."

"You said you don't think Lee's the bomber."

"Well, what do I know? Sometimes it's the least likely people. In Mount Olive about ten years ago, there was a mother who was a registered nurse who kept losing her babies in crib deaths, and everyone felt awful for her because she was such a nice woman, and she'd nursed people's relatives and was involved with her church and all that, and it turned out she'd smothered every one of them. She did five in a row."

For some reason this anecdote made him want to escape her, though it was no more gothic than any number of others she'd told him, being also a fan of true crime. Now he said good-bye to her with such haste he was more than halfway home before he realized he'd left the Waugh and Wodehouse books behind. If he didn't turn back, he'd have to wait almost a week, until Saturday, and he was out of light reading at home. Yet the paper sack of slightly stale newsmagazines had the greater hold over him. Once in his living room, he read through them quickly but carefully. Most of the articles were devoted to the so-called Brain Bomber, who seemed not so unlike Mark's childhood hero the yeti, composed as he was almost entirely of hearsay and speculation. Investigators opined that he was "a male," of "between forty and seventy years of age;" that he was "fit" if "reclusive," "with strong attachments to the West or Midwest." No evidence was offered as the basis for this portrait, perhaps because it wasn't a portrait at all. A member of a group comprising just under one-half of humans, the males; the same age as any one of over a third of them, the forty- to seventy-year-olds; uncrippled, unsocial, with a tendency to wander the region defined by the exclusion of East and West coasts? (*The yeti hunts alone,* Mark remembered. *The last of his kind, he has no friend, no mate. . . .*) One eyewitness was sure she had seen him, a big, "fleeing" man with wild hair and long beard. Another eyewitness was sure *he* had seen him, a small, "furtive" man in a cap and sunglasses. That at least didn't flatly contradict the image of Professor Lee, whom the newsmagazines seemed to treat with a gingerly bafflement. He was always outside the main story, inside his own one-column box, usually under a headline like WHO IS THIS MAN? He was a Person of Interest, whatever that meant, a professor of math, colleague of the man who'd most recently died, unmarried, near retirement age, lived alone, "kept to himself." "We've never gotten to know him. He's not very outgoing," complained one of his neighbors. Mark examined the picture again: the slight, wary brown man with his eyes concealed under his hat. Mark couldn't even tell if he was wearing sunglasses. That was the first thing the professor should change: he should take off that hat, get a haircut, and gaze frankly into the camera. Mark could better sense the motives of the unseen photographer than those of the captured professor. The photographer must have wanted the subject to appear evasive, hiding under his cap. And Mark thought of his Morro Bay mug shot, an opposite portraiture style but with much the same outcome. Anyone—trapped by that pallorous light, slightly cringing away from the necklace of numbers, forbidden the plea of a smile— appeared not just guilty of crime but grotesquely depraved.

He wasn't sure what confirmation he sought until he'd stumbled upon it. The professor had earned his doctorate from U of I in 1969. A year Mark and his father and Ruth had been living an ocean away in Kenya.

It was just past four when he got back to town. Dorothy, who manned the library from ten until three, had gone home, but the general store was still open. Mark bought two calling cards and, back outside, fully closed the door of the telephone booth, despite the day's heat. He felt furtive himself, somehow like an impostor, even during the preliminary call to directory assistance to get a general-information number for the campus. Then he was stammering a fractured explanation to the campus operator, although she was just as impassive as operators everywhere. "My father was a student, I think. It was a long time ago. I'm just trying to find out, is there any possible way, he's been dead a long time—"

"Undergraduate or graduate?"

"I think graduate. I think."

"What department?"

"I'm not sure. I think math."

"I'll transfer you to math. I don't know if there's anyone there at the moment, it's summer vacation, and they keep shorter hours."

But there was someone there, someone who answered so promptly and sang out "Math department!" so gaily that Mark's overheated discomfort now edged into panic. He felt trapped, not just in the booth but in a chain of events that, though slackened briefly since the day that he'd talked to the FBI agents, now seemed to have pulled taut again and was hauling him forward. He could have hung up the phone but felt foolish to even consider it, and at the same time deprived of the strength that would let him accomplish it. The slim box of air had grown stifling around him. He explained himself as minimally and calmly as he could to the secretary, who said, "That's well before my time, but you're in luck, because Helen happens to be here today," as if he should know exactly who Helen was, and so grasp the extent of his luck, and before he could ask, she had called out, "Helen! I've got a young man on the phone whose dad was here in the sixties. . . . No don't move, dear, I'll transfer him to you. No, Helen, don't move! You stay just where you are! I'm transferring him. You just—"

For a moment Mark floated alone. Then the line opened again.

"Hello?" inquired a very old voice.

Perhaps he'd missed a cue; he was sweating, the handset of the phone slipping over his face. It had strangely fallen to him to integrate the person named Helen. "Is this . . . Helen?" he asked.

"Yes, dear. How can I help you?"

"I'm not . . . sure. I'll just tell you what I told the other person, is that all right? My father, I think, was a student there, back in the sixties, and I'm wondering if there's any way I can confirm . . . You see, I'm not completely sure—"

"What was his name?" she interrupted, politely, but when he spoke it, her manner decisively changed. "Oh!" she said.

"You . . . you recognize—"

"Oh, my land!" she cried. "You're Lewis's little boy? Can I really be that old?" He heard a peal of affectionate laughter, the pert woman, in the background. "You be quiet," Helen admonished. "You're Lewis Gaither's little boy! This is mortifying, dear, but what was your name?

I used to brag that I never forgot a student, but I'm eighty-two years old now. I'm so thrilled I came in today! I don't come in every day anymore. I'm eighty-two now. What was your name, dear?"

"Lewis," he heard himself saying.

"Of course. And how is your father, dear? He was such a handsome young man. So tall and so handsome! He brought me camellias once on my birthday. You see? I'm famous for remembering students. How is he?"

"I'm afraid . . . I'm afraid he's passed away—"

"Oh, my goodness."

"It was many years ago, almost ten years ago. He had a heart condition," Mark told her, almost apologetically.

"Oh, my goodness. I'm so sorry. Are you calling about a bequest? We're often honored by bequests from our students."

"I was really just calling to confirm that my father attended, just . . . to get the facts straight."

"Of course he attended. He was a wonderful student, like all of our students. So handsome. I remember him like yesterday. And your mother."

"You knew my mother?"

"Just to say hello, but I remember her. Such a beauty. Like a page out of *Vogue*." A note of discomfort had entered Helen's voice, perhaps the strain of supporting the fiction that plain, stern little Ruth would have ever glanced at *Vogue*, let alone appeared in it, but Mark only remotely heard this. Perhaps it was the sticky public handset in his fist, or the last exhalation of the hot afternoon in the stifling phone booth, but he felt himself linked not to unknown, nostalgic Helen but to his own ghostly mother, at the same time as being aware of his distance from her. A globe's thickness, across which his judgment could not fully reach. Was it true, as he suddenly felt—as he had always felt, but only now lingered over—that there had been the slightest tinge of a queasy uncertainty, a shifting of sands, a nervous improvisatory haste, to his childhood milieu? He'd attributed it to their vagabond lifestyle: a new nation of natives each year, sometimes even a new continent; a new shabby house long since soiled by previous tenants; a new school out of which to be thrown or to flunk. These circumstances were the cause of the feeling, of course, or were they in fact the effects? The effects of that queasy sensation, which had its cause somewhere else?

"And what was her name, dear?" the old woman, Helen, was say-ing. "Emily, Ellen . . . I'm sorry, I'm known for my memory—"

"Ruth," Mark supplied, and then even more brusquely, "What were the dates? Can you tell me exactly the dates he attended?"

"Ruth," the woman, Helen, was repeating forsakenly. "Was that really it? Ruth?" Now a new note of tentativeness: the long tapestry of the years coming fully unrolled, and beginning to turn into dust . . .

It was the younger woman, joining them on an extension, who got him the dates. "'Lewis Gaither,'" she read into the phone. "Matricu-lated September 1963. Attended five semesters, through January '66."

"Yes, that's right," Helen confirmed, relieved that here at least her memory did not fail her.

"Three years before Professor Lee got his degree," Mark heard himself saying, without adding that his father's time as a student had also lasted, illogically and impossibly, until two months after he, Mark, had been born.

"Oh, *God,*" the younger woman said. "Don't get me started on that. We've had reporters calling all hours for weeks. How do you think I found your dad's file so fast? The sixties drawer has gotten quite a workout lately."

"A terrible thing," Helen said quietly. "And they were such good friends," she added.

"They were?" Mark snapped. "Lee and my father?"

"Oh, yes. At least at the beginning. Isn't it hard to believe, how two friends could turn out so different?"

He couldn't end the call quickly enough; they were sending him a copy of his father's transcript, but he didn't give a damn about that anymore. He would throw it away when it came, his mother's son to the core, because didn't she, too, retain nothing? No documents, no photographs, nothing picturing herself as bizarrely remembered by foggy-brained Helen as head-turning and worthy of *Vogue*—

"Who's Lee?" he asked as soon as she picked up. The middle of her night again, but he didn't apologize.

A slight, perhaps entirely imagined, hesitation. "Who?" she said.

"Not Who. Lee. Don't tell me you've become a late admirer of Abbott and Costello." Of course she didn't grasp this, and he wasn't actually trying to be funny. He was angry, a physiological cluster of symptoms with no clear intellectual basis. Clenched jaw, clenched gut, clenched hand around the telephone handset. "Who's Lee?" he repeated.

"I don't know, Mark. Isn't it the man that the FBI agents were asking about? I told you I'd never heard of that person."

"Don't lie to me again."

"When have I ever lied to you, Mark?"

"You've always said Dad never went to grad school. *Three weeks ago* you said it. Now it turns out those FBI agents weren't mixed up at all. Dad went to the U of I for almost three years, and you must have been right there with him, and me too, since he was still going there on my birthday. What's going on here, exactly? Why'd you lie about this?"

"I don't like your tone, Mark. I don't like it at all. I don't suppose you've been drinking."

"If by 'drinking' you mean my occasional enjoyment of a bottle of beer, no, I haven't been drinking. Answer my goddamn question."

The line went dead.

"Oh!" he roared at the graffiti-scoured, heat-warped, sweat-steamed Plexiglas walls of the telephone booth. "So that's worse? So I took the fucking Lord's name in vain and that's fucking worse?" The fucking Lord only knew what he might have said to her, his rage as powerful as it ever had been in his volcanic teenage years, if she'd answered when he called her again, the next moment, but she didn't; she let it ring and ring and ring, and she never picked up. There was so much here not to believe: that his mother was turning her back, walking quickly away from her phone; that the phone really could keep on ringing for five minutes, six, with each shrill iteration exactly the same, with no chance of a lengthened or truncated pause, with no expressive ascent in the key, just the same harsh mechanical noise, his entreaty repulsed—and it was finally that, the monotony of it, that bludgeoned his anger to nothing, that left him bled out and unfeeling, and let him hang up.

22.

IT WAS FROM AN OLDER HIKER NAMED GENE THAT
Mark had learned the art of keeping a pack always ready, inside the
front door. Grab and go: he still remembered how powerfully this notion of preparedness for flight had impressed him. He'd met Gene
playing pool in a bar and soon they'd been hiking together at least
once a week. Despite Gene's seniority of at least fifteen years, they'd
struck up an easy sympathy rare in Mark's life. Grab and go: until seeing Gene's pack, Mark had never desired to emulate any person in any
respect. The canteens always full. Dry food portions to last for a week.
In the short time Mark knew him, Gene would often be gone, without
warning, even longer than that. Mark would drop by with his own
pack hike-ready some morning, or with a bottle some evening and
find Gene's door unlocked, as always, his house as always submerged
beneath friendly disorder, but the opaque, knotted, soldierly pack
would be gone from the hall. Gene's truck or his motorcycle, a 1969
Triumph Bonneville to which he was devoted, would be gone from the
driveway. Mark would labor to quell his hurt feelings by extracting a
lesson he hoped to absorb. Later he would reflect that, though he'd
scarcely known Gene, he'd admired him. For Mark, admiration had
never come easy, perhaps because it had been urged on him from a
too-early age. Ruth had urged him to admire his father, and his father
had urged him to admire her, and although he had loved them, he had
striven with increasing difficulty to guard this flame of childish adoration in the face of their exhortations. Meeting Gene, admiration had
been a reflex; he had seen in the other man his idealized self, calmed
with age and the self's acceptance of the things it can't be.

One night, when he had known Gene a couple of months, and they
had been playing cards and drinking Jim Beam in Gene's living room—
an unapologetic bachelor's nest with sagging couch and gigantic TV
and stacks of firewood in the corners, and the beloved Bonneville
dominating, with Gene's tools scattered in a sort of worshipful sunburst
design all around it—Mark had gone to take a piss and found that the

shower curtain in the bathroom, which he realized he had always until now seen closed, was open, exposing a tub full of bright plastic boats.

Coming out, he'd heard Gene taking a hammer to a sack of ice in the kitchen, and in obedience to an intrusive impulse almost foreign to him, he'd opened Gene's bedroom door, which, like the shower curtain, he had always seen closed. Within was the familiar disorder of the unmarried man, laundry of unknown condition in heaps, but on the walls near the head of Gene's bed were framed photographs, in great number, of two boys. A range of ages: three and five, perhaps; five and seven; seven and nine. Flannel shirts and blue jeans, or shirtless in swim trunks; spray of freckles; a familiar, self-confident, open expression that somehow contained a remoteness: the complete self, enthroned in its place, far in the future of—or deep in the soul of, or in both places of—each small boy.

Mark had suffered an inexplicable sense of betrayal. Hearing Gene coming out of the kitchen he'd left the room quickly, shut the cheap hollow-core door noiselessly, rejoined Gene, played a couple more hands, and then told him good night. In the months that followed, he'd never asked Gene about his children, nor had Gene mentioned them, although now, on the occasions that Mark found Gene gone, and the pack gone, and the truck, not the motorcycle, absent from the driveway, Mark sensed that Gene was off with his sons.

Later that year, in the winter, Mark learned that the boys were named Wesley and Drew. They were, at that time, ten and twelve. They lived with their mother, whose name Mark never heard. Walking into the bar where he first had met Gene, Mark was told that Gene, on his motorcycle, had been struck by an eighteen-wheeler, pulled beneath it, and killed. Gene had been on his way home from seeing his sons. Their existence was so generally known in the bar—indeed their likes, dislikes, habits, hobbies, funny sayings, all were discussed—that Mark wondered if Gene had only thought that Mark must know them, as all the town did. He wondered if Gene had not spoken of Wesley and Drew because they went without saying.

Mark had given notice on his rented room and his job that same week, had moved away from that town, and had never gone back there again.

It was also true, Mark reflected now, that he had never told Gene very much of himself. They had spoken of the lean-to on the pond, of the fish that were biting or not, of half-baked DEP regulations, of the woman still weeping alone at the end of the bar, of the blazes that hadn't been fixed on the trail, of the people those blazes got lost, of the wasp's gray balloon in the tree, of the cherry's great age, of the old growth, the clear cut, the jewelweed coming in bloom.

They had spoken of those aspects of the immediate world they shared. For Mark it had been an intimacy of perfect clarity and perfect simplicity, devoid of anguished barings of the soul. And wasn't this what he sought? The sense of having found his snug place, without having to pay in disclosures, in endless confessions and self-revelations? That was what repelled Mark from religion: all that supposedly selfless obsession with self, with self's failings and sins and past lapses and present resolves. Mark never could bear all that speaking of *self,* all that cleansing of *self,* all that woebegone self-proffering in the hope of forgiveness. More than anything it had been the necessity that he constantly yield his *self* that had propelled his resistance to church, not, as his parents had wanted to think, the necessity that he believe in God. Such belief, if it could have been his, was something he would have enjoyed. He knew that he yearned for the truly great thing, the One thing. He'd yearned for it in drugs, and in gypsy crisscrossings from West Coast to East, and most happily down the trails with Gene. Perhaps it wasn't his particular birthright; every human must have it. But Mark had gained from his parents an outsize preoccupation with that yearning and a tendency to put it ahead of all other concerns.

Perhaps he'd felt injured that Gene had not told him about Wesley and Drew because his contentment with Gene had been almost monastic. He had loved Gene not as a father or friend or sibling but as if they'd been two mendicants, a pair of Franciscans with backpacks, allied in their choice of essential aloneness, and free of all ties to the world. And yet all that time Gene had his sons.

Mark had been steadily climbing for almost two hours, as the tender coolness of early morning was swallowed by heat, and the chirr of the insects rose up into such an unvarying roar Mark soon stopped hearing it. The trees all around were the color of spring, that impossibly fresh, vibrant green that could make Mark's chest ache, as if the leaves were too young to be out in the weather and should have been packed up in cotton at night. And yet the woods were impenetrable to his eye; the leaves were youthful, but they were full size, and when Mark gazed between the tree trunks, the leaves filled up the spaces between like a depth of chartreuse-colored water. Mark knew from his map that the trail, which was ascending the flank of a mountain, was going to level off soon in a sort of a saddle between two higher peaks, but he couldn't make out any sign that the saddle was near.

All at once he was there, as if he'd stepped off a staircase. The ground was level beneath his feet, and he'd entered a natural clearing, with long, silken grass underfoot and the trees that marked off a perimeter mingling their boughs overhead, so that in spite of the clearing below, there was no patch of sky overhead, only sun-dappled shade. Mark's strange sense he was underwater intensified. Somehow an expanse of old growth had survived here, so that he seemed to stand in an arcade, or a mosque, with the columnar trunks rising out of a verdant prayer rug. It took him a moment to realize that his impression of a temple wasn't entirely fanciful metaphor. At one side of the clearing, thick segments of tree trunk about two feet across had been crudely cut into chairs, one cut crosswise to just over halfway, a second cut lengthwise to meet the first, so that a chunk was removed and the segment became a squat L, its seat not much more than a foot off the ground. There were eight of them, ranged in a circle, around the vestige of a fire pit so overgrown that it probably hadn't been used since the previous summer.

Mark turned around, slowly, but he didn't see any cut stump nearby. The maker of the chairs must have lugged the fat logs here from elsewhere, perhaps already cut into chairs, perhaps with a chain saw to do it on site. But as obvious a process as it was that had led to these chairs—the fat logs, the two cuts with the saw—Mark couldn't envision it. The circle of chairs seemed ancient and ordained, as if they'd grown out of the earth on their own, or been conjured by nonhuman force.

He stood hesitating so long that all the exertion of the past few hours had the chance to catch up with him, and his legs became meltingly tired. He squatted, freed himself from his pack, and then, as if it might bite or collapse, gingerly sat down on one of the chairs. Once settled, he felt all the clandestine excitement of his boyhood, inventing tales of castles and broadswords and strange amulets. The other seven empty chairs seemed to quiver in expectation. The clearing had a contrary atmosphere that mingled secretiveness with exposure, so that Mark felt he'd tripped through a portal and tumbled away from the world and at the same time was sure he'd be intruded upon any moment. He'd seen no one on the trail this morning; no other car had been parked at the trailhead. But he was in the northeastern United States of America, never far from his fellow humans, no matter how he might try to sequester himself and pretend.

Although splintery, sharp-edged, and unaccommodating, the chair seemed to embrace him; he found himself falling asleep. The chirr of insects swelled and ebbed like a tide, but it might only have been his drowsiness that found a rhythm in the drone. He felt certain that something happened here, that this Stonehenge of logs must mark a site of conjunction, a seam between worlds, where the one, every four thousand years, would reach into the other. . . .

He had fallen asleep. When he jerked awake, he felt the same embarrassment he might have if he'd started to snore in a movie, to the unseen but palpable displeasure of persons nearby. He couldn't quite persuade himself he was alone here; he checked his map, shouldered his pack again, and spent several minutes probing the perimeter of the clearing for his trail, which he finally found winding off very faintly in the direction of the modest peak—thirty-eight hundred feet—where he meant to eat lunch. Perhaps he'd come back here and camp for the night. Perhaps not—he brusquely shook off the enchantment once walking again. He didn't owe the place any additional tribute. The more distance he gained from it, the stronger his sense it was someone else's, with no space for him, although the land was public and no one could have claimed it.

After another half hour of steady climbing, he was astonished to find himself in a froth of pristine mountain laurel. All tidy-cornered and white like so many fresh handkerchiefs sized for a wren; when Mark brought his giant's nose close, he could see needle pricks of deep pink, each so small it seemed strange to be able to make out their color. He could not understand this return to the last weeks of spring, when the summer had already poured the woods full of chartreuse; it was at his back and a few hundred feet below him, the high heat and dense bug drone of June, and yet here he was spirited into the past, before the FBI came to his home, before his mother had hung up the phone. . . . His camera was locked in his van at the trailhead, three hours behind him. This fresh evidence of his lucklessness choked a groan from him, and the wild, wounded sound startled him, as did the fact that he'd started to cry, tipped forward to counter the weight of his pack, with his face in the flowers.

Mark was aware that a crisis of unprecedented type and degree was fomenting in him. His lifelong habits of near solitude, of having very few friends at any one time and never keeping any for long, of speaking little of himself even when he was given the chance, were due only to a distance between him and others, not between him and himself. Hence his distaste for self-centered religion. Such believers, Mark felt sure, did not know themselves; they viewed themselves with a mix of fascination and dread; they made their business their own re-demption as a way of avoiding any real confrontation with the stuff of their souls. Mark's father had been one of these: his aloofness from others was a function of his aloofness from self. But Mark felt he was more like his mother: tight-lipped toward others because all too aware of the unruliness of himself. Of course, Mark had never confirmed this with her; the members of the Taciturn Tribe don't jaw on about how they don't talk. But little as he understood Ruth, the one thing he'd felt sure of was that she understood herself and was just keeping quiet about it, the way that Mark did.

That Mark was aware of the fomenting crisis did not mean he knew when or how it would break. This wasn't due to insufficient self-knowledge but to insufficient time. The crisis was on the horizon, making steady advance, but at a speed that could not be determined.

Mark stopped crying, broke a pom-pom of blooms from a branch, and stuck it into his chest strap. He started climbing again. Right away the terrain grew so steep he really was climbing stairs, jagged blocks piled up on each other, the slim trunks of the laurel growing almost straight out, so that Mark could use them as handholds to pull himself up, which loosed a snowfall of petals.

Gene would have known what to do about the circle of chairs, by which thought Mark meant that Gene would have known what atti-tude to take, and what manners to use. Gene would have known whether it was an honorable or a dishonorable thing to have colonized the woods in this way. Gene might have known, just from examining the logs, if they'd been deadwood or a live tree cut down for that purpose. Gene would have known whether to treat the chairs as a public amenity, to which all had rights and for which all were responsible, or as a private vandalism—the circle to be broken, the chairs scattered, the fire pit filled in, covered over, so as not to be used.

But the object Mark really pursued by this indirect train was that Gene would have known what to do about Mark's brewing crisis. As little as he'd let Gene know him, and as little as he'd known Gene himself, Mark had mourned him as if somehow realizing that a time would arrive in his future when he'd need a priest. And given that Mark had dodged priests all his life, Gene was as close to a priest as Mark had.

Still, it was because of his solitude, and the undisciplined, off-trail wanderings of his mind—and not because he thought such an exercise in hokum would do any good—that Mark found himself narrating for Gene the events of the past several weeks, as if they were sitting across from each other at Gene's card table, with the bottle of Jim Beam and a bowl of ice, while Gene cut and shuffled the cards and Mark refilled their glasses. They were not on the trail, where no serious hiker enjoyed conversation; the trail was for hiking, not talking. So that as he climbed through the clouds of white laurel, until they slowly thinned out and he had come to a place of stunted chestnut and black gum and oak and longer grass and an opening sky, Mark was two places at once and two times at once: with Gene both before him and lost to him, and his mother both as she had been all his life and as she was now—for which Mark had no words.

We're all mysteries to our kids. That's the way it should be. Those two—Gene gestured toward the bathroom, from which came sounds of squealing and splashing—they'll never know who I was. And they shouldn't. I knew too much about my old man, and just enough about my mom. I loved her, and I hated his guts.

If we don't know the people we came from, Mark said, how do we know who we are?

I can't agree with you there. You're not those people. Lighting a fresh cigarette, Gene added, I struck the match, but that flame isn't part of me. It doesn't need to ask me, "What is fire?"

That, Mark said, is a stoned thought if ever I heard one. They both laughed.

I'm not stoned, Gene remarked, but I sure wish I was. Just another thing my boys don't need to know. Gene went to get Wesley and Drew out of the bathtub and into pajamas. Mark listened to their easy rough-housing, the boys' protests and Gene's admonitions, small wet feet slapping down the hallway, water sucked down the drain.

Mark was crossing a meadow, all long golden grass lying flat in the wind and huge lichen-stained boulders left there by some thundering glacier; thigh-high blueberry bushes just forming the first sour green fruits. He was on the summit: no dramatic triangular point, but a vast tableland swept by wind and pressed upon by the sun. He knew he was high from the neighboring peaks he could see, dark ever-greened masses like motionless waves, or the spines of humped beasts, bursting up from the edge of the prospect. He'd chosen this peak for its openness, as described in his book; the other summits were higher, but entirely forested. Blind.

Only God can give you knowledge of yourself, said Mark's father. He made you.

I don't believe in Him, Mark said again.

You love Creation. Look at this place you've sought out! You must love the Creator.

It's not math, Dad. It's not "*if P, then Q.*"

So says my atheist son who flunked math, Mark's father observed, not without bemusement.

Your mom's hiding something from you, Gene observed, coming back. That's a reason to be pissed off, sure. But it's really her problem, not yours. You don't need your mom to be honest. You have your own life.

I don't know who I am.

Sure you do. You're the kid who always went his own way, always rogue of the herd. Climbed out of your crib at ten months and walked out the front door. Tanzania.

I never told you that shit.

You could have.

They were silent.

Though I have to say, Gene added after a moment, ten months is pretty early for walking. You must have been crazy.

I have a feeling I was older, Mark said. I have a feeling I *am* older.

Yeah? How do you mean?

Like something's missing. Some part of my life.

Mark kept moving across the meadow, pushing through the tall grass and the islands of high-bush blueberry, passing groves of little gnarled hardwoods that gripped their scant leaves against the strong wind. It was a summer wind, warm in his face. He was drawn on by his sense that the meadow's exact center point lay just beyond, and again just beyond where he was. The dark, distant neighboring peaks shifted slightly. He'd lost the trail long ago, upon coming out into the open.

Gene's house now felt brighter, and smaller, and less comfortable; and those parts of it Mark noticed were entirely different, as if a lens had been placed on his memory that enhanced, for some reason, the woodwork, the plush velvet leaves of small plants with impossibly dark, purple flowers, like pinches of night sky brought cringing and puckering into the day. (Mark closed his eyes now and knew: these were African violets. But where? Not Africa. These flowers he saw were in little round pots, beneath long lightbulb rods that were casting a harsh, bluish glow.) The doorframes, the legs of a piano, the legs of a chair were all shiny and brown, as if coated in syrup. A hooded lamp on the piano he's told not to touch. He's no longer with Gene. He is younger, even, than Gene's sons. The quality of the light at a sliding glass door fascinates him. Somewhere a door slams, and then, after a silence, two voices, of women, grow louder and louder, and he slips down the hallway to find them, trailing one hand on the wall.

His mother and the older woman, the one he's been told is his grandmother, are standing in a back bedroom, the door not quite closed. "And what about his mother?" his grandmother cries, as he shoves the door open. They turn and look at him.

And what about his mother? As if she's not there in the room.

And then he is older, he is Wesley or Drew's age, he is ten, perhaps twelve, he and his parents have stopped off in some Asian country, who can guess which one now, but it's next to an ocean, with steep cliffs that plunge to the surf. Their local hosts are full of pride for a lo- cal temple, it is built in the cliffs, it involves a cliff cave with a mouth facing east, some devotional object, and at dawn once a year, when the sun rises out of the ocean, its rays pierce the cave, strike the object in just such a way that the pilgrims and priests climb cliff steps in the four A.M. darkness, to be there and prostrate themselves, and it's happening during their visit, a great stroke of luck.

Mark is desperate to go. His father has no interest and even, Mark sees, an aversion, though his father professes to be a Christian with enormous forbearance for those of debased pagan faiths. His mother is afraid it is dangerous, cliff steps in darkness, and Mark never gets up before eight, and they would have to get up at three-thirty, and Mark will be crabby and clumsy and plunge to his death. It is out of the question. The subject is closed. In his fury Mark does not go to sleep until some shocking hour, perhaps midnight, so that he is indeed crabby, cotton-brained and bewildered when his mother, her stern, homely face made bizarre by a flashlight, wakes him with a hand on his cheek. *Don't make noise. We'll just do it without telling Dad.*

They go, bleary-eyed, tripping over their practical foreigners' shoes tightly laced over thick woolen socks. Through the tumbled little streets in pitch-darkness, until they have merged with a firefly parade, old people and toddlers and genderless parents in culottes, every age wearing cheap rubber flip-flops. How can they walk, let alone climb the cliffs, in such footwear? Mark's mother is afraid they will trip, and the rock is volcanic, its harsh surface can slice up your shoe soles—but here is the whole village, hauling shopping bags heavy with offerings, laboring upward, four-year-olds, ninety-four-year-olds, everyone in between, their huffed breaths audible, all eyes glued to the twinkling and wavering chain of flashlights of which each is a part, and which makes up the sole trail to follow, a lifeline of stars.

The surf booms invisibly somewhere below. And though it has been years since Mark has willingly held hands with Ruth, he and she are conjoined, fused together by their damp, anxious palms, even as they climb single file, Mark first, Ruth behind stretching up to keep hold and to catch him in case he falls backward.

He loves her. She is a strange, remote, distracted little woman, but she is all he's ever known. He doesn't remember the cave, the miracle of first light. They probably didn't make it inside at the optimal moment—there were too many other pilgrims—but he is not dis-appointed.

By the time Mark had eaten his sandwich and pottered around the meadow for a few hours, thoroughly lost, until he'd spied a faded blaze of paint across the face of a boulder, and then found his way to another, and so to the trail, it was late afternoon. He could get off the trail by nightfall, and yet everything seemed to incline him to spend the night here. Descending again through the cloudburst of fresh mountain laurel, he was surprised by the excitement he felt at the prospect of seeing the circle of chairs from this new angle, headed down-mountain.

The voices reached him just before he broke out of the trees, into the saddle clearing. A percolation of high notes and low; without see-ing the people, he knew that it must be a family. It was clamor without raucousness, perhaps another way of saying it was a large group of campers not narrowly focused on drinking and sex. And then as he entered the clearing, the voices of children rang out from the rest, and he saw them rushing through the trees, skinny legs, bright T-shirts and shorts, whipping hair. Three girls and a boy, in a frantic pursuit where all four were both hunters and prey.

His refuge of a few hours before, where he had seemed to sit alone at the beginning of time, or in a parallel world, was completely trans-formed. The clearing and the grass and the trees were still lovely but at the same time mundane, scaled down and reined in. At a glance he saw five tents set up near the circle of chairs, a disorderly scatter of backpacks and bedding, a plastic garbage sack already dangling half full from a tree branch. There were men and women from late middle age to Mark's age, all of them somehow alike, browned and vigorous and in constant movement, some pulling deadwood toward the fire pit, some sorting through food packages, some striding after the chil-dren. "Hey, you imps!" yelled a woman. "Get back here, we're not done setting up!"

One of the older men came toward him. "Were you planning on camping?" he asked. "Don't let us drive you off. There's plenty of room, and we'll try to be good neighbors, though I can't vouch for everyone." A younger man had joined them, equally affable, and the older man clapped him on the shoulder to demonstrate that he was an element that could not be vouched for, and both laughed.

Mark was struggling to contain an upwelling of such uncomradely irritation, of such petulant disappointment, he wasn't sure he could speak. Of course it was all public land—it was theirs; it was everyone's—and he'd sensed such a coming intrusion when he'd sat here before. But something had happened to him on the summit. It had ruined him for other people, perhaps just for the next several minutes, perhaps for a lifetime.

"That's okay," he rasped, not sure whether he meant, That's okay, I don't want to camp anyway or That's okay, I'd be glad to camp with you. He hadn't spoken aloud, he realized, since his furious curses when his mother hung up on him, almost four days ago.

The two men, and now a pair of women who were also approaching, seemed as accustomed to solitary, unwashed, unshaven, shellshocked solo hikers as they were to this campsite. "Were you just on High Peak?" called the older of the two women. She had smooth gray hair cut in a pageboy and the antic eyes of a person much younger. When Mark nodded wordlessly, she added, with vehemence, "It must be *spectacular* up there right now. Don't try hiking with kids! We meant to get there, but we reached camp so late we won't make it. We'll have to drag them up there in the morning."

"Is it your camp?" Mark managed as they all began walking back toward the fire pit. He didn't know how he'd fallen in with them.

"We live as if it were ours, but of course it's the state's. We try to camp here at least once a year."

"Did you make the chairs?"

"Oh, no. We don't know how those got there. But we like them. We old folks need our lumbar support."

"Like you're such an invalid, Mom," razzed the younger woman affectionately.

Once they had absorbed him, they scarcely noticed him any longer. They were building a fire in the pit, which they'd freshly redug and expanded, and this beacon drew the four children out of the trees and kept them hovering just clear of the flames, eyes gleaming, like oversize moths. The makings of a camp dinner were being assembled, Coleman lanterns were being rewicked and lit, sleeping bags unfurled in tents in preparation for nightfall. The brighter the fire grew, the more quickly the indigo light sifting down through the trees seemed to lose all its color, so that the forest grew murky with shadow and the gaudy encampment stood out like a stage. Mark had put down his pack at a slight distance from them, outside the circle of chairs and the comforting beacon of flame, but not so far away that he couldn't hear the murmur of their voices, the outbursts of their laughter. He was part of the dim margin now; perhaps he'd pick up his pack, turn on his flashlight, and go, and they'd never remember he'd been there.

He had time to count them, as they drew toward the fire and each other. The four children, all long-legged but not yet teenagers. Maybe the youngest was six and the eldest was twelve. Seven adults: the noticeably older man and woman with whom Mark had spoken, three younger women within a decade of Mark's age who were probably sisters, and two men who were presumably husbands to two of the women and fathers to the children, in some combination that Mark couldn't parse. The third young woman had a baby bundled to herself in something like a snug hammock that tied over one shoulder; at first Mark had thought it was a side pack she inexplicably hadn't removed, until he saw the bundle erupt in a struggle and a small head pop out.

The light was failing and failing, and he still hadn't crawled off to make his own den in the darkness. Nor had he gone forward to reciprocate their welcome with some friendly act of his own. They were clearly experienced campers, if not in Mark's style. They knew protocols. They had opened themselves up to him, but they weren't going to hound him. The next move, if any, was his.

He watched the woman with the baby pacing slowly in the dim space between where the firelight expired and where he was sitting. She had the baby still confined to its bundle and was bouncing it gently, but its displeased exclamations grew louder and louder, or perhaps it was that she drew closer and closer to Mark. On an impulse he stood up and crossed the few yards that still lay between them and, as he did, felt the night dew that had weighted the tips of the long grass, brushing over his calves.

"Hi," he said. "I'm over there. I didn't want you to stumble on me and get scared."

"I knew you were there," she said. "You're the poor solo hiker whose peace we've destroyed."

"No, not at all," Mark managed, suddenly anxious to dispel this impression. "It's nice not to be here alone. I just don't want to intrude. It looks like a family thing."

"That it is, but believe me, you wouldn't be intruding. My mother must be sitting on her hands to keep herself from dragging you up to the fire and making you toast a marshmallow. She's the original den mother. She and my dad had three girls, but she didn't let that stop her." The baby, which had been sounding more and more like a bobcat and thrashing with abandon, gave a last desperate yowl, and the woman took it under the armpits and began to try to liberate it from the tangle of cloth. "Okay, Esme," she said. "You're not being strangled, good grief."

"Can I help?"

"You can pull down on the sling, yeah, like that, so I can get her out of it."

A thrill of self-conscious anxiety prickled his skin as he stepped near to do what she asked, which felt strangely like helping her out of her clothes. But it was the baby he'd freed, and once that was accomplished, he stepped away quickly, blushing so much he was sure she must feel the heat from him, even though it was too dark to see. "Feel better, Esme?" he asked, to conceal his embarrassment.

Esme was now sitting very upright and alert in her mother's arms. Mark saw the fire miniaturized in her eyes, which seemed uncannily keen, tigerlike, gleaming out of the darkness.

"And I'm Laura," the young woman said. "Do you even want to know the rest of our names? No one should have to confront our whole family at once."

Mark wanted to. "I'm Mark," he began, and as he was saying it, and thinking of how strange it sounded, of how uncertain a statement it suddenly was, a blotch of light came bouncing wildly through the night, and a great cry went up.

"Oh, my God!" Laura cried, bounding away with Esme in her arms. "Are you crazy? I thought you were going to wait until morning!"

"Who wants beer?" a new male voice was shouting. "Where's Esme—there's my girl! Look at you! Look at you, little camper!"

Mark turned and walked back to his pack, his heart beating wildly, as if the pack might have vanished. But it was there, though it took him a moment to make out its bulk. His hands were trembling, it must be with hunger, though he felt he had no appetite. He hauled the pack a little farther away over the wet grass and began to dismantle it in the darkness. He lighted his candle lantern and rolled out his ground cloth and found a Baggie of trail mix that smelled strongly of socks. He swallowed sun-warmed, brackish water, forcing it over the lump in his throat.

He was almost scared out of his skin when the children approached, their eight eyes and the stripes on their sneakers reflecting his candle. "We brought you some chili and rice," the oldest girl said, holding out a bowl that was temptingly steaming and had a spoon stuck on top. "Our moms say you're welcome to join us."

Mark had the happy feeling that they'd fought over who got to carry the bowl. He reached out to accept it, and the girl gave it to him, with the other three looking on closely.

"Hey, thanks," Mark said. "That's really nice. Tell them thank you, okay?"

"Are you coming?" the girl asked after a moment.

"I think so. I might."

But he didn't. After he'd watched them reluctantly leave him, he wolfed down the chili and washed the bowl from his canteen. Then he got into his sleeping bag. He lay a long time, sheltered by their voices, before falling asleep.

Laura's family had made a conquest of the mountain. Not by any aggression but only their forceful reality, their uniformity, their geniality, they'd made the woods into their backdrop, and apart from anomalous Mark, nothing alien to them remained. Gene was gone. Gone were Mark's father and mother, and his forgotten grandmother, whom he had encountered only that once, and of whom he had not been reminded again until his mountaintop vision. They had all drawn the lid on their chamber of ghosts. Mark did not even dream. When he opened his eyes in the morning, the interval didn't exist anywhere in his body. Thunderclap—the sun stood overhead. He sat up.

Laura was pacing and bouncing Esme, who was bundled again. Esme sat straight up from her pocket of cloth, like a mirror of Mark sitting out of his sleeping bag.

"You probably think that we've been here all night," Laura said. Behind her, on the far side of the clearing, the rest of the camp lay silent, giving off a luxuriant aura of sleep.

"Have you?" Mark asked. He was aware of foul fuzz in his mouth, the ripeness of his armpits and crotch, the fact that he was speaking to her from the intimacy of his bed.

"Believe it or not, she does sleep. She just doesn't sleep until way after midnight, and then she gets up at five, and then she'll doze all day long and come to life around sundown. She's a total vampire."

In the daylight Esme was very beautiful and sagacious and not at all vampiric. It was clear to Mark she wasn't going to sleep anytime soon. Perhaps Laura was walking and bouncing her because too exhausted for anything else. "Want to put her down?" he said.

They disentangled Esme again, a replay of the previous evening's proximity, with Mark keeping his lips clamped this time so she could not smell his breath. At the end of the ordeal, he found that it was he, and not Laura, who held the baby by her sides, with her feet dangling down. He quickly stooped to put her on his sleeping bag, where she sat very steadily plumped on her bottom and took a fistful of fabric. Mark and Laura sat down to either side of her, off the ground cloth, and Mark felt the dew soaking his shorts.

"What time is it?" he asked after a moment.

"Just past six." Laura lay down, heedless of the wet grass, slinging one arm over her eyes.

Both females seemed settled. Mark pulled his pack near and furtively dug for his toothbrush. Each item he removed, Esme reached for, and a furrow of concentration and annoyance appeared on her forehead. Finding toothbrush and toothpaste Mark scrubbed his teeth and was able to complete the operation without Laura's seeing him, although he knew she must hear him. But that seemed less humiliating. "I should get going," he said, just for something to say.

Laura lifted her arm from her eyes to squint at him. "Really? That's too bad. You should at least stick around for breakfast. My mother bakes bread in a can in the fire. It takes until noon, but it's pretty darn good."

Esme tipped suddenly forward, and Mark moved to catch her, but she was only shifting onto all fours. Once there she examined his sleeping bag closely. Laura propped her head on one elbow. "You going to crawl away, Esme?" she asked.

"How old is Esme?" Mark wondered. He'd never felt the least curiosity about a baby. He'd never touched one, he realized, until just a few moments before.

"Almost ten months," Laura said. "She'll be a year in September."

"Do you think she'll walk soon?"

"God, I hope not." Laura laughed. "I need a little more time to prepare."

"When do they usually start?"

"I don't really have any idea. My sisters' kids all walked between fourteen and seventeen months, so I'm hoping I'll have a few more months of immobile Esme. Not that she's really immobile," Laura added as Esme, with resolute thrusts of her arms, began crawling the length of the sleeping bag.

"Do babies ever walk when they're just ten months old? Or even, climb out of their cribs?"

"If they do, then I pity their parents." Laura laughed again. "No, I don't know. I'm sure some do."

"But it's uncommon."

"I'd say so. Why? Are you hoping to see her first steps? In that case you should definitely stay for breakfast."

The impetus for these questions was so personal he was sure he had not been oblique, but a true exhibitionist, and that he'd confessed that the myth of his own babyhood now seemed flawed, far too mythic for him to believe. At the same time, he knew he had not told her this, and he longed to. He felt he was obeying ever more reckless impulses when he asked, "Was it your husband who got here last night?" But Laura didn't seem to notice the color he felt coming up once again in his face.

"Yeah, he's crazy. He had to work late, so he was going to hike up this morning, but instead he comes up in the dark, with all his gear on his back and a twelve-pack of beer on his shoulder. I'm taking pity and letting him sleep. Usually he gets up with Esme, to give me a break."

Her casual evocation of a domestic routine had much the same effect on him as the photographs of Gene's sons had once had. "That reminds me that I ought to be hitting the trail myself," he said, not having come up with a destination but simply wanting to be gone.

"What's your plan?" Laura asked him as he began reassembling his pack. "Are you doing a long-distance hike?" She'd pulled Esme onto her lap so he could roll up his sleeping bag.

"Not really. Just driving around, checking out a few places I've wanted to see."

"Sounds nice. A vacation?"

"I'm not really working right now." He'd left Pine Hill without giving notice to his boss on the house-building crew and without seeing Dorothy—because, he now realized, he hadn't yet understood he was leaving.

"Do you live near here?"

"No."

"Sorry," she said after a moment. "I'm not trying to pry."

"You're not." Mark paused in his packing, an unpleasant thought crossing his mind. "I'm not a fugitive or something," he assured her. "I'm just in between houses and jobs. I'm sort of wandering, I think."

"I envy you. If you've got the freedom to do it, that's great."

"It doesn't feel as free as you'd think." He paused between yanking his pack's straps and then yanked them tighter. "Have you heard of the word 'hegira'?"

"That's a record by Joni Mitchell." They both laughed. "No, I've never known what that word means."

Mark closed his eyes, trying to picture again the word's full definition, as he'd read it in Dorothy's library. The word had recurred to him recently, for no obvious reason. But he'd noticed that this often happened: a word he'd brushed past long ago, ignorant of its meaning, somehow found its way to him again and then felt uncannily apt when he learned what it meant. As if the word had returned to reveal to Mark not just its meaning but a meaning in his situation, of which until then he had been unaware.

"Hegira," he told her. "It's from the life of Muhammad, but it can mean any 'journey or flight from danger, to a more safe or congenial place.'"

"Is that what you're doing? Hegira?"

"I guess. Yeah," Mark said, and then he grinned foolishly, and Laura grinned back, while Esme looked sternly from one to the other.

"And how's it going? Your hegira?"

"Better. I mean, I don't think I'm quite there. But it's going okay."

"I'm glad."

"Me, too," he said, meaning he was glad she had been part of it, and knowing, as he felt he almost never did with women, that she understood his subtext. She was flirting with him, wasn't she? He had assembled his pack and was hoisting the heavy weight onto his back when he heard children's voices drift out of the tents. Perfect timing.

"Have a nice life," Laura said.

"How about 'See you next year'?"

"That's much better. See you next year."

"See you next year, Esme," he said, crouching down to make eye contact with her. "You'll be walking."

"Oh, yeah," Laura said.

And what was most remarkable, Mark thought, gazing into the baby's clear eyes, was that they took it all in, lucid and attentive, and yet nothing remained. She was just ten months old. In her future this time of her life would be severed from her, no less than Mark's sleep of the previous night had been severed from him. All that fierce striving and wakeful intelligence, and what would she keep? Not a thing, not the fire or the tent or the trees or the unshaven stranger. They might tell her that anything happened, and she would have to believe them.

23.

"...WITH A COAT HANGER," LEE REMEMBERED HER saying.

The poor man had undone the wire coat hanger and sharpened one end, so that it worked like those pokers the park rangers used when they picked up the litter. And that's the way he'd done it, too: one page at a time, with incredible patience, stretched out full length on the pavement with an arm down the storm drain.

The first year of their marriage; the first house; Sawyer Street. "The poor man" the one other young college instructor who lived on their block, a painfully thin, tall and angular, bearded historian who reminded Lee of a tormented artist, something like D. H. Lawrence. The young historian's agonized efforts to complete his dissertation and obtain his degree were well known on the street, although for obvious reasons the young historian didn't mix much with his neighbors. He was already overwhelmed with offspring: a toddler and an unexpected pair of twins. He would never finish; this was Lee and Aileen's prediction. Tidy and efficient in their freestanding home, mistakenly convinced by Aileen's seven-month pregnancy that they, too, were practitioners—but more calm and successful—of family life, it was their fleeting privilege, or folly, to pity their floundering neighbor. His toddler had taken the single copy of his thesis-in-progress and disposed of it in the storm drain.

"Sheet by sheet," Aileen clarified, miming the arduous salvage, as Lee laughed helplessly.

Lee's own dissertation was finished, and Aileen was in charge of creating the precious clean copies. There would have to be three: one for Lee's adviser and committee, one to live in the stacks of the library, one for Lee to retain. Each page typed three separate times, no mistakes, on a special typewriter with math symbols they'd rented short-term. When she was typing English, she could read as she went and so work with astonishing speed, but not here. All Lee's handwritten pages of numbers were gibberish to her. She had to check every character, back and forth, to be sure it was right. And she wasn't contending just with an illegible language but with Lee's often illegible writing. When at last she completed a page, she proofread it again, and if it still seemed correct, she enshrined it in the relevant stack on the top of the bookcase. No toddler yet, but there were all sorts of other mishaps that could befall a typed page. She'd considered storing the finished pages in the refrigerator, in case they had a house fire, but was afraid that it might be too damp.

This was tedious work that had gone on for months, while Aileen incurred headaches from eyestrain and cricks in her neck and funny cramps in her fingers and wrists, and the chair that she sat in progressively distanced itself from the typewriter table. Soon she was reaching for keys with completely straight arms. She and Lee had a joke that the stacks of clean pages expanded more slowly than she did. But they never would have likened their own situation to that of their hopeless neighbor. To the contrary: the longer it took, the more triumph to savor.

It was possible, running a fingertip over the page, to feel the indents where the keys made their marks. Although not the key striking down on the paper, or the surprisingly strong slender finger striking down on the key, or the arm a tense bridge from the hand to the shoulder, or the sleeveless green dress, the slight body within like a stalk when observed from behind. Then the enormous surprise of her, viewed in profile. Lee chose not to remember a previous time when she'd been thus transformed, but forgetfulness wasn't an effort; this was all new to him. He was no less transformed; perhaps more so. Watching his wife, her smooth brown hair tied back, as she made his work real. The elating gunfire, the metallic hailstorm, the repeating mechanical slaps of the small metal hand (and the sagging depletion of ribbon); but there was no sound it was really akin to, Aileen's typewriter noise. Once it had sutured the seams of his world. Now no comparison quite brought it back.

The horror he'd felt, upon seeing page twenty-four sharply folded in thirds, was for her, not himself. For her squared little pile of successes and the haystack of failures. He'd just missed, as it faded again, the forgotten typewriter percussion. But now, even with the disfiguring folds, the page felt like a gift. He would never have thought Lewis Gaither could have given him this: the reminder that Lee and Aileen had been happy together. Not for a year, or a few months, or even the length of a day; but there had been tiny bright grains throughout, like those flashes of mica that wink at the beach.

For hours, since leaving the library, he'd been afraid to stop driving, but by early evening he was so hungry he thought he would faint at the wheel. He'd gone without food for more than two days. At an interstate rest-stop McDonald's, he braved the drive-through hunched under his cap and then devoured the burger and fries in his car at the outermost edge of the vast parking lot. Every once in a while, a car parked within a few hundred yards, its weary passengers emerging and trudging indoors toward the bathrooms, and when this happened, Lee lay sideways, the gearshift impaling him, until the intruders' noise faded away. He himself waited, more and more painfully, until nightfall and then hurried over the grass toward a margin of trees and pitch-darkness, and peed there, looking back at the rest stop's bright lights.

Once he'd both eaten and emptied his bladder, the purely physiological burden removed was enough to pass for a momentary lessening of his anxiety. His hands still trembled; his heart still fled and tumbled headlong; his mind still raved with imprecations and pleas; but at least he felt able to take a brief rest before driving again. After a few empty moments, during which he cleaned and recleaned his fingers on a paper napkin, he allowed himself to gently unfold the dissertation page again. He didn't even read what it said, his own work; he only gazed on the sharp little marks. He could almost have felt he was sheltered, in the teeming rootlessness of the vast parking lot. Perhaps he was camouflaged here, a flat flounder ensconced in the seabed of night, just the unnoticed beads of his eyes shining forth alertly. His own creeping tranquillity brought him up short. As if to gaze any longer might amount to a heedless and dangerous idyll, he quickly put the sheet away and forced himself to turn to the other, its replacement, its dark opposite, its intended negation.

This was not excellent-quality letter-size stock, with a watermark, but a cheap little slip of notepaper. And no specialized keyboard for math had been used, but a standard typewriter, in very poor health. The lack of salutation still struck Lee, as it had when he'd first gaped at it in the library, as violent, a sort of verbal ambush, although now, squinting at the truncated, single-spaced lines piled atop one another, he could also imagine that it might have been to save space:

If you're reading this then we both might feel pleased with ourselves. My last letter to you: I was agitated, I failed to include my true post office box where you might write to me. No matter. This is better, if it works. The post office is too insecure. Do not think I choose this location because it is perfectly safe, i.e. rarely if ever sought out. Not at all. It is fine work, I'm sure, though I will not have time to read it. In my situation there is no "perfectly safe." I weigh risks against benefits. I do hope you are first to get here, after me.

Then a small space, a white void of emphasis, below which the note concluded:

Inquire Marjorie, Sippston Idaho Public Library.

Once he'd recovered again from the shock, the audacity, of it, he could not help lingering over "It is fine work, I'm sure, though I will not have time to read it." *Fine work, I'm sure.* That was Gaither to the core, that condescension ill-disguised as politesse. Very southern, very "gentlemanly." He would let the mask slip just enough to help Lee understand he was being insulted, but not so much that Lee could have pointed the slight out to anyone else. The work was *fine*—read: adequate. Not simply good. *I'm sure* painted Lee as the supplicant, eager for praise. After more than three decades, Gaither still pulled the strings with his oversize hands; he allowed Lee his few skirmish triumphs, but he still won the war.

Lee's fingers had stained the little sheet with perspiration. He was no longer the secretive flounder on the floor of the sea, but a cork at its surface. In fatigue his aged body was such a horribly exquisite barometer of shifting conditions. When had he simply been hale, and unaware of his flesh? Now it was past eight at night by both Nissan and Seiko, and suddenly cold; his teeth began to chatter at the slimy, frigid touch of his own sweat as it rolled down his sides. And, what seemed paradoxical to him, the McDonald's lot had grown more and more crowded. Who were these hundreds of people, on the move after dark? With a twitch from the chill, or from horror, he realized suddenly that Gaither must be among them, as concealed as Lee hoped he himself was. Gaither must drive, on his sinister errands—to plant goading notes, to mail letters and bombs. He couldn't possibly fly. Or did he opt for the long-distance bus? Lee remembered the interstate bus rides of his earliest days in this country: the dispossessed ridership, the poorest of his new nation's citizens. Men who had just finished serving in prison and girls who were running away. That faceless milieu was well suited to a killer with a bomb in a box. Perhaps this was why the "Woodmont" envelope was postmarked from Spokane, the "Lumberton" from Pocatello—in each of his postal personas Gaither hoped to appear to be from a small town, but no interstate bus went to such little places, so he settled for something nearby. He was subject to the approximateness of the poor person's method of transit. Or did he mean to create this impression? Was Gaither dropping false clues, to lure Lee toward erroneous Holmesian thoughts? Lee's first idea must have been right: Gaither must drive a car. After all, he'd gone to the town he and Lee had once lived in as students, and slid into the library stacks, and sliced open Lee's book. That was far from approximate.

Now Lee put the little slip away also, and closed his eyes—not to rest, not as salve to his soul, but to rile himself further, by reviewing that first diabolical dart, that had pierced him so many weeks back, and reduced him to where he was now. He remembered it all.

Dear Lee,

What a bittersweet pleasure to see your face after all of these years, even if through the mesh of newsprint. You are still a handsome man. "Princely," I believe, was the word sometimes used around campus for you. I know that you, like me, are rational, and that you won't be offended when I say that the sight of my grad school colleague almost seventy years (is that right?) from his start in this life, was a bracing reminder to one of his peers as to how many years of his own life have passed. Let me compensate for the great gaffe of mentioning age by asserting you wear it admirably well, a lot better than I do. I wonder if you would agree that there is some relief, in becoming old men. What poet wrote "tender youth, all a-bruise"? I can admit that you bruised me, that last time we met.

Of course I was laughably innocent then, of the workings of human relations. But I am not a sentimental man—nor are you, I've long assumed and admired. I only press on the point (on the bruise!) to impress how I'd like to revive faded fellowship now. Now you are probably angry with me, as I once was with you. Please don't be. There's a reason my arrow grazed you. I can learn what my long-ago colleague has done in the long years since we last had contact.

I hope to hear from you soon. Until then I remain,
Your Old Colleague and Friend

He only missed having the actual object when it came to the illegible thicket with which it concluded. He wished he could pore over those slashings and scratchings again, perhaps under a microscope. Morrison hadn't been able to make "Lewis Gaither," or anything else, from the tangle; perhaps it actually read "Jesus Christ" or, for that matter, "Brain Bomber." It occurred to Lee that this might be a fresh affectation. Lee didn't recall Gaither's writing as being dramatically bad; he didn't recall any notable characteristics. Perhaps the new style strove to indicate scholarly brilliance. Or perhaps it was unintended, a sign of deepening madness.

Did it go without saying that Gaither was mad, to have done what he'd done?

For the first time, Lee's fury at Gaither was laced by a fear that was almost dispassionate. He had been accustomed to viewing Gaither as a combatant, a reviled rival, long before these most recent events. The recent events had disinterred the rivalry, had infused it with blood and then heated that blood to a boil—but they hadn't fundamentally altered the bristling relation Lee felt toward a man he had not seen in thirty-one years. For all the reluctance with which Lee admitted the fact, rivalry implied an equality, a contest between rational men. One might be malicious and self-righteous, but he couldn't be mad.

I know that you, like me, are rational.

Lee's will to conjure the other man was so powerful that for an instant he felt he'd succeeded, though Gaither didn't appear in the form of a man—who might threaten or be threatened, might crumple the hamburger bag, might revile Lee or cower before Lee's revilement, might pace the pavement, might weep, might take a piss on the grass—so much as in the form of an assessing intelligence, an observer who passed judgment. But who was judged? Lee? Oh, Lee abhorred Gaither's precedence!—Gaither who had discovered and married Aileen, had impregnated her with his child, all before the decades-old evening Lee first set eyes on her. Gaither had preceded and created and possessed, and it must mean he knew something, at which Lee was not able to guess; it granted him a power; it loosened the keystones; it had always left Lee feeling less his wife's husband, despite having won her away. He'd been too proud—too "princely," as Gaither put it—not to be galled by his second-place status, even if it was only temporal. And perhaps he was still too proud, now, to believe that the man who had ruined his life at a stroke was no genius of vengeance, but only insane.

He realized he was nodding off, drained, when his chin struck his chest. His body seemed lost in his clothes: he had the lap of a little old man. *I wonder if you would agree that there is some relief, in becoming old men.* There could be, Lee thought, his eyes filling with tears. Perhaps that was all he was seeking—not the revenge of a lifetime, but simple relief.

The interstate highway can be a sweet sanctuary, between towns and in darkness. Making his way westward, Lee was reminded of this. His entire career as an American driver had been one of timorous caution that nevertheless often failed to guarantee safety; at best he prematurely exhausted his brake pads; at worst were the small accidents at low speeds, at least a couple a decade before this most recent one that had officially ushered him into a fugitive's life. But there was also an alternate history, embedded in the first, as distinct as a patch of bright color on the reverse of the familiar drab cloth. In this history Lee is a long-distance driver at night, and his usual fidgety glancing at mirrors, his nervous pulsing of the brake, his defensive and dangerous jerks of the wheel are as absent as if here confined to the one other car, half an hour and many miles now distant, Lee has seen in the whistling tunnel of night. The car's sleek hood parts the waters of speed; the pale cones of light probe the void. Distance is conquered, devoured, almost effortlessly. This time of his life feels so lost as to be prehistoric, yet in years it's not so long ago. Lee isn't yet driving the Nissan, but one of the Nissan's isomorphic ancestors, probably the Toyota Corona. Lee isn't halfway through his sixties, but just in the door of his fifties, although he was amazed, now, to reinhabit that past self and remember how old he'd felt then: at the outer limit of experience and unwanted wisdom.

Then he'd been driving not west but east, every Thursday night after his last summer class of the week. He would have had an early dinner, begun to drive around seven, only let himself stop for fitful, unavoidable sleep after daylight in a rest area somewhere in Pennsylvania. Almost always the trip that began with such fragile tranquillity,

himself solitary and swift through the dark, would conclude in a caul-
dron of afternoon traffic on the New England Thruway, with the
pumping of brakes and the shaking of fists and quite often the shed-
ding of tears, all of which was an apt preparation for the weekend
ahead.

At that time Aileen and Esther had been living in Providence,
Rhode Island, for five years. When she'd left him, Aileen had first
taken Esther to Tampa, where Nora was living. But after only six
weeks, she'd gone to Providence instead, where she and Nora had
grown up. Their parents were dead and Aileen no longer knew anyone, but at least it wasn't Florida, she'd told Lee on the phone, and
Providence was a clannish place, so that she'd gotten a good secretarial
job up at Brown—reward for the prodigal daughter—and put Esther
in a school with enough nonwhite kids that she might finally get cast
as a Pilgrim in the Thanksgiving play.

This informative phone call hadn't been unusual for them, and it
would be some time—well after the time of those nine-hundred-mile
weekly drives—before Lee understood that it was unusual at all, that
most divorced couples did not speak by phone with a frequency ex-
ceeding that of many couples still married. In one sense at least, he
had considered that his marriage to Aileen had been improved by divorce. When they spoke by phone, there was a sense of shared en-
deavor, as if divorce had been imposed from without and required
their joint ingenuity. Of course this was because of Esther—but it remained that for however much they bickered and sniped, a collabora-
tive quality underlay their conversations that had been absent from
their shared domestic life. It might have proceeded only from the fact
that, in all the new arrangements, there was no one else logically to
consult. Yet it still felt to Lee like a renaissance, and perhaps he
wouldn't fully understand they were no longer married until she was
dead.

Arriving at Providence Hospital after changing his undershirt,
rinsing his face, hacking his skin with a razor at the Days Inn motel,
the devastating shock he endured undiminished each time came less
from Aileen than from Esther. He had seen Esther at spring break or
Christmas, and for an endless and uneasy and precious full month in
the summer, every year since the marriage had ended. But as if some-

one meant to ensure the worst conditions imaginable, it was this most recent year, when she'd gone from thirteen to fourteen, that had swept away all continuities. Gone was the child who had placed her small hand inside his. Gone, even, was her hair, to Lee an unparalleled treasure, its rich color like that of a piece of expensive wood brought to a mirrorlike shine. Esther's long hair had been chopped up at random, producing a dingy, rough plumage that made Lee think of unkempt barnyard chickens (perhaps because "it's called 'feathers,'" Aileen had explained). In her five years away from the town of her birth, Esther had not just excised all her memories of it but had substituted an imagined contemptible version, a pathetic hicksville that was revealed as the butt of her jokes. She had acquired a "gang," an assortment of both boys and girls who exhibited insolent stares, strange asexual puffs of dyed hair, sadistic chain mail of bright little buttons with such exhortations as PLEASE KILL ME PLEASE down the fronts of their jackets. And yet they pretended, with what to Lee was insufferable ostentation, to human compassion; they turned up at the hospital, day after day, did not just loiter with Esther in far corners of the grim cafeteria but were presumptuous enough to sit beside Aileen's bed, to—as it sounded to Lee from the hall—complain to her, burden her with their germy, self-centered concerns. Aileen who, in her rapid descent, seemed not so much saintly to Lee as promiscuous, turning the same smile on her husband that she gave Esther's friends, who were "wonderful," whose conversation engrossed her, who seemed to prize her in turn, because she listened to them, for what reason Lee couldn't discern.

Lee taught only in the first summer session that year. By the time of the break, at the Fourth of July, Aileen's condition had worsened so much that Lee gave up his late-summer class and lived entirely in the Providence motel. This was the end of his solitary night driving, the end of what had been an inexplicably cherished and tranquil commute. A dilation, he understood much later, of the unfinished moment; no verdict, no final decision. Illness could not lay its claim, death could not be the answer, so long as one lonesome night in the car must give way to another. He did not fill his pressboard drawers at the Days Inn with his grayed cotton T-shirts and shorts, with his plastic disposable razors, thinking this was a short-term encampment, awaiting the end. He was still in his car, all alone. A nimbus of light showed the instant ahead, but beyond that was merciful darkness, in every direction.

He and Aileen spoke of things that did not seem to matter. In her second life in Providence, as an adult and parent, the town had revealed its charms. She described these to him, and he listened, as if they were strangers discussing a place to which random travel had brought them. The stern little houses, the surprisingly nice nearby beach. Rhode Island was the Ocean State, Aileen observed. What a contrast this summer must make to Lee's summers back home, in the landbound Midwest, amid tedious furrows of corn. Lee had always missed the ocean, hadn't he, since he'd come to this country? The ocean and the mountains—she remembered him saying he loved those landscapes; what an irony he'd lived for decades exiled from both. When she wasn't pursuing this train, she was singing the deluded song of praise for Esther's near-delinquent friends. They were misfits, Aileen said, as if this were something to cherish. All too smart or too creative or too morally distressed—*By what?* Lee thought scornfully. *Hamburgers?*—to get along with the rest of their peers, but this was the miracle of it, that they had all found each other. They were passionately loyal to Esther, the brave tribe to which she belonged. In retrospect Lee would hear the wheedling in Aileen's voice and cringe, at the portrait of him it suggested. Was he really a person who had to be probed, softened up, caught off guard by sly, slantwise suggestions? Could his own wife not speak to him frankly about what she desired? He liked to think that bluntness would have served her well. It was clear indirection had not. At the time he had only been affronted by every separate proposition—Esther as "misfit," delinquency as "creativity"—so that he'd entangled them both in his refutations. He hadn't had any idea what Aileen really wanted until Nora, his unlikely ally in this one particular, told him.

"She wants you to move to Rhode Island, so that Esther can stay with her friends. They're all supposed to start high school together this fall. She doesn't want Esther to go somewhere new and start over again. Especially because it's such a frightening prospect, high school."

Lee was too amazed by this idea to grasp its substance; his first objection was peripheral. "She's not going somewhere new, she's going home," he said, as if this latter idea, that Esther was returning to live with him because her mother was going to die, was by contrast a simple idea that provoked no distress. He and Nora were sitting at a corner table in the hospital cafeteria. Beside Lee were the final exams from his one summer class, which he still hadn't managed to grade. Nora had been in Providence for two weeks, during which time she and Lee had not bothered to speak to each other, even when they were both seated outside Aileen's room in the hallway. Aileen's own relations with Nora had been arctic for the duration of her marriage to Lee, and Nora's appearance in Providence had been another unnerving reminder to Lee that not only had Aileen left him, but she had altered all aspects of her existence to an extent that not even the phone could reveal. Nora and Aileen were sisters again, and Esther was most definitely Nora's niece. On entering the cafeteria this afternoon, instead of taking a table by herself as far from Lee as existed, Nora had come straight to him, and he had squared his exams and set them aside, as if he'd known as well as she did that consultation between them was inevitable.

"She's been here five years. The way it feels to Esther, she was a little girl when they moved here. Providence is her home."

"Even if I wanted to, it's impossible," Lee finally said. "I have tenure. Aileen knows what that means. I can't just quit there and get a job here." That it was so beyond his capabilities to get tenure wherever he wanted made him angry at Aileen for underscoring the fact, and his face, he knew, grew unattractively hostile.

Nora didn't bristle in response. She only said, in a mild tone of correction, "It's a pipe dream. She wants to think that Esther's friends are all she needs, so it's all right that she's losing her mother." Without any warning, Nora started to weep, but it was a phenomenon of tears and not sobs, so that their conversation didn't need to pause. Nora drew a paper napkin over her face, as if wiping at rain.

"What do you think?" Lee asked, and he heard his voice betray the humble fright he thought he'd concealed in his chest. He wanted to cry, too, but he wasn't capable of such decorous tears.

"I think," Nora said carefully, still wiping her face, "that it would be better for Esther to leave here. High school is a big upheaval anyway. She doesn't think so, but everything's going to change. Might as well change the scene. I don't think her friends here are so wonderful."

"Neither do I!" Lee exclaimed.

"I won't tell them if you don't." Nora had regained her composure, but now Lee felt that something had shifted between them; she had opened to him; she agreed with him about Esther's friends. He hadn't realized how lonely he was for a partner in fear, anyone strapped next to him for the sickening plunge; the disaster was Aileen's and secondarily Esther's, and only then was it his, and he couldn't go begging solace from them when he couldn't return it. He needed someone very slightly off center in the same way he was, someone neither an imminent corpse nor an imminent motherless child. Now he saw that this person had always and only been Nora. In the space of a moment, he regretted their two weeks, really almost two decades, of frosty reserve, and grandiosely imagined they were already making up for it. He sat forward, eager for more consultation. "Why hasn't she mentioned it to me herself? This idea I should move to Rhode Island."

"Afraid of you," Nora said flatly. Then she added, "As usual."

The reversal was so abrupt it took Lee a beat to realize there had been no reversal at all, but a misprision of his and resulting interior tumult, which he was confident Nora's obtuseness had kept her from seeing. "Aileen has never been afraid of me," he said calmly, appending, "you dumb bitch."

"There's Exhibit A for why she's frightened of you," Nora said, also calm. "Your disgusting temper. You control yourself about as well as a two-year-old child."

"I don't need you to tell me how to treat my wife!" Lee said, turning heads in their direction, though briefly; it was a hospital cafeteria, and there were often scenes of rage or grief playing out at its tables.

"'Your wife'?" Nora echoed primly. "It's just like she told me. You don't notice anything. You don't even notice she left you, five years ago and only ten years too late."

"Too late for *what*?" Lee snarled, not caring at all, but too caught up in the rapid exchange of hostilities.

"Oh, for everything!" Nora finally lost her composure as well. "It's too bad she didn't leave you before you ever met in the first place! She's dying, and she'll never see her little boy again, she'll never hold him, she'll never know who he was. *John.* I don't suppose you remember. I don't suppose you remember her child."

He was completely unprepared for this tangent, and for a moment something shifted again; he gazed at Nora's flushed, contorted face with theoretical sympathy; he thought she might be insane, her habitual reserve a madwoman's inspired façade. "That was her choice," he said carefully—taking care not because the idea was fragile and might fail beneath hard scrutiny but because he knew that the idea was a bedrock, in the face of which Nora would likely collapse.

"Garbage. Garbage. Bullshit!" Nora raved. "She knew you didn't want him, and she was too frightened, she thought if she kept him you'd leave her and then she'd have nothing. She should have known that would be better than marriage to *you.*"

"Goddamn bitch," Lee hissed, raking his papers together and leaving. Bursting out the cafeteria door, he ran into Esther, with a few of her coterie, on her way in.

"What?" Esther cried when she saw him. "What's happening? Daddy! What's happening?"

It had been easy and instinctive to reject Nora's words to her face—no other course of action had entered Lee's mind. But with the quarantine between him and Nora restored, and their lunchtime encounter receding, and Aileen's death advancing, day by day larger on the horizon but the same unknown distance away, like an optical trick, Lee became exasperated with Aileen that she didn't sit up from her pillows and resolve what for him had grown into a grating dilemma. Wasn't it true that the child of her marriage to Gaither had effectively ceased to exist, by their tacit agreement? All the empirical evidence Lee could discern still supported this view. Aileen lay at the threshold of death watching afternoon talk shows with a rapt entourage of teen vandals. It was dismaying and embarrassing, but it was also a new kind of proof: Aileen never looked up from her circle of waifs and said, Find my son. Bring him to me before it's too late. On the other hand, if Lee studied the actual years of their marriage, he was confronted with ambiguity, hostile allusion, slantwise assignings of blame—and so he didn't study these years. As if he'd come late to some well-meaning gospel of family life, he let every morning be new, with no ink on its back from the past; he reinvented his marriage, with the help of a cleansing divorce. He was deluded with regard to most aspects of his life with Aileen, as an innermost self that he brusquely ignored was aware. Years before she'd left, he had known that Aileen hated him, because he'd done nothing to help her keep John. But her hatred for him was obversed with hatred for herself; she had been his accomplice. She'd allowed Lee's indifference to paralyze her. Like Lee she had put up no fight when her son disappeared. The difference lay in their reactions: for Lee, shared disgrace didn't cancel but in fact even nourished his love. For Aileen it killed love so completely that once she had finally left, she no longer even felt hate, just the lesser emotions—impatience, trepidation, annoyance. The regular phone calls denoted not passion but passionlessness: another fact that Lee chose to ignore.

Yet one thing remained that even Lee's inmost self, his harsh jurist, affirmed was no product of Lee's self-delusion and self-justification but fact, and somehow for this reason it unsettled Lee most of all: Aileen's time remaining continued to shrink, and she still didn't ask for her son. Lee almost wished that she would. He would say, A little late, don't you think? You must not really care! Or perhaps he would say, Right away. You only needed to ask. It could have happened a long time ago.

At night, sleepless at the Days Inn, he thought it must be the easiest thing in the world to walk into Aileen's room the next morning, at the first stroke of visiting hours, and take the chair to her right, and perhaps take her hand, and just ask her, the same way one might ask if she wanted some orange juice, *Don't you think that we ought to find Gaither? So that you can see John.* Eight-o-five by the clock. Esther swaddled in sleep for another two hours and Nora her sentry, so that Lee and Aileen were alone.

Morning light beating in through the window. The unending hospital sounds that are so harsh by night somehow hushed by the influx of sun.

On several occasions it happened, precisely the way he had worried it over, so industrious in his insomnia, as he sometimes had risen and showered and made himself coffee and graded his pile of exams before twitching awake in his knotted pajamas, a few hours or perhaps just a few minutes into long-deferred asleep. Over and over he sat with Aileen, took her hand, and she understood him, and he understood her, and the thing was decided somehow, and he felt such enormous relief that perhaps he did actually sob—and then felt his heart racing, his sweaty, pajama-trussed body again tripping over the threshold, ejected from dreams.

One such morning he got to the hospital and she was dead.

And although he continued to think, at irregular intervals, perhaps for a year afterward, that the conversation was still possible, obviously it wasn't, and realizing this was just one of the thousands of ways she kept dying for him. Once again at the door to her bright, empty room, the bed stripped, the nurse scissoring toward him as if to deliver a scolding, and the usual grocery-store nosegay as dead in his hands.

24.

ALL ACROSS THE STATE OF COLORADO, HE IMAGINED HE might find Esther, sitting on the bright swell of grass that rose away from the interstate's shoulder, her feet in a carpet of wildflowers, a heavy pair of binoculars held to her face. The warm sun still reminded him of holding the back of her smooth newborn's head in his palm. Now he was surprised to find that even amid the demands of driving, of keeping his eyes on the road, of maintaining at all costs the speed limit, of checking the rear mirrors regularly, he often noticed magnificent birds, with their great wings outstretched, hanging motionlessly in the air. Could these be Esther's eagles? They conveyed that nobility to him, with the fans of their tails and their planar perfection of wing, through which he could see the sunlight when they passed just above him. He saw one surveying the road from its perch on a post like a conquering Caesar, big as a fireplug with darkly caped shoulders and a weaponlike hook for a nose. They weren't brown with white heads like the eagles he'd seen on TV. In truth they were probably not all the same. But they were equally awesome to him—glimpsing Caesar, he'd heard himself gasp. Some were dark brown all over, but with an incandescence, a gold gleam in the brown, that reminded him of Esther's hair. As he pushed west through grassland, the ground near the highway was often churned into furrows and holes, as if drunks had been trying to put up a fence, and amid the fresh dirt Lee saw comical rodents, sitting up on their haunches with their little paws clasped, as if the road offered great entertainment. The eagle's stark shadow would be rippling closer and closer. Lee was almost convinced all these eagles had been raised by Esther from chicks. In their brief helplessness they'd looked up from their nest and seen her, watchful, looking back down.

Since crossing the Mississippi, he'd also harbored the imprudent belief that he'd eluded the last of the FBI's agents: he'd found a hole in their net. Nothing like elation or triumph accompanied the idea, but beneath the titan sky of Colorado—Esther's sky, with her sentinels in it—he could dare to believe that he'd vanished. He left Colorado driving to the north, the mountains keeping their distance to the left and west of him. When Lee looked away from them out the passenger window, he seemed to see all the way back down the featureless plain past the anticlimactic elbow of the brown Mississippi to his house on its own dingy elbow of Fearrington Way. But this brief union of the old and discredited world with the uncertain present disturbed him, and he turned his eyes back to the road.

At Cheyenne, Wyoming, he joined Interstate 80 and turned west again, driving into the sun until he so needed to rest his seared eyes that he parked on the shoulder—just for a moment, and to look at the map—and woke up again hours later, with a distended orange sun in his face, the few other cars on the road dragging shadows like capes. He'd collapsed against his door, his cheek pressed to the glass, which was cold against his face, though it had been a sultry afternoon. He had a crick in his neck and deep aches at the base of his spine and in the hidden sockets where his legs met his trunk, and his bladder was pained. He clumsily righted himself, flipping down the sun shade, which revealed a small mirror, and his own shocking image: an old, shriveled apple, strangely shiny skin carved by creases and sunk with deep hollows, eyes beady and vague from the depths of a fringe of gray hair. No one had bothered him, perhaps even noticed him, while he'd been sleeping.

Utah was a mud flat, a few poorly organized piles of stone standing off in the distance like islands of a long-vanished sea. As he crossed from that state into Idaho, his brief oasis of calm burned away. A swarming sensation tormented his skin, anticipation and dread as a dermal outbreak. In his motel that night, he barely slept, leaving the lamps on so that he could move his miserable, tension-coiled body between every station the furniture offered, very possibly talking out loud to himself, as he thought about Gaither. He remembered the chill sanctimoniousness, the gigantic deft hands, the insufferable air of the patriarch meting out justice. He recalled his own shameful sensation of being the victor, because Lewis and John had retreated—when in fact this retreat might as well have been Gaither's first bomb. To destroy from a distance, without fouling his oversize hands—that was Gaither's brilliance. Whitehead had Dieckmann, and Gaither had death, and Lee felt once again he had nothing.

He was even farther from Sippston than he'd realized. The next day he had to continue north, across the east end of the state, leave it and spend tedious hours tacking north by northwest through Montana before he turned west to reexperience the horror of crossing the fateful state's line, as he entered the handle. By now it was late afternoon. The landscape no longer seemed neutral, but hostile. The highway just narrowly threaded through plunging pine walls; it wound gingerly, held aloft by immense concrete stilts, sometimes briefly revealing a glimpse far below of the steel-colored river it followed. Rarely a precipitous slope touched the road, or vice versa, and at these points of contact, Lee twice saw huge corpses of deer stretched out dead on the shoulder. Since crossing into Idaho the second time, through the shadowy pass of the Bitterroot Range, Lee found he drove more and more slowly, as if the car had gained weight or was dragging its fender. Whenever the grade ran downhill, the huge trucks thundered past with their horns screaming warnings, like freight trains. It was cold, as if he'd ascended past summer to autumn, and with the car's windows tightly rolled up he felt bathed in a pocket of palpable dread. Whatever pithy or courageous declamations to Gaither he might have rehearsed had escaped him. His mind was a blank.

Abruptly he saw the sign he had been looking for and scarcely made the turn, pumping his brake in a panic as he slid down the off-ramp. He had to turn again on the road that he found at its foot, two wet-looking lanes of asphalt. The highway closed its curtains, as if it had never existed.

Sippston was only a few miles north by the map, but it was more than forty minutes of slippery driving before the pines fell away and he had entered the unwelcoming utilitarian town, larger than he had expected and at the same time extremely alone in its long, narrow valley. There were snowmobile dealerships and gas stations and a Woodsman and generic motels, a stingy assortment of orange lights beneath a gray sky. The library was unavoidable, a squat brick building on his right just before the first stoplight, so that he was almost forced to turn in and take one of its four parking spaces. Then he sat for a moment in the harrowing silence left behind by the engine.

The town felt wrong to him. Never having spent time in the West, he had envisioned Gaither's hideaway in northeastern terms, a sort of Smith College amid soaring alps, with cottages and cow pastures and most particularly lots of churches, a veritable arsenal of spires. Gaither himself in this vision was a pseudonymous priest, beloved by a duped congregation, leading a satanic double life. But if there were any churches in Sippston, they were unsentimentally located in brick boxes like the library building; Lee saw no spires or crosses straining for the sky. It was a town of chain saws and snowplows, and the fact that there was a library at all was surprising, if not the emptiness of the small parking lot. There was only one other vehicle, a truck with an occupied gun rack.

"My God," Lee murmured. He was frightened again, by the unfamiliar Gaither who was adequate to live in such a place.

The only welcome detail was a sign on the door indicating that the library would close at five P.M. The Seiko and the clock in the dashboard agreed that it was only ten or twelve minutes to five. Ten or twelve minutes was certainly not enough time, Lee realized with relief, to conduct his inquiry of Marjorie, or even to determine who Marjorie was. He would find a motel, as he'd done every day for five days, pay in cash, find a drive-through McDonald's—nowhere lacked one—eat his rubbery hamburger hunched in his car, and then, back in his room, curl his limbs painfully between chemically sterilized sheets—except that tonight would be different, because he was in Gaither's town.

A person emerged from the library, a woman, perhaps close to Lee's age, less petite than severely pared down, with extremely straight carriage. If not for the style of her clothes, she might have been mistaken for a slightly built man. She was wearing white running shoes and a fuchsia windbreaker zipped to the neck. Her white hair stood coarsely off her head like a ruff, and she apparently owned the shotgun. She unlocked the truck before glancing in Lee's direction. Lee had been paralyzed by the possibility that in starting his engine he might make her notice him, and so he hadn't, but now she had noticed him anyway.

"Already closed," she called. "Sorry. Eight-thirty tomorrow."

Lee gave a wave through his closed window to indicate that he had no objection and started his engine, but now she had jutted her head slightly forward, as if she had not understood. Emboldened by the running engine, Lee rolled his window partway down, and cold dampness poured into the car. "That's okay!" he called. "I'll come back in the morning!" He was trying to get into reverse when she came swiftly toward him. She bent slightly, squinting into his open window.

"You're the Oriental gentleman," she said.

Lee was so astonished he couldn't say anything.

"I'm Marjorie. Sorry," she added indifferently, "he didn't tell me your name. He just said a friend of his, an Oriental gentleman, might be coming to visit. That's who you are, am I right? Dr. Burt's friend?"

Lee's mouth hung slack in amazement. Not just an alias but a degree: *Dr.* Burt. He gaped at his questioner, seeking the answer.

"Something about mathematics," she supplied, with a note of distaste—not for mathematics but for the protracted discussion.

"Yes," Lee finally said. "Dr. Lee."

"Pleasedtomeetyou," Marjorie ejected, the blandest formality. "He did tell me you might visit sometime this month. He didn't tell me today."

"I wasn't able to call ahead," he began.

"You wouldn't be, seeing how he doesn't have a phone." She abruptly returned to her truck, and he saw her displacing a series of items—boxes, bags, and coats, though not the gun—from the cab of the truck to the bed. It was too late to leave: she had seen him. She would tell Gaither she'd seen him, even spoken with him, and that he'd then fled, a coward.

"I apologize it won't be comfortable," she said over her shoulder, "but Dr. Burt said that I had to drive you. He was absolutely clear about that. You can leave your car here. I can come fetch you back in the morning."

"I'm not planning to sleep there," Lee said in alarm.

She stopped working a moment to look at him. "That's your call. But I'm not at your service all evening, I've got things to do. I can fetch you back down in a couple of hours if that's what you prefer. He would probably prefer it too though he's too polite to say so. There's good motels you can stay in. I heard the Woodsman's all full with a big group of hunters, but there's the Timberline, which is perfectly fine, and Super 8's on the far side of town, if that's what you're used to."

"I can't leave my car here," he protested, astonished. In the onslaught of the moment, it had taken the whole of her speech for him to locate his central objection: he couldn't be at their mercy. He'd been one with his car for five days. Now he'd finally crossed over enemy lines; he couldn't possibly cast off that armor and go forward naked.

"Nope: he was very specific about that," Marjorie said, brushing past him to stretch a tarp over the items she'd thrown in the bed. "You must know he's really particular. I'm not trying to be rude, I'm just telling you. I'm sure it's for your own safety anyway."

"My safety?" Lee cried.

"The last leg of the road to his place isn't really a road. That little car there"—she cast a scornful glance toward it—"won't do it. What, you think that he wants to kidnap you? More like no one wants to be hauling you out. It's already starting to rain, and the temperature's dropping. It's going to be snow. Lots of it, if you trust the forecasters."

After this she made clear she was giving him a chance to come around and stop giving her trouble. *City person,* she seemed to be seething as she yanked on her twine and tarp corners, or perhaps, *Foreign person.* Lee tried to overmaster himself. He groped for the script of the visiting friend. "Does Dr. Burt live alone?" he wondered, in the most offhand tone he could muster. But his question had the opposite effect from what he had intended. When Marjorie turned to him, her face seemed for the first time suspicious.

"How did you say that you know Dr. Burt?"

"We were graduate students together."

"From the university," Marjorie translated. When Lee nodded, she seemed to consider a moment. "Haven't seen him in a long time," she surmised.

"No."

"Well," she said, and now an entirely new aspect entered her face. Her narrow eyes glowed. "I'm sure you'll find that he's still the same genius as back when you knew him."

She might have bared her shriveled breasts; Lee opened his mouth but then failed to pronounce any words.

"I'm ready," she added, with a peremptory gesture toward the truck's passenger seat.

At his own car, Lee stood a moment staring at his suitcase and briefcase and seeming to feel and see all at once the few paltry items that comprised his existence—and then, like a man stepping out a window, he locked the car's door and left them behind.

He was trembling as the truck rumbled onto the road. In the course of their negotiations, purple twilight had come, bringing with it a fine mist that shrouded forms and condensed into zigzagging rivulets on the windshield. It wasn't the way he'd imagined reunion with Gaither. He had never imagined the exacting gatekeeper, whom he supposed wasn't so unlike Ruth. He had never imagined the coarse, remote town. Yet what form had expectancy taken? He could only say it had featured its own thorough absence. The dream sensation took the form of an ambush, a thunderbolt falling. It in no way included a rumpled old man, unshowered, unslept, uncourageous, conveyed like a poor supplicant to the feet of the pope.

"Turn off," Lee said. "Please turn off. Turn around."

"What?" she said, over the staticky hiss of the tires.

Shame was struggling with panic; he could hardly push words from his mouth. "Please turn around, ma'am. I'm not feeling well. Turn around."

"That's the Woodsman," she indicated, calling out as if acres of space separated the seats. She had taken his inaudible plea for a visitor's question.

They left the zone of bleeding fluorescents, the Exxon, the Super 8, so that the black night, now complete, settled sharply around them. The mist hardened into rain, and the few taillights and headlights they saw seemed to glow more intensely. Then there were no other cars on the road, as if they all had been swallowed. The road began to climb and wind. There was nothing to see, but Lee had his vertiginous innards to show him the terrain. Marjorie put on her turn signal, and after a long interval she began to slow down, and then kept going more and more slowly, until they were almost merely idling without moving at all. Just as the waiting grew unbearable, she gave a pull to the wheel.

They bumped off the asphalt.

"I can't," Lee admitted with shame.

"You see," she mistook him, agreeing with satisfaction. "It's so little a road even *I* almost miss it each time."

Now branches were scraping the truck on both sides. The grade had grown steeper than seemed possible, and yet the truck still ascended, masticating what sounded like large rocks and even tree limbs. With each shudder Lee thought they would peel backward off the hillside. They clawed upward at barely the rate of a walk, scraped around a hairpin, clawed again. At one point the truck actually stopped, and Marjorie shouldered open her door and was devoured by darkness—the sighing treble of the rain briefly joined to the noisy bass drumming of drops on the roof—only to startlingly reappear in the fan of the headlamps, amid translucent strings of water, her hood tightly cinched on her face. Marjorie ducked out of sight; there were sounds of a struggle. Then she'd swung herself briskly back in, slammed the door, and their glacial ascent had resumed.

"You get a branch caught in the axle, that's it," she remarked.

Lee said nothing; he stared through the twitch of the wiper blades into the dark. Any thought of escape had left him; he only wanted it done. He felt dread, in the form of an almost unbearable pressure exerted on him by the forthcoming moment. His ribs buckled under its weight. The abyss of the very near future; he could say to himself that tonight he would find someplace decent for a glass of red wine and a plank of pink steak and a local potato coal-hot in its jacket of foil, but it was an idle extravagant dream, severed from actual life by the next several minutes. No continuities made the transition. Nothing from now, damp and cold and dreadful, and nothing from the past.

By contrast to his silence, Marjorie seemed more and more pleased and gregarious the more like a vision of hell grew their route. "You bring that foreign car of yours up this way," she was envisioning, shouting at him to be heard, "there'd be no one to help you get out. With this weather that's coming, they might not've found you for weeks. Nobody lives up here. No one. That's how Dr. Burt likes it. Oh, there's a hunting shack not far from him," she acknowledged, imagining Lee's shudder of horror as an attempt at refutation and lifting one shoulder to point the same way that he twitchingly had, by coincidence, "but nobody's ever in there. The owners are city people like you, I think they live down in Boise. Get a place in the mountains, they think it's all fun. Then they find it's hard work and they never come up. That suits Dr. Burt fine. To be frank I was very surprised when he said that he had a friend going to visit. I didn't know that he knew anyone. He keeps to himself, besides me. Even I've never been in the house."

"Never?" Lee said, his presentiment of horror so great his voice finally wrenched free, seemingly on its own. Too late he realized this was a wound to her pride.

"He never lets anybody come near," she shot back. "Only me. And with me it was years of him hoofing it all the way down into town to get books before he ever accepted a ride. He hasn't even got a car, you know. He's always managed everything on his own."

"When I knew . . . Dr. Burt, he was married," Lee risked, not to further antagonize her but in the hope she could somehow explain Gaither's transformation. Instead she reverted to taciturn scorn.

"Dr. Burt's never been married," she said, in a tone that made clear she would not endure any more nonsense.

"It was a long time ago."

This drew no response at all. Lee felt the land slowly righting itself, scaling down to a less deadly angle. The truck in response gained comparative speed. Now perhaps they were walking, not crawling. Lee

had no idea how much farther there was, but the minuscule acceleration made him feel that his time had grown short.

"How do you know him?" He suddenly felt he must know this
himself.

"I told you. He needs books. For his work."

"His work?"

"His mathematical work." The way she uttered "mathematical,"
with excessive precision, managed to be both reverent and ironical, as
if to imply that in Gaither the pursuit was sacred, while in Lee it was
silly, if not contemptible.

"Yes, of course, but these are . . . very specialized texts. You have
what he needs, in your library?"

"I write other libraries on his behalf and I order things for him."
All at once the truck turned and achieved a plateau of some kind, and
Marjorie struck the horn quickly three times, as if repeating a code, almost scaring Lee out of his skin. "We're here," she said, cutting the
engine.

The truck's headlights dimly suggested a tiny structure, lodged in
the trees; more discernible by far was a woodpile, almost as tall as the
structure and wider, beneath a blue tarp. Then the truck was answered
with a flame, a surprising small light that unswallowed itself to reveal,
from within, a window, and someone moving behind it.

"Thank you," Lee said, throwing open his door with resolve. The
rain angled in, stinging him. He was zippering his own, nonwater-
proof, windbreaker and settling his cap on his head. Now it was all
mundane actions. Securing himself against rain. Getting out of the car.
He was going. He slid out and stood pinned between truck and tree
trunks, being pelted by rain.

"Hang on," Marjorie said, making to leave the truck also.

"Don't come with me!" Lee barked, with such force that she actually stopped and swung around to look through the truck's cab at him.
"I'd like privacy, to be reunited with this very old friend. Please," he
added, aware he sounded unhinged.

"But you can't just go up to his door," she said, actually cowed. "If
I were you, I would wait till he fetches you in."

A pale rectangle appeared. "Marjorie?" called a rough and yet reso-
nant voice.

"And I've got books for him," she added, but these had been riding against Lee's left thigh all the way up the mountain, and he seized them before she could, several backbreaking, sharp-cornered tomes in a limp plastic sack. "Please leave us alone!" he said, slamming the door. He turned toward the cabin, willing her disappearance, clumsily shielding the books with his body, stumbling through oozing terrain toward the cabin's front door.

"I've brought that friend of yours," Marjorie called. Whether because she was decent after all, or just impatient and sufficiently soaked, after a moment's hesitation she got back into the truck and restarted the engine. Lee heard her negotiating the awkward reversal, commencing the mud crunch back down. Two moss-slickened steps raised him out of the mud to the threshold.

"My God, you've come!" The man beckoned, marveled. "Please, please! You can see I don't often have guests in my humble abode. 'My pallet is the bracken and my lamp the distant star.' What opium-addled old poet penned that bosky line? Forgive me if I feel I've wrought a small miracle. The hermit has his garrulous streak as the jester his tears. And you can see, now you've seen at first hand, what I'm limited to. We can start there: my humble factotum. Marjorie. She is blameless, Lee. If you have quarrels with me, they cannot touch on her. She doesn't know she abets a lone huntsman. Please, give me the books! And you're drenched by our welcoming weather. Here is the woodstove, Lee, here is the peg for your jacket, here's ancient raiment of mine you can wear while that dries. My diet of berries and roots seems to suit me so well I can't button it up anymore, which has spared it hard use and preserved it for you. Forgive me, Lee. I possess an advantage. I have seen your graven image. I've digested the work of the decades. I'm not shocked by you, just delighted, but you're shocked by me."

A blast of wood smoke and intimate odor scorched Lee's eyes and nostrils; yet despite the strength of these foul exhalations, the houndstooth jacket drooped, a windless flag, from Lee's hand.

It was true he had grown bulkier, but by way of stored power. The thick chest and arms of someone who maintained his own woodpile, yet the hunched shoulders of someone who read by poor light. Or who ticked his own sinister clocks.

"A queer paradox of the hermit's existence: we live in a state of expectancy. Keep the hordes at the foot of the mountain, but what if an elegant Martian descends from the sky? Or a friend from the past. I have tea, nothing Japanese, sadly, just bitter Lipton's and a fruit distillate called Red Zinger. I had just, before Marjorie bore you to me, poured a glass of my apricot wine, and it stands there untouched as if hoping to lure Elijah."

The face almost completely concealed by leonine hair and tremendous gray beard, but the eyes—although Russianized somehow by proximate hair—still the avid, self-satisfied eyes Lee recalled, though he wouldn't have thought that he could. The eyes hurtled to him from a vault, on the wings of the jacket.

"Lewis isn't here," Lee said—telling himself, reprimanding himself, wringing the jacket with fury.

"Lewis? My God: Lewis *Gaither.* I'm astonished Mnemosyne yields the name. You weren't expecting a full class reunion, I hope?" Whitehead laughed with delight. "Lewis *Gaither.* I wonder where he ended up. As I remember, a Christ-hyping dimwit. They can be the most dangerous people, but he seems not to have managed to do any harm."

"You killed Hendley," Lee blurted.

"The 'Minister of Information'? Yes. Not one of my prouder experiments. I don't like them to linger and suffer: that is barbaric. But it brought us together."

Perhaps this was what Lee required, the repugnant suggestion of fellowship, or perhaps it was just that they heard something, a vague engine noise briefly mixed with the sound of the rain.

"That can't be Marjorie again," Whitehead mused. "Don't tell me you're the posse comitatus after all."

Lee had only stepped over the threshold into the cavelike and flickering room, cramped and dark as a mouth, which he now stroboscopically grasped was enclosed on all sides by bookshelves, exotically floored by a miscellany of overlapping mats and pelts, enlivened by examples of handmade furnishings that conformed cleverly to the space—a hinged worktable, a hinged single bed—and centered snugly on the woodstove, the room's ardent heart, in the pulsating light of which towered a miniature city of boxes and cans, cartons, cylinders, spools of wire, plastic bottles and jugs, lengths of pipe, squares of screen, jars of matches, narrow towers of small blocks of wood almost touching, with their pinnacle points, the stalactite-like pendants that hung here and there from the ceiling, the hacksaws and hand drills, an upside-down forest of tools; he absorbed these impressions instantaneously, his mind's shutter held open, as he turned for the door, half an arm's reach away, and plunged through it, skidding down the two moss-slickened steps, belatedly rejecting the houndstooth jacket and then tripping over and trampling it into the mud. A weak, limited glow seemed to mark the far side of the clearing. Lee felt one knee fail beneath him but was still thrashing forward, the sluiceway of rain blinding him, he had smacked into something—

Arms seized and bundled him into a car, some kind of tall sport-utility vehicle. He saw the eerie green glow of a dashboard display, varying concentrations of darkness, heard doors slam and felt the see-saw movements of a three-point reversal—

"Had to wait till the pickup left," a voice near him was saying. "He went in and came out. Yeah, I have no idea. You're breaking up, wait a sec."

From far away Whitehead was calling, "Who is that? Who's there?"

Then they were crashing down the narrow declivity, the tree branches snapping like fireworks. Surprisingly soon, they were back to the tranquil rain hiss of the two-lane paved road.

"Are you injured?" a new voice was asking. "What happened in there? Are you injured? Can you tell us what happened in there? What were you doing in there anyway? What's your name?"

". . . No idea, no, I don't. . . . Yeah, I don't. Heard, not saw. Tell them sit tight, I guess."

"Can you talk? What's your name?"

". . . like a bat out of hell. Doesn't seem to be injured."

"What's your *name,* sir?" The dome light snapped on, an explosion of brightness. Lee gasped and sheltered his eyes. From beneath trembling palms, he saw three men, one driving, one craned around from the front seat, one in the back beside him, all of them wearing brownish green, hunterlike clothing, caps with flaps, lace-up boots, bulky vests. The man beside Lee was holding a rifle, its end pointed out the back window.

"Speak English?" demanded the man in the front passenger seat.

Lee was still heaving for breath. His heart smashed his rib cage. He was soaked to the skin, he had a pain in his knee, he was shaking so much it seemed possible he was in shock. "Lee," he ejected with effort.

Instant darkness again as the dome light blinked out.

"Says his name's Lee," the voice said. A beat later the voice said in surprise, "Oh, no shit?"

There was definitely something wrong with the seats of the car: they had lost all their springs, or their backs rose at too sharp an angle. Whatever it was, it enforced an uncomfortable senile posture, pressed the ribs to the guts, wrung the abdomen, crumpled the spine; he was forced to curl up like a fetus yet ached from decay.

He was sobbing. He pressed his hot face against his cold hands.

". . . possibly injured," the distant voice reevaluated.

Whoever was driving was speeding, or at least the night seemed to rush awesomely past. The rain had grown viscous; it battered the roof of the car like many thousands of handfuls of mud being constantly hurled. The car swung through a turn, moved more slowly, then came to a stop. His elbows pressed onto his thighs, his face onto his palms. These conjunctions seemed eternal and unalterable. Doors unlatched, the dome light blazed on, doors slammed, the dome light was extinguished, doors were forcibly unhinged again, the dome light reignited—he perceived it with no more interest than he might have sensed changes in weather from the depths of a vault. A familiar voice said, "Tell them to meet us in the room. And I want some hot tea. Not that shit that the restaurant serves. Get the stuff that I brought, it's on that chest-of-drawers thing on the left when you come in the door. Yeah, you'll get the *water* from the restaurant. Make sure it's boiling. And a chicken soup and the burger and fries. Medium. No, say medium rare. They overcook everything."

Lee sat up, hugging himself. His clothes were drenched. The air pouring into the car felt much colder. His cap was gone; he wasn't sure when he'd lost it.

"Okay," the familiar voice said. "Can you stand up, Professor? Take my arm if you need to. The room's just this way. You're going to have a hot shower and put on dry clothes and drink some hot tea and eat dinner. The Woodsman's food isn't half bad, but I'm afraid there's no

sushi." Jim Morrison laughed as he led Lee along. Morrison was wearing crisp camouflage slacks and a sweatshirt that read EDDIE BAUER. He
looked every inch the rich dilettante hunter, enjoying a wifeless
vacation.

"It's reassuring to see you here," Morrison added. "I bet it's an interesting story. But first the shower and dry clothes and dinner. I'll be waiting outside." He'd steered Lee through the door of a room. There was a
made-up bed, western-themed amateur paintings. Lee crept to the bathroom, his mind echoing with the series of tasks that had been laid
before him—shower, dry clothes, and dinner—and locked himself in.

The water pressure was good, and the temperature scalding.
Cocooned in a geyser of heat, he had the vague sensation, not unpleasant, that his flesh was being cooked. Donald Whitehead did not recede
so much as succumb to suspension, his figure dangling in his rough-
hewn doorway, his baroque words of greeting unlaunched on his
tongue. Somewhere the path forked. Where had Lee stumbled? What
wrong turn had he taken?

A loud thumping. "Professor!" Jim Morrison called. "Doing okay in
there?"

He had fallen asleep, or perhaps he had fainted, tipped against the
wet tiles.

When he was finished, he cracked open the bathroom door as
slightly as he could. The room was empty, but some clothes had been
left on the bed. Lee drew them onto himself almost unconsciously, like
a sleepwalker. The boxer shorts ballooned around his groin. The pants
had to be rolled several times at the cuffs. He drew the belt all the way
through the buckle, to the innermost hole.

He was slumped on the end of the bed when a tactful knock came
at the door, like the doctor's when one has been forced to strip naked
and put on a stiff paper gown. Morrison entered bearing a plastic tray
with a bowl of soup and a hamburger on it, and he was followed by
another man bearing a tray with a plastic teapot and two cups on it,
and that man was followed by so many additional persons, mostly
men but some women, all dressed in brand-new hunting togs, that the
room was soon full.

"I hope you don't mind company while we talk?" Agent Morrison
said.

25.

SOMETIME IN THE COURSE OF THE NIGHT, THE RAIN turned to snow. Even during Lee's ride down the mountain, the change was occurring. The heavy strings of rain that had framed Marjorie had lost speed, devolved into stiff soup, approached ever clumsier, sloppier mire, and then at the apex—or nadir—of this process, as if at the touch of a wand, all began to reverse, to flow *up,* to become weightless. Snow.

It wasn't such an unusual thing at this altitude, a snowstorm in May. It wasn't usual, no. Not unusual either. It happened. Every once in a while.

The man who had voiced these laconic analyses was very long and narrow, with huge hands and shaggy white hair, but if not for the hair he might have looked Agent Morrison's age, even younger. The hair was a strange foreign growth on his head. He must be only in his late thirties, or early forties at most. He wore a plaid work shirt that, unlike Agent Morrison's, looked soft and faded with washing, although it was still stiffly bulky, because of a thick quilted lining. Lee could see the lining where the man's cuffs were unbuttoned and turned back at his bony, red wrists. The man was sitting in one of the room's two mustard-colored chairs, at its brown wood-grain laminate table. Agent Morrison, in his too-new-looking wilderness clothes, sat in the other. A third man, who had not even tried to appear to be rustic, was lying across the end of the other bed, perpendicular to the normal direction. Lee could see only the soles of his wing tips and the limp cuffs of his slacks, darkly stained with moisture.

Lee himself was rolled up at the head of the other bed, the one nearer the window, at the foot of which were the table and chairs. At some point during his long and confused conversation with the roomful of people, he had grown so light-headed with fever and so incapable of speech from his chattering teeth that eventually he'd been lifted, like a sack of potatoes, and matter-of-factly inserted beneath the bed's covers, and this was where, after an unrestful dreamscape, people letting themselves in and out, loudly talking, even using the foot of his bed to sit down—he would bounce as if floating on turbulent seas—he had awoken, he didn't know how much later. A gray light had been struggling into the room. For a long time, he'd listened, not with any intent to eavesdrop but only because he had felt so abraded as to have been made unbearably porous, unable to shield himself from the sounds. The overnight babble of voices reduced to just three, whose owners he saw when with effort, and briefly, his eyes fluttered open. Agent Morrison, the prematurely white-haired man, and the pair of wing tips.

"EOD flying in . . . the Team Leader . . . a tactical entry . . . bomb techs . . . damage radius . . . decent assessment . . . clear out neighbors . . . SWAT launch . . . maintain radio contact . . . Would we need Hostage Rescue? Your call, but I don't think there's time for those people to get here. . . ." The voice of the man wearing wing tips had been rambling and droning eternally; Lee dozed and awoke and dozed again to its unending stream.

"He's not going to have anyone in there," the laconic voice broke in, sounding slightly annoyed. "That place is barely big enough for him to fit. Ask your professor."

"He awake?"

"I don't think so."

"You'll need a doctor for him." Wing Tips yawned.

"It's just a fever. He'll sweat it out."

"At that age pneumonia's a danger. My dad almost died from it two months ago."

"I didn't know that, Tom. I hope he's doing all right now." This was Agent Morrison's voice.

"Old age is a bitch. If it isn't one thing, it's another."

"And you don't need to clear out the neighbors, because there aren't any neighbors. Just that little log cabin a quarter mile down that your three guys were using." White Hair again, audibly testy.

After a few silent moments, Agent Morrison said, "Why don't you tell us your take on it, Dave? This is your turf. You know him."

"I'm just local yokel," Dave demurred with sarcasm. "I'm not Task Force."

Another pause, slightly shorter. "You're saying we don't need Hostage Rescue."

"I'm not saying what you need and don't need, I'm saying what you can and can't do. You can't launch your SWAT people from the neighboring place because there isn't a neighboring place. There's an eight-foot-square cabin where your three guys have been freezing their tails off. The only reason they haven't got frostbite is because they've been sitting on top of each other."

"SWAT'll have to hike in," Agent Morrison admitted.

"Crunch, crunch," Dave replied.

"This guy can pack a bomb in a matchbox that'll blow off your head. You need a tactical entry," Wing Tips said.

"Have you looked out the window? There's no fucking leaves on the trees, and there's a foot and a half of new snow on the ground. Now, the snow has a nice crunchy crust. If he doesn't see you coming a mile away on the nice white backdrop, then he'll hear you."

"Crunch, crunch," Agent Morrison echoed.

"I'm not disagreeing you've got to be delicate. He never let me within twenty feet of his door. I always thought he was hiding something. Never dreamed it was this."

"What'd you try and run him in for?" This was Wing Tips asking.

"Game violations. He's just got a few acres, but his place backs onto Forest Service land. We were pretty sure he'd been poaching for years but never could catch him at it."

"Lucky you didn't," Wing Tips said after a while.

"Anytime I walked near his property line, he came striding right out. He's got the ears of a dog."

"That's what needs to happen," said Morrison.

"What's that?"

"We need to lure him out of the house empty-handed. Unarmed. Out of reach of any mechanisms he might have prepared."

"I don't know how you're going to swing that. He senses danger now. He knows I'm law enforcement: if he sees me, he'll start throwing grenades. At this point he'll probably do the same thing if he sees anyone. Your guys made too much fucking noise when they grabbed the professor."

"He awake?" Wing Tips asked again.

"It doesn't matter if he is," Agent Morrison said. "He's not leaving this room till we're done."

And why not? Lee wondered as he subsided back under the waves. Because he might rush to warn Whitehead? Because he might tip off the press? Morrison constantly seemed to mistake him, this time for a person within reach of the wild-spinning wheel that was steering the course of events. While Lee was still just tangled in the chassis, more mangled the farther it dragged him along. For a short time, the previous night, he had harbored the terrible thought that he himself, in his flight to find Gaither, had led the agents to Whitehead's front door— the thought terrible not because it meant capture for Whitehead but because it meant Lee, all those miles, had never been undetected, never free of the Furies, never outside a gaze that was that much more awful for being unfelt. But soon he'd realized that his appearance in Sippston had been just as surprising to Morrison and his colleagues as theirs was to him. It hadn't been Lee who had led them to Whitehead. Their breakthrough had been an unemployed poet and soapbox orator who'd befriended Whitehead in his brief time at Berkeley and then exchanged philosophical letters with him for three decades. An old man himself, one of the unchanging "characters" left from the sixties well known to the students on Telegraph Avenue, the poet had first followed the Brain Bomber story with anarchic glee and had then read the whole manifesto when it ran in the papers. It was easy to imagine his vertiginous doubt at this point of his own sanity, the same doubt he might feel if a specter of his poet's invention had materialized. Whitehead's repertoire of metaphor and allusion was vast, but not so vast as to avoid repetition in thirty years' worth of letters, let alone in a manifesto of thirty-five thousand words. The poet's proud exultation—he *knew* the Brain Bomber!—was brief; he'd then suffered intense paranoia and called the police.

He'd also, just after his first lengthy interview with local FBI agents—and just before the Berkeley police, at the FBI's request, took him into custody on vagrancy charges to prevent precisely such an indiscretion—called a San Francisco network news affiliate. The national network had prepared a story on a Brain Bomber suspect in the Idaho mountains and, as a courtesy, informed the FBI and offered a one-day delay before broadcasting. This was why the three men had been talking all night in Lee's room, about how to seize Whitehead, without Whitehead's exploding himself or his cabin—in which the evidence against him must be—or any number of arresting agents, and it was also why no one could wait for the new snow to melt.

"Fuck these people!" exclaimed Morrison, of the network news show, in a tone of exhaustion. Lee remembered the first time he'd heard the generally courteous agent use the same expletive. Then, exhausted himself from his fever, he went back to sleep.

Lee had absorbed the conversation between the three men as thoroughly and indifferently as a lifetime prisoner might absorb the game of chess being played by his captors outside his cell door. He was aware of every move and countermove, in possession of complete understanding of the contest so far, but his soul was elsewhere, in a furnace of fury and shame. He viewed his fever as the outward expression of the fire in his brain, which, having been so diseased, was consuming itself to clear ground for fresh growth, like a scorched mountainside. In their shallow penetration, the roots of his reason had at least knitted tightly together, like a mat of crabgrass, so that everything baffled and wrong came away in one piece. Lewis Gaither's death wasn't some sort of trick being played by Agent Morrison on Lee or by Gaither on both of them. It was simply itself, the ungraspable fact of a canceled existence. Lewis Gaither was dead. He had been dead for years. There was a wholeness to Lee's brokenness, as there was strange love in his old, worn-out hatred: Lewis Gaither was dead, and Lee was surprised by real grief. He knew he wasn't noble enough to grieve Lewis for Lewis's sake. And yet he felt grief, perhaps for their brief, awkward friendship or perhaps for an ardent believer in God who could still be as clumsy and mean as a sinner when his love was repulsed and his pride was destroyed—but who was far from a monster of vengeance or a killer of men.

Gaither could never have been such a thing, yet Lee knew he'd seen him this way long before Hendley's bomb, and the letter. Lee's thoughts of Gaither had taken their shape from his thoughts of Aileen, which had gouged him for years with sharp edges of blame and regret. Without the deep channel they'd carved, all his torrents of hatred for Gaither might have spread themselves thin and evaporated. But Lee had never cured himself of the shame that he felt toward his wife, which had causes as stark as his gladness her child had vanished and as nebulous as the mistrust that had poisoned their marriage. He'd needed Gaither's villainy to excuse his own ignoble acts, and perhaps just to feel comparatively like an adequate husband.

That Lee could have imagined it all, that he'd housed such unruly emotion as had made him extrude—like the spider he'd thought Gaither was!—a delusional web that enmeshed the two men in a decades-old dance of revenge, compared only to Donald Whitehead's astounding misprision of Lee. How could Lee ever have known, while he thrashed through a past that revolved around Aileen and Gaither, that he of all people loomed large in Whitehead's memories? How could he have realized that for all the loneliness and pain he'd endured in his days as a student, his life—which had included not merely a friend to betray and a lover with whom to effect the betrayal but so many other quotidian ties, to persons who'd had him to dinner or with whom he'd drunk beer and shared warm conversation, that until now he'd so far taken them for granted as not to recall them—had in fact been as normal and varied and full as Donald Whitehead's had been irregular and narrow and empty? He'd known Donald Whitehead so little he'd never suspected that their glancing acquaintance, for Whitehead, qualified as a singular friendship. He'd been so quick to assume that Whitehead's social unease was aloofness that he'd acted aloof in return—to Whitehead's eyes seeming "princely," as Whitehead admiringly recalled in his letter. All those decades ago, Lee had been so impressed by Whitehead's brilliance and promise and stature as the rarest of students that he had never perceived it might be Whitehead who trailed after the Byrons, unwanted, and not the reverse. Perhaps it showed something touchingly innocent in Lee's thinking that he had assumed Whitehead's genius must be an elevating, not an isolating, force. Lee had associated with that blessing of genius a large number of other, unrelated conditions he had longed to possess for himself—like wealth and taste and self-confidence—that he now understood Donald Whitehead had not possessed either. In severely jarred retrospect, Lee could admit that Whitehead had been not aristocratically eccentric but awkward, not proudly aloof but alone. Perhaps it helped explain why, after Whitehead's departure from grad school to his plum teaching job, Lee had never heard of him again. Something in Berkeley had been unbearable, or perhaps something had always been unbearable. A few years after taking his job, Whitehead had resigned with no explanation and effectively vanished. At around the same time, "Dr. Burt" had appeared in the Idaho mountains.

Now the very few people who shared that vast wildness with him, whose POSTED: NO TRESPASSING signs came in contact with his, were to be astonished by sharpshooters noiselessly trespassing over their property, with computerized guns and headsets sprouting out of their ears. At least this was the hopeful idea that Wing Tips entertained. But even Lee, as he came to again in the unwholesome fug of the room, knew that this had been Wing Tips' attempt to constructively rile his colleagues, to produce the argumentative heat that might forge a real option. He must not have succeeded. The lanky, irate, white-haired man had departed. Even Wing Tips had finally departed. An abrasive silence pained Lee's ears that he realized was the drone from a fluorescent lightbulb. Agent Morrison had pulled his chair close to Lee's bedside and met Lee's awakening gaze thoughtfully. Morrison's square, solid face, at its best like something knocked from granite with a hammer, was in a worse condition than Lee would have imagined this face could achieve: the ruddy skin had gone green with fatigue and seemed pitted all over, made spongy by some cellular breakdown that a bristling, half-gray, day-old beard only partly concealed. If this was how the younger man looked, Lee himself must be gruesome. The thought wasn't dismaying, as it would usually be. All vanity, all shame, all fear seemed steamed out of the husk of his body.

"Feeling better?" Morrison asked at length.

Lee felt helpless to utter his answer, whatever it was. He was still negotiating phlegmy deposits and the peculiar uncertain sensation of the voice after fever when a single knock came at the door. A boyish-looking man entered, not having waited for any response. He wore a dress shirt with dark armpit stains, a tie pulled slack like a noose, and suit pants so crumpled they must at some point have been dampened and crushed into a ball. "He's awake," the man noticed, and from his voice Lee understood that this was Wing Tips, now standing upright.

"Just this instant," said Morrison.

"So . . . you float it?"

"He's just come to this instant. He'd just opened his eyes when you came through the door." Morrison's face twitched a little, as if in suppression.

"It's past noon. We're gonna screw the pooch here if we don't make a timely decision."

For a moment they faced off, until Morrison said, "There's no decision to make, Tom. This is not on the table. It's unacceptable risk."

"Not if it works. Besides, what's on the table? I feel like for the past twenty hours you've been saying, 'No, impossible, Tom. No, it can't be done, Tom.' "

Morrison stood. "Let's keep talking outside. Professor Lee needs his rest."

"He looks rested to me. Why not ask him?"

"No!" Morrison barked startlingly.

"What's the harm?"

"The harm," Morrison said, but all at once something seemed to obstruct him, as if what he wanted to say weren't too minor but too vast to compress into words. He looked so depleted that Lee sat up abruptly in bed, thinking to catch Morrison before that man collapsed.

After the slightest of pauses, the merest gesture toward awaiting the rest of his colleague's remarks, the agent whose name was apparently Tom said to Lee, "You must already know what we're driving at, don't you, Professor?" And before Lee could say he did not, "Our friend on the mountain is homicidally hostile to most everybody but you."

"Tom," Morrison said warningly.

"You he welcomes," Tom went on. "You he *invites*, if you can be believed. You go up there today and call 'Yoo-hoo,' I'm thinking he comes out, our guys pounce. It's all over."

"I go back there?" Lee exclaimed huskily.

"Dr. Lee is not a law-enforcement agent," Morrison interrupted, his own voice very calm but with such unnerving cords of tension expanding the girth of his neck that he might have swallowed a massive explosion just under his tonsils.

"And he's happy to see you," Tom answered. "His 'Old Colleague and Friend.' "

Lee felt goose pimples quicken his skin.

"He comes out, our guys pounce—"

"We don't invite members of the general public to help us execute arrests," Morrison continued, a viselike pressure in his voice now, as he turned himself fully to Tom, as if to signal that the scorn in his face was directed at one object only, and not at any members of the general public who might happen to be in the room.

"We take them into our confidence when they're useful to us," Tom countered.

"We don't put them in harm's way."

"There's a lot of things we don't do that we do. It's called being creative."

Another compact, buzzing silence fell here, like a noise of its own, but Lee only remotely heard it. He didn't disbelieve in the prospect so much as he needed, urgently, to grasp everything perfectly clearly. "I would be alone?" Lee persisted.

When Morrison turned away from Tom again, it was as if he'd shut a door in that man's face: only Morrison and Lee now remained. Resuming his place in the chair, Morrison trained his oppressed, weary gaze upon Lee. "Lee, this isn't an option for you to consider."

"I know that," Lee said. For him it was also as if Tom were no longer there. "I know you want me to feel there is no obligation." He had not known, until speaking this particular word, what species of word he might try to say next. But "obligation" seemed to offer an anchorage. It pertained in no way to his entanglement with Morrison and Tom—he was not obligated to them—yet despite this he seized hold of it. Obligation fulfilled; had he ever been able to say this? The persons he longed to oblige himself to were all gone, or his chances with them had all passed. He could no longer be Aileen's comrade or her son's guardian. He could not restore Hendley to life or assuage Rachel's pain. He could never erase the charnel of that burned, spattered office, much less the sight of the victim himself, from young Emma Stiles's mind. A martyrdom here wouldn't ever make up for the lapses he saw there and there and all those other immutable elsewheres now lost to the past. Perhaps all Lee really felt now was the need to escape from this bed, where a lifetime's distillate of shame had enrobed him for hours—and, more simply, that as cocksure as Tom might behave, his idea was right. Tom had outlined a logical plan. And Lee, every once in a while, could be logical, too.

"I know that," Lee reiterated, "but I'll do it," he finished, almost winded by what he had said.

"I'll get moving," said Tom, startling them both with his ongoing presence and punching keys on a phone he'd snatched out of his pocket.

"Just hang on a goddamn minute!" Morrison said. "Lee, I think I can understand, better than anyone else, why you might feel under pressure to do this—"

"Jim, what Tom says makes sense," Lee put forth, his voice a rattling tea tray that was certain to scatter its cups. His resolve felt so precious and frail; he knew that the stronger, authentically brave man could dash it to bits without ever realizing.

"If you'd never been here, we'd still be where we are, and we'd still move ahead."

"Into a shitstorm," Tom said.

"You'll have a shitstorm when Professor Lee is injured or dead."

"I never said it was ideal. Ideal is no network news yanking our pants down, we get to wander around in our mountain-man clothes while we nail down probable cause, I do some skiing, the jerk finally gets hungry, and we cuff him in front of the grocery store—"

"He really did invite me," Lee murmured as the two men resumed arguing. "He went to so much trouble. He must have taken a bus all the way to our school, so he could put that note inside my book."

"You're gonna have to let me kick it upstairs," Tom was saying to Morrison. "He's volunteered. It's not my call or yours."

"It is a logical plan," Lee whispered, less to the other men than to himself. *I know that you, like me, are rational.* He heard those words again in his mind and cringed from them. Now they were spoken by Whitehead's stentorian voice.

He scarcely noticed when the two men banged out of the room. Once the noise of the door ceased to echo and the fluorescent's flat buzz filled his ears, he might have waited three minutes or thirty. His Seiko seemed unreachable, on the farther nightstand. He lay on the chemical-scented motel pillows and felt the drifting movement of the mattress over calm, windless seas and realized that his body and not the mattress was the source of the feeling. He grew aware of voices outside his door, both raised and suppressed—high emotion, low volume. He couldn't pick out distinct words. When he heard the door open again, he jerked upright, his gut sick with dread. He'd wanted this limbo to last, and perhaps never end.

Morrison reseated himself in the chair. For another long time, another three minutes or thirty, he didn't speak, until he finally did. "We're off the map here. This is not the way I like to work."

"I know," Lee said in a rush of compassion, for a moment forgetting himself. "You like to have all the i's dotted and all the t's crossed."

"SWAT will have to do a wide perimeter. A big loose circle, several hundred yards from the house so he doesn't detect them. But they're the best shots in the world. You'll be protected if he tries anything."

"I know," Lee said, by which he didn't mean, I know SWAT is the best in the world, so much as, My personal safety does not matter now. He didn't mean he didn't care if he died; he did not want to die. But the shock of what he'd offered to do had transformed him somehow. He felt weird imperviousness, as if a spell had been cast.

"You'll be wearing a bulletproof vest. Dave and I will drive you up to within about five hundred yards on a snowmobile; then we'll have to hike up. But once we get to the clearing, you step out on your own. No closer to the house than necessary. Think of the cabin like it's radioactive. You can't approach it. Can't touch it. Persuade him to come out to you. And you can't let him know that you're with us. You have to talk to him just like you would, Lee. He has to think you're alone."

"I know," Lee said.

"And if you get killed or hurt, I will make you regret it." This said not in jest but almost in anger, as if he expected to have to make good on his threat.

"I know," Lee said a last time, though he wasn't confident or courageous. He was just the one person to do it, the one way that the thing could be done. As if the whole misbegotten equation added up after all.

The prematurely white-haired man, Dave, was a law-enforcement agent of the United States Forest Service, and it was he who fitted Lee, from his own closet, with snowshoes and a winter coat, the coat reaching almost to Lee's knees but cut narrow, so that it fit somewhat better than Morrison's clothes. The snowshoes were not the rustic wooden tennis rackets that Lee had envisioned. They were ungainly rectangular frameworks of aluminum pipe with a welter of buckles and straps with which Dave struggled while Lee sat sideways in the passenger seat of an SUV, either the same one that had plucked him off White-head's mountain or its identical twin, the car door standing open and the chill air, ominous with moisture, probing Dave's coat, seeking points of entry. Dave squatted on the icy asphalt while he worked, in the same plaid shirt he'd been wearing before, cuffs rolled back, his only concession to being outdoors a thin black knitted cap on his head. When he had finished, he helped Lee to his feet, and Lee, leaning hard on Dave as if he were an old woman and Dave were a Boy Scout, scraped with a horrible noise across the asphalt to a vast, pristine stretch of meringue at the parking lot's border. Dave had to roughly hoist Lee, holding him under the armpits, to get him over the filthy bulwark of plowed snow that hemmed the lot on all sides. When Lee touched down on the level meringue, he clung to Dave across the bul-wark, certain he'd sink to his knees, and felt Dave's fingers matter-of-factly prying his loose from the sleeve of Dave's shirt. Morrison watched from the lot's farther side. Dave pushed Lee, the stronger ani-mal calmly imposing its will on the weaker, until Lee stopped bend-ingly reaching for Dave and stood straight, miraculously afloat on the bright crust of snow.

Dave handed Lee a pair of spindly flexible sticks made of plastic and rubber. "Use them for balance, not leverage," he said. "Pretend you're walking on water. Go light. You'll have to put your feet wider," he added, as Lee, confused by the width of the shoes, almost fell on his face.

There wasn't much time to practice, or rather there was no time at all. It was one-thirty; Lee had done his best to eat a ham sandwich and a cup of chicken noodle soup with Morrison at the wood-laminate ta-ble in his motel room, but the sandwich bread had stuck in his wind-pipe and the smell of the ham made him nauseous; he'd gotten the soup down his throat at the rate of an eyedropper. The national net-work would air their story, blowing Morrison's and all his colleagues' cover, at six-thirty. But dusk would have already fallen an hour be-fore—SWAT had to work with just visual contact between the team members, because radios were too loud. And really, visual conditions would already be hopelessly lousy an hour before that, given how shoehorned in mountains Donald Whitehead's place was. And to cap it, the forecast was calling for even more snow. At best they had three hours remaining; at worst it was already over—

This overheard information impressed itself upon Lee about as well as might a discussion of wind speed if he was about to be pushed from a plane. He knew it impinged upon him, but he couldn't digest it. He took a step, swayed, waved his sticks like a flailing insect, felt the protest in the small of his back and his groin and his calves. He had to spread his feet wider. And up there he'd be climbing: that same final ascent that felt grueling enough from the inside of Marjorie's truck.

Now another huge SUV, which gleamed like new despite radial spatters of road salt and mud, drove into the slush-flooded lot with a trailer in hitch that had a snowmobile on it, and at the same time Agent Morrison came striding as fast as he could through the slop. "We've got it," he told Dave, "so let's go," and because Lee understood all the prerequisites of their mission, like a rank-and-file soldier whose sheer petrifaction has paradoxically honed his perceptions, he knew this meant that the warrants had now been obtained from the district court judge, and the next instant Dave had boosted him back to the parking-lot side of the bulwark of snow and then boosted him again, a clumsy and clattering scarecrow in his overlarge coat and aluminum shoes, into the SUV's passenger seat, and with an angry slamming of doors all around they had "launched," as had the SWAT team already; Lee and Morrison and Dave would drive as far as a defunct wood mill and wait there for confirmation that the SWAT team had formed their "loose ring," and then the three men would continue on the snowmobile and then on their snowshoes, and then came the point when the smallest and last rocket stage tumbled off all alone.

Lee's bulletproof vest seemed too long for his torso; it dug painfully into his armpits. He struggled to bring into his mind all the parts of his life he would have hoped might enfold him and solace him now. He was disappointed; his life did not "pass before him," although he could feel, when he closed his eyes, when he let the cement-grinder noise of the tires drown out the terse exchanges between the other men in the car, Esther's small, glossy head, beaming warmth, in the cup of his palm. . . . He did not mean to be melodramatic, only as acknowledging, as undeceived, as Agent Morrison was. Before, over lunch in the room, Lee had said to him, "Jim, are you nervous?" and Morrison had said, "I always am."

Lee knew he was nervous also, so nervous that the word seemed absurd when proposed as the name of his inner condition. If he had felt this before, he could not recall it, in the way that some say one cannot recall physical pain, so that pain is always brand-new, lacking all precedent, laying siege to a body unsuspecting of it and so that much more vulnerable. Lee only knew that his feeling was entirely different this time up the mountain. In the truck with Marjorie, his awareness of the impending encounter had been so acute he'd felt bruised on all sides, as if by an onslaught of sensory hail. Now a featureless pad seemed to muffle him from his surroundings, even silence his breath in his throat. When he did choose to listen to Morrison and Dave and the third agent, whose job was to drive, the substance of their conversation was received by his mind with the indifference of a pond stretched beneath a light rain. Explosives ordnance detonation, command post, device signature—Lee might already have been on his own, already climbing the mountain, wizened and hunched and impervious, like the monks he remembered from boyhood: serene with indifference, their life in this world and their life in the next mere conditions, marked off by the slightest of membranes, through which one might pass anytime, no big drama, no tears, no regrets. . . .

At the defunct wood mill, they unloaded the snowmobile, put on their snowshoes, watched the SUV leave them behind. The SWAT team was in place, too far away to give alarm and so too far away also to give comfort. At least four separate law-enforcement agencies, represented by more than two dozen persons, with countless more en route, from East Coast and West, from a nearby army base, were secreted in Sippston; yet it was really just three mismatched men, in the sighing near silence of a pine mountainside. Two of the men hadn't slept for two days, and one was sick with the flu, underweight, over sixty, and his cold-weather clothes did not fit. Two were armed, and one could barely stay upright in snowshoes and while supporting the weight, which seemed to double and double again, of his bulletproof vest. It seemed to Lee, every moment, that in the next moment they would sit and discuss in detail what was going to happen, but they never did, because they never could have; future time had taken on a strange, truncated quality, and there was only the immediate moment, in which shoes and sidearms were adjusted, and the subsequent immediate moment, in which they awkwardly climbed on the snowmobile—Lee in the middle, Morrison behind him, and Dave at the controls—and the subsequent immediate moment, in which this physical intimacy felt almost comical, but the comedy was remote, out of reach, like the V-shaped black bird drifting far overhead, and then the subsequent immediate moment when the snowmobile came to life with a racket like that of Lee's ancient lawn mower, and then Lee was no longer aware of immediate moments.

Nothing looked as it had the night before, in the darkness and rain. At every bend and ascent in the track, Lee expected the cabin to leap onto them, a devouring monster of shingles and boards. They roared and whined, throwing snow divots, seeming to fissure the earth with their noise, his terror that Whitehead would hear them endurable only because demolished by the even greater terror he'd be pitched from the bucking machine—but after they'd abruptly stopped, and dismounted, and started to slog on their own, he understood that they'd never been anywhere close to the cabin, that in fact they would never come close. It was Zeno's snow hike. Lee felt, within ten or twelve marshy, up-straining steps, that he'd been pushed to the limits of his body's endurance, that now he'd passed into the dissociated state of a victim of torture, that the vest, which seemed made of lead plates, was sawing his arms from his shoulders, and the shoes, which seemed glued to the snow, were uprooting the tops of his thighs from his hip joints, and that feverish unconsciousness was about to submerge him. He seemed to see himself, and Agent Morrison and Dave, from some swirl-inscribed distance, across which their three forms, bent in effort, appeared scored by a swarming of little white worms. It was snowing again, he realized: tiny featureless pellets this time instead of feathery flakes. The sky seemed to have closed like a lid. It was harder to see. Beside him, their gasping breaths drowned out by his, Agent Morrison and Dave were lumpen blocks of dull color, of browns and sickly army greens, camouflage tones that made them not less visible but more inexplicable against the backdrop of whitish gray soup. What were these shuddering, khaki-clad lumps? Lee was no less visible in his borrowed parka, which was navy blue, with an edging of mangy fake fur on the hood that had clotted with snow and his own frozen spit. And he remembered, suddenly, that the Communist soldiers had worn white cotton clothes in the winter and crawled through the snow while invading his country, and this was why no one had seen them in time to repel them.

"Do you know what a hemlock is?" Dave was asking. "Like a feathery pine?" Lee managed to show that he did. "Once you've climbed to that big hemlock there, that's about fifty yards, you have a clear line of sight to the cabin. But go slow. Me and Jim'll go the long way to come out at the back of his woodpile, but we need time to get in position."

No admonition had ever been less necessary. Watching the other two men hunker off, Lee experienced a sudden inversion, all the alarming sensations of being knocked off his feet, as he sometimes did when nodding off to sleep. Perhaps he had actually fainted. But when he jerked back to awareness, his heart rampaging, his limbs turned to rubber, he was upright. This was the form defeat took. He might have been a dead piece of tree that had fallen upright in the snow. He would stand here forever, immobile, and not even rot.

And yet he must have clawed his way somehow, from the place they'd left him to the hemlock and from the hemlock to the cabin's little clearing, which drew him miragelike, alternately appearing and fading, assembling and dissolving, through the snow and the trees. When he was a young man, he'd walked from his invaded, fallen city all the way to the sea. He'd walked, amid corpses and stragglers, completely alone, his family swept untraceably from him as if by a tsunami. And that had happened to a separate man's body, perhaps even a separate man's soul: he retained only the dry knowledge of it, as if acquired from history books, the same way this ordeal was being swiftly excised, so that even as he endured, he diligently forgot.

He didn't so much bravely enter as fall into the clearing.

The snow here was almost two feet deep. Exhausted, he sank into it, his knees buckling, the tangled snowshoes partly under his buttocks, his left hip canted out so that it quickly grew wet. Gaither was dead, he remembered. His own Aileen was dead. Brilliant, unbearable Hendley was dead. Lee was alive, but in a moment he, too, might be dead, just another condition, the boundary of his life a mere membrane through which he would pass. He was aware of the cabin's door opening; the snowflakes had grown larger and lighter, and the wind had died down, so that the whine of the cabin door's hinges was as audible to him as if he stood just on the threshold, though he was possibly ten yards away, a few pickup-truck lengths. Marjorie had turned around in this space; she'd had to squeeze, but she'd done it. Now came Whitehead's boots scraping onto the threshold; if in the snow hush Lee could hear their abrasions this clearly, wouldn't Whitehead hear two other men creeping past his woodpile? But Lee wasn't thinking of this. He was remembering instead something Whitehead once said in a class they had taken. They'd both been interested in simple group classification, which held that of those phenomena known as multiply transitive permutation groups, only four existed. That was a given; it was not controversial; but Donald Whitehead had once scoffed at it, and when their professor had asked what he meant, he'd replied, with strange heat, "I don't like to be told there are only so many of something. I don't like to be told things like that," and Lee had been both disturbed and impressed by that peculiar, self-certain outburst.

"I must admit I am less overjoyed," Whitehead said now, from his doorway, his voice sounding very different, wary and thick, as if congested with feeling it fought to suppress. "I've assumed, since our strange reunion, that your trustworthiness went without saying. But perhaps I'm sentimental after all, and deceived. Who fetched you last night? And how did you get back here now?" Lee saw Whitehead reaching for something, brushing fingertips over some item to be assured it was there. From behind Whitehead's bulk, a white plume of misvented woodsmoke escaped out the door, and Lee remembered the stench of the cabin, or smelled it again, as it made its way across the cold to him. Whitehead's attire, as well as his manner, had changed since the previous night. Lee realized he was wearing the old houndstooth jacket. He must have ventured outside to retrieve it from where Lee had dropped it in the course of his flight. And then dried it, perhaps carefully draped on the smoking woodstove. It was true that the decades had made it too small for his frame. It barely stretched shoulder to shoulder and winged out on both sides from a gap where it should have been buttoned. Even the sleeves ended short of the thick, hairy wrists. Now Lee knew, from Agent Morrison and Dave and Tom, that Whitehead had never been the scion of a moneyed and lettered East Coast family, as Lee once romantically thought. He was the midwestern son of a husbandless mother, who had raised him in sooty brick houses against a background of smokestacks. The jacket must have come from a secondhand store, like Lee's briefcase. Perhaps it had never quite fit.

He could only ignore Whitehead's questions and accusing assumptions. "Donald," he said instead, hoarsely, around chattering teeth. "Did you ever do it? Did you ever manage to prove a fifth group?"

Lee was not near enough, but he sensed something disrupt Whitehead's threatening face. An impulse of eagerness: it made a tentative showing, lingering in the background of the forbidding expression, as Whitehead lingered in the doorway of his cabin. "You mean a quintuply transitive permutation group?" Whitehead finally said.

"Yes. Like we discussed in seminar."

"Well, Mathieu says that the problem is settled," Whitehead countered, a note of irony lifting his voice.

"You didn't think that it was."

"I still don't. I think Mathieu's approach lacked generality. It's very strange you should remember I said that."

"I remember very well," Lee said, although he hadn't remembered, not for thirty-one years, until now. But now he did remember very well. Now it came to him envelopingly, as memory often did.

"Your memory didn't serve you so well yesterday. You seemed taken aback. I notice you still haven't explained how you got here alone."

Lee stabbed his spindly, flexible poles through the snow until they struck solid ground and then began struggling to pull himself upright, although he remembered Dave saying to use them for balance, not leverage. "Maybe that's because," he managed, heaving breaths, "I remember you differently. To me you were like an aristocrat."

He saw Whitehead start forward to help him and stop short. Whitehead stepped back into his doorway and made a brusque noise of scorn. "The prince saw me as princely."

"I was no prince," Lee said, giving up for the moment and sitting back heavily, his legs splayed in front of him now, his rear soaking and numb.

"Nor was I."

"You were the best of us," Lee rebuked. "You were brilliant." He remembered Fasano's words to him: *So bright they seem radioactive.* "All my life all I wanted was what you threw away."

"All you wanted was the chance to work on weapons contracts, or build supercomputers? I doubt you wanted that, Lee."

"Is that what you were doing? Those aren't the only choices. When we studied together, we did pure mathematics. We ignored applications."

"Certain applications I've found interesting." Whitehead cocked his head slightly. "These are things that I was very much looking forward to discussing with you. Come in, Lee. Cross over this untouched snowfield, on your surprising snowshoes, and come into my home. But perhaps some misgiving is making you pause."

"You could have done brilliant work," Lee persisted. "You were given such gifts, and you wasted them. It's awful to someone like me, who never had them at all."

"Or perhaps you are tired, or hurt, and you need my assistance," Whitehead added. "You wonder why I don't come to you, with my own hand extended. Are my misgivings a mirror of yours? Or do I misjudge my friend?"

Whitehead had not contradicted Lee's own claim to lack scholarly gifts. After a moment Lee said, not to wound the other man but from an opposite impulse, an authentic concern for his soul, "You could have used your own mind, instead of trying to get rid of others."

Now Lee saw, for the first time, Whitehead's inchoate suspicion coalesce into anger. "Is that your assessment of me? If so, it's sentimental, not rational. Every human life is not sacrosanct. I hold this is true. I think you do. I know our society does. It will want to remove me for my so-called crimes, and if you agree with that punishment's premise, then you agree with me, Lee. Some humans must be removed, for the good of the whole. We all concur on the principle. We only disagree on how it's put into practice. Society will condone my removal, to avenge the removals I've accomplished myself, which had far greater value. How can one judge? You'll be lucky not to. If the atom bomb hadn't existed, would the people of Hiroshima have been able to *judge* the superior outcome, on August sixth, 1945, when nothing particular happened?"

"Hendley never would have harmed other people," Lee protested, meaning to continue, *and even if he had, it's not your place to judge any more than it's mine: you're not God,* but the rest of the sentence was stuck in his throat. For the first time since Hendley had died, his death pierced Lee with intimate force. Lee was as stunned by the taste of his tears as if from the top of this mountain he'd found himself thrashing around in the sea.

"Hendley's world of computer junk food for the brain would have been, and probably still will be, despite my best efforts, even worse than the atom bomb was, because it will come on by stealth, like a cancer, and be fatal before it's detected. Oh, my friend," Whitehead said in remorse, crunching down the two steps and plowing powerfully through the deep crust of snow, arm outstretched, toward where Lee found himself not just crumpled on spent legs but weeping. "Oh, my friend, I've been touchy and rude. I've been pacing all day like a cat in a cage, your departure last night made me think—"

Lee's tears had seized hold of him so ruthlessly, were wringing him so unrelentingly, he discerned even less than Whitehead the approach of the two hidden men; he was equally shocked, more afraid, as they came flying clumsily forth, wallowing through the snow, leaping on Whitehead like cooperative ambushing beasts. Whitehead was a singular beast of his own, for a moment majestic and doomed, his leonine hair standing out as he fought to twist free of his captors, who had snared him ignobly, with handcuffs snapped open like giant fishhooks, and with guns. It seemed to Lee that despite all the roared imprecations to *Get down!* and *Hands up!* and *Lie still!* and *Don't move!* the event was silent, a wild mute tornado before which he cowered, but perhaps this was only because Whitehead in his fury was silent, never looking at Lee, never calling to him, not with threats nor with supplications. By the time Lee was lifted back up to his feet, the little clearing was teeming with people and bristling with guns, but Whitehead himself, the caught beast, had been carried away.

26.

IN THEIR FIRST EXAMINATION OF THE CABIN, EOD—THE explosives ordnance detonation team, or bomb squad (but Lee now felt it very important to use the professional term, as he would want any interested outsider to say "quadruply transitive permutation group" in discussing that aspect of his field, rather than something approximate and for that reason useless)—found, with the help of a robot, a fully armed bomb, just inside the front door. Lee must have seen it, perhaps even brushed it, as he'd entered and fled. It took the form of a beautifully made wooden box, its trigger mechanism attached to the lid. It would have blown up the cabin, and the bomb-making workshop squeezed into the cellar below, and anyone to a distance of about twenty feet, leaving only a crater, if its lid had been lifted. Once the explosive interior had been disarmed and separated from the exquisite encasement, Morrison got to handle the box and to study, on the lid's underside, the Japanese characters calligraphed there as if with a tattoo needle. That had been Whitehead's "signature," Morrison said. Every bomber, whether he or she means to or not, has a signature, a characteristic manner of building a bomb, that a good analyst can detect. But Whitehead, whether because he desired recognition or merely to please his own sense of aesthetics, had elaborated his bombs with intentional signatures, little captions or titles, always in Japanese. Enigmatic things like "reliance" or "stones in a field." "This one translated as 'divine wind.' " Morrison smiled, already pleased by the quick understanding he knew Lee would show.

"*Kamikaze,*" Lee said.

"A rare case where the Japanese word is required, for us Americans to get Whitehead's meaning. He was saving that one, in case enemies came to the door."

The cabin in fact was so wondrously full of evidence against Whitehead—Lee remembered its dizzying riot of objects, its stacks of containers of the jagged and shiny, the disassembled and coiled, a mad magpie's overstuffed nest—that Morrison and his colleagues had decided to peel the whole thing from foundation to shingles off the lot in one piece, and to scoop out the cellar in its bowl of dirt, and ship them east to the FBI lab without a mote of dust altered. Lee thought of his lost cap, entombed with the evidence, traveling on a flatbed truck thousands of miles under state police escort. Another scrap of his life that was forever entangled, through error and chance. Since the announcement of Whitehead's arrest, thirty-six hours before, Sippston had been overtaken by press, by fleets of TV trucks with satellite stalks straining toward the gray sky, by reporters in unbroken-in snow boots running races on foot or in the rental cars that a shortage produced by demand had obliged them to share with their fiercest competitors, rushing from one spurious, self-declared Marjorie-like intimate to another (but not to the only authentic one, Marjorie; she wasn't talking, on the advice of a lawyer), from the federal building four counties away to the foot of the road Lee had turned down with Marjorie eons before, and which now was a sentries' encampment, protecting the evidence mother lode being mined from that small snowy clearing to which Lee had somehow ascended, not just once but twice. Their frantic movements interested Lee only insofar as they meant that the roads were clear enough for him to leave. All the roads weren't just plowed but restored to wet asphalt by warm temperatures. Lee had persuaded two of Morrison's lesser colleagues to drive to the library—staked out by reporters who still hoped for Marjorie—and caravan back with his Nissan. And there it sat now, in the slush-streaming lot, some vestigial snow crust still adhered to its roof like a crown in reward for its valiance. It had waited for Lee through his amazing ordeal, and would now take him home.

When Morrison heard he was leaving, he'd come to have room-service breakfast with him. It was a lively, enjoyable breakfast, despite the overcooked eggs in their oil slick of grease, and as he and Morrison talked, Lee almost felt he'd been reunited with a countryman, or a soldier with whom he had served, or a colleague with whom he'd been students, a long time ago. "I can think of a lot of reporters who'd give their right arms to hear how you helped nab him," Morrison added as he scraped his plate clean. Then his gaze met Lee's with new gravity. "Lee, I realize you might want to talk to the press, but I'm asking you please to hold off. Wait until he's been tried. Understand, it's not over, it's only beginning. It's critical we not jeopardize our case against Whitehead—"

"I don't want my name mixed up in it at all," Lee broke in, scraping his own plate. He was unusually hungry. "Please don't ever mention me in this case again, Jim, if I could ask you this favor. Never say I was here."

Morrison put down his fork. "You helped capture the Brain Bomber, Lee. You'd never want people to know that?"

Lee remembered his peroration on the hospital sidewalk, the day Hendley was bombed. "I've learned my lesson, with TV and these things. I'm really not interested. I'd rather stay a short poppy, if you know what I mean." He felt Morrison's thoughtful eyes on him as he peeled back the plastic membrane on his last jelly packet and applied the clear purple substance to his last piece of toast. Then Morrison pushed himself away from the table.

"Before you go, I've got something for you," he said. "Back in a minute."

When he returned, he was holding a manila file folder, like the one from which he'd taken the list of Lee's mail the first time he'd come to Lee's home. "Of everything from your house, this was the only item that contained the name Gaither, back when we thought the name Gaither might be a real lead. So I had it with me because it seemed like it might be important, and then I still had it with me when we realized it was completely unimportant, and I've been on the move ever since." Morrison paused, and Lee put down his toast and met the other man's gaze, and for the first time in their acquaintanceship—could Lee call it a friendship?—he saw Morrison's eyes seem to search, beneath the noble Neanderthal shelf of his brow, for some place of concealment, some refuge in which to recompose the generally unwavering beam that they cast. But in the next instant, the recomposure was effected, and Morrison looked at Lee without hesitation, but also with acknowledgment. "There's a bureaucratic process you go through, a formal process, to reclaim possessions. It can be slow. And since we happen to be here together . . ." He finished the sentence by holding out the file folder. Lee cleared aside his plate and cutlery and wiped his hands on a napkin before taking it. He didn't need to open it to know what it contained, but he did anyway. Aileen's letter to him.

"Thank you, Jim," he said, and found that though he'd meant to go on, a sort of valve in his throat seemed to close, a physical punctuation mark that didn't allow for additional words, and so he didn't attempt any.

"It's been a pleasure to know you, Professor."

"Please, just Lee," Lee reminded him, finding his voice, as they shook a last time.

Driving again, his restlessness wasn't the sort that he usually suffered while on the road, of thinking constantly about when to stop for a stretch or to use the toilet. An effervescent agitation bubbled up from his gut, constricting his rib cage in such a close imitation of fear it took a while to realize he in fact felt unbearable eagerness, straining him forward. The past five weeks kept returning to him in a fractured kaleidoscope form; he saw Emma Stiles recoiling, and Peter Littell's shifty gaze of distaste, Sondra's injured coldness, his neighbor with the baby on her hip and contempt in her eyes. And somehow this took him, by way of a shudder of realized negligence, to his house and its punctured window. He had felt that his place in the world was unsteady and worthless, a perch best abandoned and, more than that, not even his. But a peculiar sensation of ownership was overtaking him now, that was directed toward not just his vandalized house, but his life.

He still couldn't break the speed limit, but haste imbued all of his actions, and back in the limbo of a rest-stop McDonald's he even tried to wolf down his burger, without much success. All her life Esther had been a fast eater, dispatching her meals in a fraction of the time that Lee took, not from gluttony but a chilly efficiency that let her push back from the family table as soon as she could. Esther's manner of eating had horrified Lee. "Slow down, honey," he had implored. "No one's going to take it away from you!"

"The way you eat makes Daddy feel like we're poor," Aileen commented once.

"Bullshit!" Lee replied angrily, surprising his aged reflection in his car's dirty windshield. As had been the case years before, the observation angered him in direct proportion to its accuracy. The burger was thrust back into its bag, only halfway consumed.

Perhaps love can't surrender to loss, but at least in that tireless rebellion it recognizes itself. Before losing Aileen, Lee had not understood that her merciless knowledge of him was a rare antidote to aloneness that he would only be privileged with once. Since her death he'd grown more and more able to cherish the aspects of their marriage he had once found intolerable, and he couldn't help but wonder, as if she were not only still alive but still married to him, if she wasn't having the same change of heart. Whether or not, he found her wonderfully willing to restage their old arguments, as he crawled across their daughter's Colorado and then nobody's Kansas and even blander Missouri, hardly aware of how long the drive took, or how little the landscape varied, now that all the topographic events of the West were behind him. He knew that the refreshed vividness of her ghost was the product of different infusions, but mostly the absence of Gaither—his having been slain, finally, in Lee's mind. Lee was able to admit, with a dread that was bracing, because brave, that the failure of his marriage to Aileen hadn't been Gaither's doing. It was Lee's fault alone.

Because he'd felt so companioned while driving, at first it didn't seem completely strange, as he cautiously pulled up in front of his house in the gathering twilight, to see that his front window had been closed with a sheet of plywood. Aileen had always been good at rough practical things, like constructing a trellis or unclogging the toilet. But Aileen was also dead, Lee reminded himself, as with a rush of trepidation he turned in to his driveway and returned to the sullied remains of his life.

The inside of his garage, with its exposed two-by-fours and plasterboard and the Mower of the Ages against the back wall, was almost poignant in its ignorant sameness. But when Lee entered the actual house, pushing off his shoes by habit to leave on the mat, he was conscious of difference. He smelled a persistence of cigarette smoke.

Otherwise there was a baffling cleanness, to surfaces and the carpet. Lee's telephone notepad was turned to a fresh page and centered on the kitchen table:

> *I came as soon as I could: got some adjunct to proctor my finals, got here in time to stop your local hoodlums from turning your place into their private clubhouse. And who got the ticket for trespassing? ME. Cleaned up what I could, patched your window. Hope to God you're all right. At the Holiday Inn next to campus.—FF*

An arrow bisected the rest of the page, pointing toward where a picture postcard lay in careful alignment just offshore of the notepad. The photograph showed a hideous bird. Chicken-beaked and baldheaded, with parched ridges of flesh dangling down where a chin might have been, and a small, cunning eye. The distressing head poked from what looked like a white ermine collar. The rest of the bird wore Grim Reaper attire, a dusty black enrobement like a funeral hot-air balloon around the implied skeleton hanging down from that head, the full effect reminiscent of portraits of Elizabeth I. He was thinking all this—ugly bird, Queen Elizabeth choked by that huge wheel of lace—and also digesting the words printed under the picture—ANDEAN CONDOR *largest flying bird in the world*—but really he was hesitating at a perilous threshold, hand extended, heart stilled in his chest, both lungs empty and limp like the condor's weird wattles, because he knew he couldn't bear the disappointment if it wasn't from her.

He wanted a beer, to give strength, but this was so pitiful that with a reckless exertion of fingers he flipped the card over.

Dear Daddy

Lee dropped into a chair and devoured the postcard. He read with such greed he'd seen all of the words several times before having any idea what they said.

> *Dear Daddy,*
> *You'll never believe where I am: Patagonia. We are saving the condor, I'll explain it all later. A tourist came here with a copy of* TIME *and I COULDN'T BELIEVE IT. When the tour leaves I'll get a ride out, then a bus, flight from Santiago, layovers Houston & Chicago, I should be there 5:30 pm 6/14 pick me up if you can but if not it's ok.*

She'd been running out of space, but she managed

> *I love you,*
> *Esther*

When he telephoned the Holiday Inn, tears were cresting the rims of his eyes. "Frank?" he said. "Frank, I'm home."

"I got your mailbox back up just in time," said Fasano. "You saw the card, right? She's a good kid, Esther. But half Gypsy, not sure how that happened. Christ, say you're hungry. I came all the way here, and I'm still eating dinner all by my damn self."

When he and Fasano went for sentimental, tough steaks and cheap purple wine at the Wagon Wheel, the bartender momentarily paused in his labors and gave Lee a long stare, as if to say to everyone who was watching that he wasn't going to make a big scene, but that he hadn't been fooled. The waitress who served them was tight-lipped and carelessly hostile with glasses and plates, and kept her gaze slanted away. The other patrons were momentarily paralyzed and then fervid in conversation with one another, putting their heads close together. But no one came to their table with squared shoulders and hot coals for eyes, as the young mother had come to Lee's door, and beneath the superficial opprobrium was a sense of excitement, as if everyone hoped Lee would stay a long time, and drink heavily, and do something bizarre, so that the story would be even more singular when told to a person who hadn't been there.

So this is notoriety, Lee thought. He'd become untouchable in every sense of the word. Not just at the Wagon Wheel but everywhere in town he was shunned—looked away from as if his face were a male Medusa's, while at the same time cold gazes were flung at his back— and surrounded by a sphere of silence, so that even in the loquacious grocery line all the shoppers for ten yards around were struck mute. But to the same extent that people found him repulsive, they left him alone. Whitehead's arrest hadn't dispelled the suspicion that hung around Lee, but the suspicion had altered in texture. Every assertion that Lee must have been "somehow mixed up" in the Brain Bomber's crimes was countered by the uncertain notion of Lee's having been somehow mixed up in his capture. Had Lee turned state's evidence, winning immunity for his share of the guilt? Or had Lee been undercover on the FBI side all along? Whatever the answer, to his neighbors and his fellow townspeople and even some of his colleagues, Lee was now a completely ambiguous person, and if no one felt able to judge him, no one wanted to absolve him either.

He told himself he didn't care: he was far too old to start caring now about what people thought. He was tenured, wasn't he? So there was no reason to fret if his colleagues shunned him. He had citizenship, didn't he? So it wasn't important if readers of *Newsweek* and *Time* thought his foreignness made him a threat. He was a sane man— it wasn't his problem if the world was crazy. But he was aware of a theatrical swagger to such sentiments and was also aware that he didn't feel them, so much as he tried to collect them. He might be rehearsing, for Esther; the prospect of comforting her, of reassuring her that his ordeal had done no real damage and that in any event it was over, was the most comforting, reassuring prospect that he had. But there was nothing pretended about his avoidance of the handful of reporters who still wanted his story. These few insisted to him they were different, and indeed they behaved differently. Instead of camping on his lawn, they left hopeful and courteous messages; instead of asking an FBI agent for damning details about him, they asked him to help them in damning the whole FBI. There was an appealing intentness to them; they seemed more like young scientists on the verge of a breakthrough than like the mob that had eagerly watched as his house was dismantled. All the same, he declined; he said "Thank you" and "No comment" and "I'm sorry" and hung up the phone.

Apart from the stubborn reporters, there was one other surprising exception to the rule that Lee now was persona non grata: his summer-school class, made up, as it was every year, of precocious high-school students and particularly stupid undergraduates. Reclaiming the class had been the opposite of a satisfying self-vindication; no sooner had Lee appeared than Littell thrust the class at him and fled, the way a nurse might thrust gauze at a leper. Littell saw him now with even greater dislike, as the possible source of a lawsuit, and though Lee had never cared for Littell, that man's desire to do whatever it took to get away from Lee quickly was initially so demoralizing that Lee wandered into the classroom in a fog of depression, failing to notice the responsive alertness of some of his students. Finally one of the high-schoolers, an actually bright boy camouflaged as some kind of vandal, in a slashed T-shirt depicting an A in a circle that Lee intuited wasn't a reference to grades, raised his hand and smirked, with an air that everyone, including Lee, must now want to dispense with formalities. Variations on the smirk appeared throughout the classroom, on a spectrum from eager to gigglingly anxious.

"So, Professor," the vandal began. "We're all dying to know what that guy Donald Whitehead was like. I mean, you know him, right? You, like, were his friend from a long time ago?"

"I don't know who's saying that," Lee exclaimed, flustered by the idea, which seemed to him just as far from the truth as everything else people seemed to believe.

"But you thought he had a point, didn't you?" asked a blond girl, also high school and also quite bright, but as tidily groomed as the vandal was aggressively unkempt. "I mean, in terms of his beliefs?"

"No joke he had a point," cut in someone else. Now everyone was talking at once. In their eagerness to state their opinions, they all seemed to have forgotten they'd solicited Lee's.

"This world is completely *diseased.* You don't need to go to med school to figure that out."

"I thought a lot of what he was saying, like about technology and the breakdown of society, was right on," announced one of the stupid undergraduates, who wore a tiny tape deck and a pair of headphones into class every day, and who was there because he'd failed calculus in the spring. "I agree it was totally uncool and insane that he killed Dr. Hendley. But history is full of visionaries and messiahs and things who were pretty insane."

"Blowing people up is like: we go to the Middle East and blow, like, tons of people up so we can get gas for our cars, but then this guy blows up a few people and it's a total double standard," the vandal observed.

Lee needed a few moments to locate his footing. He was actually dizzy, he would have liked to say in response to the groundless ideas he was hearing, but it wasn't quite that. He realized, with a tinge of dismay, that his heart had grown light on the wings of classroom badinage.

"One of the excellent things about life in this country," he began carefully, "is your freedom to say things like that. In the country I came from, if you said things like that, you'd get thrown into prison."

They all burst out laughing, but Lee wasn't insulted. "Oh, I'm not kidding," he rebuked mildly as they went back to calculus.

For all his discomfort and unhappiness, he knew that the misplaced admiration of his students was still a consolation, and not the only one he enjoyed. There was Esther's impending arrival, and Fasano, who'd put off his departure. They were both aging men in whom difficulties of the body had been recently added to historic difficulties of temperament, and so Lee had invited Fasano to stay at his house rightfully confident that Fasano preferred the hotel, and Fasano had said so with no less accurate confidence that Lee would not be offended. They both knew that this didn't mean their esteem for each other was flawed. And they hardly spent less time together than if they'd been roommates, that enjoyable week, eschewing the Wagon Wheel to cook steak with green peppers and Fasano's Italianish bachelor food, and drinking cans of light beer and talking, with inexhaustible fluency. There had been nothing that Lee misremembered about their friendship, and if he was amazed that they'd both let it drop for almost twenty years, he could also reflect that this further revealed their alikeness. There were no false conceptions or deluded projections of one toward the other, not even those small conversational gaps that the friendliest duos will need to locate a fresh subject. Lee and Fasano enjoyed a shared context and similar personal lives, and at the same time each lacked knowledge of all of the other's compelling details. The result was a festive companionship very unlike the intense rapprochement Lee had felt with Aileen as he'd been driving home.

Under the circumstances it wasn't surprising that Lee told Fasano much more about his marriage to Aileen, and her marriage to Gaither, than he'd ever told anyone else. "So Aileen's son would be about thirty?" Fasano observed. "Wonder how he turned out."

"I hope not like his father," said Lee, having made the full circle and come back to his original, sensible dislike of Gaither, on the grounds of his self-righteousness.

"It's pretty hard to imagine Aileen with a Bible-thumper," Fasano said, laughing. He had met her on a few occasions, at the very beginning of his time as Lee's colleague, which had also been the very end of Lee's time as her husband. Lee was aware, without wanting to dwell on it much, that no small part of the solace of Fasano was the fact that Fasano remembered Aileen, *"vividly,"* as Fasano had said, and with admiration.

"She was very young when she married him," Lee pointed out. "And very angry with her family. And they were Unitarians. To them an evangelizing Christian like Gaither was almost as bad as a black man."

"Or an Asian," Fasano said, laughing again.

"She was young even when we got married," Lee said. "Still making youthful mistakes." He didn't want Fasano to insult him by protesting this, and Fasano did not.

"And very young when she died," Fasano said instead.

Perhaps there were, after all, a few conversational gaps. They sat with Aileen's death, her absence, between them. Lee drained the rest of the beer from his can. "When I got here and saw the fixed window, I thought that she'd done it," he said.

"Even I'm a better carpenter than a dead woman," Fasano replied.

Another gap, which Lee filled with his sadness, both heavy and light, like those ground fogs that sometimes appear at dusk, filling the ditches.

Fasano said, "You still own running shoes?"

"Oh, my God." Lee waved off the implicit suggestion.

"What? You don't look so decrepit to me."

"Then your eyesight's as bad as my feet. I have shoes. And I have tendinitis and bad knees and ankles and pains in my shins and my back. And my toes."

"Christ, you sound like my mother. Where's your shoes?"

"I guess I wouldn't mind a little run on the riverside path," Lee said when they'd found them. "For old times' sake."

"I was thinking right here in your neighborhood. Right through these streets."

"Forget it," Lee said, for the first time annoyed with his guest.

"You went to the Wagon Wheel. You went back to campus."

"And you see what I got," Lee said, pulling the tab off a fresh beer.

"Don't do it with me and you'll never do it."

"I quit jogging years ago, Frank."

"I'm going back to the Holiday Inn," Fasano said. "For my shorts and my shoes. I'll be back at eight. Perfect time for a jog. Nice and cool."

Lee sat drinking his beer when Fasano had gone, watching the minutes tick by on the clock. The emptiness of his house was unbearable to him. He wondered, for the first time, if Esther really would come. And if she did, was it only from pity? And was that why Fasano was here?

By seven-twenty he had finished his beer, urinated, and changed into a T-shirt and sweatpants. He lifted his foot toward his buttocks, seizing hold of his heel, almost losing his balance. He caught sight of himself in the sliding glass door, twigs for limbs and a mop of white hair, the opposite of Fasano, whom age had thickened and depilated.

Hamstrings groaning, he laced up his shoes.

By the time Fasano returned, night had descended on Fearrington Way, revealing the suburban constellation of streetlights and porch lights. They might have risked meeting more people on the riverside path, but then it wouldn't have felt as it did—audacious—more as if they were teenagers streaking and shouting *Up yours!* than unsteady men huffing, in yoked spheres of effort, heads reeling, pains blooming, toes cramping, conferring pared down to harsh nods, nothing seen but Fasano's form hunched alongside, nothing heard but the thunder of blood. They went farther than Lee could conceive, past the no-man's-land trees among which he'd once hidden his car, through the neighborhood portal, down streets whose inhabitants might have winced with disgust if they'd seen Lee pass by. He didn't care— no, he truly did not!—because there was power in this willed self-destruction, which was how the run felt when they'd flung themselves back through his door. He sank onto a chair, his bones smashed in the sack of his skin, his large muscles dead, while small spasms surprised him all over, as if they were being dispersed by his veins. They couldn't speak. After some time Fasano limped into the kitchen, to get them fresh beers.

When Fasano had gone back to California, Lee had a few days to prepare for Esther's arrival—by making the spare bedroom more comfortable, by stocking up on fresh fruit and cookies, the sorts of foods he didn't normally keep in the house but that he knew she would like—and it was on his return from one of many disorganized trips to the Sears or A&P or Klaussen's, always for one more item he'd forgotten before, that he reexperienced the unsteady sensation of seeing an unfamiliar vehicle in his driveway and a stranger waiting on his front step. But this time the stranger was a young man in a limp, dirty T-shirt, with a week's worth of stubble that still hadn't turfed itself into a beard, and a stolen and breathtaking face—it gazed not from under the stubble but out of the eyes, eyes Lee could never have mined from his mind's eye, but only from his gut. Were there ice floes this color, Antarctic fragments, floating off Patagonia's coast? (He'd been reading about it, and about the condor, and its mighty wingspan.) Esther had wanted those eyes; Lee knew this about her. His proud, brown daughter, who had sometimes suggested he, Lee, was a self-hating Asian and improper role model. She had wanted those eyes, less to assuage vanity than an unequaled love. He knew who this was, and wondered if he had always expected this meeting, in some secretive bodily way, so that now, though he hardly believed it, he felt he was ready.

"I'm sorry to bother you," the young man began. The young man wasn't ready. He was aware he ought to be, that a moment had come, but he didn't know what it contained, and he wasn't prepared. Lee could see all of this and at the same time could see that the specter, around which the young man had seemed like a transparent casing, was dwindling away. It was the voice that had done it, a voice all its own, although the feminine predecessor still gazed out for a moment, resigned and bemused. Lee gazed back as if his gaze might entrap, though he knew that this was just as hopeless as the nose's efforts, with its greedy inhaling, to imprison the ravishing scent.

"Please don't apologize," Lee said. "It's me who should apologize to you. I should have known that someday I would meet you, and yet I have no idea what to say."

This declaration had a startling effect on the face that was told it had long been expected. It cringed into a mask neither comic nor tragic so much as affronted, although Lee could sense that the offensive idea was not quite what he'd said but some generalized ludicrousness the young man now found newly confirmed. Lee could not remember his name, he realized. Once he'd struggled to expunge it, and now a mental ransacking could not bring it back. In a sort of physical echo of Lee's interior efforts, the young man began struggling with an envelope he'd been holding pinned under his arm. It was the regular kind of large manila envelope with two tines of a metal brad holding the flap, but the young man sought entry with quaking fingers, as if breaking into a vault, or defusing a bomb, and Lee found himself breathlessly willing the process along. The young man's hands, now that Lee's gaze was fixed so entreatingly on them, were large but graceful, with long fingers that must have been otherwise dexterous, though they were less Gaither's for the deeply browned backs and the pocks from bug bites. The envelope surrendered its contents, a birth certificate identical to one Lee recalled having seen several decades before, and in fact this one said DUPLICATE, stamped across it in red.

John Allen Gaither—that was right, that was vaguely familiar. The name had always equaled a pang of reproach, a swift wincing-away; sometimes it brought him that day in November when a weirdly hot wind had spun cyclones of garbage across his landlady's lawn.

But the young man, John, was not pointing to that name, his own, but to the name on the line marked for "mother."

"Who is this?" John demanded.

"Aileen. That's your mother."

"So you're saying that's me?" Stabbing now at the other name.

"John. Yes, that's you."

"That is *not* my name!" John said. "My parents named me Lewis. I changed it to Mark."

"Mark," Lee said readily. A strange intuition had seized him, so strongly he wanted to call it an insight: the changeling had authority here. Like some child lama plucked off the Mongolian steppe, Mark's self-ignorance was just short of total, yet all power was his. The best Lee could do was provide any service he could. "Come inside, Mark," he said gently. "Your mother named you John, your father changed it to Lewis, I think, but without even knowing the problem, you've found a solution. You've named yourself Mark."

"You're saying *this* is my mother?" Mark still stabbed the page. "Who is she? Where is she?"

There was no varnishing this; to attempt it, to hesitate even a handful of seconds with a handful of stammering words, might be just enough time for the onrush of hope, for that phantom who perfectly loves us to shimmer to life.

"She's dead," Lee said. And then he was able to lead the boy into the house.

The folder that Morrison had given him, with the letter from Aileen inside, had been on the telephone table in his kitchen ever since he'd come home. He knew that it might have been considered a strange place for something he'd once wanted buried, near at hand but locked up, safe not only from Esther, whose days of possibly coming across it were years in the past, but from himself, and his incurable weakness for self-punishment. Yet lately he'd found in the letter less punishment than a slow revelation. It was possible he'd never read it correctly, back when it most mattered to him; that, as with the letter from Whitehead that he'd thought was from Gaither, he'd only glared fearfully at the words through a mesh of defenses. Reading a paragraph here, a page there, while preparing his dinner, he sometimes fell into a trance of enjoyment and reemerged to the pasta water boiled away and the noodles adhered to the pot, or to his steak turned to smoldering charcoal, or his broccoli steamed into pulp. John's closed eyelids, Aileen wrote, *aren't a "half-moon" or "fingernail" curve or other things people say. As a mathematician perhaps you know the name of this curve. Almost straight but the ends turn a little. Like the surface of the water in my glass where it clings to the sides and lifts up. I've just recalled the word for this: meniscus! But already that's wrong. Without my even noticing the curve just transformed, into more a triangular shape, as if something in his sleep surprised him and his eyeball bulged out.* John's gaze, when awake, *doesn't see me, that's plain. Or doesn't see me in any clear way and think "Mother!" and all the special ideas that are supposed to go with it. But I'm not disappointed or impatient, as Nora says most women are. It's as if I'd stowed away on the spaceship of a little Martian, and he's speeding along, and I can see all the things that he sees, and I can tell what he's thinking somehow, because I'm not really there—* And, with a vehemence in her voice that Lee relished to clearly remember, *This world hasn't yet taken up his attention, so he still can see backwards, to where he came from. And I don't mean "Aileen Adams" or "Lewis Gaither" but some place only he still remembers. And if I don't remember it now, how will he ever know?* Once Lee had skittered all over its surface, he went back and read from the beginning, and once he'd finished, he started again, not out of repentance but just because the letter did what she must have intended it to do: it conveyed her to him, thoroughly, without any constraint. It wasn't tainted with distortions, like their marriage, to satisfy him. The truth was, it scarcely involved him at all. And it was this, once offensive and baffling, he found he liked most.

Now, like that miraculous curve of an eyelid, it had subtly but completely transformed into as familiar a household object as its telephone-table companion, the recipe box. Yet after Lee managed to seat the stumbling, mute boy at his kitchen table and place these two items before him, his explanation of the epistolary grew quickly confused, while the culinary sturdily came to his rescue. In preparing for Esther's arrival, he'd combed the box for her childhood favorites and then bought all the ingredients required for five nights' worth of dinners, so that it occurred to him now that he could make shrimp jambalaya for the boy—Mark—and himself, because the bag of frozen shrimp was enough for six servings, which left Friday's planned menu intact. "After Aileen and I divorced," he told Mark, relieved to the point of garrulity by this plan to make dinner, "I phoned her one day with this terrible craving for this very dish, 'shrimp jambalaya.' I had to know how it was made. She didn't even know what I was talking about. Then she finally remembered—it was just an idea she'd gotten off the shrimp bag. She'd never written it down! She said, 'Put in some chopped onion and pepper to start,' and I said, 'But how much?' I'm a mathematician, I've always been very methodical in my cooking. I can't improvise." But he was improvising now, as he spoke to Mark in the tone of a distant relation—an acknowledgment of tie; a careful disregard, for the moment, of bewildering intimacy. Lee spoke as if Mark were a second cousin, visiting from Spain, inquiring after a long-dead great-aunt; perhaps, in a while, Mark would be a first cousin, or from Canada, or the great-aunt only recently dead. Perhaps they'd inch up to each other by little degrees. Lee also thought of death, and all the humble, homely acts in the face of the howling abyss that had seemed so contemptible to him when Aileen had died, the crusty casseroles lined end to end on her kitchen table. Now he knew that such small things were the only things that could be done. Watching Mark slowly empty a bottle of beer, his eyes blankly trained on the patio door leading to the backyard, Lee thought, This boy's mother has died, and I'm making him dinner. And for the moment that seemed like enough of a plan for them both.

But just before the shrimp was ready, Mark asked for a bathroom where he could wash up. Lee's week of preparation helped him here, too: there were brand-new towels and bars of soap and an absence of dust in the upstairs bathroom, next to Esther's bedroom. After Mark had left the kitchen, and climbed with slow steps up the stairs, Lee noticed that the file folder was gone from the table.

Half an hour later, Mark had still not come down. By nine P.M., with the shrimps hard as rubber erasers in their garish red sauce, Lee sat down to eat by himself. He had set two places at the kitchen table: two breakproof Corelle plates, two plastic Tupperware tumblers, two forks and two knives—in the pattern of the house of Penney, went the joke of Aileen's—paired on paper napkins folded into triangles. All the deep memory of the fingers, time-traveling two decades into the past. The ceremony of the family table. He gazed at his symmetric place settings a long time before he finally sat down.

He'd been shifting the last morsel of shrimp across the dirty plate when a sound made him stand up again. Nothing sudden or startling; it had stolen on his senses like the cry of a child in the night as it dredges a parent from sleep. Yet he went with the same urgency he remembered, his heart in his throat, the short distance impossibly long. Upstairs, Mark lay sobbing upon Esther's bed, made for her that morning, folded and pleated fastidiously like a gift. Mark was curled as if nursing a wound in his gut, but with his heavy boots carefully hung off the side of the bed, as if even in grief he would not claim much space for himself. The letter lay on the bedside table. Lee felt the piercing return of an instinct unused since Esther's babyhood, yet he could not presume to stroke this boy on the nape of his neck, or even to sit down next to him on the bed. After a moment Lee removed the austere wooden desk chair from under the desk, turned it around, and sat there, feeling, as he made this indication of patience, true patience come down over him, like a craved sedative. He could wait, he did not know for what; he could wait until he knew.

"I didn't know I'd lost something," Mark sobbed. This was all that he said, though he said it again and again, broken into fragments.

Did it solace Mark, to be witnessed like this? Or was Lee an intruder to him? Lee didn't know, but he tried to trust instinct, which told him to stay. Even after Mark had gone to sleep, Lee remained in the chair.

The airport hadn't changed much in the three decades that Lee had known it, mostly as a point of collection for the occasional guest professor, shakily dismounting the staircase-on-wheels with a briefcase in hand and an ashen complexion if the plane had endured thunderstorms. It was still, as Agent Morrison had joked, mostly a slab of cracked runway and an egg carton testing the wind. Although it

occurred to Lee now, as he parked, that for all its bareness and smallness the airport was the opposite of utilitarian; it was entirely devoted
to the romance of coming and going. If that wasn't true, then what
was the purpose of the long, low building, a little curved at its ends
like a solo parenthesis, the better to obstruct any views, from the parking lot in front, of the platform of arrival behind? Certainly, that building, with its faded linoleum flooring and its single squeaking luggage
carousel, its single unmanned rental-car booth and its plastic floor
plants every once in a while on the unneeded length of walkway, had
not been designed for shelter. It was always, even when flights came
in, almost three-quarters empty. It was there as stage curtains are
there, to create ceremony.

"How will I know her?" Mark asked, his voice croaking. Mark had
shaved, ineptly, and gougings marred his uncanny face. That morning
he had asked for directions to the mall and returned two hours later in
a striped shirt, still creased from the package, and a pair of awkward
slacks and stiff, cheap-looking loafers; he must have bought the
clothes, but they looked borrowed or, rather, donated; it was as if he'd
never tucked in a shirt or had to fasten a belt in his life.

"I hope *I'll* know her," Lee said honestly. They both stood as alertly
as they could at the smudged wall of glass. Black vinyl conjoined seats
were behind them, unused. A ponytailed girl, the only other human in
evidence, moved purposefully out a door, wearing some kind of ear-
muffs; she must be the combination air-traffic controller and unloader
of luggage, deliverer of salutations and mopper of floors. They had
been very early, as was always Lee's habit when dealing with travel,
whether or not he himself was the traveler involved. He might have
sat in the airport all day if it weren't for Mark's shopping-mall errand.
But today the high-strung agitation Lee was accustomed to feel—
whenever he saw the twinned words "Arrivals/Departures" let alone
on the far rarer occasions he set foot on a plane—while as pressing,
was a different sensation. The difference seemed directional; instead
of a downpulling dread, there was a reckless uprushing of . . . what?
Perhaps Lee was finally riding the swift wing of travel, though for the
moment quite still. He had never felt the excitement of airports before, the joy of a sudden displacement in space, like the jumbled-up
logic of dreams. The glaciers appended to jungles, the rooms in his

home he had not known were there, the dead strewing oranges on blankets to nourish the living. . . .

"Right on time," Mark burst out, and Lee startled away from the glass, where his forehead had pressed him to brief, gorgeous sleep, like a vitamin shot of renewal. Indeed, other people had been sifting in, a serene scattering of co-greeters, and the drone of propellers had grown in volume at the same time as it lowered in tone, until the loudest and most guttural tone said the plane had touched down. It was a very tiny plane—they always looked so small as they came careering around on toy wheels, but this time Lee exclaimed in amazement and apprehension. Could she really be in there? And what if she wasn't? He felt a stab of sadness for Mark next to him, trembling also.

"Anything might have happened," he offered. "Coming all that way, from South America. You can miss a connection. . . ."

She'd often said she didn't look like her mother, and Lee had never known if the remark was a complaint or a question, nor had he known if he'd answered correctly in saying, with the pride the fact caused him, "You have your own face, Esther." Not entirely true: she was perfect Aileen at the jaw. Sometimes she glanced sidelong in scorn and shape-shifted, and Lee's heart seemed to bleed. As a child she'd accused them of denying that she was a changeling. The children at school, seeing her pale, blue-eyed mother, had explained that she must be adopted, and she had agreed.

As always, a remarkable number of people emerged from the plane. A joke or a miracle: the scant tube kept squeezing them out, eager returnees and uncertain newcomers and perhaps some who had boarded the plane by mistake and now waited to see what new world it was, all making their way down the little staircase with palms shielding their eyes from the sun. When Esther ducked out, not quite last, Lee knew her not by her face but her whole silhouette, her very contour in space; he would know it at the edge of his vision, in motion, in darkness. She knew his as well. Across yards of concrete and through the glare of the glass, she saw the shape of her slight, rumpled father—and someone else, she would soon see him also—and thrust her arm up, to wave.

"There she is," Lee said, waving triumphantly back.

ACKNOWLEDGMENTS

I am indebted to the John Simon Guggenheim Memorial Foundation, the Sidney Harman Writer-in-Residence program at Baruch College, and Ledig House for giving me money and time while I was writing this book, and to Denis Frawley and Jon Novick for giving me space; to Semi Chellas, Jhumpa Lahiri, and Pete Wells for tirelessly reading, rereading, and responding to drafts of the manuscript; to William Finnegan, Tom McDaniel, Mark Rossini, Kevin Sack, and Julie Tate for invaluable information; and to Lynn Nesbit, Molly Stern, and Laura Tisdel for their endless assistance and unflagging enthusiasm. Thank you all.